"Tom's an expert storyteller." —F. Paul Wilson

"A highly engrossing, wildly surprising thriller with a stunning premise that thoroughly grabbed me."
—David Morrell on *The Blood of the Lamb*

"[Monteleone has a] knack for the right phrase, dialogue, and imaginative depictions of violence."
—*West Coast Review of Books*

"*The Blood of the Lamb* is daring. Monteleone grabs the reader with his first paragraph and never relaxes the tension." —*The New York Times*

"[The author] has a gift for complex characters."
—*Library Journal*

"*The Blood of the Lamb* is a vastly entertaining novel of horror and suspense [that poses] difficult questions about the nature of man, God and the devil."
—*Los Angeles Daily News*

"A terrific book that's as fun to read as it is difficult to put down."
—*The Washington Times* on *The Blood of the Lamb*

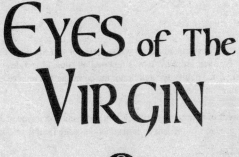

EYES of The VIRGIN

THOMAS F. MONTELEONE

TOR®

A TOM DOHERTY ASSOCIATES BOOK
NEW YORK

This is a work of fiction. All the characters and events portrayed in this novel are either products of the author's imagination or are used fictitiously.

EYES OF THE VIRGIN

A Tor Book
Published by Tom Doherty Associates, LLC
175 Fifth Avenue
New York, NY 10010

www.tor.com

Tor® is a registered trademark of Tom Doherty Associates, LLC.

ISBN: 0-765-34028-3

First edition: December 2002
First mass market edition: November 2003

Printed in the United States of America

0 9 8 7 6 5 4 3 2 1

This one is for

Al Molinaro,

a friend

who became

family.

ACKNOWLEDGMENTS

Nothing I write is done without the continuing support of those who believe in my attempts to be an entertaining teller of tales. And so in a spirit of total and heartfelt appreciation, I would like to thank Matt Bialer, my agent at Trident Media Group; his assistant, Cheryl Capitani; and my longtime editor, Melissa Singer.

I would also like to highlight the unending efforts of my harshest critic and biggest fan, my collaborator in all things larger than a mere book—my wife, Elizabeth, who is easily the most intelligent, generous, and sensitive person I have ever known. Thank you, Baby. . . . I love you.

Prologue

*S*enhora Maria Carrera knew immediately the men were dangerous.

She had just excused herself from the home of Father Julio, where she worked till evening as the parish house-keeper, and had begun walking toward the Fatima road. Tall hedges and the long shadows of dusk rendered her invisible to anyone approaching the Cova.

Maria heard their raspy voices long before actually seeing them. Although she had lived in the county of Ourem all of her long life, none of them sounded fa-miliar. Other than the pastor's house, there was nothing along the main road between here and the *Capelinha*. Whoever these men might be, they either had business with Father Julio, or they intended to pay a visit to the little chapel. Whatever their intent, thought Maria, it was obvious they did not care if anyone knew they were coming. Indeed, they spoke and laughed loudly as they drew ever closer to where she crouched in hiding.

Had they no fear?

Apparently not.

Although the sun had already wedged itself behind the hills of Torres Nova, there was still barely enough light for Maria to peer through the hedges. If the men were coming to see Father Julio, she would be able to see them turning up the carriage lane. From the shadows, she could see them now—four men, dressed in dark clothing and floppy hats, two of them struggling with a handcart obviously weighed down by something heavy. From the sounds of their voices, they were all fairly young and full of strength, and even in the failing light, Maria could see they were all tall and muscular.

Tensing her wiry body, she held her breath as she watched them reach the intersection of Father Julio's lane and the main road from Fatima.

What were they going to do now?

If they were coming to the priest's house, they would surely catch her crouching in the hedges. And she knew in her heart these men were up to nothing good.

But they did not even pause at Father Julio's lane, grunting and cursing the handcart they pulled.

Maria felt her breath easing from her thin chest, only then aware she'd held it for so long. The tension drained out of her, but left a thick residue of dread. Even though she was safe for the moment, she could not shake the sense that something terrible was about to happen.

Turning quickly, silently, she crab-walked back up to the priest's door and rapped as loudly as she dared. The sound of her knuckles' impact on the wood seemed to reverberate across the yard and down the slope to where the brigands moved along the Fatima road. Sure they could hear it!

In truth, Father Julio had barely heard it. The old priest, short and full in the belly, slowly unlatched and opened his door. He was surprised to see his house-keeper again so soon.

"Maria? Are you all right? What are you doing back here?"

She pushed past him and spoke in a whisper, quickly recounting what she'd just seen. And when she finished, she could easily read the fearful comprehension in the old man's face. Whatever was going on, he knew about it.

"Father," said Maria. "What is it? Please, tell me . . . !"

He shook his head as he began wringing his hands atop his abundant stomach. "This is very bad. Very bad."

"What? Who are those men?"

"They are probably sent by Mayor Santos—"

"The mayor?" Maria could not hide her confusion. "I don't understand."

Father Julio walked slowly to his large oak desk and began fishing through the piles of letters and envelopes heaped there. "You are aware of the atheistic nature of our government . . ." he began. "They send me threats on a regular basis."

"It is no secret Arturo Santos was not happy with the children and the apparitions," said Maria.

Father Julio chuckled nervously. "The processions and the crowds have angered the civil governors as well. You probably have not bothered yourself with the politics, and I don't blame you. But you should know there are people who wish to fashion a godless republic in Portugal, and the Catholics stand in their way."

"The men, Father . . . you know where they go?"

"I think so."

Maria had not wanted to even think about the possibility. There was only one thing which lay beyond Father Julio's cottage. "Oh, no," she said. "Not the *Capelinha.* . . ."

"They have spoken against it ever since it was built," said the priest. "You remember when the municipal guard stopped our procession?"

Maria nodded. The previous spring, the people of the surrounding villages had planned to install a beautiful statue of the Blessed Virgin in the "little chapel" that had just been built at Cova da Iria, on the exact spot where Our Lady had appeared to the children. Already *la Capelinha* had become a special shrine, a place for thousands of personal pilgrimages. But the government had stopped them, and the mayor had proclaimed an end to all public demonstrations of religious fervor. Since that time, Father Julio had kept the statue in the study of his tiny house, to await a time when the climate would be more appropriate to have it installed.

"What can we do, Father?" she said after a desperate silence between them.

Father Julio's jaw muscles tightened beneath his jowly cheeks. "I will follow them," he said. "Maria, I will need you to go into the village and tell Doctor Formigao what is happening. See if he can gather some of the parishioners."

"I will try!" she said as she gathered up her long skirt and headed for the door. Turning to look back at the priest, she was shocked to see him lifting a strange object from one of the drawers in his desk. The light of the bronze oil lamp held everything in slashes of orange light and deep shadows.

"Father, what are you doing?" She could see the object for an instant as he stuffed it beneath the folds of his cassock—a pistol.

"I am just being careful. Go, Maria."

Father Julio Enrique watched the woman slip outside into the brisk night air. He waited a moment, then followed her. As he reached the knoll overlooking the wagon lane which twisted down to its joining with the Fatima road, he could see Maria's fragile silhouette moving against the light of a pale quarter moon. She minced her steps, a combination of stealth and fear, but Julio knew she was safe. There would be no danger on the way back into the village.

No. The real trouble lay three kilos in the opposite direction at Ira da Cova where the rough men were pulling their dark wagon.

Pulling his coat collar high against a rising breeze,

Julio took out after them. He walked along the shadowed road with a long, determined stride. His gait was strong enough, he hoped, to close the gap between himself and the men who labored with the handcart at a considerably slower pace.

In twelve minutes, he had indeed caught up with them, but they had already reached their target—Julio had been ruefully correct—the *Capelinha*. But what were they doing?

Crouching at the corner of a stone wall, Julio kept his cover as he tried to determine their actions, their intentions. Although he was no farther than half the distance of a football field, he had great difficulty seeing much through veil of darkness. The men spoke in short grunts as they dragged several objects from the wagon and placed them in various places, and even though Julio could not see them clearly, he knew he was witnessing a crime of great evil. The men were planting firepots or, worse, explosives. . . .

And then they were all speaking in unison. A prayer or the rote words of ceremony. Straining, Julio could barely make out the cadenced foolishness of a Freemasons' ritual.

The bastards!

The heathen, left-footed *bastards!*

He could feel his breath ratcheting in and out of his lungs, and as he carefully reached for the Prussian pistol from his cassock, he realized how much his hands were shaking.

Could he be serious? Did he actually think himself capable of using a weapon? Against his fellow men?

The notion punched a blow deep into his soul, and he bent low as he lay the pistol in the cool grass. He felt like a coward as he wrestled with his rationalizations. Even if Maria could stir an army of parishioners, they would not reach the little chapel in time to stop the marauders. It was up to Julio . . . to make a stand, or remain hiding in the shrubbery like a terrified little boy.

He should—

Suddenly the four men were running. *Fast.* Leaving the handcart next to the *Capelinha*, they ran full tilt as if the devil was in their tracks. For an instant, Julio was startled and confused. It appeared for a moment the men were headed straight for him and he could see the bulging whiteness of their eyes.

But they ran right past his recondite position, angling across the meadow to the Fatima road. Instinctively, Julio had reached for the pistol, and it hung limply in his hand when the first bomb went off. . . .

The darkness had been suddenly pierced by a blossom of white heat and ripped by the sound of splintering thunder. Then in quick succession, three *more* shuddering explosions lighted up the Cova with an instant of terrible daylight. And in that photo-flash, Julio had seen the little chapel consumed by the billowing concussions, reduced to a storm of pulverized stone and splintered glass.

As the debris ripped through the limbs of the trees and raked the grass like grapeshot, Julio sprawled behind the short stone wall, else he himself might be shredded by the onslaught of the bombing. But even as he protected himself, he felt riddled with thoughts of pain and outrage. He could not believe they'd actually done it . . . to destroy the little chapel that the people of the village had constructed so lovingly . . . stone by stone, brick by brick . . . a sacrilege of the greatest order!

The silence which now swallowed the Cova was suddenly oppressive. Feeling as though he'd tumbled into a vast and terrible vacuum, Father Julio struggled to his knees, listened intently for any sound, any sign that he was not so utterly alone with the smoldering pieces of Fatima's gift to the Virgin.

But there was nothing . . . nothing but the darkness and a void within his spirit.

He stood and walked slowly towards the wreckage of the *Capelinha*, and as he drew closer, he gasped in pain.

So complete had been the work of the heathen bombers that the entire chapel had been obliterated, reduced to nothing larger than the pebbles you would find in a roadway.

Get away from this place, the thought suddenly pierced him. *It has been defiled and it reeks with the stench of great sin.*

But Julio also felt a great sadness and questioned his superstitious fear. He only wished he had not been so helpless, so weak . . . perhaps—

His notion faded as something caught his full attention. Lying ahead of him in the debris, something seemed to be reflecting the pale light of the moon. But Luna was a mere scythe in the heavens tonight—weak and illuminating little. As he approached the object, Julio wondered if it might be glowing from *within*, rather than reflecting any light at all. He felt a shudder pass through him as he imagined a final explosive, a final booby-trap left to snare the first on the scene of the explosions.

But he brushed away his fear as he reached the object, which softly pulsed with an inner energy. Perhaps ten or twelve centimeters in length and a third as high, it appeared to be roughly rectangular, and when he touched it, he realized what it was—a shard of stained glass from the window of the *Capelinha*.

As he lifted it close to his face, to examine it in the dimmest of light, Julio suddenly froze. The object was *looking* at him.

Compose yourself! he chastised himself. Exhaling softly, he realized he was holding the piece of stained glass that had been part of the Virgin Mary's face, a jagged panel that depicted her beautifully serene eyes. Julio could not stop staring at the blessed fragment he held—there was something powerfully compelling, attractive, and at the same time mysterious about it. As he looked directly into the glass, its soft glow seemed only an illusion, but if he glanced in any other direction, he swore he could detect it in the periphery of his vision.

Quickly he scanned the grass for any other pieces large enough to be identified, but there was nothing else but tiny crystals of shattered glass.

How odd and wonderful that Mary's eye had been preserved. Julio took this to be a sign from God that the tragedy just witnessed was not as terrible as it seemed. Perhaps he'd received a message that the Virgin still watched over this place.

Father Julio smiled at the notion, and removed a kerchief from his back pocket. He wrapped the piece of glass into his cloth as carefully as if it were a saintly relic.

Yes, he thought with great conviction. *I have been given a sign that this is something special.* As he walked away from the wreckage, back towards Fatima, he decided he would contact the Knights of Malta.

The crime of the Freemasons would be avenged.

PART
ONE

ONE

The home of Harold Wieznewski
Potomac, Maryland
June, the present

"**O**kay, pal . . . hold it right there." The voice shattered the silence encircling Kurt Streicher.

Male. Middle-aged. Tremulous. Fearful. Unsure.

Streicher instantly noted all these things and felt better, but remained extremely angry with himself for being caught. This *never* happened to him.

He heard the *click!* of the hammer of a revolver being pulled back into firing position. And then: nothing.

For a moment, Streicher stood listening to the silence as one listens to some terrifying but brilliant atonal symphony, as one listens to an approaching storm at sea.

Then slowly, he raised his hands like the bad guys in the old Westerns, and waited for whatever came next. Whatever it was, he would have to come up with the correct response. Streicher eased his hand towards the back of his head, resting them there, only inches from a Navy Seal blade tucked neatly into a shoulder harness.

"Turn around, real slow, and keep your hands up," said the voice. Good. He had not noticed the knife.

Streicher pivoted, grateful for the chance to assess his adversary. That was the guy's first mistake. Far better to have kept Streicher turned around. But most amateurs can't resist the opportunity to see what their opponent actually looks like.

The man pointing the gun was tall and reed-thin. He had a receding chin, big ears, and wore thick glasses. Wearing billowy seersucker pajamas, he looked like a caricature rather than a real person. The heavy .357 revolver wavered slightly in the man's two-handed grip—a combination of its weight and his anxiety.

Streicher risked a half-smile. "Did you actually call me 'pal'?"

"You just stand right there," said the thin man as he sidestepped across the kitchen toward a wall phone.

Streicher nodded and waited for the man to move his left hand off the gun's grip to reach for the receiver. In that instant, the barrel of the Colt dipped, and Streicher's right hand dropped to the handle of his knife. In one fluid and often-practiced maneuver, he fell to his knees and launched the blade at his target.

The thin man's hand never reached the phone. When the serrated edge of the Seal knife entered his throat with the force of a major-league fastball, it stunned him, severing his vocal cords and right carotid artery. The .357 clattered to the floor, the man grabbing for his savaged neck, trying to hold back the dark flood of his life.

In short order he would bleed to death, but Streicher couldn't wait. Stepping close to the panicked man, Kurt broke his neck in the grip of hammerlock-nelson. A sound like a broomstick wrapped in a wet towel—snapping. The victim's eyes bulged for a second as the light of sentience left them, then the husk of his body collapsed to the floor.

Striding over the body, Streicher entered the hallway which led to the sleeping chambers of the other servants. The cook lay snoring in her bed as he loomed over her, a heavy-boned woman insulated by a thick layer of fat. This did not keep him from lifting her head and twisting it violently, severing her spinal chord, killing her instantly.

When he reached the maid's room, she must have sensed something, even in her slumber. Because as Streicher reached the edge of her bed, standing there like a guardian angel, the Hispanic woman's eyes popped open, insanely white and wide. As she opened her mouth to scream, Streicher caught her across the face with a left hook that lifted her from the mattress and the bedclothes, almost hurling her completely from the bed.

So stunned that her eyes began to roll backwards into her skull, she could not move nor make a sound. It was all the chance he needed to kneel over her and cut her throat from one ear to the other. And so leaving her body to convulse and flop like a fish pulled to the deck, Streicher headed for the opposite wing of the large house.

The pajamaed butler had already done him the favor of disarming the alarm system, so his passage through the corridors and rooms to the central staircase was quick and silent. Moonlight seeped into the house, casting his path in the palest of pastels.

There was an odd and terrible beauty to the light, making the interior and its fixtures seem almost transparent, ethereal. And when he ascended the thickly carpeted steps to the second floor, he found he had to pause to absorb the stark aesthetics of the scene, as though photographing a surreal tableau of mirrors and paintings, chairs and chandeliers.

But enough of that.

When he reached the bedroom of his targets, he paused outside the door to listen to the machinelike rhythms of their breathing. Soft. Measured. Peaceful.

With practiced quickness, he padded into a large room with a canopied, king-sized bed forming its focal point. Defined under flimsy floral sheets were the twin shapes of typically overfed Americans. Like basking sea lions, husband and wife's bulk dwarfed the dimensions of the large bed. Streicher hefted a sap in his hand as he bent low to the sleeping woman. A snap of his wrist, and the thin leather pouch filled with lead shot *thunked* the fragile bones at the base of her occipital lobe. Sudden, instant unconsciousness.

The man beside her grunted, shifted his position in the bed, but did not awaken.

Soon enough, thought Streicher as he produced a Glock 9 millimeter from his belt, screwed a silencer into the end of its barrel, and drew in a deep breath. Then, without flourish or hesitation, Streicher reached out to a bedside table to click on a reading lamp. As warm, yellow incandescence washed over the husband's face, his eyes fluttered.

"Wha—?"

"You'll have to excuse me, Mr. Wieznewski," said Streicher, "but I need to talk to you. . . ."

"Huh . . . ?" said the heavyset man as he rolled over and opened his eyes squintingly against the light, still not really awake.

Streicher watched the man's rounded, doughy features change from dull awareness to sudden fear. His mouth tightened into a tiny circle and his pinched eyes strained in their sockets as he registered the sight of a lean, black-clad man holding a very mean-looking gun on him.

"Who the fuck—?" Harold Wieznewski pushed back on one elbow, quickly assessing the helplessness of his situation. He looked to the stilled form of his wife, spoke her name fearfully.

"She's all right," said Streicher. ". . . for now."

"What did you do to her?! What do you want?" Wieznewski's attention had shifted back to Streicher and his weapon. "How'd you get in here?"

Streicher smiled. "So many questions. . . . Let's see, where do I start? Well, I hit your wife on the back of the head . . . I want to get something from you . . . and I climbed in through the kitchen window in the servants' wing. Anything else?"

Wieznewski edged away from him, and sat up to drop his legs off the edge of the bed. Although still in his early forties, he looked absurdly out of shape and flabby in his T-shirt and boxers.

"I don't keep much money here," he said, running his hand through his thinning hair. "Please, don't hurt us, we—"

"I don't want your money. I want the glass."

Harold Wieznewski looked at him with a dull stare. It was a good piece of acting, and the only thing ruining it was the sparking short circuit of fear behind his eyes. Streicher always looked into the eyes of his targets— there was never any hiding whatever lurked there.

"Glass?" said Wieznewski. "What're you talking about? We have some Waterford . . . several Chihuly—"

"Waterford. Oh, that's a good one." Streicher sighed audibly. It was a labored stage sigh, the way a villain might do it in a bad play. "You know," he said. "I'm not one of these guys who likes to talk a lot. Just get me the glass. *Now*."

"Look," said Wieznewski, trying to erect an engaging, I'm-just-your-friendly-lobbyist smile. "I don't know what you're talking about. We don't have any 'glass' anything—"

Streicher nodded as he reached into his belt and pulled out a pair of needle-nosed pliers. "Okay. . . ." he said very softly.

Without another word, he reached out to lift Lorraine Wieznewski's limp left hand, adorned by an ostentatious diamond, a wedding band, and exquisitely manicured nails. Working like a surgeon, Streicher used the needle-nosed pliers to nimbly grab the Chinese red fingernail on the woman's index finger.

Wieznewski screamed *No!* and tried to stop him, but Streicher had already jerked back his hand, stripping the nail completely away from her flesh. As the sudden pain yanked her into consciousness, blood seeped from the wounded finger. Lorraine Wieznewski was so terror-struck she could do nothing but scream hoarsely as she sat staring at her spurting, savaged hand.

"The glass," said Streicher ever more softly, barely audible below the screams of the woman. "Now."

"I *can't!*" said Wieznewski, panic now staining his voice. "Please try to underst—"

Like a snake striking at its prey, Streicher's hand uncoiled, grabbed Lorraine's upheld, bloody hand.

The pliers flashed and another nail ripped free. Blood gouted from the end of her hand and she writhed away from him in high-octave agony.

"Jesus Christ!" yelled her husband. "All right! All right! Leave her alone!"

"The glass," said Streicher.

Wieznewski staggered to his feet, his face a sagging mask of horror and surrender. "This way," he said dully.

Streicher followed him from the bedroom to an adjoining study, replete with mahogany bookshelves, overstuffed wingback chairs, a massive desk, and carefully arranged baronial clutter. Wieznewski touched a hidden latch and a section in one of the bookcases swung outward to reveal a wall safe with a small keypad. With a palsied hand, the man tapped in a series of numbers and spoke deliberately into a small speaker/mike: "Until The End Of Time."

A green LED was his only response, but it was enough. Wieznewski opened the minivault with a familiar tilt of the finely-machined latch. Like a refrigerator, the interior of the small vault was illuminated in harsh halogen light as the door opened fully. Streicher watched his prey move mechanically, reaching past several stacks of banded cash, folders and documents to what appeared to be a dark, metallic strongbox. Its dimensions were perhaps eighteen inches by five by two.

In the background, the sounds of his wife's pain played on dimly, but Wieznewski seemed to be ignoring it. He removed the metal box of polished, dark metal and held it outward with both hands. "Here. Take it."

"Open it. Let me see it."

Wieznewski carefully opened the machined case. Its interior was lined with a soft green cloth, protecting a piece of stained pale amber glass. Floating in its center were a pair of beautiful eyes.

Streicher nodded. "Close it. Give it to me."

Wieznewski did, and as Streicher accepted it, he noted its density, its weight. Holding it tightly, he motioned Wieznewski back to the bedroom with a subtle wave of the automatic pistol.

"Don't hurt her anymore," said Wieznewski. "Please . . ."

"I won't," said Streicher, following the man as he shambled ahead like a broken windup toy.

When Wieznewski reentered the bedroom, his wife looked up to see Streicher behind him and she began working up another rising crescendo of terror and pain. "It's okay," said her husband. "It's all right now, honey, he's going to leave us alone, now, aren't you?"

With a silly smile, the man turned to look at Streicher and seemed genuinely surprised to see his intruder's weapon aimed at a point somewhere just above the bridge of his nose.

"No. . . ." he said softly.

The woman began to wail like an Irish fishwife at a wake.

Streicher said nothing. Readjusting his aim from Harold Wieznewski, he squeezed off a single, silenced slug into Lorraine's forehead. There was a soft *phffft!* and a popping sound, then nothing.

To his credit, Wieznewski remained facing his executioner. A terrible sadness had replaced the horror in his expression. Streicher interpreted it as a kind of relief, an acceptance, and perhaps even an ironically pleasure in knowing the grand game Wieznewski had been playing was finally at an end.

"Just tell me one thing," he said.

"What's that?" said Streicher as he calmly pointed the weapon.

"Who are you? How did you know?"

"We have no name," said Streicher. "And we know everything."

"That's no answer!" said Wieznewski, pleading.

"It will have to suffice," said Streicher, pulling the trigger.

TWO

KATE HARRISON

Kate had been sitting on the deck overlooking the lake, anticipating another late summer postcard sunset, when the telephone chirped from the kitchen. The electronic sound broke her contemplative, Thoreau-like mood, and it made her think of a time not so very long ago when phones still had bells in them.

Pulling herself from the Adirondack chair, she entered the patio doors and plucked the portable receiver from its wall cradle. "Hello?"

"Kate?! You're *there!* Oh, Christ! I'm glad I got you." The voice ran all the words together in a scary, out-of-breath way. It sounded like her sister, but as Kate had never heard her.

"Justine, is that you? What's the matter? Where are you?" Kate felt her body slipping into that strange state where you become keenly aware of normally autonomic body functions like breathing and heartbeat. Before her sister (and she was certain it was her sister on the line) could answer, Kate felt a spike of cold fear pass through her like a winter draft.

"Yes!" said Justine. "Kate, just listen to me! I don't have much time. . . ."

"Justine, what's wrong?"

"Domenic and I are in a lot of trouble. Very big trouble. I can't explain it right now—not over the phone."

"Domenic? Trouble? What're you talking ab—?"

"Please!" Her sister was half-shouting into the phone. "There's no *time*, Kate! Just listen to me: I'm in Boston. Meet me at our old rendezvous, remember? From college?"

"Yes, okay," said Kate, unsure what was going on, feeling a thick column of panic trying to surge up like lava through the center of her thoughts. "I remember."

"Okay! Then leave now," said Justine. "I'll meet you in an hour!"

"Justine, wait a minute—!"

But the line was dead. Either her sister had slammed down the receiver or it had been cut off. Neither explanation offered Kate much consolation.

Staring off through the patio doors at the lake, she took a slow, deep breath, then let it out even more slowly. *Calm down.* Whatever was wrong, she couldn't do anything constructive until she understood more about it. She stepped out to the railing of the deck, scanning the placid mirror of Eastman Lake. Somewhere out there sat her husband, the great Lawrence Copley Harrison, hunched and alone in his LakeMaster skiff, casting and reeling for largemouth bass and pickerel.

Damn him and his fishing! she thought as she began walking aimlessly about the deck, trying to decide what to do. She couldn't contact Lawrence because he refused to take the cell phone or even a pager with him when on the lake. It was his only time alone, and he would simply not allow any intrusions from the rest of the world. He always said that if he didn't have his "safe house" on Eastman Lake, and his time to fish, he would have gone insane long ago.

But she needed to talk to him. *Now.* Kate respected

his keen judgment, his coolness under pressure, and his almost preternatural sense of the truth, of what was really happening in almost any situation. They were qualities that had made Lawrence Harrison one of the most successful American industrialists of the last three decades. In that sense, he was a dinosaur, an example of the way a family business used to be run. But he could always cut through the crap, as he liked to say, and make the right decision.

She needed him right now. Lawrence would know what this all meant. He would know what she should do. . . .

But there was no time for that. Justine had said to meet her in an hour. If she left immediately she would just make it. Kate leaned against the railing hoping to see a trace of her husband's boat, but it was no use. The plaintive cry of one of New Hampshire's beloved loons drifted across the surface of the water. The fragment of a sad and tragic song, it touched Kate as it never had before.

I've got to go. Justine's in trouble.

The thoughts galvanized her into motion. After scribbling a quick note to her husband, making sure it did not sound too drastic or dramatic, she took the keys to the Mercedes, and ran from the spacious house.

By the time she reached Interstate 89 and headed south towards Concord, she was starting to get scared. She'd never heard Justine sound so . . . so *terrified*, so absolutely desperate. She kept trying to imagine what could have made her sister place such a call. A stalker? A rapist? No, she said Domenic was in trouble too. Could it be something about their son, Vincent?

Pushing down on the accelerator, Kate felt the black Mercedes respond by surging forward, deepening its grip on the Interstate like a sleek jungle cat stretching out its claws.

Or was it Domenic? Maybe he was the one? She tried to imagine what Justine's husband could have done to get them in "very big trouble." Kate's sister, two years older than she, had turned forty last May. She'd been married for eighteen years to Domenic Petralli, an engineer who'd been working for Kendall Structures, an international construction company specializing in bridges, tunnels, and broadcast towers. Ever since Vincent had entered high school, Justine had worked fulltime as an accountant for the Archdiocese of Boston. Now, with Vincent off to college at Holy Cross, they were looking forward to a lot more freedom. And now this . . . this trouble?

Kate couldn't help it. She could feel a wave of terror rushing toward her like a storm beating up the highway from the coast. And she was heading straight into its center. But she *had* to go. Justine had been her best friend all her life. They'd grown up so close, sharing secrets that nobody else would *ever* know. She thought about this as she drove to their rendezvous—one of their most minor secrets, but still a piece of them no one else could possibly know about.

When Justine enrolled at Boston College, it was generally assumed that two years later, Kate would be following her big sister to the same school. But that all changed the summer Kate graduated from Saint Anselm's. She shook her head as she allowed herself the bittersweet memories of what followed that graduation summer. . . .

. . . when her family had taken their annual vacation to Lake Sunapee, renting the camp at water's edge. It had been such a natural and comfortable ritual for all of their lives; so predictable, so stable. But that summer, everything changed. That had been the summer she met Charlie Powell. He was what the summer people called a town-boy, who worked at the Lakeside Inn, one of the best tourist restaurants at Sunapee. Tall, athletic, and smart too, Charlie was the whole package; and he took a giant fall for Kate and her srawberry blonde hair and freckles. Summer love. It was the first and only time in her life Kate ever understood the words. The first time she couldn't bear the thought of being separated from him; the first time the idea of being separated from her sister did not seem like the end of the world. And so instead of attending B.C. that autumn, Kate had her father pull a few strings, call in a few favors, and get her a very late admission to Colby-Sawyer College in New London, just down the road from Lake Sunapee and Charlie Powell. She studied Literature and Computers Stuff at Colby-Sawyer while her dearest Charlie labored to get a degree in business administration at Plymouth State, while he continued to work odd jobs around the lake.

And so, Kate engaged in a small rite of passage, if not letting go of her big sister's hand, at least reaching out for the touch of another as well. Thankfully, Justine didn't seem to mind, and devised a clever, direct way to stay in contact with Kate. On the Interstate into Manchester, which marked almost exactly the halfway point between Boston College and Colby-Sawyer, Justine selected a rendezvous for them. A huge New Hampshire "state store," where every imaginable hard liquor was sold was located at a rest stop off the highway. It was easy to reach, impossible to miss, and a favorite gathering spot of college kids from all over the area, especially on the weekends. Justine would call Kate every week or two and arrange for them to spend a day or a night together, trading college tales and general girl-talk. They called their meeting place "the Voo," and it was one of the special secrets that even years later neither had ever thought to share with anyone else.

How many years had it been since she'd met her sister at the Voo? Kate shook her head as a flood of memories crested over her. And who would have imagined they would be doing it again? Life was indeed a strange and sometime nonsensical journey, and she was so glad she'd had a companion like Justine alongside for most of it.

Kate continued to urge the Mercedes down the darkening and practically desolate stretch of I-89 south before the Concord interchange at I-93. There was rarely much traffic on the road at any time, and this evening proved true to form. To punch through the darkness at eighty or eighty-five was most motorists' rule rather than the exception, despite the always possible sight of a deer in the headlights. But now, just after sunset, even the high speed and unimpeded traffic made her anxious because she needed to just *get there* as soon as possible.

She tried not to think grim thoughts, but as she pushed onward through the solitary darkness, Kate could not avoid thinking that something very bad lay in wait for her. It was funny, in the weird, strange kind of way, that she'd only felt that kind of clairvoyant (or was it prescient?) sense of tragedy one other time in her life . . . and it had been connected even more directly to poor Charlie Powell.

Kate had just gotten back to her dorm after ice skating with some of the girls from her building. It had been the winter of her junior year, she would never forget it. There was a message attached to her door: *Kate call Mrs. Powell right away.* She could remember standing there, staring at the simple note, and sensing a terrible darkness, a void, swirling just beyond the sense of the words. She hadn't wanted to call Mrs. Powell, and she'd wished at that moment she'd never known Charlie or his mother or anything about them. But she did make the call, and when there was no answer, she became even more convinced of the utter wrongness, of the *badness* of what the message implied. Kate wanted no part of it, as if by simply avoiding it, she could keep it from infecting her, from hurting her as she *knew* it would. However, she could not just turn away, and on that far away night, just as on this current one, Kate found herself driving, alone, down a dark road to a place of hideous uncertainty.

As she drove into Sunapee Harbor, toward the Powell

house, she saw the police and the town men in their parkas and Sorrels, and in the lightly tufting flurries of snow, sparkled by the flashing lights of the police cruisers, she knew they'd assembled because of Charlie. And she'd jumped from her car to push her way through the ring of onlookers, where she saw Mrs. Powell crying on the sheriff's shoulder. Just seeing the woman like that was all Kate needed to know—that Charlie was gone from all of their lives. Later she learned the details of how he and four of his friends had knocked back a few "frosties," then rigged up Bill Smith's antique sleigh with a sail with the idea of running it across the frozen surface of Lake Sunapee like an old schooner. But the old sleigh was too massive, too heavy, and its rails had sliced right through the ice and taken the five college boys into the frigid, dark center of the lake. The sleigh had gone down like a torpedoed ship, said one of the state policemen, and once it disappeared beneath the black water, that was it. Not a sound, nor a trace. Charlie and the others were never found, and Kate had never been able to look out on that lake . . . not ever again.

She exhaled slowly and blinked back a single tear as she stared through the windshield at the empty road ahead. Back then, when she was caught up in the blank unbelieving dead weight of the tragedy, Kate hadn't faced what she knew now—that she knew Charlie was dead as soon as she'd seen the note on her dorm room door.

But why was she retracing such old steps? Was that same feeling returning like a bad dream to haunt her through this night as well? Was she trying to tell herself that something very bad had happened to her sister?

Stop it, she told herself. *Just get through this damn drive and find out what's really happening.* She wished she'd been able to bring Lawrence along. He'd provided her with the stability that had always been missing in her life. Kate had always believed the simple truth of that—and not the obvious notion of feeling good because of all the Harrison money. Lawrence hadn't been the first wealthy man she could have married, and she had taken a pass on all of them, despite the sometimes outrageous advice of her more flamboyant sister.

Justine.

It was funny how your thoughts could always loop in on themselves. Always come back to the business at hand. No matter what she did to distract or entertain herself, there was no escaping it.

Justine was in *very big trouble*, and she had reached out to her baby sister for help. *Well, just hang on till I get there*, Kate thought. She'd just passed a sign that warned of the connecting ramp to I-93 south to Manchester. She couldn't remember exactly how much farther, but she knew she was getting close. After the sun slipped below the treeline, it was hard to tell where you were on the Interstate because it was so damned dark out there. No lights, no landmarks. In New Hampshire, if you didn't see a familiar green sign marking the next exit, you may as well be on the dark side of the moon.

Checking her watch, she was surprised to see that she'd been on the road for almost an hour exactly. She must be—

And suddenly there was a huge sign on the right side of the highway for the rest stop and the State Liquor Store. The exit ramp appeared quickly and she had to brake down. Kate felt her heart hitch up for an instant as fear and excitement merged in her. She tugged quickly on the wheel of the Mercedes and the sleek sedan almost jumped off the Interstate instead of merely slipping into a brief high-speed powerslide.

For an instant, Kate was certain she was losing control of the car, but its heavy chassis and superior suspension system wouldn't allow any severe body sway or roll, and the tires regained purchase as though everything was part of some smoothly running machine. It wasn't until she reached the bottom of the ramp that Kate released her breath.

Take it easy. You're almost there.

Through the windshield, she could see signs and stores that keyed old memories. She could have been nineteen again—so much about the place hadn't changed at all. Kate followed the access road into the liquor store's sprawling parking lot. Justine had always beaten her to the Voo, and had always parked in the lower end of the lot, as far from the store's entrance as possible. There was no reason to think she would play things any differently tonight; Kate headed for the lot's farthest corner, where there were practically no cars at all.

As she negotiated the final turn at the end of the last line of spaces, she saw Domenic's maroon BMW sitting by itself under the sallow light of a sodium streetlight. Tapping the accelerator, she speeded up, lightly beeped the horn, and flashed her lights. The old ritual came back from a forgotten parcel of memories.

Kate slowed down as she approached the driver's side of the BMW. There was no one seated behind the wheel, and the car looked somehow ... abandoned instead of just unoccupied. Kate stopped, allowing her headlights to fix the other car in their beams like a jacklighted deer. Something told her not to just glide in and park next to the empty car.

Something was wrong here. Her own extra sense, her prescience or whatever the hell they called it, was kicking like a bad habit. An alarm light strobed maniacally down the emergency corridors of her mind.

Just keep going. You can't stop now.

Part of her inner self urged her onward, while another less vocal side signaled caution, if not outright panic.

Justine, where are you?

Maybe she'd gone into the state store for a cocktail? Sure, and maybe she took the Tooth Fairy and the Easter Bunny along for company. . . .

She knew she couldn't just sit there staring at her sister's car and not do anything. It was time to get moving.

Slowly, Kate unhitched her seat belt, reached for the door handle, and slid her legs out from beneath the wheel. Long and pale in her baggy Land's End khaki shorts, her bare legs reminded her how vulnerable and nearly naked she was to any real danger. But there was no turning away now.

Standing up, she tried to see into the BMW but the glare of her headlights on the driver's window prevented it.

"Justine!? Are you in there?"

No answer. Not a sound.

Kate moved to the window, blocking the headlight glare, and peered into the car.

"Justine, what're you—"

Her voice was cut off in midsentence just as her sister's life must have been.

Without thinking, despite what she saw through the glass, Kate grabbed the handle, unlatched the door. As she pulled it open, her vision blurred, as if her eyes refused to focus on Justine's body.

So much blood. . . .

The thought saturated her, holding her. Against her will she was seeing everything clearly now. Too clearly. Justine's body lay sprawled across the driver's seat, heaved across the center console. Her throat had been cut from one ear to the other, and the wound gaped obscenely as her head lolled back, her eyes open and staring out through the passenger's window, but seeing nothing. Her T-shirt and jeans were stained almost black from the tide of blood, which had pooled thickly in the carpeted footwell and imparted a pungent metallic odor to the interior. Kate's stomach lurched, and she staggered back for an instant to gulp a breath of air.

So much goddamned blood. . . . Oh Justine. . . .

She knew she had to get somebody, get some help, the police, but she couldn't make herself move. She couldn't stop looking at the twisted, savaged form of her sister, hardly believing anybody could be transformed so thoroughly into something so ghastly. And then, just as she was feeling able to turn away from the body, to finally say good-bye in a sense, she noticed Justine's outstretched index finger above the passenger seat.

There was something about the way her hand was poised over the smooth leather that forced Kate to move slowly, mechanically, and walk aound to the other side of the car. Opening the passenger-side door, she crouched down to see that her sister had written something on the tan leather—in her own blood:

5508 0854 9888 9879

Even in her dulled state of emotion overload, Kate knew it was some kind of desperate message from her sister. Something she'd believed was so important that it was the last thing she'd tried to tell her. Something that someone else had believed was important enough to kill for. . . .

Staring at the numbers, Kate realized their format meant something, but she couldn't make herself think that rationally right now. And she knew she could never memorize such a long string of numbers.

Fumbling in her jacket pockets, she found what she knew was there—a pencil and an old scorecard from Eastman Golf Course. Exactly what she needed. Kate quickly wrote down the sequence of numbers in the blocks of the scorecard. To anyone looking at the card, it was nothing more than hastily-scrawled scores. But Justine's message had to be terribly meaningful and she must preserve it.

But only for herself.

Kate stuffed the card back into her poclet, then using the sleeve of her sister's chambray shirt, she rubbed at the numbers on the leather until they were nothing but an illegible smear.

Slowly, she backed away, careful not to further disturb her sister's body. She looked into Justine's face, now rendered down into a pale mask of who she'd really been, one final time. *Whoever did this to you . . .* she thought with a bitter resolve, *I'll get them. I promise you.*

A knot of nausea twisted through her insides as the initial shock started to wear off. She didn't want to allow herself to be sick, to be so weak. But the onrush of conflicting emotions was making it hard to keep it together. She just couldn't believe it. That her sister could get herself into something that could get her killed, that she'd actually done it, that she was oh God really dead. . . .

Leaning against the outside of the BMW, looking up into the black sky, Kate thought about praying for the first time in many years. But if there really was anything like a God up there, how the hell had he let something like this happen? Just exactly what was going on? She would have to—

The sound of approaching sirens broke the surface of her thoughts. The air felt cool, crisp; and despite the warmth of the August night, a chill ghosted through her. The sirens grew louder, closer, and she saw the flashing lights of police cruisers angling into the vast rest stop parking lot at high speed. Three of them, fishtailing and powersliding, the cars split up and approached her position from three different directions.

How could they know she was here?

Kate faced the cruiser coming straight at her and began waving her arms. The car skidded to a halt, its doors springing open as two cops appeared with their handguns drawn and pointed at her.

"Stand away from the car, Ma'am!" squawked a bullhorned voice. "Get your hands up where we can see them, and don't move!"

Kate took a step forward as the other two vehicles boxed her in from both flanks. "My sister's been murdered!" she screamed. "What're you doing!? My sister's been—!"

Somebody rushed her from the side, body-slamming her against the front fender of the BMW. He pinned her arms to her hips, then drew them back, slapping hand-cuffs across her wrists all in a series of slick, precise motions.

"You have the right to remain silent . . ." said the cop, reciting it like an altar boy's familiar litany.

ThREE

MATT ETCHISON

*I*t had been a very long, very tough day for Matt Etch-
ison, and it wasn't getting any better because the Red
Sox were taking a pounding from the Orioles down in
Baltimore. And it was only the sixth inning.

Leaning back in his executive chair, he remoted off
the TV in the wall unit across the room, and looked back
to the computer screen on his desk. He'd just finished
printing end-of-the-month invoices on all the clients who
still owed him money. The accounts receivable report
sported a very handsome bottom line and life was good
even if he didn't like light beer.

He double-checked that he'd saved all the files, and
made a backup, then powered everything down. He liked
computers because they allowed him more direct, hands-
on control of his business and even his leisure. Once
he'd crested the learning curve, the faxmodems and
scanners and printers and all the other crap saved him
immense amounts of time and money. He'd liked his
receptionist and his bookkeeper, but he really didn't
need them with one-key accounting, voice mail, pagers,

and cellular phones. Etchison Investigations was now a one-man band and showing no signs of stress or fatigue.

Standing up to stretch, he had an urge for a Nestor 727, but thought better of it. Way better. It had taken him *years* of frustration to finally quit cigarettes and he wasn't going to allow the mildly euphoric pleasure of a fine cigar drag him back down into the quag of addiction. One of his many lawyer friends had given him one at the Excelsior Club the other night to celebrate the successful wrap on a case, and Matt had accepted the cigar against his better judgment. Days later, it seemed, he was still feeling the effects of the nicotine jolt he'd given his system, and that was plain bullshit, my friend. No way he was giving in to that old weakness.

He smiled to himself. If he had to find a weakness, better to find a *new* one like overabundant amounts of money, or a far older one like green-eyed redheads. . . .

As he reached for the pull cord on his desk lamp, the phone rang and he debated whether or not to answer it until he noticed it was his private line—the one reserved for close friends, top-level colleagues, and the few relatives he'd allowed to remain in his life.

Ah, what the hell . . . it was too late to go anywhere; the call wasn't really keeping him from anything. And besides, he always had this weird feeling that the call he ignored was the one that would launch him on the adventure of his life.

"Hello?" he said softly.

"Matt! I was hoping I might catch you there. I was going to try the pager next."

"Jonathan, what're you doing working so late?" Matt sat back down in his desk chair, smiling as he chided one of his oldest friends and best business contacts in Boston.

Jonathan Markley chuckled perfunctorily on the other end of the connection. It was a mannerism which meant he was in full-blown mega-lawyer mode. "I've got some trouble with one of my biggest clients, and I'm going to need your help. I've already told them about your fees and everything's been approved. You're on—if you want it."

Matt nodded to himself. Sounded interesting. "Details?"

"Although it's not widely known, I've always handled all the personal and business affairs of Lawrence Copley Harrison," said Markley.

Matt whistled. "Very powerful guy," he said. "What's he done?"

"Actually, his wife, Kate is the client. . . ." Markley paused for a fine dramatic moment. "Mr. Harrison has gotten himself killed, and so has Mrs. Harrison's sister, Justine Petralli."

"Jesus, all in the same day!" said Matt. "Anything else you can tell me?"

"Lawrence was shot with one of his own deer rifles."

"The proverbial 'hunting accident'?"

"Ah, no, actually," said Markley. "He was fishing at the time."

Matt smiled. "Christ, Jonathan, maybe I should just go down and read the police reports. What's Mrs. Harrison's part in all this . . . besides being the prime suspect?"

Markley cleared his throat. "That's what I've always liked about you, Matt. You can cut right to the core of just about anything."

"Where's Kate Harrison now?"

"Manchester Central District Police Precinct. New Hampshire."

" 'Bout an hour's ride," said Matt.

"I know. I'm preparing to drive up there to attend her interrogation and to arrange for bail."

"Is she innocent?" Matt picked up a pencil and began doodling dollar signs on his memo pad.

"Yes, I think so." Markley sounded sincere.

"That's good enough for me," said Matt. "You want some company for the ride?"

FOUR

Roma, Italia

JAGEN KERSCHOW

*H*e adjusted the windsor knot on his $300 silk Brioni tie, then returned his hands to the edge of the small alfresco table at the Ristorante Nino. Just beyond him, on the sidewalk of via Borgognona, he watched the crowds of tourists intersect at via M. di Fiori to brawl their way either to, or from, the Piazza di Spagna. Once there, they would take pictures of each other sitting on the Spanish Steps, and then begin wondering why it was such a famous attraction.

Jagen signaled for his waiter, ordered another gin and tonic. Such a plebeian drink, and English to boot, but damn it, it *was* the perfect drink for the muggy days of late summer in the Mediterranean. Jagen checked his watch, a Vacheron Constantin Chronograph, and smiled as he realized his appointment was now twelve minutes late.

Looking across the table, he shook his head with subtle drama at his companion, Renee Beauvais, the most powerful member of the Euro-industrial cartel. She was what they called a "handsome" woman. Early forties, thin and fit, ferociously bright, and far too stylish to be coquetishly attractive or sexy. She always conducted herself with the demeanor of the cool professional, and it was that lack of warmth that distanced her from most women. She and previous members of her family had been guild members for centuries, and her rise to one of the board positions was no sop to political correctness or some fatuous social "movement." Renee Beauvais was a shrewd, brilliant, and completely necessary component of the guild's highest eschelon. Kurt liked her enough to respect her and maybe even fear her a little.

"Streicher . . ." he said to her. "Other than an assignment, he was *always* late. I think if he ever showed up on time, I would be convinced he'd come to kill me."

Renée smiled and looked at him over her titantium-framed sunglasses. "That's good information to know. We wouldn't want him tipping you off, would we?"

"You are so clever," said Jagen.

Picking up the luncheon menu, he carefully donned his reading glasses and scanned the offerings, trying to decide how he wished to stimulate his palate. Ristorante Nino was admittedly not as elegant as the vaulted ceilings and arches of El Toula, but he preferred their Tuscan entrees and the open-air ambiance. The waiter returned with his cocktail, then discreetly vanished.

As Jagen sipped beneath its dry bouquet, he looked at her again. "Sorry, madame, in my distraction, I forgot to ask you if you would have liked a refill."

"I am quite capable of taking care of my own needs," said Renée.

"Yes, I agree," he said. "But my aristocratic upbringing precludes me from not being a gentleman."

She smiled in a very small fashion. "You have always thought highly of yourself. I suppose that is a good thing."

He saluted her with his glass, then scanned the crowds for anything unusual. He did this as much out of a natural curiosity as necessary paranoia. Although he believed he was one of the three or four most powerful people on earth, he was practically unknown to everyone in the world. Hence, there was little reason to fear the *gemeinkeit*, but his father had taught him that no one can ever be *too* careful. He began to lapse into a hazy, pleasant memory from his childhood in Buenos Aires when he saw Renee's gaze sharpen and focus on something behind him. Almost simultaneously, a hand lightly touched his shoulder and a voice announced its presence.

"Good afternoon, Herr Kerschow," said a silky baritone of great familiarity. "And of course, to you, Madame Beauvais."

Jagen removed his reading glasses, and looked up to see the broad-shouldered Streicher pull out a chair and prepare to take a seat. At forty-two, the man was in peak physical condition, as revealed by the exquisite tailoring of his Mondo di Marco suitjacket, the thickness of his neck, and the grace with which he moved. His dirty-blonde hair was combed straight back, accenting his strong forehead and steel-blue eyes. Jagen was certain that Streicher's good looks and savoir faire made him an almost irresistible package to most women and probably the faggots as well.

"Fashionably late," said Jagen with a curt nod, the hint of a smile. "What are you drinking?"

"Speyside single malt, ice," he said.

Jagen shook his head. "They won't have that here."

"I know. I just wanted you to know my tastes continue to be expensive. I'll settle for Glenlivet."

Kerschow nodded, signaled to his waiter, who'd been hovering politely out of earshot. When the white-jacketed man reached the edge of the table, Jagen ordered the scotch for his number one employee.

"How was the trip?" asked Jagen after the waiter had vanished.

Streicher shrugged. "Enervating, as usual. But my tour of the estates of 'the rich and famous' was very enriching—as you've both no doubt heard."

Renee leaned closer and removed her sunglasses, as if this would help her hear more clearly. "We've been briefed," she said.

Jagen nodded. "Yes. A beautiful job. The glass is on its way to the lab. Safe and sound, as the Americans say."

Streicher nodded. "You didn't want to see me just to give me a pat on the head."

Jagen shrugged. "Of course not. There are further concerns that we must—"

Pausing while the waiter placed a glass of amber liquid over ice, Jagen looked out on the endless stream of tourists passing by their location. Uncountable numbers of Japanese, the usual over-representation of Germans, and a scattering of Americans. It occurred to him at that moment he'd become terminally bored with Rome. No longer the cosmopolitan lodestone of Europe, but a sluggish, over priced, and baited trap for the *untermenschen*—the common rabble who polluted its streets like sewage being sluiced from the site of one religious excess to the next. Talk about ennui. . . .

"*Grazie*," said Streicher as the waiter nodded and slipped away. Then to Jagen: "You were saying?"

Jagen sipped from his gin and tonic, leaned forward to speak as softly as possible. "As you must realize, obtaining the glass is only the beginning, plus there are other developments we must now handle with our usual efficiency."

"I am listening." Streicher sampled his scotch.

"Early communiqués confirm the Vatican's outrage," said Renee. "We have poked a very large stick into that particular hornets' nest."

"No, really?" Streicher grinned. "Any details?"

"Domenic Petralli almost intercepted you at Fiumicino."

"So what? A failure is a failure."

Jagen tilted his head, the merest suggestion of agreement. "Perhaps. But his presence was an indication to me that their intelligence gathering is impressive. Not as well placed as our own, but formidable."

"I can handle Petralli and his merry band," said Streicher.

"If you couldn't, you wouldn't be working for us." Jagen toasted his colleague with an upheld glass.

"Is there more?"

"Our courier escort attempted to remove Petralli at the da Vinci terminal, and—"

"He's too smart for that."

"Apparently," said Renee, with just the right hint of sarcasm. "Not only did he get away, but he arranged to meet his wife at Ciampino."

Streicher leaned forward, obviously impressed. "The military airport."

"Exactly. She flew in on a State Department jet."

"To what purpose?"

Jagen shrugged. "That's what we don't know. He managed to lose our coverage for a short period of time. We do have satellite photos of the two of them on the tarmac, just as she was reboarding the jetliner, but we have no idea what might have been exchanged."

"What was her destination?"

"Boston. Logan," said Renee.

"Commercial terminal," said Streicher, rapidly assimilating the data. "Did we close the deal?"

Renee nodded. "Oh yes. She hadn't been able to do anything other than contact her sister by phone."

"Do we have the conversation?"

Jagen waved off the question. "Totally innocuous. She wanted to meet with the sister in person, but our man with the New Hampshire State Police prevented that."

Streicher nodded. "Any loose ends?"

"The sister and her husband. But they've been tied up." Jagen Kerschow ran his thin, delicate fingers through his silvery hair. With his trademark unruly mane, he'd been told he looked like a conductor, and he'd always liked that image. "Neither of them had any knowledge of Petralli's true identity. They knew nothing—especially concerning the current operation."

Streicher held up a cautionary index finger. "Never assume anything so positive. I have survived this long by always presuming the worst scenario. That way, I am never surprised."

"Not to worry. We have people monitoring the outcomes of our actions. If there has been any leakage, we will know it almost instantly. If there is additional cleaning up to be done, it will happen."

Streicher nodded. "Yes, but it may be a good idea for me to supervise that end of things."

"We want you here on the continent." Renee replaced her sunglasses on her thin, Hellenic nose. "Your assignment is Petralli."

"Don't worry about Petralli," said Streicher. "He is mine."

Jagen finished his cocktail. "I know. . . ."

"However, I would feel better if I could oversee the States operation. I never trust the Americans. They are too damned inventive, too damned lucky."

"Luck is merely the residue of determination," said Jagen.

"Then the bastards are dripping with residue." Streicher knocked back the remainder of his single malt. "You should both know that. Be careful with them."

"You will receive daily updates. You'll know if things start to spin off center."

"All right, what else?"

Jagen picked up the menu and readjusted his reading glasses across his nose. "I have always liked the grilled liver of veal," he said. "Or the *fagioli cotti al fiasco*."

"Have you?"

"Let us relax for a moment and enjoy the cuisine, Kurt," said Jagen with dark chuckle. "After all, we have all the time in the world, and most of the money."

FIVE

Interstate 93

MATT ETCHISON

The ride up from Boston was easy, once they cleared I-95 and picked up I-93 north, especially in Markley's new Lexus. As much as Matt didn't want to admit it, the Japanese had mastered the art of designing and constructing damned fine cars. His father had been shot up in Hellandia, New Guinea, during the World War in the Pacific, and the old man had always carried a vitriolic hatred of anything from Japan. And when you grow up with that white noise of hate blistering in your ears all the time, you don't have much choice but to believe it. But that war was more than a half-century buried, and now that his father was also in the ground, it was time to trash the old prejudices.

Jonathan Markley had his own words of caution about the Japanese—he was always saying how their stock market and their banks were keeping the American exchanges propped up like cheesy scenery flats at a community theater. And as they drove through the Massachusetts night towards the state line, Jonathan rambled on about how the Japs were unbelievably smart, shrewd, and ultimately dangerous. They could still kill us with a Zero; but this time it would be in our bank accounts instead of the skies.

But tonight, Matt wasn't in the mood for geopolitical finance, he was more interested in Kate Harrison. When Jonathan paused in his financial diatribe to catch a breath, Matt seized the opportunity: "Okay, Jon, let me ask you something."

"Sure, what?"

"What's she like?"

"Huh? Who?"

"Mrs. Harrison. Your client? The woman we're going to bail out of jail tonight?"

Jonathan Markley grinned as he continued to look at the road slipping beneath the path of his headlights. "Oh yeah. I guess I was getting a little cranked up, eh?"

"Just a little," said Matt. "You know, after you've made as much as you have, and you've got so much socked away it really doesn't matter if you never make another dime . . . what the hell is this obsession with money?"

Jonathan shook his head slowly, looking a little sheepish. "You know, that's a good question. My wife asks me the same thing, and I don't know for sure what the answer might be. When I was a kid I liked collecting stamps and baseball cards and the stuff you used to get in the cereal boxes. So now, I collect stocks and foreign currencies and options. But you're right, I don't much think about the amounts and the values anymore—it's just part of this big game, this big set of manipulations."

"I still don't get it," said Matt.

"Well, it's like peeking behind the curtain to see how the world really runs. The little guys, the small investors and the old ladies with the savings accounts, they are completely at the mercy of an elite class of movers and shakers. I mean, come on, Matt, you have to know that, don't you?"

Matt sighed audibly. "Yeah, but I don't much give a damn."

"That's why you'll never be wealthy," said Jonathan.

"I'm wealthy enough."

"Well, then, you won't be super-rich." Jonathan smiled.

Matt laughed softly. "I don't really need more money than I can possibly spend. There's a point of diminishing returns for me."

"Okay. . . ."

"Okay," said Matt quickly. "So tell me more about Kate Harrison."

"Is this for personal or business use?" Jonathan looked at him for a moment before returning attention to the dark swath of Interstate ahead of them.

"In my line of work," said Matt. "There's not much difference."

Jonathan exhaled with mock exasperation. "You're one of a kind, Matthew."

"I certainly hope so."

"So what do you want to know about her?"

"The usual stats. What do you want me to do here—play twenty fucking questions?"

"I'm not trying to be difficult, it's just that I'm having a hard time figuring out where to start, what to leave out, what to leave in."

"And you call yourself a lawyer," said Matt. "Christ, Jonathan."

"Hey, no lawyer jokes, remember?"

"Okay, tell me how you met her. First impressions."

Jonathan Markley nodded as he watched the road. "That works. Okay, listen. . . . Old man Harrison brought her with him on a routine visit to our offices downtown. It was right after they'd gotten married."

"How long ago was that?"

"About ten years ago. She looked pretty young—probably late twenties, maybe thirty—back then. Larry Harrison was probably forty-five or so. They acted very much in love, very much in synch. Seemed like a good couple."

"What about her . . . mind, her motivations? Could you get any kind of read on her back then?"

"Right from the start I thought she was a sincere woman, if that's what you mean," said Jonathan. "She was no gold digger."

"You sure?"

"Oh yeah. She'd come from a decent bunch. The family name was Manville. Her great-grandfather had made a little money in the restaurant business around the turn of the century. Most of it got washed away during the '29 Crash, but there was enough left to keep everybody's aspirations blue for a couple more generations. Her father sent the daughters to private colleges, worked as an insurance exec with Hancock."

Matt digested this, and made a note to spend a little time on the Net and its search engines. "Okay, so she came from an okay family. What else?"

"She'd waited a while to get married. That tells me she's pretty smart," said Jonathan. "She obviously had spent some time exploring the world, getting to understand how men are, and which ones to avoid."

"That was probably easy—all the poor ones. . . ." Matt smiled. "What about a profession? She have one or was she just working hard at being wife of a really rich guy?"

Jonathan grinned, shook his head, and continued: "No, she's had her own consulting business. She's some kind of computer geek. She specializes in setting up 'data havens' for multinational companies."

"What's a 'data haven'?"

Markley shrugged. "No clue."

"I can find out, don't worry about it." Matt continued jotting down his mental notes. Jonathan had just passed a sign that said deer crossing, and he wondered for an instant why they put those signs up—deer certainly weren't reading them. "Go on, Jon, you're doing great."

"Well, she kept her business going, even after meeting Larry, and—"

"How'd she do it?"

"Do *what?*"

"Meet Lawrence Harrison? Did she actively pursue him?"

Jonathan grinned. "Oh, I see where you're going here. No, nothing like that. Larry told the story all the time. One of his companies was interested in some kind of sophisticated information retrieval and storage, you know typical computer stuff—and Larry was part of this group of board interviewing consultants. He met Kate in one of the meetings, and—"

"And old man Harrison falls for her, chases her, throws tons of gifts her way, and she lives happily ever after," said Matt.

"Well, kinda, but it wasn't as easy as you're making it sound."

"Tell me," said Matt.

Jonathan shrugged. "Well, from what I can tell, Kate wasn't interested in Larry at all."

"Couldn't get past his third eye, eh?"

Jonathan chuckled. "Larry wasn't a bad-looking guy. He kept himself in great shape and had plenty of available women. He didn't have that smell of desperation on him, if you know what I mean."

Matt did. He nodded. "So she wasn't interested. You think that's maybe what got to old Larry—couldn't bear to have a woman turn him and his empire down?"

Jonathan shrugged. "Maybe a little of that. But from what I could tell, he was just nuts about her."

"Why?" said Matt. "Is she a looker?"

"Depends on your personal tastes. Me, I like 'em with long dark hair, skinny, and legs up to their shoulders. Kate Harrison is the more wholesome-looking type, and with eyes that let you know right up front she is smart and doesn't like bullshit."

Oh-oh, thought Matt. *She sounded like trouble already.*

Actually, Kate Manville Harrison struck him as a very intriguing woman, full of hard-left turns into places you never thought she'd ever take you.

"Okay," he said after a pause. "I have to ask you this . . ."

"What?" Jonathan continued to look at the road ahead.

"When I asked you on the phone if you thought she was innocent, you said you 'thought so,' didn't you?"

"Yeah, so what're you getting at?"

"I mean, why the qualifier, Jonathan? After what you've been telling me about her, she sounds like a pretty decent person. So why aren't you sure she didn't do it?"

Jonathan shrugged. "Well, I haven't seen any of the evidence. Any of the case they have against her. I mean, knowing Kate the way I do, I—"

"You're not piping her, are you Jonathan?" Matt was not smiling when he said this.

"Jesus Christ, come on, Matt! What do you think I am?"

"That's the point," he said. "I know *what* you are. And unless you've changed radically in the last twenty-four hours, you're still the same guy who proclaimed drunkenly at our last poker game that you'd fuck a snake in a boot—as long as it was wearing a skirt."

"I don't *do* my clients." Jonathan's tone had become a little icy.

Matt shook his head. "Jonathan Tyler Markley, Esquire. Don't insult my memory or my intelligence."

"Okay, once or twice, but never during the proceedings! I—"

"Yeah, well we don't want to distract the jury, do we?"

"Hey, what're you doing here, man? I mean, I can't believe you!"

Matt shrugged. "I'm just trying to see what you *really*

know about this woman. I mean, would the thought of killing her husband ever cross her mind?"

"Never."

"Because," said Matt, ignoring the interjection. "Because lots of spouses have bandied that particular solution around in the privacy of their own skulls. And whether you want to believe it or not, they usually start thinking that way in the first place because they're getting boffed by somebody else."

Jonathan put his hands up for a moment. "Okay, I give up. You're right about that. And wrong about Kate Harrison. She's way too classy to want anything to do with me."

"What about anybody else? Somebody who could use the control of the old guy's companies."

"Look, I'm sure there's plenty of potential enemies," said Jonathan. "But they're not in bed with Kate, I can tell you that."

"We'll see."

Jonathan shook his head. "You're going to be meeting her very soon. After you talk to her, I want to see if you're still thinking like a small-time divorce dick."

Matt grinned. "Oooh, low blow, Jonathan."

Jonathan shook his head. "Well, if you're supposed to be this big-time troubleshooter for Washington's elite, I just thought . . . maybe you should start talking like one."

"Okay, point for Mr. Markley," said Matt. "Sorry, I can't help it if my business has taught me one of society's saddest truths."

"Which is . . . ?"

"Always expect the worst from people."

As he said the words, Matt was looking out his side window into the trackless darkness of rural New Hampshire. Somewhere out there were all the answers he would need . . . and also all the trouble.

Six

Manchester, New Hampshire

KATE HARRISON

*H*ow could any of this be happening to her?

Eight hours ago, she'd been sitting on the deck, watching the colorful sails of small boats lazing across Eastman Lake. And now she was supposed to believe that Lawrence was dead? That Justine had been practically decapitated by a killer's knife? And that she was the number one suspect—because her sister had supposedly tipped off the police?

It was impossible. How could she *believe* it?

But she must.

Even though it all sounded so . . . so stupid, so resoundingly silly. Or at least it should . . . if it weren't a truth so heavy and leaden that it threatened to drag her down, down to a bottomless place where hope died eons ago. Kate wanted to laugh, but she knew she didn't have the inner strength to do it right about now. The drab-green, cement walls of her holding cell seemed like they were gradually closing in on all sides. Like a three-dimensional vise, preparing to compact her like yesterday's trash.

And part of her was wishing it could be that easy. She couldn't believe they were dead. . . .

Lawrence and Justine.

Gone.

Every time she thought of either one of them, she could hear their voices in her head. The two most essential, important people in her life had been ripped away from her in an instant. *Why?* What was going on that could possibly include her in its widening gyre of pain and madness?

Despite a deepening feeling of hopelessness, Kate knew she could *not* give up believing in her ability to get through this nightmare. Because she *would* get through. Just hold onto that central thought, and everything else would work out. If she would—

"Mrs. Harrison?" the voice interrupted, and she looked up to see a familiar face. Young. Short, sandy hair and blue eyes. It was the detective who interrogated her when the troopers first brought her in. She couldn't remember his name.

"Yes?" Kate stood up from the bunk and folded her arms defensively. "Is my lawyer here?"

"Not yet. But I think we're going to need to talk a little more," said the detective.

"I don't have anything to say unless Mr. Markley is with me."

"I understand that," said the cop, as he adjusted the knot on his cheap tie self-consciously. "But I thought you might be more comfortable waiting in the conference room."

He smiled diffidently as she studied him for a moment. "I've forgotten your name, Detective." Kate hoped she sounded strong, confident.

"Dorr, Detective Sergeant Terrence Dorr." He stood there, beyond the bars of the cell, waiting patiently.

Kate paced to the far end of the small cubicle, turned to face him. "Why are you suddenly being so nice?"

He shrugged. "We just got a call from your lawyer. He'll be arriving in a few minutes."

Kate nodded grimly. "And you're anxious to put me under the hot lights again, right?"

"Listen, Mrs. Harrison, if it means anything to you, I'm not real convinced you've done anything wrong . . . but at the moment, you're the only suspect we've got. And I'm sure you know the spouse is *always* a primary suspect . . . and you can imagine, we would like to be able to locate your sister's husband."

"You still can't find him?"

"Not yet."

"At any rate, we need to take a walk down the hall. You have some people here."

Kate nodded, watched the jailer unlock the cell door and slide it back. She walked past him and Detective Dorr, then waited to be escorted off the block. He led her down several corridors to the bullpen of the precinct house, then beyond it to a small room with venetian blinds at the windows and a table with six chairs around it. After closing the door, the detective took a seat opposite her.

"Coffee, soda?"

"No, thank you." Kate maintained her demeanor of indignation, despite his attempts to make nice.

Screw him, she thought in a sudden burst of renewed anger. *How could he possibly think I killed my husband and my sister! Could he really think I could do something like that?*

"Mrs. Harrison, I'm sorry it has to be like this. I really am."

She looked away, as though studying the lack of decor in the room. "Why do I think this is a setup? Where's the two-way mirror and the hidden mike?"

Detective Dorr allowed himself a small grin in spite of the situation. He looked a little like a younger Dave Letterman when he did this. "Mrs. Harrison, I think you've been watching too much of the old tube. We don't do stuff like that. We're too busy to be that clever or dramatic."

She looked at him, but remained silent as her anger continued to surge through her like a low-level current.

He shrugged. "No kidding, I think you've been set up."

Looking at him squarely, she sensed he was being sincere. If he was trying to really be helpful, he'd have his chance after Jonathan arrived. She looked at her watch, its face ringed in diamond chips. He should be here any minute.

"Why do you say that?" she heard herself ask, in spite of her desire to seem as aloof and outraged as possible.

"Just a feeling. You get 'em all the time in this job. This guy's lying . . . this guy's telling the truth . . . guilty . . . innocent . . . you know what I mean?"

"No, not really. I've never been in this business."

Nonplused, Detective Dorr continued. "Too many things look too 'pat,' and we realize this. Everything unfolded by the numbers, and the state police even admitted to us they felt like they were being manipulated. It was like everything was timed out on a prearranged schedule. Crimes aren't usually unraveled that easily.

"So what is going on here? What could this possibly mean?"

"It's still early . . . we're still trying to put things together," he said in an attempt to make sense out of their lack of leads or clues.

Just then, a uniformed officer tapped on the door, opened it and leaned in just far enough to announce the arrival of her attorney.

"Bring him in, Al," said Dorr, as he stepped back.

Kate felt a sudden rush of relief, as if she no longer had to be as tough, as strong, when she saw Jonathan Markley enter the room. With his charcoal Pal Zileri suit and his briefcase from Barney's, he looked exactly as a modern day rescuing knight should look. He was your standard high-priced, family-and-business attorney, and she was glad to see him even if she had no enthusiasm to show it right about now. She was about to greet him when a second man followed Markley into the room, and she paused to quickly assess Matt Etchison, the highly recommended private investigator.

Where Jonathan was all smooth and polished, Etchison appeared slightly rough with a studied casualness. He was of medium height and a good athletic build for someone his age. He looked like he was in his early forties only around his dark brown eyes. His hair was cut short and simple in a form-follows-function kind of way.

"Jonathan," she said, standing up to accept her lawyer's hand and then a perfunctory hug.

"I'm so sorry to be seeing you under such circumstances, Kate. I'm really sorry."

"I know, I know. . . ." she said softly.

Turning smoothly, Jonathan gestured towards his companion. "This is Matt Etchison."

"Kate Harrison," she said. "Jonathan has spoken very highly of you. Thank you for coming on such short notice."

"Short notice is part of the job specs," he said with a polite nod, as he shook her hand. "Sorry to hear about all this. . . . We're going to help you."

He spoke with a quiet confidence that immediately touched her, and she found herself disposed to *want* to like this Matt Etchison. If Jonathan Markley trusted him, then he must be well-qualified and competent.

"Thank you," said Kate. "That's about all I can say right now."

"All right," said Jonathan. "Let's get started by getting you out of here."

They did.

Within thirty minutes, Jonathan had taken care of everything. Kate had been released on bail, pending further investigation; the media had been efficiently diverted; and funeral arrangements were already in progress.

Her car needed to be released from the impound yard, but she was far too distressed and distracted to want to do any driving by herself. It could wait until the following morning.

"Oh God, I have no idea what to say . . . what to do now?" she said, feeling suddenly exhausted with the release of all the tension that had been jacking her up. All three of them were standing on the front steps to the Manchester Northern District Precinct. Despite being close to midnight, the air was pleasantly warm.

"You feel like doing a little more driving?" said Etchison to Jonathan.

"Why? Where?" The lawyer looked puzzled.

"Back up to the lake house," Etchison said. "I think it's a good place to start."

"Start what?" asked Kate.

"I've been thinking about what we know so far," said Etchison. "And I have no idea what we're dealing with. Is there anything at your summer home that . . . somebody might want or need?"

"What do you mean?" Kate wasn't thinking all that clearly, and her normally logical mindset was absent.

"Well, your sister was trying to reach you. . . . Do you think she was trying to get you away from the house for some reason? Was something going to happen there?"

"I . . . have no idea," said Kate. She knew Justine had wanted to tell her something, and in fact *had* given her those numbers, but her instincts were telling her to hold off on that bit of data for now. It seemed like that was something she should confide to them when they were not so . . . so out in the open. Someplace more private, more . . . safe.

"I know it's late," said Etchison. "But I'd feel better about checking the place out before too many other people have a chance to go over it, to go through it. Even the police."

"Why? What do you mean?"

"When you don't know what you're looking for," said Etchison as they began walking toward Markley's car, "you have no idea what might turn out to be a clue or evidence and what's not. . . . You have to trust me on this one, I guess, but I'd feel better if we could get a look at your place as soon as possible."

Jonathan Markley looked at her. "Kate, I think you should think about staying in Boston for the time being . . . until we get things sorted out."

"All right," she said. "If you think that's a good idea. . . ."

"So maybe, we could use this chance to get a few things done. You could gather up anything you might want to take with you back to town, and we can close the place up good and proper."

"That's right," said Etchison. "Few birds. One stone. That sort of thing."

Kate nodded. Admittedly, she wasn't thinking as clearly as usual, and everything the two men were saying sounded reasonable enough.

"All right," said Jonathan. "We'll stop back here tomorrow and get your car released, then I'll arrange a time when the detectives can have another session if they want one, but with me onboard this time."

"Then we'll all head back to Boston and get to work," said Etchison. "We've got to start figuring out what's going on."

"Okay," said Kate, her voice sounding weak and faint, even to her. "Thanks. Both of you."

Jonathan led them around the back of the building to his black sedan. As soon as Kate settled into the soft leather cradle of the backseat, she felt safer, if no less confused. There seemed to be a numbness in the center of her thoughts, an unwillingness to think about what had happened tonight. She felt as if she were skirting around the perimeter of the hard, unthinkable truth that her husband and her sister were gone.

No one spoke for a few minutes, until Jonathan had maneuvered the Lexus onto Interstate 93 heading north. Then, Matt Etchison turned in his seat to look back at her. "I know you might not be in the mood right now, but I have a few questions, if you don't mind."

"No, of course not," she said.

"Okay, thanks. First off, would it be okay if I called you Kate?"

"Yes, that would be fine," she said.

"Okay, good . . . and just call me Matt, okay?"

She nodded.

"Some of what I need to know, to ask you, it might be . . . uncomfortable . . . and—"

"It's all right. I understand. Go on."

She appreciated his effort to be as inoffensive as possible, even though it wasn't necessary. And she knew his questions were inevitable and had to be asked.

"Okay, thanks," he said, and paused for a moment, then: "Now, can you think of anyone who . . . who would want to murder your husband?"

"I've been thinking about that myself," she said. "I can't get it out of my mind, actually, and no . . . he didn't have enemies like that. Not that I could imagine. I mean, of course there had to be people who didn't *like* him . . . he was in business, that means competition, and a certain amount of . . . oh, I don't know what you would say . . . ruthlessness?"

"But not enough to start killing people?" said Etchison.

"I can't imagine it," she said. "And my sister . . . whatever all this means, it has to involve both of them, right? There's got to be a connection."

"Maybe. Maybe not."

Kate shook her head. It was all so awful . . . so unbelievable. . . ."

"That was my next question," he said. "Is there anything you can tell me that might connect both victims . . . in any way? Other than the obvious one of being related to you?"

"I'm sorry . . . but I haven't been able to come up with anything."

Etchison nodded, pausing before continuing. "What about your sister? Did you see her or talk to her on a regular basis?"

"Not what you would call *often*, I mean . . . maybe once a month or two. . . . We saw more of them in the summer than the rest of the year."

"Them?"

"Justine and her husband, Domenic. They have a son in college, but he's not around much."

"What does her husband do for a living?"

"He's an engineering consultant for Kendall Structures. They have an office in Boston."

"What do they do—build stuff?"

"Yes. It's an international firm. They design and build large structures—tunnels, bridges, broadcast towers . . . things like that."

"International," said Etchison, considering what that meant. "So he travels a lot?"

"Yes, he always did." Kate couldn't remember a time in her sister's marriage when Domenic was ever home for more than a few days at a time.

"And that's why they can't find him right now," he said. It wasn't a question.

"You know," said Jonathan, who had been silently assaying the conversation till now, "that might be an angle to pursue. The international thing—maybe Petralli got into something way over his head?"

"That's a possibility," said Etchison. "It'll be hard to get some leads into it, but we can get to work on it when we get back to Boston." To Kate: "You can tell us enough to get us started, right?"

"Yes, I should be able to."

"And your sister, she never told you anything that

would make you think she or her husband was in any kind of trouble?"

"No, never. Nothing." She looked out the car's window, into the perfect darkness. It was hard to imagine it being any darker in her life or in the world. ". . . not until she called me, and then she sounded absolutely terrified. And she said she *had* to see me right away."

Matt looked at her, obviously thinking. "Usually, when people are frantic to see someone in person like that, they have a damned good reason."

"Like what?" said Jonathan.

"They need a face-to-face meeting," said Etchison, "which can be an uncconscious need for the most personal contact possible. Your sister needed to tell you something very important—maybe about your husband. Maybe she knew people were planning to kill him? Or they were trying to kill her, or she had some kind of information she wanted you to have.

Kate didn't respond immediately as she thought about the numbers Justine had written in her own blood. She knew she would need to share this with Etchison and Markley, but she wanted to think about it on her own first. If the numbers meant something personal, something dark and secret that her sister had wanted only Kate to know about, perhaps Kate should at least try to honor that dying request for secrecy for a little while, until maybe she could figure out what it was about.

She didn't know what to do, and the act of being so confused, so indecisive upset her even more. It was not like Kate to be wishy-washy. A part of her knew she would have to eventually share everything with Etchison and her lawyer, but not right now. Take things slowly, so she might have time to give them her usual focus and attention.

Etchison continued to log in more routine questions and Jonathan gave her a short course on criminal law, and his assessment of the legal ground whereupon they all now stood. By the time he had outlined their legal strategy for the police and the courts—if that ever became necessary—they were reaching their exit off Interstate 89.

"Exit thirteen, right?" said Jonathan.

"Yes," said Kate. "Take a right at the bottom of the ramp, at the stop sign."

"It's been a while since I've been up here," said Markley.

After Jonathan turned right, Kate leaned forward between the front seats. "Right up here, on the right, there's the sign for Eastman Village."

"I got it," said her lawyer, gliding the Lexus around the turn and up onto a road lined with tall evergreens and graceful, towering white birches that glowed like ghosts in the headlights.

"Just stay on the main road for awhile," she said. "It kind of winds around for about a mile or so."

Kate shook her head and blinked away the suggestion of tears as she realized the last time she negotiated these twisting, tree-lined roads Lawrence had been alive, sitting behind the wheel, laughing and talking about his damned fishing. It seemed like something from another lifetime now, another world. All gone now.

They passed a sign for the golf course and the clubhouse, and a side road where another sign announced the need to use the boat wash before launching anything into the lake. The road continued to meander through the dense woods that made it one of the most beautiful places to live in all of the Dartmouth-Sunapee region of New Hampshire.

"It's really *dark* in here, isn't it?" said Etchison rhetorically.

He was right, thought Kate. It was incredibly dark. All the years of coming here, she'd become so used to it. Newcomers always noticed it.

"We go down past the lake and the south cove beach, right?" said Jonathan.

"Yes," she said, clearing her throat. She had to stay

focused, try not to dwell on the worst right now. She had to be strong. She had to help them catch whoever it was who killed Lawrence and Justine. "Stay on the road around the lake, when you pass the firehouse, it's the fifth road on the left—Autumn Hill."

They rode in silence for another minute or so, past the entrance to the beach and the firehouse, and finally the left onto Autumn Hill.

"Take it all the way to the end," she said. "To the cul-de-sac, and down our driveway."

"This must be rough in the winter," said Etchison, keeping his attention focused on the exterior, always observant.

"We never came up that much, except for a few weekends to ski," said Kate. *So sad*, she thought. *They would never be doing that again. . . .*

"If possible, it's even *darker* back here," said Etchison as they passed several driveways disappearing into the woods. "And the trees are thick."

"Oh yes," she said. "You can't see anything back in here until you're almost right on top of it. "There's our driveway, Jonathan."

"Got it," he said, guiding the Lexus around a short turn and down a drive lined with pines and spruces, the occasional thick-boled oak. The leaves and the bluestone gravel flashed for brief moments in the headlights as they trundled down towards the house.

"Hold it!" said Etchison suddenly.

Jonathan tapped the brakes and the car slowed almost to a stop. The tires grinding on the driveway stones sounded incredibly loud.

"What's the matter?" Jonathan's voice was almost a whisper.

"Cut the lights!" Etchison grabbed the handle of the passenger-side door, but did not open it.

Jonathan punched out the headlights and stopped the car, plunging them into total and utter blackness. Ahead, just for an instant, Kate saw lights illuminating the interior of her home's second level, by the back deck.

But just for an instant.

Then they abruptly winked out.

"Did you see that?" said Etchison, who manually switched off the interior dome light before opening the car door and slipping out. He reached inside his jacket, and she presumed it was for a weapon. She hoped she was right.

"Jesus. . . ." said Jonathan, his voice a harsh whisper. "We've got company. Do you think we should—"

The question expired on his lips as Kate heard a soft *klink* of glass breaking combined with the soft, dull thud of a silenced slug hitting something. In the glow of the dashboard lights, she saw Jonathan Markley's head snap back and sharply to the right as something *wet* sprayed across her face like mist from a Windex bottle.

"Get out of there!" yelled Etchison, as he pulled her through the open rear door, gripping her upper arm roughly. As she felt herself being pulled out and down, she heard the car's windows imploding as more silenced bullets spattered it like a hard rain.

PART
TWO

SEVEN

FATHER HECTOR ACCARDI

*H*ector entered the area beneath the San Marino Church that had once been a small catacomb for the medieval priests of the Tuscan town. Recently, it had been reengineered to accommodate the twenty-first century and its nonsectarian technology. His telephone in the rectory had rung in a distinctive irregular pattern, which told him he was needed in what he still called the catacombs.

Subdued lighting de-emphasized the rack-mounted electronics, console keyboards, and monitors of the room. It could have passed for a missile launch bunker anywhere in the world. Hector sat in his customary chair and said *"Through Him, In Him, With Him"* softly into a small microphone. A vox-rec program displayed his voiceprint on the monitor screen, analyzed it, and blinked at him with a bright green rectangle containing a one-line phrase—*Hector Accardi: verified.*

Then the message blinked into oblivion, replaced by the face of a bald man in his late forties or early fifties. He had the bull neck and sloping shoulders of a very well-conditioned athlete. Although he wore the brown habit of a monastic, he looked like a military man who'd seen his share of action. His name was Sforza. No title. No way to tell if it was a first, last, or code name. As long as Hector had been a member of the Elder Knights of Malta (which had now been more than ten years since he'd been invited into the elite order), this man had been its visible leader. If there were others in power above him, then they preferred to remain invisible and speak through him.

"Good afternoon, Father Accardi," said the Sforza. "You will have a visitor this evening."

"Who?" Hector was not surprised at this. His city's church was a frequent way station for Maltese operatives.

"Domenic Petralli."

"Very well. Any special orders?"

"Just give him whatever he needs—if you have it. His wife was murdered last night."

"What? *Why?*"

"He has been incommunicado, and probably has not been informed. You will have to tell him, I am afraid."

"Oh no . . ." said Hector Accardi, shaking his head with genuine sadness, a heavy pain tugging at his heart. Then: "Very well . . . is there anything you can tell me about it?" He listened as his superior filled in all the details as currently known.

"This is terrible news," he said as Sforza finished. "Justine Petralli's sister has been arrested for the crime? That seems unlikely, yes?"

"A very low probability. The local police are following standard procedure, but nothing fits or really points to her. We have some of our people checking the area and personnel. From what we can determine, Justine Petralli and Lawrence Harrison were both professionally terminated. And we are fairly certain she was the primary target. Her sister's husband was most likely removed to make the frame-up look good or to complicate things—nothing more. We have seen this sort of thing before—something to slow the police down, just a tactic to give the real killers more time to disappear."

Hector nodded. "Do we have any idea why these people were killed?"

"We would only be speculating at this point. There is not enough data coming in yet. The most obvious reason in situations like this one is usually *information*. Either the killers wanted to prevent Justine Petralli from passing something along to her sister or her brother-in-law . . . or they were not able to interrogate her in time—to retrieve the information for themselves, and felt termination was the only alternative."

"Better to have *no one* know, than your enemy alone. . . ." said Hector.

"Yes, precisely. An age-old dictum."

"But I am troubled," said Hector. "What kind of information would Petralli's wife have? Why would his wife have *any* information of value to us . . . or our adversaries?"

Hector knew that Maltese operatives *never* compromised their mission to God in any way, including a confidence with a wife or family. It was one of the tenets of the Order handled with the sanctity of a vow. Only in the most extreme of circumstances would a mission be shared with outsiders.

Sforza nodded grimly. "A very good question. We must assume here that Domenic Petralli believed he had a good chance of being killed. If he told her anything, he must have believed it was the only way to preserve it for us."

"But it looks like his opponents were one step ahead of him," said Hector.

"Obviously. Otherwise, he would not have put his wife in such danger."

"That means he will blame himself for her death."

Sforza nodded. "Most certainly. But if he is still a true Knight, he will not allow that to alter his performance."

He had little to say in response, since he had been on a need-to-know basis with all Knights of Malta business. It was standard operating procedure, and worked well for many centuries. If Sforza wanted him to know more, he would tell him now.

And he did. . . .

. . . by talking about a religious artifact—a surviving fragment of glass from the Virgin Mary's little chapel near Fatima. Hector was vaguely familiar with the story of how fascist sympathizers, fearing the power of the Vatican over the Portuguese people in the decade after World War I, had destroyed the pilgrimage site with sticks of dynamite.

When Sforza paused for breath, Hector spoke. "What is the significance of this glass?"

Sforza paused, as if considering what he should say. Then: "There are those who believed the Holy Mother had attempted to speak to us through this artifact. Although, it was speculation as to whether anyone had ever deciphered any real messages."

Hector nodded. Typical miracle talk. He had heard most of it over the years. From the Holy Grail finally rediscovered all the way to finding a crashed UFO with a dead Jesus at the controls.

"I see," he said. "Do *you* believe it?"

"What I believe is immaterial," said Sforza flatly. Hector noted that his superior's tone and demeanor never varied, never revealed anything he didn't want revealed. "Just be satisfied in knowing that the artifact has been very important to Rome. The Pope had entrusted it to our care many years ago, and we have kept it and its location safe over the decades. But now it has fallen into the wrong hands."

"Petralli had been assigned to get it back?"

"Technically, he had been responsible for its safety— it was being studied by a team of scientists and other specialists in a suburb of Washington, D.C., in America. One of our knights, Harold Wieznewski, had been in charge of the project. They had been working on a way to decipher its messages. That's when it was stolen. Petralli is our sector chief for the States. The assignment falls to him."

Hector nodded. He knew Petralli was a well-respected operative, but had no idea he'd been elevated to such a position. "Do you have any leads?"

Sforza nodded. "Yes, but the rumor mill and our usually reliable sources are strangely quiet on this one. That is why we think something big is taking place. Information flow is *never* this tight." Sforza lit an unfiltered cigarette, ashed it in an overflowing circular ashtray with chrome penguins standing on opposites poles of the rim. Even on the monitor, the ashtray looked oddly out of place. It had to be a momento of some significance; for something so ugly, Hector hoped it was of *great* significance.

"You have no ideas?"

Sforza shook his head. "That is not what I said—there is a difference between having evidence and suspicions. Let us be frankly honest with ourselves. There are only a handful of entities powerful enough to do what they have already done. I do not rule out the alphabet agencies of the United States and China and even Russia."

"Should I bother to ask you why they might be interested in this artifact?" Hector smiled sardonically.

"When Pope Peter II was assassinated in Egypt . . ." Sforza paused for effect. ". . . he had been watched very closely by many of the world powers, but they did not understand what was really happening—they had theorized that Peter Carenza had been some kind of mutant, some kind of super-human with special abilities."

Hector shrugged "Perhaps they were correct."

"Regardless . . . some of them suspect we had our own pope eliminated."

"I still don't see where you are going here," said Hector.

"Only to make this point: The other global powers are

apt to pay more attention to what the SSV and the Vatican are doing. And if they know much of the KOM, then they are watching us as well. Many of the most powerful governments now know they were *totally* in the dark on the situation with Pope Peter II, and they know now it was a grave error."

Hector digested this theory. It made sense. Suddenly, another question occurred to him. "Do you know what information Petralli may have given his wife?"

Sforza nodded. "We have an educated guess. In any case, we are expecting him to tell you. If he does not, you will ask him for it."

"And if he will not tell me?" Hector watched Sforza ignite another cigarette, and he felt a long-dead urge to join him.

"We cannot allow for the possibility he has either (a) allowed his judgment to be clouded by the execution of his wife, or (b) become a 'rogue agent' who believes he is the only one who can rectify the problem."

Hector swallowed with difficulty. "Which means I must do . . . what?"

Sforza exhaled into the lens. "You must determine what is happening in his heart."

"You are giving me a great responsibility."

"You know this man. He trusts you. He will speak to you if he will speak to anyone," said Sforza.

"If he is already unstable, we must pray the news of his wife will not push him off the edge, into the Pit," said Hector.

"We are all close to the edge, all the time," said his superior. "Only the power and the grace of God keep us from being pulled down."

Hector nodded at this normally unspoken truth. "But tell me . . . what happens if he refuses to cooperate?"

"We have his son," said Sforza.

"If our training remains in place, that would not stop him in his beliefs," said Hector.

Sforza nodded. "True, but if our training remains in

place, then we need not fear Domenic Petralli."

Hector truly believed this was true. He had known Domenic for many years, and the man's faith was as unbreakable as his will. And because of that, Hector knew Domenic Petralli was a very dangerous man.

EIGHT

Arezzo, Italy

DOMENIC PETRALLI

Everyone was looking for him.

The thought haunted Domenic as he parked his rented Fiat Punta outside the gates of the old medieval town. Although it had swelled far beyond its sloping fortress walls, Arezzo's inner city had remained much as it had been five hundred years ago. Domenic had always liked its simple charm and its quiet acknowledgment that it could never compete with the tourist magnets of Pisa and Siena and Firenze.

Rainclouds flirted with the idea of a shower, and a subtle dampness had seeped into him as he passed through an old wooden door large enough for pedestrians only, and slipped down a narrow, twisting side street. He would wind his way to the back entrance of the church slowly, carefully. He had come this far from the military airport without detection, and it was extremely important that no one pick up his trail now. He was dressed casually in a Polo pullover and tan Dockers, which hung on his lean frame as if he were a well-proportioned window mannequin. He was in great shape for being forty-one years old, and he figured as long as his thick, dark hair remained on his scalp and did not turn gray, he could pass for a much younger man.

Stopping at a small grocery, he purchased a prosciutto *panino* and a bottled water, then used the break in his journey to survey the length of street he'd just traversed. The sliced stuffed meat in the bread tasted so good, it distracted him from his focus on the task at hand. He hadn't realized how hungry he'd become. . . .

And the pause also gave him a chance to dispatch a short prayer to his God. Please, allow Justine to arrive safely in Boston. He desperately needed to know she'd slipped through the net he'd sensed was being raised around both of them. More than twenty-four hours since he'd left her at the Ciampino airport. A long time to be moving in silence. But it was necessary; Father Accardi would give him any updates that may have come through on secure channels.

As he finished the bottled water, he checked the street one more time before leaving the shop. Another six irregular blocks of shadowed lanes and he crossed a small park and playground. Evening had mantled everything in dim, gray, half-light, but he still felt vulnerable as he moved in and of the darker shadows.

On the other side of the playground was the modest stone edifice of the Church of San Marino. He walked to the rear entrance of the sacristy, held by the half-circle of a small garden. The place had a "safe" feel to it. Ever since Domenic's earliest days in the KOM, training in Corsica, he had learned to trust a kind of extrasensory ability he'd developed to pick up danger. It had always proved to be more of a general, proximity sense than any specific premonitions, and it sometimes allowed him to "anticipate" problems. Some of his colleagues called it instinct, others a sixth sense, but names didn't matter. The people who survived in the business of espionage and global intrigue were the ones who possessed a special, largely unarticulated ability to foresee danger.

Even though everything appeared normal, he could not ignore the need for one last, obligatory check of his surroundings before slipping into the rear entrance of the church. Once through the narthex and the sacristy, in the failing light, he felt for the latch inside a tall cabinet which held a variety of vestments. The latch clicked and the interior back panel of the armoire swung away into darkness. Like a character in a C.S. Lewis novel, Domenic Petralli eased himself into the wardrobe and another world.

Down old stone steps to a steel, elevatorlike door. "Until the end of time," he said in a clear voice.

Somewhere, a digital sound recognition registry matched his voiceprint to its database file and sent an affirmative message to another automated cybersystem which opened the steel door. He entered a compact, economically fixtured room lined with workstations and the usual panoply of electronic equipment—monitors, keyboards, communications consoles, phones, etc.

A man was seated at one of the consoles. Domenic watched him slowly rotate in his wheeled chair to face him. "Good to see you, Signore Petralli."

"*Buona sera*, Father Accardi," he said, regarding the man who was probably closer to him than his real father.

Father Accardi was stocky, but still had a full head of silvering hair. He had a strong jaw and sunken eyes that made him look predatory—even when smiling with sincere warmth.

But the priest accorded him no smile this time. "Bad news. Very Bad."

Something had gone wrong, and Domenic felt a stab of anguish violate him. "Justine . . ." He could not finish the sentence, but Hector Accardi's expression revealed the worst.

"*Bastardi* . . . they followed her from Logan. . . ." said Father Accardi, who spent the next few minutes giving Domenic the details of Justine's assassination, the murder of Lawrence Harrison, and the arrest of his sister-in-law, Kate.

Domenic reached down into his soul for solace. Deep into that place where his faith burned like a steel-mill furnace. There he tempered the pain of the loss of his wife with the knowledge that he would someday again be united with her, and on a more elevated, spiritual plane. He tried to make himself feel that transcendent joy that Justine now knew—the metaphysical completeness and eternal peace of being in the presence of the Creator. He knew the pain of loss, of separation, was only beginning, and he knew he would be pushed to the precipice of enduring it. He could already feel the barrage of conflicting emotions raining down on him, and he knew the one most dangerous was guilt. If he allowed it, the burden of responsibility for his wife's murder could destroy him far more efficiently than anything his adversaries could ever dream of doing.

And he could never allow that. He was a soldier of the Lord, one of the world's last, true knights, and above all else he must honor his vows to that service to the Divine.

Closing his eyes, he gathered strength to continue. Even though he'd prepared for this possibility all his life, this was going to be very difficult. In addition, he knew there was one final way they could try to reach him. . . .

"What about Vincent? What about my son?"

"Knights have been sent to his dormitory in Boston. He is safe, and he is being protected . . . without his knowledge. I have spoken with Sforza, and he believes your son will remain safe."

"Why?" Domenic could not allow himself to feel so comfortable.

"Because they probably concede he knows *nothing* of your affairs, and if they know as much about us as they appear to, then they are most surely aware of the vows of the Knights of Malta. They know you would sacrifice even your son to the service of our Lord."

Domenic nodded. This was indeed all true, but it did nothing to lessen the penumbral dread in wait to consume him. It did nothing to make him feel any better about what was happening to the small circle of his inner life, his private world of family that had remained isolated from the terrible realities of his sworn profession.

"Perhaps he is right," said Domenic after a long pause. "Our enemies have a larger agenda than toying with me, punishing me."

"Yes, but they fear you, Domenic. They fear the power of your convictions, of your faith. They know you are one of the keys capable of unlocking the success of their plans . . . or shutting them down forever."

Domenic grinned weakly. "Yes, I'm sure I will be a very popular figure in certain circles."

Father Accardi nodded, made a sweeping gesture at the consoles behind him. "Your wife's death had caught the attention of . . . well, everyone who would take notice of such a thing—"

"—and attach significance to it."

"Precisely."

Domenic shook his head slowly and looked at his mentor of almost twenty-five years. "It's so ironic—how we all know *about* each other, all the alphabet agencies, all the secret societies, the cartels, and even all the cabal-driven fanatics—and yet, we all go insane trying to figure what we're all going to be doing *next* . . . without . . ."

"Without what?" Accardi said softly.

"Without ever wanting to know *why*."

"Why . . . why what? You mean why we do it?"

"No," said Domenic. "I mean *why God allows us— all of us—to play these absurd games*."

Father Accardi nodded. "Some would say because God himself is absurd."

"And others might say because God is dead, or never existed in the first place." Domenic spoke the words with contempt. "But we know better, do we not, Father?"

"Oh . . . most certainly."

Domenic Petralli steadied himself on the edge of a nearby computer desk as he stood up. He drew in a deep breath, exhaled. "But," he said finally, acerbically, "we are not philosophers and we should not waste God's time. Tell me something practical; I assume Sforza has brought you up to speed?"

Father Accardi told him what he knew of the theft of the piece of glass some called the Eyes of the Virgin.

"Do we know who took it yet?"

"No, but this list of candidates is understandably small."

Domenic nodded. There were only a handful of entities throughout the entire world who were (a) smart enough to know about the Fatima glass, (b) bold enough to steal it, and (c) arrogant enough to believe they could employ it towards their own agenda. "We will narrow that list to one," he said softly.

"We always do," said Accardi.

"Anything else we know?"

Accardi exhaled. "This is all new to me, but I was told you would appreciate the importance: The last lab session, conducted by Wieznewski's people near Washington, confirmed that new messages are beginning to appear."

"You are sure?"

"The American lab was certain of it, yes."

This piece of news only made things more complicated. Domenic knew it did nothing to change his primary task—getting the artifact back under the aegis of the Vatican, under the protection of the Elder Knights of Malta—but he *hated* complications.

"Does that mean there is *new* data?"

Accardi nodded. "Most likely. But we know nothing about it."

"And the thieves may already have it," said Domenic. "We could be in deep trouble, if they discover the keys to unlocking it—"

"I know," said Accardi. "Acquiring knowledge is one thing. Knowing how to use it can be quite another."

"If they realize things can be . . . altered . . . that changes everything."

"Precisely," said Accardi. "Sforza has briefed me fully, and the other cells as well—he emphasized the dangers implied here. We must find the thieves and retrieve the glass at any cost."

Domenic replayed the priest's final words over and over. He knew already about the high cost of operating against their adversaries. He made a large down payment on the cost when he lost Justine. He had no choice but to trust in the abilities of his fellow Knights to protect his son, but it did not stem the fear of failure growing in his heart.

Trust in the Lord, he thought. *Remember your vows. Patience for the present.* There would be time for a proper grieving, but it was not now.

"There is one more thing," said Accardi.

"What?"

"Sforza wants to know what you told your wife at Ciampino."

Domenic nodded, knowing now he had unwittingly arranged her execution. "Yes, I'm sure he would want to know. . . ."

He seated himself in front of a communications monitor and adjusted a set of headphones to his skull. "I'd better check in with Sforza," he said softly.

After several password and encryption entries, the face of Sforza appeared on Domenic's monitor. "Good to see you made it in," said his superior.

"You wanted to debrief me personally?" Domenic said.

"Yes, we have reached a critical mass."

"Then, may I make a suggestion?"

Sforza leaned closer to his screen. "Go ahead."

"Based on what has happened to me and the glass itself, we have to admit the possibility of our encrypted communications being cracked. Even this one."

Sforza nodded, allowed a small grin of approval to show on his face. "I was hoping you would be the one to bring this up."

Domenic understood what was being implied. If he had started unloading the critical data across channels that may be compromised by an adversary, it could be a sign he didn't care anymore, or worse—that he was deliberately trying to leak sensitive information to whomever might be tapping into their system. Domenic believed this possibility would be highly unlikely, but he simply couldn't be certain any longer. The enemy, whoever they were, appeared to have discovered things about the Fatima artifact that no one had ever known.

"Very well," said Domenic. "I suggest a Protocol Seven. Do you agree?" Protocol Seven was a well-planned operation for passing ultra-secret information by personal, digitally-identified couriers moving from station to station on seemingly random travel itineraries. The routings of the two couriers were mapped out to appear totally unconnected, which were then interlaced with a series of drops and pickups that could not be traced. There was no way anyone other than Sforza or Domenic could even know what the term "Protocol Seven" meant. It was a term the two of them had devised privately to describe the method of data transfer required. A contingency which acknowledged an interesting principle: utilization of high tech almost *always* removed the use of older, obsolete technology. But Domenic and his colleagues had discovered that returning to older, slower, less complicated methods was sometimes most effective.

Sforza nodded, keyed something into his board. "Duly noted. Make preparations to begin the sequence at your station. We will do the same.

Domenic continued his debriefing through the standard scrambled and encrypted channels, feeling immensely more secure knowing his most critical information—

the location of the deciphering key to the Eyes of the Virgin—was protected.

He listened closely to Sforza's priority list and agenda, then signed off.

Accardi had been waiting patiently until he finished. "My orders are to get you whatever you need for your new briefing."

Domenic smiled facetiously. "I cannot tell you how happy I am to receive a new set of plans. Mine did not seem to be working anymore."

NINE

KATE HARRISON

The previous three minutes had passed without her awareness, cooperation, or understanding.

Somehow, she had avoided the surgical application of high-energy slugs into the Lexus; maybe it had been Matt Etchison who'd done it. She had a vague impression, but not really a memory, of the investigator literally dragging her into the thick woods to the left of her driveway. The soft staccato of bullets impacting all around her had sounded as gentle as afternoon raindrops, and Kate had, for a few moments, decided to simply *let go* of what was really happening.

Why not? she thought. In less than forty eight hours, her entire life had been turned inside out, yanked up and eviscerated like a deer hung on one of those hideous "dressing" tripods. There was just so much she could endure before deciding it wasn't worth it, right? Kate realized this was atypical thinking for her, and she knew she should be fighting it because she'd always been a fierce competitor, both in school, in athletics, and certainly in business.

But somebody, it seemed, wanted her as dead as her sister and her husband . . . and Kate was beginning to think it wasn't such a bad idea. She couldn't get the image of Jonathan's Markley's death out of her mind. It seemed at once unreal and yet, horribly definite and final. She wished she could make it all go away. It would be so easy to give up, to just let them get her. . . .

Then suddenly, she felt a hand grabbing at the collar of her jacket, tangling in her hair. Matt Etchison was tugging on her, snapping her up to a sitting position. She looked at him and his hair was wild and his eyes were wide, and his face shined with a patina of sweat. He looked like a madman. "C'mon!" he said in a whisper that somehow also sounded harsh and frantic. "Don't do this to me now!"

"What?" she heard herself speak, and hated how dazed and stupid she sounded.

"Listen, I need you to be paying attention—right now!"

She looked at him, feeling a combination of embarrassment and indignation. He was taking charge, ordering her around, and a part of her didn't like it; but then she felt so damned helpless at the same time. She hated that feeling and—

"Tell me!" he said, interrupting her thoughts. "If we keep going this way, down to the lake, what's down there?" The woods had become incredibly quiet since they'd fled her lawyer's car, and she only noticed after he'd spoken.

"What do you mean? Water. The lake—"

"No! Anything else? A boat, a dock, boathouse?"

Kate shook her head. "My husband had the boat. . . . I don't know where it is now."

"Is there a dock?"

"No."

Etchison continued to edge toward the lower ground that sloped to the lake's shoreline. He half-walked, half-stooped, moving like an agile chimp. She tried to mimic his movements because it just looked right. The woods were impenetrably dark, but the surface of the lake reflected enough light from the half-risen moon to give them an objective target, a phantomlike beacon that called out with the promise of possible safety.

"What about the neighbors? Any of them have boats?"

"I don't know. I never paid attention," she said. "I never really cared about stuff like that—you know, like who had what—"

"You will now. It might save our lives."

Kate felt an insistent tug on the sleeve of her jacket as he moved her along. The lakeside appeared very close now. As they grew closer to its glassy, shimmering surface, she could see the silhouette of a fairly large gun in Etchison's right hand. Like their attackers, he had attached a silencer to the end of the barrel.

Ten more yards, and they were at the water's edge, listening to a soft slapping sound as the lake teased the soft mud of the shore. So quiet. And then he was whispering in her ear at an even lower level: "We don't want to make *any* noise now. We tell them where we are . . . they get us. Stay here and *don't move*."

She neither answered nor moved; Matt slipped into the darkness to her right. In seconds, he was so undetectable, he could have been miles away from her. Time quickly lost all meaning, and Kate had no idea how long he'd been gone. The air temperature had been dropping since sunset, and now, with little else to hold her attention, Kate could almost swear to *feeling* the degrees plummet. The woods, which had seemed so silent only moments ago, now *teemed* with tiny noises.

Cracklings. Wheezes and sighs. Snaps. Thumps and rattles.

Something could be scurrying away from her or headlonging itself right toward her, and she had no way to tell. But she was not scared; she was not that kind of person. There had always been a heavy I-beam of resolve welded into the frame of her soul. It was a *will-*

ingness to face whatever the world decided to throw her way. Her sister had always said it was her sheer, hard-headed "moxie" that made her special.

Things were no different now, she thought calmly.

If she was going to die tonight, she would do her best to do it kicking and screaming and clawing her way through the exit doors. She wouldn't make it easy for them.

But where in hell did Etchison go?

And how much longer did he think she could stay hunched down on her lower legs, almost afraid to exhale each breath?

Kate didn't have a chance to answer her rhetorical question. The next instant had her occupied with a far more vital problem—that is, how to continue breathing *at all*.

She hadn't heard or felt a thing until the man's fore-arm clamped down across her larynx. The shock of the sudden contact short-circuited her mind and body for an instant. The pressure on her throat increased with no suggestion of stopping and if it continued much longer, the cartilage and small bones would be crushed, and she would be dead. Pale spots began to flash in front of her eyes and she knew she was either beginning to float upward like a balloon or she was being lifted off her haunches to a standing position. An eerie calmness suddenly embraced her as she teetered on the wall between consciousness and death. A single, nonthreatening thought drifted across her mind: *So this is it . . . this is the way I'm going to die. . . .*

She seemed to be considering the notion from afar, physically as well as psychically detached. None of the stark terror or dread she would have always imagined should be there . . .

In such a state, she was only numbly aware of what seemed to be happening the next moment. The pressure on her throat tightened, then *released* completely and something damp and warm covered her cheek. Kate realized she was standing up, wobbling from side to side as she tried to turn to face her attacker who had, for some reason, let her go. When she stepped back and turned her head, she saw Matt Etchison's face only inches from hers. His dark hair was matted with sweat and he'd smeared something dark around his eyes. He looked like a raccoon, a very angry raccoon. His breath heaved in and out of him like a bellows.

Looking down, she saw a man collapsed at Matt's feet. The man's head was turned at an impossible angle and there was a gaping crevice where part of his throat should have been.

"Take this," said Etchison, handing her a compact-looking chrome handgun with a matching silencer. "He's not going to be needing it."

The hazy, dreamy quality of the attack and rescue was fading fast, replaced by hard edges of terror. Even though her husband had insisted on her learning self-defense by taking shooting lessons, the gun felt heavy and awkward and very ugly in her hand. She didn't want it, but dared not let it go.

"The safety's off, watch it," he said in a very soft voice. Then: "You ever used one of these before?"

"Yes, but not exactly like this. It was bigger . . . a thirty-eight."

"Okay, no problem. Keep it out and away from you. You point and squeeze. This is a nice one. You won't even feel it kick."

Etchison was replacing a very evil-looking serrated blade in a scabbard under his jacket. Then he held her upper arm just forcefully enough to lead her along the shoreline away from her house.

He said nothing, even after they reached the pipe which held a selection of canoes. One of them was already beached in the sand, nosing towards the water.

"I found this in my travels," he said.

Kate looked at the shallow drafted sailboat. "Where are we going in that thing?"

"For starters—anywhere but here." he said. "Once we are far enough out on the lake, we make a better plan."

Kate followed him onboard and together they pushed off across the moon-silvered surface. She stayed in the center of the boat, being careful not to alter the balance point. Matt used a single paddle first on one side, then the other, noiselessly slipping it in and out of the water. Their progress was slow and deliberate, but eventually the distance between themselves and the potentially deadly shore increased.

Intermittent clouds turned the moonlight on and off like a wall switch, and she felt terribly visible under its pale-blue wash, but Matt said they would be hard to spot against the black background of trees on the opposite shore.

Time stretched out and she had no idea how long they pushed further and further across the center of the lake. She thought about the last time she'd been out this far—it had been on cross-country skis with Lawrence, last winter on a getaway, fireplace-and-brandy weekend. A tear eased from her eye as she thought about how distant and unreal that time was now.

Never again.

"You can start paddling now," he said, intruding into her thoughts.

"Okay."

"We're far enough away. They won't be able to hear us or see us."

"How many of them *are* there?"

"No way to tell. . . . I only saw one, and he won't be bothering us anymore."

"What are we going to do now?"

"Head to the opposite shore, and get as far away from here as we can. At this point, we have to hope for two things."

"Which are?"

"One," he said, "that they haven't seen us . . . and two, that even if they did, they won't be waiting for us on the other side."

They hadn't; and they didn't.

TEN

Paris

KURT STREICHER

Most people walked past the small cobbler's shop and didn't even notice it—tucked in between two much larger storefronts. Streicher knew this was an advantage when you wanted to hide something—put it in plain view, but in such a way as to make it invisible. Make everything natural, and no one will notice.

He carried a pair of worn Bruno Magli broughams conspicuously in his left hand as he pushed through the door of the shop. But beyond its dingy, flyspecked windows lay a tiny vestibule and customer counter, atop which sat an old cash register from an earlier, simpler era. A thick, pleated curtain separated this area from a back room, where presumably the proprietor hunched over a shoemaker's bench. Placing the shoes on the Formica counter, Streicher cleared his throat.

"Anyone here?"

After a moment, the curtain was pulled to one side by an old man whose fingers looked permanently stained by leather dye, his face by age. His glasses were practically falling off the end of his large, mottled nose. "Can I help you?" he said in accented English.

"These are probably beyond repair," said Streicher with measured breath, "but they're my favorites."

The old man pushed his Ben Franklin glasses up closer to his eyes, stared at him for only an instant, then gave him only the suggestion of a nod. "I see. . . . then perhaps you should come into the back. Let me show you what I can do with them."

Streicher waited till the cobbler picked up the shoes, held back the curtain, and ushered him through. The rear end of the shop smelled of the richness of leather, the sting of dye, and the sweat of a hundred years' labor. Pigeonhole shelving held footwear of every style and color and a pock-marked wooden bench lay strewn with fragments and tools.

Tossing the expensive shoes on the end of the bench, the old man walked quickly to the corner of the room, where he pushed a concealed button in one of the pigeonholes, behind a pair of heavy boots. Silently, a section of shelving swung inward to reveal a tunnel lined with crudely cut stone and illuminated by a string of naked bulbs. Without saying a word, Streicher entered the passage and the old man closed the panel.

The tunnel's interior sloped downward at a slight angle, imperceptible unless you were looking for it. The walls were covered with phosphorescent mold, which suggested an age measured in centuries. Streicher had heard the boasts of his colleagues that the tunnel had at one time connected a Guild shop with one of the organization's "star chambers," which would place it in the mid-fifteenth century.

It was inwardly pleasing to know the works of the Guild had been built to last. It bespoke a belief in the system and the philosophy that had held the organization together for so long. He was proud to be part of something with a legacy, with a sense of permanency, especially since he did not think in terms of such things. He was a highly pragmatic man who dealt with each contingency of life as it confronted him. He'd never been a worrier, a hand-wringer, someone who played out a variety of scenarios; which also meant he was not a great strategic talent. Tactical ability was what he'd been designed for, and he was superb at such operations.

He continued down the tunnel for another five minutes, ever descending lower beneath the streets of the European town above his head. Gradually a burnished metallic door appeared out of the vanishing point of perspective and grew larger, more distinct with each step. Streicher had visited this facility infrequently and was not as familiar or comfortable with it as he would like. He continued walking until the door was only a foot away from him. To its left, in an alcove in the stone wall, rested a sophisticated video camera, which he turned to face. An instant passed as his image was recorded, registered and compared to a visual image database. When his facial features passed a rigorous pattern-match, the large steel door began to slide to the right on silent bearings.

He entered a white-walled anteroom, where he stood motionless until the steel door sealed behind him. It was a small, antiseptic sallyport, and a second steel door awaited him. "State your name," said a cybernetic voice through unseen speakers.

"Streicher, Kurt Loren."

A dark blue fan of light swept over him and the second door slid into the wall to reveal a wide foyer, beyond which were several large bullpens filled with personnel. A woman in a dark, tailored suit stood waiting for him. He stepped past the threshold to greet her with a firm handshake. She was probably in her late thirties, and looked only spectacular. Dark hair and huge almondlike eyes. Trim waist and legs that couldn't have been turned any better on a lathe.

"Mr. Streicher, welcome!" she said brightly. "I am

Shahrnaz Safavi-Martin. I am the chief cryptanalyst at this installation."

"I am most charmed to meet you," he said. No one had bothered to tell him he'd be working with a woman; he considered it a pleasant surprise. He actually preferred working with women because they never wasted time trying to prove any of the usual macho nonsense regarding their toughness or their courage. Quite the contrary: Capable women brought intelligence and competence to the table . . . *and the bed*, he thought with a smile.

"You will follow me, please," said Safavi-Martin.

Streicher gladly did so. Her purposeful stride was a pleasure to watch. They turned off the main corridor and entered a large, well-lit lab. Only two other technicians were present, both young men, both totally absorbed in separate tasks. In the center of the room was a large glass rectangular enclosure that resembled a laminar flow cabinet. Inside the case, small stainless steel brackets floated a small fragment of stained glass in the center.

Streicher leaned forward, looked at it and smiled. "Yes, that's it. . . . Just as I remember it."

Staring more intently, he noticed the piece of glass was subtly backlit to reveal a pair of brilliantly blue eyes. Lapis lazuli. Stunning, but more than that. There was a totally *arresting* quality about the eyes of the Virgin. The stained glass artisan who'd created them had been quite the genius at his craft. Although flat and two-dimensional, you could not stop staring at the eyes, with an accompanying sensation of falling *into* their gaze, as if drawn into the vanishing point of a cosmic black hole.

"Incredible, isn't it?" said Safavi-Martin, who stood close enough so that he could smell the intriguing mixture of Chanel and her own pheromones.

"Yes, very impressive. But I did not come here to view a work of art. My message indicated something more . . . more sensitive, shall we say?"

The woman smiled. "That is an interesting way of

phrasing it. We have kept the object under a constant array of measuring and observation devices, covering the total array of visible and invisible spectra."

"I would expect as much," he said. "Go on."

"The image of the eyes changes. Sometimes it disappears altogether."

Streicher smiled. "Our sources were correct. That is excellent. But they said there are times when actual *text* can be seen. Have you seen it?"

Safavi-Martin nodded. "Oh yes, we have also recorded it. I think it might be Latin, or perhaps a lost dialect."

"Can you read it? What does it say?"

The woman gave him a look of total dismay. "Under normal circumstances, it should not be a problem. I am fluent in seven languages, plus I possess a plausible familiarity with the 'dead' tongues of Latin and early Turkic."

"Impressive," he said. "But . . . ?"

"But the five different notations we have seen appear to be a fairly complex code . . . maybe not a language at all."

"How complex? Can you break it?"

"Well," she said, pausing to choose her words carefully. "That is why I am here. I have access to the finest equipment and programming in the world. If the code can be broken, I can do it."

"How long do you estimate?"

Safavi-Martin smiled and gave him an expression as if he were a five-year-old asking for a shot of bourbon. "Now you know perfectly well I cannot even *begin* to give you a time frame. It could happen in the next few minutes, or it might not happen for another year."

"If it takes that long, there are many people who would be very unhappy with you," he said.

"You are familiar with the Rosetta stone?"

He shrugged. "Somewhat. Why?"

"It proved to be the key to unlocking the Egyptian

hieroglyphic code," she said. "We could very much use such a thing here. You didn't bring me a Rosetta stone. It would have provided us with what we need."

"Like a key," he said, inwardly angry that Guild intelligence had not uncovered the need or the possible existence of such a thing.

"Precisely," she said. "A key. Did you bring me the key?"

"No."

"I am certain there is a key that unlocks this code. Where you 'obtained' the piece of glass, is it possible you might also obtain the key for me?" She looked at him with the hint of a wink. "You could save me a lot of work, you know."

He looked at her, but said nothing. He liked her sardonic sense of humor, her respect for him, but also her lack of fear of him.

"Have you been briefed on the true nature of this object?"

"No," she said. "But it is obviously a piece of stained glass, most likely from a religious shrine or ruin. That we have observed unexpected and thusfar unexplained phenomena associated with the glass, I could make the intuitive leap we are dealing with something of an otherworldly—if not divine—nature."

"And you believe in such things?" Streicher looked at her closely, searching the place behind her eyes for sincerity. He admired the ability of scientists from non-European cultures to mix equal parts of empiricism with their mysticism.

Safavi-Martin shrugged. "Let us just say I am open to possibilities. And I suspect that usually you are not."

"Why do you say that?"

"Only because I can see you are not in touch with your mystical side," said Safavi-Martin with a wry smile.

"I don't have one."

"Oh, I believe everyone does," she said. "But in many of us, it is allowed to atrophy."

"Are you saying there is no hope for ones such as me?" .

"Not at all, Mr. Streicher. Sometimes, we experience a reawakening of our spiritual nature when we are confronted by mysteries beyond our comprehension."

"Is that what you think this is?" He gestured towards the case containing the glass.

"I don't know *what* it is. I am on need-to-know, as usual. If those serving the Guild at echelons above me wish me to know more, I am confident they, or *you*, will tell me."

"You are correct. How many on-staff have knowledge of this?"

"At this installation?"

"Yes."

"Only me . . . and my two assistants. They are both cleared."

Streicher grinned. "I would be shocked were they *not*. That would mean I would have to exact dire consequences."

Safavi-Martin replied with a cool stare into his eyes. She didn't flinch or blink.

He liked this woman. She had accepted her training in the Guild very well. "Get me a hard copy of your findings . . . now."

Without a word, she moved to a console, tapped a key and reached into a bin where several laserprint pages appeared. Streicher grabbed them and scanned them quickly. Although his people had not been able to extract any real, hard information from the glass, it had been confirmed that the rumors had indeed been true—the artifact the Catholics called the Eyes of the Virgin contained lettering, writing, perhaps actual messages.

Safavi-Martin's report contained a detailed physical analysis of the artifact, and described physical changes which appeared irregularly in the images within the glass. Sometimes the eyes would fade away, to be replaced by snatches of text—words which so far eluded their understanding. He tried to appear nonchalant, but his pulse was racing. If this glass could possibly do what the rumors claimed, it would be a tool of unlimited power . . . and *he* would be one of the elite who would have absolute access and utility to it.

He could not help but feel he was part of some vast and exciting adventure. And whenever he thought of how the Vatican had kept this object, this powerful relic, from the rest of the world, a terrible and righteous anger shot through him. He had been proud when Kerschow had tagged him for the job of removing it from the sphere of those medieval prigs.

Looking up from the pages, he saw Safavi-Martin staring at him, as if awaiting new orders. "You are certain *no one* has seen this material other than the four of us here now?"

"I am certain. I could swear to it."

"I want this area notched up to the highest security level. I must get this information to the proper channels ASAP."

Shahrnaz nodded. "I am correct then to assume I am no longer authorized to discuss the data with you or anyone else?"

He looked at her with a combination of protocol awareness and his obvious interest in her as a woman. "You are correct. If I bring up the subject of this data, you will discuss it with me—otherwise, you will not."

"Understood," said Safavi-Martin.

"Destroy all paper records of the data, including this one," he said, handing her the laserprint. "From now on, e-data only—with the usual encryption."

"Of course."

"Do we have any video or film records of the events you have observed?"

"Yes, it is standard procedure."

"I think it's best if we destroy those as well."

"Consider it done." Shahrnaz Safavi-Martin paused

before returning to her workstation. "Is there anything else?"

Streicher paused. "Yes, perhaps you can help me. I have been traveling all day. I will require a substantial dinner. . . . Do you have any suggestions nearby?"

Her expression was totally noncommittal. "There are many places in the neighborhood. But if you do not mind driving out past the suburbs, there are some very nice village inns."

"That sounds worthwhile," he said. "Tell me, would you mind very much accompanying me? I . . . I may have more to discuss with you about this project by then."

"Yes, I could do that," said Safavi-Martin. Her expression remained businesslike, and he tried to determine how she really felt about his invitation. But she continued to be completely unreadable.

"Very good," he said. "I will arrange for a driver. Be in front of the Banco di Argentina at seven—I will pick you up there."

That evening, she was waiting for him on time. He liked punctuality, and besides, he did not wish to think about what he would have done if she had not been standing in front of the ornate entrance to the bank. They exchanged small talk as the Guild driver maneuvered the sleek Mercedes through the early evening Parisian traffic. They spoke of the kind of banalities he normally found repugnant—the weather, the architecture of the city, the snooty personality of the natives, and the abundance of museums—and was surprised to discover he was actually enjoying the social exercise. He noticed her ability to keep the conversation flowing with an almost effortless lilt in her voice. This was a woman who had obviously been as much a world traveler as himself, and who was no stranger to culture and art, as well as science.

When they arrived at the appointed village of Arigny, situated in the rolling meadows of the incipient farms beyond the metropolitan suburbs, the driver left them at the local inn with orders to disappear until called by electronic pager. Shahrnaz's call ahead had succeeded in preparing a private table for them—an immaculately set table with fresh cut flowers and unscented candlelight.

Streicher became determined to dispense with ritual conversation as they looked over the menu, and even after the first courses were served. He was interested in finding out more about this woman, who was attractive not only because of her exotic features, but also her intelligence and ability. Gradually, she allowed veils of information to drop, as if she were entertaining him with a seductive dance.

Her father had been a general in the Persian army, and was in fact related to the shah by blood—which made her a member of a royal family that stretched back into Middle Eastern history for more than five-hundred years. She spoke of this lineage with deserved pride, tempered by an attitude that told him it mattered little what he might think of it. He had no real opinion of the geopolitics which changed the name and posture of Persia into a place called Iran. When stacked up against the concerns and operations of the Guild, such minor international intrigues were almost laughable.

But Streicher did not bother to voice his feelings on that particular subject. Instead, he steered her into stories of how she became an expert in cybercryptanalysis and how she came to be recruited by the Guild. Both tales were as mundane as he'd expected them to be. Shahrnaz was one of a hundred thousand midlevel "employees" who believed they worked for one of the growing multinational corporations beginning to pepper the twenty-first century's geo-economic landscape. She didn't volunteer any information about a current husband or family, and Streicher noted this with complete neutrality. Such things simply were not important to him—although he planned to obtain a complete dossier on this woman, anyway. Within twenty-four hours, he would know more about her than her most familiar friends and family.

Conversely, he had skillfully managed to avoid telling her much about himself. She did not need to know his real title was Chief of Field Operations, Northern Hemisphere—a feat he'd accomplished by the time he was thirty-nine years old. And there was no chance of him ever telling her he'd originally received his training right out of secondary school with the East German army's elite commando unit, *Krieg*. Those kinds of people did not officially exist any longer, and he would do nothing to defeat that myth. He almost grinned openly as he recalled a memory from his days at the Krieg academy, when he was clandestinely recruited by a neo-Nazi group with financial connections to the Guild. He'd joined them while remaining an officer in the East German army until the reunification in 1991, when he'd opted for getting pensioned out. There was no way he could have remained under the thumb of those reform-minded welfare-statists. From there, he'd been officially on the payroll of Balkan Metals, a highly successful mining and ore processing conglomerate owned by a powerful visionary, a man named Jagen Kerschow, a man he'd come to respect like a stern but fair patriarch.

During the course of the dinner, however, he had allowed her a few glimpses into his character. His love of World Cup Football and boar hunting was typically masculine enough, but he balanced it with an admission that he not only appreciated classical music, but played it passably well on his own cello. His preference of the moderns such as Bartok and Kodaly marked him as a maverick to most, and he relished the appellation. Perhaps later in their relationship, he might share an etude with her, or even more intimately, allow her a glimpse of his fervent fascination with history and his admiration for the Third Reich's attempt to impose a lasting *order* on the world.

But not tonight.

No. The only thing he would require this evening would be some laughter and uncomplicated feminine companionship. He might even ask her to dance, but this would be done with great ceremony and cordiality. He knew how to treat a woman when he wanted to be gracious and charming. This evening he would allow her to think she was in control of the level of intimacy they might share. There would be plenty of time for his will to dominate.

ELEVEN

Boston

MATT ETCHISON

"*I* don't get it," said Kate as they drove into Boston on I-93. It was the middle of the night and it was one of the few times you could find the roadway clear as you passed Copley Square, Storrow Drive, and the Fleet Center.

"Get what?" asked Matt idly.

He'd been driving for almost two and a half hours from a place called Newport, New Hampshire. After emerging from some of the thickest, darkest woods he'd ever imagined, they slogged their way across some sandbars in the Sugar River, and worked their way back to State Route 10. The moon had fallen and the rural road through Croydon Flat was so dark, Matt could not see his hands in front of his face. Every time they detected the lights of an approaching vehicle they'd ducked into the roadside brush because he couldn't take the chance it might be more of their pursuers. His cell phone didn't work because of the all the mountains, and they didn't come to a public phone for almost three miles of stumbling along the shoulder of the road.

"We can't call the local police," he'd told her.

"Why not? This is a small town!" she'd protested. "Lawrence and I knew everybody—we can trust them."

He'd told her she was most definitely right, but if the creeps who were after her were as slick as they were making themselves up to be, then he could make a good bet they were monitoring all calls to local authorities, gas stations, and cab services, and anybody else who might answer an emergency call.

"Okay," she'd said in a voice that did nothing to hide her frustration. "So who do you suggest we call?"

"A friend," he'd said. "Somebody close enough who can help us. Right now. Is there anybody you can think of who fits that description?"

"Only one," Kate had said after giving the problem some thought. "And I don't know him very well, but he was a good golfing buddy of my husband's. . . ."

Kate's choice and her instincts had been perfect. The man she called, a local businessman named Tom Canfield, picked up the phone on the first ring, and had been absolutely overjoyed to hear Kate's voice. He owned the Ford dealership in Newport, the next town over, and he'd not even taken the time to change out of his pajamas before driving over to personally pick them up in a new Explorer, loaded. He didn't even want to hear any of the details. If Kate told him she needed help, that was enough for him.

Then it had been back to the dealership in the middle of the night, where Canfield opened up the offices, grabbed the keys of a demo Taurus off a salesman's desk and pressed them into Kate's hands.

"Your husband was one of the good guys, Kate," Canfield had said solemnly. He had thinning hair, a long, angular jaw, and an always-ready smile. "I can't believe what's happened to you and your family, and I'll do whatever I can to help."

He'd told them to take the car and use it for as long as they needed it. "When you're done with it, just call my manager and tell him where it is—I'll arrange to have it picked up. Absolutely no problem. I just want to be able to be some help."

Matt had been impressed with the way people still watched out for each other and did business in a small town. Kate had told him that was one of the reasons she liked where she lived—it was the way more of America used to be.

Matt debated whether or not to warn Canfield about the possibility of being approached by anybody who might find out he'd helped them. It might be better to make it look like they'd *stolen* the car off the lot. He mentioned it to the owner, and the man waved off the suggestion emphatically.

And so after thanking Tom Canfield one final time, they had driven off his lot with one of his cars with nothing more than a handshake. Canfield stood there waving at them. "Be careful, Kate, and don't worry about that car—" he said cheerfully. "I know how to find you."

Better you than those bastards with all the guns, Matt had thought.

"Get what?" he repeated. Kate hadn't spoken much during the drive, lost in her own thoughts, he'd figured. She'd seemed to be holding up damned well under the stress and exhaustion of their earlier escape across the lake and a dead-reckoning hike through the woods until they'd hit the state road leading to Newport. It had been a harrowing grind, and he was feeling it now.

He'd been trying to concentrate on his driving, fighting drowsiness with only his thoughts to keep him company, and the major concern he'd been turning over was whether or not Kate's attackers knew anything about him.

"I'm sorry," said Kate, interrupting his thoughts. "I must have been mumbling, you know, thinking out loud."

He looked over at her and nodded. Her fashionably cut dirty-blonde hair didn't seem to mind the tussled tangling it had taken in the woods, and her complexion was clear.

"You said you 'Didn't get it' . . . and I was inquiring about the nature of the it, that's all."

Kate chuckled softly. "Oh, right, I remember. . . . I was just wondering why they—whoever *they* are—tried to kill me tonight. I mean, if they wanted me dead, why did they go to the trouble of framing me? It just doesn't make sense."

"You know," he said. "It's funny, 'cause I was thinking along similar lines. Want to know what I came up with?"

"Sure, that's what I'm paying you for, isn't it?"

Matt grinned. "Oh yeah, that's right, I've been having so much fun, I'd almost forgotten. Anyway, listen: The first thing you're doing is assuming that the people who killed your sister and set you up are the same people who shot at us tonight."

"Oh my God," said Kate. "Could there be more than one group after me? Why? I don't understand all this. . . ."

"Well, I'm not saying I do, either. Just that you have to consider all the possibilities." Matt pulled off the interstate at Atlantic Avenue and headed for the Marriott on State Street down by the water, checking his rearview mirror almost constantly. Atlantic Avenue was practically deserted and if anyone was following them, he would definitely know it. "The second possibility is they are the same guys, but that they *didn't* try to kill you at the house—only Markley and me."

"Really?" She looked at him with genuine surprise. "With all those bullets flying? They're *that* good?"

Matt chuckled. "I used to know a couple of Army

Ranger sharpshooters. With the right equipment, they could pick a fly off your nose at a hundred yards without even thinking about it. If these guys are the professionals I think they are—then, yeah, they're that good, and a hell of a lot better."

"Okay, any other theories?"

"Sure, I got plenty of theories . . . not a lot of answers, though. The other angle is this: They set you up with the murder of your husband and your sister . . . even though it looks like a silly case, maybe just to keep you out of the picture while they went through your house and your sister's place without any time constraints. The more I think about it, the more sense that makes to me."

Matt pulled the car into the Longwharf Marriott lot, headed for the portecochere. She ignored this, homing in on what he'd been talking about. "What do you mean—'went through'? You mean ransacking my house? Robbing me?"

"No, these guys aren't burglars. I mean, try this: Let's work from the assumption they needed something from your sister or her husband. When they didn't get it or find it, and she tried to contact you out of the blue, they figured that, hey, maybe she gave it to you! Or how about you had it all along, and she was trying to get it back from you . . . or something like that? Or maybe you have something they all need, and you don't even know you have it? How's any of that sound?"

Her expression, a kind of shocked realization that he'd touched on something sensitive, told him more than any of her words ever could. He waited.

"Ah, that sounds like a possibility," she said. "But I swear to you—I don't know anything! I don't know why anybody'd want to kill Justine, and I have no idea what Domenic was up to. Could it be possible he was in organized crime, maybe he owes somebody a lot of money? Could it be something so . . . so sad and ridiculous as that?"

Matt was about to speak when the doorman appeared

out of the darkness, putting a hand on Kate's door handle. It startled him and he was automatically going for his Sig-Sauer 9 mm when he realized the man was an employee of the hotel. He opened the door and waited for Kate to slip out of the Taurus.

Moving around to join her, he gave the keys and five bucks to the doorman.

"Any luggage, folks?" he asked.

"No, not tonight," said Matt, watching the guy nod with a touch of an approving grin. *It ain't like you're figurin' it, man,* thought Matt.

As he escorted Kate up to the front desk, he whispered to her quickly. "You have cash?"

"No, I left my bag back in Jonathan's car. Why?"

"Because we don't want to use any credit cards. Too easy to get traced. Okay, let me handle this."

He signed her in as his sister, who'd been visiting in the city. No ID, no nothing. Then he rolled out a fake name and address somewhere in Indiana and frankly, the desk clerk couldn't have cared less. If he'd questioned anything, Matt would have mumbled a few words about being robbed, but that would be it. One of the best things he'd ever learned in his work was that most people simply don't give a damn, and they only get suspicious when you try to give them too *much* information.

When they reached the room and he'd locked them in, he handed her the room key and several hundred-dollar bills. "Add this to my expense account," he said with smile. "This place will probably be as safe as anything for a few days. They have some stores right in here where you can get some stuff you might need. You know, some extra clothes, stuff for the bathroom . . . things like that."

"I get the idea. Thank you."

"And you should figure on staying here a day or two, at least, if that's okay with you?"

"I defer to your professional judgment," she said, sounding upset over the situation.

"Okay, good. Let's plan on it, until I can get a handle on what kind of danger you're really in."

Sitting on the bed, looking very tired, very stressed, she looked like she wanted to throw herself across the comforter and stretch out, then thought better of it. "Thank you," she said. "You've been worth every penny."

"I know," he said. "I saved your life and all that . . . but I have to tell you, Kate, I am still very much in the dark, here. I need some answers pretty soon, or we will get outsmarted. Whoever we're up against knows an infinite amount more about what's going on than me—'cause I don't know *zip*."

She looked at him, biting he lower lip, as if considering what she might say. He had no idea what the truth might be, but it was worth taking a shot. He decided a little coaxing wouldn't hurt, a little poker-bluffing maybe.

Matt cleared his throat: "So why don't you tell me what you've been holding back."

Again that startled little expression. "How do you know I–I might be?"

He shrugged. "It's my job to figure stuff out. If you don't *know* what these people might be after, I have a feeling you were at least told *something*?"

"Not exactly." She fumbled around in her Slazenger jacket and pulled out the golf course scorecard. It was still there, which meant the police hadn't searched her belongings when she'd been arrested, or if they'd seen the card, figured it was nothing, and left it. "I mean, it might be the numbers on this card . . . but I don't know what they mean, or what they are."

She offered him the card, and Matt took it, scanned the numbers. Four sets of four digits. Could be just about anything. She told him how she'd copied them off the seat of her sister's car, how she tried to cover them up.

"That might not work," he said.

"What?"

"They have staff called luminol and special lamps that they radiate at just the right wavelength in the spectrum so they can see where blood *has been*, even after it's been wiped up."

"Oh no, you're kidding." Kate sounded horrified.

"Serious as cancer," he said. "And I assume you . . . 'forgot' to tell them about the numbers, just like you did me?"

"I just wasn't sure how much I should say, especially when they were making me a prime suspect."

"Good thinking, I guess, but you should have kept me in the loop from the beginning. And listen, I'm not sure they can read the numbers or not, but if they're looking, they'll find *something*. You have no idea how good forensic science is getting."

"But who would be looking at things that closely? The police? The Feds? Or do you mean just our unknown Bad Guys?"

Matt began to slowly pace across the length of the room. "For now, I wouldn't rule out *any* of them. Depending on when your sister's car was impounded and where it is now might have a lot to do with who's been able to crawl all over it with sophisticated gear."

"Any ideas on how to stop them?"

Matt chuckled. "Short of sneaking into the Manchester impound lot and setting the seats on fire? Well, no, not exactly any *good* ideas. What about you?"

"I already told you, I have no idea."

"I mean about those sets of numbers. You told me you're in computers, right? Those numbers mean *anything* at all to you?"

"They could mean lots of different things. They could be numbers to specific lines of machine language code, but without knowing what program they referred to, they're completely meaningless."

"But the numbers *have* to mean something," he said. "Something your sister believed you would understand, or could use. I mean, I don't want to upset you, but don't forget—it's the last thing she was able to tell you. She knew she was dying and something made her want to tell you those numbers."

"No," said Kate, nodding her head. "You're right."

"So what exactly do you do in computers? Maybe we need to look at this from the other end."

She looked at him as a high priest would an initiate. How could she possibly explain her arcane binary rituals to a compu-dummy like him? He remained expressionless, waiting. He knew enough about computers to be thoroughly dangerous, and he was betting he had a good chance of understanding what she was assembling to tell him.

"It's complicated," said Kate.

"Yeah, I figured it might be."

"No, I didn't mean that to be a slight."

" 'Course not. . . ."

"Anyway," she said, "I worked with a company that creates and manages databases. When I figured out a few new wrinkles, and a system of improvements to the way information can be retrieved, I decided to try to open my own development company. Small, but more fun and more challenging than clanking along with a giant corporation."

"I agree. . . . That's why I left government service." Matt leaned against the credenza. "But what exactly did you *do*? What kind of skills do you have that we may need to talk about? That we may need to look at more closely?"

"Well, I would develop the software for storage and retrieval systems."

"Jon Markley said you create 'data havens,' is that right?"

"No, not really. I try to figure out the best way to make them operate efficiently. Creating a data haven is an engineer's job."

"Funny, I didn't hear you *exactly* like that. Now, please, what's a data haven?"

Her expression brightened as she warmed to the topic. It was a little piece of body language Matt had learned to appreciate years ago. When people talked to you about a particular subject with that certain *look*, you knew they weren't lying. Kate glowed as she began to tell him about data havens.

"Basically, they're like safe deposit boxes for digital information—but much bigger."

"How much bigger?"

"Usually, they're set up in underground bunkers. Your basic cube laced with corridors and elevators. And filled with thousands of redundant storage devices—hard drives, CDs, even tapes."

"Redundant meaning what?—lots of backup copies of the same stuff?"

Kate nodded. "That's right."

"Sounds expensive as all hell," said Matt, trying not to be charmed. "What's the reason for putting it underground—EMP?"

Kate could not hide her surprise. "That's right! I'm not trying to be funny, but how do you know about something like that? Most people would never have heard of something like that."

"Goes back to my Navy Seal days," he said. "Actually, the military's been experimenting with electromagnetic pulse weapons technology for a long time now. Ever since they first discovered that nuclear blasts create EMP, and that it can knock the hell out of digitally stored and controlled data."

"There's a lot I obviously don't know about you, Mr. Etchison." Kate said this in a tone that communicated professional appreciation.

"Yeah, people tell me that all the time." He cleared his throat, and began to pace slowly back and forth across the room. "Tell me more about the data havens. I have a hunch they're important somehow. I mean, think about it—we have to assume the Bad Guys are after information, and data havens are where people store *information*. What about your sister, or her husband, ah . . . Domenic, right?"

Kate nodded. "Go on . . ."

"Did either of them know much about what you do?"

"Sure, we would talk shop when we were together once in a while. And recently Kendall Structures—that's the company where Domenic works—won a contract to build a DHI—a data haven installation—on a small island in the Mediterranean. And in the best tradition of nepotism, Domenic had gotten them to hire me. I helped them put together a consortium of companies to make it happen."

"When was that?"

"More than a year ago. The project's practically finished now." Kate said, then paused to give this some thought. "There might be some kind of connection there. I wish I had my notebooks or my computer files."

Matt chuckled ironically. "Our friends have crawled all over your house—don't you think they've already had a look at all that stuff?"

"If they can get into it," she said. "I use some pretty sophisticated encryption routines."

"Okay, so how do we find out more about Domenic and his work?"

"I'll have to sit down and make some notes. Remember names and places, I guess."

"Okay, if you're up to it, try to start thinking about it tonight. We'll get to work on it tomorrow." Matt checked his watch and headed for the door, stopped there and pulled a small object from his pocket. "Oh yeah, almost forgot . . . take this."

"A pager?" she said, pausing to apprise the small object attached to a thin cord necklace.

"Something like that. Just wear it all the time, even in the shower—it's waterproof—and hit that big button on the side if you need me. I'll come running, guns blazing."

Slipping it over her head like a talisman, she looked

at him wearily. "I'm tired of playing this whole I-spy game, and you know what's the worst part?"

"What?"

Kate folded her arms and looked as weary as she sounded. "I know it's not a game . . . that it's something deadly serious and the only way I'm getting through it without going completely crazy is to keep acting like it's some dumb game."

Matt stared at her, but wasn't sure what he might say to make her feel any better.

"Sorry," she said. "Does any of what I just said . . . does any of it make any sense? I just realized I might have sounded like I was insulting you or trivializing what we've already been through, and it's not like that at all."

"Relax, I understand what you're trying to tell me," Matt said. "Frankly, I've been wondering how you've been keeping it together. You've been through a hell of a lot. You're handling everything a lot better than most of my clients—and I've had some people who were supposed to be pretty wily customers."

"Yeah, well I guess I'm tough," said Kate.

"Yeah, maybe you are, but for now, I think we'd both better get some rest."

"Okay."

He looked at his watch again. "Oh yeah, one more thing. Give me the room key for a minute."

"What for?"

"You'll see. I'll be back in a minute. Stay here. Don't open the door. Don't do anything."

He slipped from the room, down the desolate main corridor until he found the ever-present vending room with the ice machine and the machines full of junk food. He fed them their base-metal offerings and they coughed up enough carbohydrates and saturated fats to keep Kate alive for the next twenty-four hours.

When he reappeared in her room, she was standing there, patiently waiting where he'd left her.

"I bring gifts," he said. "In case you get hungry, this stuff will have to do. Please, don't think about leaving the room, or even opening the door until I get back."

"When will that be?"

He shrugged. "I have some stuff I want to follow up on, check out. I'll call you in the morning, and check in every once in a while. After I get a little more information, check on a few of my sources, we see what we want to do next."

And with that Matt said goodnight and headed down toward the lobby. He kept thinking about how resilient she was. She said she was tough, and he had a feeling she was right. He'd worked with lots of clients, especially the inside-the-Beltway types in D.C. who would have been feeling pretty helpless by now, but Kate Harrison was still standing in there, taking their best shots, and wondering what would come next.

Matt hoped they wouldn't know the answer to that one for a while. They at least needed time to catch their breath.

TWELVE

Arezzo, Italy

DOMENIC PETRALLI

*T*he guilt would not leave him any time soon.

As he maneuvered the rented Punta out of the twisting streets of Arezzo, he let his thoughts wander where they might. The theft of the artifact and the wholesale slaughter at the Wieznewski home had been a real wakeup call to him and his superiors. Prior to that singularly horrible event, they had believed the secret of the Eyes of the Virgin had been safe for more than eighty years.

No one could possibly know about it after all that time. Especially since all the connections and references to it had been carefully altered or erased by the Vatican and its sworn protectors. But then, almost precisely when the Commission on Miracles had asked his sector for help in procuring a new analysis of the artifact . . .

Someone appears out of nowhere, and takes it from them.

Although Domenic had avoided discussing what this act implied with Sforza, it must certainly be an unspoken understanding: There was a serious breach of security within either the *Servicio Segretto Vaticano* or the Knights of Malta. A possible alternative could be the Americans or another world power had launched a new generation of espionage technology that rendered the communications of Domenic and his colleagues totally transparent.

Either answer made him feel weak and ineffective, and he was not certain what he should do next. If there was a mole within the ranks, there was nothing he could do on a short-term basis—that would fall within Sforza's sphere. But if he faced a technological menace, then he would have to permanently change the way he communicated with KOM as well as anyone else.

He replayed his debriefing with Sforza, and his previous observation that technology rarely looked back. Once a new, faster, cleaner, cheaper, better way of doing something—anything—is developed, it becomes highly unlikely that the world ever would revert to doing it the "old" way, which is precisely why the KOM would be quick to do exactly that.

It was a good bet he would be very safe sending Morse code, regular letters, or couriers. He nodded to himself as he downshifted the small car and headed west on a two-lane highway. He was driving toward *autostrada* E78, and taking a generally southeast direction to the coast. Ultimately he had to get back to the States, and he would not be able to do it through the usual channels. Without his normal communications available, he had no choice but to assume that Corsica Station had prepared the way for him.

He grinned as he thought that there were far worse alternatives than throwing your trust to the ancient order of the Knights; then shifted thoughts again. There was definitely something to be said for the retro-approach from here on out. If his adversaries were able to read e-mails, intercept faxes, and penetrate "unbreakable" encryptions with supersatellites and other third millennium miracles, then he would stop using them. Things would be slow, but they would remain secure, and none of his enemies would be the wiser. And besides, *slow* was a relative term. It would allow him extra time to plan and execute.

Domenic was hungry and he was tired. It was probably best to head southwest to the coast as directly as possible to catch the boat at Follonica. If anyone was following him, and they attempted to interfere, he would take the appropriate action. He reviewed what he'd received from Sforza's last briefing about Justine's sister, Kate Harrison.

1. The attack on her home and murder of the family attorney;
2. The escape with the private eye; and
3. Their appearance in the Boston hotel.

He hadn't seen or spoken to her in months, and he couldn't imagine how she was reacting to the chaos that tornadoed around her. Kate was such an analytical, levelheaded person, the amount of insane tragedy suddenly thrust upon her must be close to unbearable. She was the type that likes to have things under control, to have things in order. To have so much unpredictability in her life right now must be infuriating and frustrating. Domenic would do what he could to change that. He would take her into his protection, and arrange for her safety until the artifact was retrieved.

Regarding the assault on Kate's home and its subsequent ransacking by their enemies, Sforza did not believe they had any idea what *kind* of information they were looking for. That, at least, was to the Knights' advantage. However, it was quite clear the enemy *knew* Domenic had passed something vital to his wife, which made it something they would *de facto* want very much—whatever it may be.

The enemy seemed to *know* everything Domenic's

people knew. He wondered if it were possible they had already tracked Kate to the Boston hotel?

No way to tell. It was therefore very important for Domenic to reach Kate Harrison ASAP. He needed to know if Justine had given her any of the data, and if she had any idea what it meant or how it could be used. It was frustrating to not have all the cards in his hand; a position out of the norm for him.

For instance, in addition to not knowing if Justine had succeeded in giving her the data, he wondered if Kate now knew anything about his true profession? Did Justine tell her about the Knights of Malta? Not having these answers crippled him severely, and he found himself worrying about decisions to be made.

Which was absurd when you thought about it. He'd spent his career assessing situations and moving on them instantly. Never a second thought; never anything even vaguely resembling worry or a lack of confidence. Now, after getting compromised at Ciampino, then managing to get his wife murdered, and losing a sacred relic of the Church, he was giving serious consideration to the possibility he was losing it.

At forty-two years old, he'd been in the field for eighteen years. That was a very long time to be so deeply immersed in deadly, clandestine activities. To last that long, you had to be extremely lucky or extremely competent. And he didn't believe in luck. But he'd lived the hours and years in the self-imposed prison of almost total detachment. So many things about himself he'd had to keep hidden from everyone, even Justine. And when he'd finally confessed to her, in a moment of abject desperation and danger, it contributed to her death.

Maybe it was time to step down from his sector chief's position; maybe this would be his last operation? After all, the Eyes of the Virgin had been stolen on his watch. He recalled with regret that he had suggested Harold Wieznewski's testing facilities in Potomac, Maryland for the latest analysis of the artifact. Wiez-

newski had been a loyal member of the KOM for more
than twenty years. Any way you regarded it, he'd been
embarrassed and exposed in a way that had never happened in his long career.

But he kept telling himself there was no percentage
in doubt and recrimination, as he pushed the little Fiat
through the layers of night. He tried to keep his attention
on the road, but with little success. When he entered the
coastal village of Follonica, more than two and half
hours had passed and he had little memory of the trip.
He didn't even remember the torturous detours around
Siena or the twisting hillocks of route SS322. Darkness
conspired with a sleeping blanket of fog to half obscure
most of the town's landmarks as he drove the car down
ancient, narrow back streets and alleys barely wide
enough for scooter traffic. Leaving the lights of via Cris-
toforo Colombo, Domenic killed the engine in an alley
adjacent to a wharfside nautical supply warehouse.

Before he could even reach for the handle to open the
driver's side door, a long, craggy face had materialized
from the dim light to stare at him through the glass. It
was a face he'd expected to see, and was not surprised
by it.

"Signor Petralli . . . buona sera."

"Ciao, Giacomo," said Domenic to the old man who
looked to be made from hawser rope and sun-rotted sail-
cloth. Sinewy and thin, he looked frail, but Domenic had
seen him kill men half his age without breaking a sweat.

"You gave us no advance warning," he said to Domenic as he held the door open and waited for him to
clamber out.

Domenic apprised him of the possible leaks in their
communications protocols as they slowly walked to the
side entrance of the warehouse, which was attached to a
low, dilapidated boathouse.

"I need to get to Scioffino tonight."

Giacomo smiled to reveal several large front teeth, top

and bottom, and lots of hideously abscessed gum. "Nobody at the airfield tonight. . . ."

"I want to be there for the next flight—whenever it goes out."

Giacomo nodded and ushered him into the boathouse, where a low, sleek Ocean Marauder bobbed and tossed in the light of a kerosene lantern. Its black, shining hull looked like the carapace of a giant waterbug. Domenic followed the old man into the cabin of the powerboat, then waited as he remoted open a door to the sea.

Within minutes they were half-skipping across the choppy waters toward the Corsican coastline. A bank of sophisticated navigational and guidance equipment practically steered the craft without Giacomo's expert seaman's touch. He'd been fishing and sailing the Ligurian Sea for several of Domenic's lifetimes, and knew its moods and moves better than those of his wife.

Skirting south of Elba, then cutting past the tiny Pianosa, the boat accelerated through the black waters like a torpedo trying to become airborne. The moon was high in the black dome of the sky and its light fell dim and scattered across their path as if doing its best to ignore their passage. As they approached the coastline, Giacomo reached for the radio, and Domenic stopped him. "No, my friend. Get me the semaphore lamp."

"What?" said the old man, then nodded as he remembered Domenic's earlier words of caution.

It was several minutes before his compatriots at the Scioffino Station were convinced he was who he claimed. They exacted an extra layer of code clearances from him to be extra certain, then finally okayed his landing—also by semaphore lamp.

A young man whom Domenic recognized from previous visits to the underground hangar waited for him on the dock. He had one of the brand-new HK-50 automatic assault rifles unshouldered, but not aimed at Domenic, and his young features expressed unabashed relief when he recognized the sector chief.

"Signor Petralli, I am so sorry to greet you this way, but your arrival . . . it was not expected."

"Yes, yes, I know. I would have been surprised if you did *not* greet me with such suspicion."

Domenic reprised his need to remain electronically invisible, then asked to be taken to the debriefing center. If his superiors were surprised to see him, they would be even more startled by his demand for immediate transport.

"Can't it wait until morning?" said Armando Cerami, the flight op director.

"Well, if you don't have the man or the equipment, I guess it would have to . . . but I'm willing to bet Sforza will give you a top priority on this one. It's need-to-know stuff—you know that, 'Mando—and I wouldn't be pushing for it unless I had an extremely good reason."

Cerami grinned, and shrugged. "Okay, I give up. I'd already gotten a white flag from Sforza to get you whatever you needed. I have pilots, but they would have appreciated a full shift of downtime."

Domenic was taken off guard. "Sforza knew I was coming here?"

"No. He just told us that you could show up at any time . . . and we needed to be ready for you."

"Okay, so when do I get going?"

"Give me ninety minutes to get your crew briefed and log in their flight plan."

It only took a little more than a hour before he was wheeling west across the Atlantic in a small cargo jet. Flying under the world famous green and white logo of International SkyFreight, the SSV and the Knights of Malta had achieved an almost perfect access to any country in the world. A plastic SkyFreight ID badge dangled from a braided cord around Domenic's neck, which complimented his white baggage-handler's coveralls, also emblazoned with the SkyFreight logo. That simple uniform and badge could get him access to just about any building on the face of the earth—as long as he was carrying a package under one arm. The presence of overnight letter and freight carriers had become so ubiquitous, so *expected*, that their trucks and uniforms had metamorphosed into part of the international economic landscape. A perfect, undetectable cover.

So far, at least. . . .

As Domenic curled up in the go-seat behind the pilot's cabin, he tried to get comfortable enough to get some sleep. Logan International Airport lay six hours distant, and he welcomed the chance to stop thinking for a while.

ThIRTEEN

Boston

KATE HARRISON

*T*he next twenty-four hours were probably her worst since she'd found her sister bleeding to death at the interstate rest stop. Immediately afterward, Kate had been swept up in a vortex of stress, confusion, and activity. There had been no time to accept any of the terrible facts about the changes in her life.

Her husband and Justine senselessly murdered.

She kept replaying that truth over and over in her mind. Ever since the distraction of Matt Etchison's presence had been missing, she couldn't stop thinking about both of them. Constantly.

After Etchison had left her room, she'd been surprised how quickly she'd given in to total and complete exhaustion. Despite her confused and stressful emotional state, her body's need for rest finally overwhelmed her mind's intention to keep running at full speed. But when she awoke to a bright sun through the gauzy curtains, the memories and the leaden reality of what had happened to her life came thudding back to her.

Etchison had kept his word and called in at random

times, but he wasn't sure when he'd return. The day became like a piece of saltwater taffy, going soft, stretching out and losing its shape and place in the real world. The hours alone had given Kate more time to ponder her fate—her past as well as her future—than she'd ever bargained for. She felt more adrift and alone than she'd ever felt in her life. The only time she could remember feeling so inexplicably isolated was when Charlie Powell had taken that final ride onto the fragile ice of Lake Sunapee. *Oh God*, she thought, *so many years ago. . . .*

Kate shuddered as she remembered how she used to lay in bed, hour after moonless hour, in the weeks and months after Charlie had slipped beneath the broken surface. She would lay there trying to imagine what it must be like at the bottom of the lake—a black, timeless place of endless cold and wet, and what her sweet Charlie must look like by now. . . .

The nightmares didn't go away for a long time, and now she was discovering that they hadn't really ever gone away. They'd simply been waiting for the best time to come back and remind her just how much fun life can be when you think nothing can be better.

Sunset was perfunctory and unspectacular from the vantage point of her room window, which overlooked a channel of water between the Atlantic Avenue wharf and the next one over. The sun had passed over the back of the hotel and the effect imparted an ever-increasing twilight-gray cast to the brackish surface and the sky. It was practically black beyond the windows when Etchison called to say he was heading into traffic and would probably stop at his downtown office before heading back down to the Marriott.

"Glad you called," she said. "I was getting ready to have my dinner of Cheese Doodles and a Hershey bar, but maybe now, I'll wait for you."

"Good idea. I know a nice place in the North End. Safe as we can be under the circumstances. Quiet. We can talk."

"Anything new?"

"Couple of interesting things," he said. "You'll see."

After she hung up, she cleaned the room, tidying up the little amount of mess she'd been able to create. The television droned on to fill in the dead air, but she regarded it as generally intrusive, rather than helpful. She never had been able to understand people who actually planned their activities around the schedule of programming on TV. Something weird and sterile about that kind of lifestyle, and she—

The sound of a key being placed in her lock startled her.

Her thoughts seized up like a broken engine, and she instinctively touched the wireless alarm hanging from her neck. The door opened an inch or two and the security catch—a hinged, brass V tapering down to clasp a brass knob on the threshold—grabbed the heavy metal door with a solid thud.

"Who is it?" said Kate, trying to sound as indignant as possible.

"Ooh, I am so sorry, ma'am," said a young woman's voice. Her accent was Latino or perhaps Portuguese. "I have to do the room. . . ."

"No, thank you," said Kate. "That won't be necessary."

"I have to change your sheets." The woman sounded apologetic and unctuously deferential, yet at the same time insistent.

"The sign says DO NOT DISTURB. I really don't need anything."

There was no reply.

As the seconds of silence tumbled away, Kate became

far too aware of the lack of response. Especially since the door did not close.

Why did she leave it open? What was she doing?

As if in response, there came the sound of something heavy, massive, and metallic. Looking to the door, Kate could not believe what she saw—the stainless steel jaws of a huge set of bolt cutters had shark-nosed through the opening and grabbed the security catch like helpless prey. Before she could move or even utter a sound, the cutters crunched through the metal and the door exploded inward.

There was a blur of motion as the two figures burst into the room, closing the door behind them all in the same furious motion.

One of them was tall, muscular; the other lithe and athletic but definitely female. The man stood in a shooter's stance, a blue-black weapon pointed at a spot in the center of her forehead.

A thought, lightning flashing through her, that her life was going to end in the next instant, that she would never feel the slug explode through her brain, that she was surely going to die.

The finality and terror of the instant had paralyzed her. She had yet to make a sound, and knew she would not, *could* not. Kate's hands rushed to her chest to press the panic button before a bullet tumbled through her skull. . . .

Then, on pure instinct, she turned to run, even though there was nothing but a wall and a big window behind her, and no place to go. She felt herself jerked roughly forward, a knee in the small of her back forcing her down to the floor where she could smell the dusty scent of the carpet fibers. A heavy weight was pressing her down. When she tried to move her head, to look up, the weight increased.

"Do not move," said a voice. The man's, smooth, calm. "If you wish to remain alive."

"What do you want with me?"

Laughter. Sardonic and venomous. The woman.

"Kate Harrison," said the male voice, ignoring his partner's amusement. "Please do not consider *not* co-operating. You have already seen what we can do."

Listening to the man's precise diction, she was certain he was a foreigner, even though she could detect no accent. Even though her heart hammered against her rib cage, she kept reminding herself to try to stay calm and keenly observant. Her short time with Matt had already demonstrated how important it was to always be paying attention to even the smallest details. And she knew they didn't want to kill her. She knew they wanted information from her.

"I'm sorry, but I'm not sure what you're talking about. What exactly have I seen?"

Suddenly, her scalp was ablaze as a hand grabbed what felt like most of the hair on her head and yanked upward savagely. Her neck arched back at an alarming angle and there was suddenly a hideously serrated blade under her nose, slowly descending to her exposed larynx. "I did this to your sister, and I can do it to you. . . ."

The words burned into her like a branding iron. *This was the one?!* Her stomach lurched as she realized how close she was to such an animal.

"Now do you know what he's talking about?" asked the woman, still unseen somewhere behind her.

"Yes. . . ." said Kate, barely able to get out the single syllable.

"Now listen carefully," said the man. "We shall allow you to rise and take a seat. Get comfortable. Compose yourself. Prepare to tell us what you know. Is that clear, Kate Harrison?"

"Yes, yes . . . that will be fine."

And with that, she felt two sets of hands pulling her to her feet and turning her around. She was directed to a chair next to the table in the corner opposite the bed, and roughly pushed down into its cushions by the woman. On second glance she appeared stocky, but her movements were smooth, graceful. She had hair the color of blue steel and pale icy eyes like those Siberian dogs. Her lips were thin, and always looked like they were on the verge of a grin. The man was tall and broad-shouldered with sandy hair and a pale complexion. He looked British or Irish, maybe, but she knew he could be anything, really.

They both wore casual clothing, as if they'd recently been playing golf. Ralph Lauren jerseys and khaki Dockers—they looked so normal, so fashionably harmless. The woman had removed her pastel lemon yellow windbreaker to reveal a double shoulder holster that carried several hand weapons. The man still wore an unzipped, hunter green jacket, but Kate could see a panoply of weapons strapped beneath its folds. These two were walking arsenals, and she wondered if they were really the ones who'd killed her sister and her husband. . . .

Because if they were, she wanted them *dead*.

The thought rang through her with a hideous realization—she'd never consciously wanted anyone dead before. A chilling and yet extremely warm sensation. Kate's acceptance both repulsed and attracted her. Fragments of thoughts sheeted through her, making her mind like the sky of an electrical storm—chaotic, yet full of some greater natural order.

And with that sense came a calmness, an almost serene detached contemplation of how she truly felt at this moment of terror. The essence of her pondering: What kind of person had she become to start thinking like this?

One who wanted to survive, came her instant self-response.

With her acceptance had come an inner control, and she realized how easy it was to *hate* these two dirtbags. These pieces of garbage who'd violated her life so completely. And she knew, with utter serenity, that if she got the chance, Kate would kill then both with her own hands.

Seated in the chair, she glared at them, and both appeared on the verge of smiling. Either her expression of anger amused them, or they were just naturally happy folk. She wanted to spit at them, kick them, claw their eyes.

"You don't know us, Kate," said the woman. "But we obviously know a great deal about you. Just about the only thing we don't know is what information you were given by your sister."

"She didn't tell me anything," said Kate. "She was . . . already dead when I found her."

The woman smiled, then walked close to within several feet of her chair. In a move so quick, so precise that Kate never even *saw* it, the woman struck her lower jaw with enough force to dislocate it. A ringing shockwave *stunned* her for an instant, before an aftershock of pain latticed her skull. Reeling, Kate could not stop tears from bursting out of her. She had never imagined such pain, and for an instant she thought she might actually pass out.

"Don't lie to me, you fancy bitch!" said the woman, leaning so close her cold blue eyes seemed to give off an icy breath. "I know how much you like all that American Express Platinum treatment—I tore your house apart! I know everything you ever had there, everything you ever *did* there! Not that it matters anymore . . . we burned the place to the ground."

The words flared through Kate as full of shock and pain as the blow to her jaw had been. Her house—gone. She couldn't believe it . . . couldn't accept that. Not after everything else. . . .

"We *know* she left you a message," said the man, who approached her within arm's length. Reaching inside his golf jacket, he produced the wide, jagged-edged blade she'd already felt at her neck. "And we do not have time to waste with you. . . . so . . ."

He placed the blade against her cheek. ". . . either you tell us what we want . . . right *now* . . . or we kill you. *Now!*"

Blurred by her tears, the image of the man wavered in front of her. Her breath was coming in short, gasping bursts, and the pain from her jaw still throbbed with dizzying effect. She was not sure she could respond even if she wanted to, and—

The last thing Kate heard was an explosion of shattering glass, and then there was nothing but darkness. . . .

FOURTEEN

MATT ETCHISON

*E*ven though he'd been hopping all day, he was glad
he'd taken the time to check in on his client. Kate
was not holding up very well by herself even though she
was trying to make a good go of it. He didn't like leaving her alone but there were things that needed doing.

One of the most imortant was to cash out some of the
very healthy expense advance she'd given him at Markley's. He filled his money belt with fifties and one hundreds, and hoped he wouldn't need to spend them. He
always regarded his expense account like that, but it always managed to disappear anyway. He also stopped at
his office safe to pick up an ATM card linked to an
account in Antigua, which was not party to any FINCEN
agreements. It also utilized encrypted PIN codes and allowed him access to cash anywhere in the civilized
world.

However, most of his day had been taken up with a
very delicate and difficult problem Kate unloaded on
him during the nighttime drive to Boston—namely the

disposition of the bodies of both her sister, Justine, and Lawrence Copley Harrison, her husband.

It was one of those *big* problems that Matt had not given an instant of consideration, and when Kate mentioned it through a gale of choking tears and guilt, he felt like a complete jerk. Originally, when Kate had called Jonathan Markley, very quickly after her arrest, the attorney had promised to take care of everything— from contacting other members of both families, all the way through permissions for the autopsies, funerals, etc.

After Markley's own death and the subsequent chaos that consumed both of them, she was half-crazy wondering what had happened to her two most loved people in the world. She had been insisting to Matt that she *must* be the one to handle everything, and he spent more than a few minutes convincing her just how impossible that was. Anyone who wanted to kill her, or worse, interrogate or torture her, would be watching and monitoring all the expected venues such as funeral homes, crematoria, cemetery administrations, obituary desks, churches, clergymen, extended families, and even florists and the Manchester city morgue. If she surfaced at any of the above places, her enemies would have all they needed to track her and ambush her at their convenience.

No way, he'd told her.

And then he had to swear on the soul of his dead grandmother, Emma Quinn, that he would pick up the task wherever Markley had left it and take it to a complete and satisfyingly appropriate end. As far as Kate's guilt for not being able to personally administer all the proper rituals, he had no quick fix, other than to tell her she shouldn't feel guilty for having to save her own life.

Not that it did much good, of course.

Pushing that small failure out of mind, Matt had been able to wrap up a few things, which in the process, revealed more of the total mystery. When he contacted Detective Dorr at Manchester Central District he was shocked to discover that Justine Petralli's body had been claimed from the city morgue by a clergyman from St. Michael's parish in Somerset. Father Phillip Winslow had introduced himself as the Petralli's family priest, and had proffered an impressive amount of information about the Petrallis as evidence he'd been asked to take care of all the funereal obligations.

Detective Dorr apparently had been convinced of Father Winslow's affiliation with the family, and hadn't done any verification other than a routine phone call to St. Michael's rectory. When the woman who answered the phone told him "Father Phil" was on his way to Manchester, New Hampshire, Detective Dorr figured everything was, in his own words, "on the up-and-up."

However, later that same day, *another* priest, calling himself Father Richard Tuxbury, showed up from St. Joachim's in Sunapee, New Hampshire, claiming to be Kate Harrison's family priest, and who had been requested by her side of the family to take care of Lawrence Harrison's remains.

"He gave me the same kind of info on Kate Harrison's family," Dorr had told Matt. "Really thorough, like he knew everything about them. And you know, even though it all sounded pretty 'jake,' I was feeling my cop instinct starting to twinge a little."

Matt knew what Detective Dorr was talking about. Sometimes, for absolutely *no* reason, you just knew things were not "right."

". . . so I call St. Joachim's and I get a routine confirmation this Tuxbury guy is who he says he is, but you know, I still don't feel right about it."

Dorr had then tried to contact some of Lawrence Harrison's side of the family, but had problems because of some misunderstandings among Lawrence's two brothers and several nieces regarding Kate. They were irate she'd disappeared, had said nothing to anyone, and had seemingly ignored the death of her husband. After Dorr had tried to explain some of the weird events which continued to envelop Kate Harrison, in hopes of assuaging the Harrisons, the family remained skeptical—especially after they all claimed *no* knowledge of a Father Tuxbury.

"So I did something I wouldn't usually do," said Detective Dorr. "I personally drove over to the archdiocese building, and asked Bishop O'Brien to get me some poop on Father Tuxbury."

Matt hadn't been surprised to learn that the archdiocese had never heard of Father Tuxbury. And Dorr, once discovering that, had asked Bishop O'Brien to check out Father Phillip Winslow in the Boston archdiocese—with the same results.

Detective Dorr had been angry with himself for being flummoxed, but also at a loss to explain how it had been done. From what Matt had seen so far, it was obvious they were dealing with extremely sophisticated operatives—far slicker than anyone the Manchester Police Department had ever imagined, much less encountered. Even with his Seal training, Matt had felt intimidated by the sheer force of the enemys' attack and the boldness of their activities. They didn't seem to care when or where they intervened; they acted with utter impunity. It was obvious they'd deployed digital fiber optic intercepts, breaching any firewalls they encountered.

Matt smiled as he pieced together the phone scam on the Manchester cops. In terms of complexity, the process was relatively low-tech and not terribly sophisticated. Matt tried to stay ahead of the curve on all the *stuff* out there for surveillance, privacy obliteration, and weaponry, but it was getting to be impossible. No sooner than someone dropped a new system into the arena, a new "antisystem" would be available before you had a chance to finish reading the owner's manual on the former.

He offered to help Detective Dorr track down the "body snatchers" masquerading as parish priests, but he got the old stonewall treatment. Stemming mainly, he figured, from the embarrassment the Manchester PD had to be feeling right about now. To get burned once was bad, but twice in twenty-four hours just proved how pitiful the Department could be.

So Matt tried to do a little hi-tech privacy invasion of his own and used his hacker skills to check usage and inquiry, tracking on items such as rental cars, casket purchases, funeral arrangements, cremations, grave-diggings, monument engravings, even organ donations and costume rentals (a stretch, he realized). He was getting blind alleys on 99% of his cyber forays, but there were a few intriguing items that were flapping in the digital wind so blatantly, he couldn't believe it. Amazingly, both bodies had been delivered to funeral homes in the Boston exburbs in a vehicle sporting the markings of the Manchester Division of Forensic Medicine by personnel wearing nondescript city employee uniforms. Within hours, the directors of the Hopkins Funeral Home in Somerset and the Halloran Funeral Services Facility in Pawtucket both received SkyFreight Express deliveries of cash and letters of explicit instruction. The letters were essentially identical in their format, syntax, and content—both supplied details for requiem masses, eulogies, guest/invitation lists and addresses, wakes, and burials.

Matt found the level of consideration and detail to be astonishing. He had to conclude that whoever had orchestrated these arrangements had done them in this manner for a variety of reasons—one, to show anyone who might be paying attention how *powerful* they were; two, to ameliorate any problems brewing among the families; and three, perhaps to ease some of Kate's terrible guilt and pain.

Hard to imagine that an international band of thugs would ever pause to be so nakedly thoughtful. In fact, the more he thought about it, there was only one person who would have the motivation to do what had taken place . . . and that was the mystery man, the so-far invisible man, Domenic Petralli.

Matt had been generating a lot of rhetorical questions for Justine's husband, and Domenic proved conspicuous in his absence. There remained the very good possibility he was also dead, and Matt had kept that choice as his odds-on favorite until he discovered all the funeral arrangements. Now he had to figure Petralli was most likely still alive. Who else would do all the stuff he'd suddenly uncovered?

Finding Petralli had been one of his highest priorities. The man was obviously involved in something very big, very complex. Either he had pissed somebody off very badly, or he represented a formidable obstacle to a larger set of plans. There was absolutely no evidence to explain the incredibly swift level of violence that spun out of the vortex surrounding Petralli. Matt hoped to isolate *something* that might give him a signal to Petralli's location. It was reasonable to assume Domenic was in the Boston vicinity for several reasons—the number and magnitude of the arrangements made for both funerals suggested Domenic Petralli cared very much for his loved ones, and that he may be intending to make an appearance at either or both events.

Which meant Matt and Kate would be planning on the same.

He was driving north to Pawtucket to take some notes on the location and surrounding environs of the burial plot site for Lawrence Harrison, when he heard the distress beeper.

Wheeling along I-95 at seventy-five, his mind on anything but driving, Matt felt an instant of total confusion. How could that thing be going off? It was one of those precautionary devices he *never* really needed. It was like that little Kidde fire extinguisher he kept by the side of his computer desk—one of those things he would absolutely not *ever* need, one of those things he kept around precisely for that reason. But the base unit he'd attached under the dash of his Grand Cherokee was doing its job—chirping and blinking benignly. It didn't look any more dangerous than a digital clock, but it could mean Kate was facing death or could possibly be already dead.

Matt pressed the accelerator to the floor and the Jeep's big V-8 roared in response. He hoped he had enough time. . . .

FIFTEEN

DOMENIC PETRALLI

*T*he window to Kate's room overlooked the oily, black water of the harbor. A moonless sky held Domenic and his rubber boat in a close, dark embrace. As a silent, bass boat, electric motor pushed him over the low chop, he watched the long, four-story facade of the hotel grow larger and larger. When he reached just the right distance, he killed the engine with the flip of a toggle, and picked up a small device that looked like a cheesy science fiction film handgun. Wearing a pair of wireless blue-tube headphones, Domenic sat in the gently bobbing boat and keyed on the handheld surveillance equipment.

A small pencil beam of neon green light needled through the darkness to dance and play against the target window—Kate Harrison's room—essentially turning it into a large, vibrating tympanum which radiated the sounds within. Instantly the audio characteristics of the headphones kicked in and the sensation of standing in an enclosed, acoustically-tailored space enveloped him. The sound of Kate's voice was at once reassuring and unnerving: *. . . not sure what you're talking about. What exactly have I seen?*

Although she sounded as if she were in control, Domenic could hear the tension stretching her words. Forcing himself to remain still, he listened to the voices and movements of the others in the room just long enough to determine their number and sex. Good odds, but from what they were saying, he knew he had very little time.

He toggled on the electric motor, and eased as close as possible to the side of the building. Then he set aside the laser audio snoop, and reached for a small weapon that looked a hi-tech mating of a crossbow and harpoon, but no larger than a handgun. Shouldering it, he aimed at a point above the hotel's roofline, and squeezed off a single gas-charged round. With a soft *whoooooosh!*, an object hurtled toward its target. Although he couldn't see it, Domenic knew the egglike casing had fractured open to allow a combination grapnel and winch apparatus to unfold itself in midair. So quickly did the device operate it was instantaneously ready the moment it cleared the Marriott's roof. There was a soft, secure, metallic grunt as the grapnel attached itself to the top of the building; the thin cable running from its winch down to Domenic in the boat formed a line which bisected Kate's window.

As Domenic attached the cable to a breakaway piton on his utility belt, he flashed back over the events of the last few hours in an instant. . . .

After arriving at Logan International, with six hours of uninterruptable, safe sleep behind him, Domenic had felt reenergized, prepared to do whatever was necessary to find Kate and the private detective. He was taken from the cargo jet to a SkyFreight Express hangar, where he entered the offices located in a far corner of the massive building.

If anyone was paying attention, they might have noticed an extensive array of satellite dishes and microwave relays on towers so plentiful the roofline resembled the spiculed back of a deep-sea predator. Not so obvious, but still detectable under close inspection would be the placements of sonic oscillators on all the windows which enclosed the office. These devices served as extremely effective jamming devices against anyone trying to listen in on office conversation with laser-targeted audio-imaging equipment. Beyond this layer of security, invisible to the casual observer, would be the bulletproof glass, plus the lead and concrete shielding under the corrugated steel shell of the hangar.

Domenic smiled as he passed through the minimaze of cubicles where the business of SkyFreight was routinely handled. All these cyberwar precautions to ensure overnight delivery of packages?—a confused observer might ask. . . . Hardly, he answered himself as he touched the tip of his index finger across a camouflaged ID scanner embedded in a steel door which ostensibly opened upon a storage closet. Once sealing himself within the small room, Domenic moved to the back wall where he repeated the fingerprint-recognition scan on a lock which caused the entire wall to slide into an invisible recess. From there, he mounted a circular steel staircase which descended to a wide concourse below ground.

He was greeted by the director of the KOM's Boston Station—a thin, almost frail-looking man with a round-shouldered posture. His closely trimmed beard, high forehead, and horn-rimmed glasses gave him a scholarly, threadbare aspect which bespoke someone of mild manner and little physical presence. His name was Costanelli, and as a younger man had been one of the most fearsome Cold War operatives in the Western hemisphere.

"We have been briefed by Corsica," said Costanelli. "There's a console ready for you. This way."

"Any success?" asked Domenic, as they walked down the concourse, then entered a small room filled with monitors and rack-mounted electronics. The room illumination was suitably low, shadowy, imparting a sinister aspect to the fixtures.

Costanelli smiled. "What do you think? We can see everywhere, hear just about anything, as long as we know what we want to look at. Sit down. Have a look for yourself."

Seating himself in a comfortable chair next to the station director, Domenic focused on the images locked in freeze-frame on the large screens in front of him. All of the visual data had been culled from satellites so sophisticated they could tell you what brand of cigarettes a subject might be smoking. One of the monitors revealed infrared images, enhancing the heat signatures of the target, while the others depicted various magnifications in the visual spectrum. He looked at one which contained the greened night-vision image of a lakeside residence and tiny fireflies of momentary brilliance—gunfire.

"That's what happened after we had tracked her from Manchester," said Costanelli. "This is when things got very dicey."

Domenic studied the images of the attack and subsequent escape, fast-forwarding through various parts, then pausing to study other segments in careful detail. "That guy with her . . . he knows what he's doing," said Domenic. "He handled that firefight pretty well."

"Yes, he did."

"What do we know about him?" said Domenic.

"Matthew Etchison. He's a one man band—private investigation, protection, soldier-of-fortune. Caters to the wealthiest clients he can find along the mid-Atlantic. Does lots of semicovert stuff for Washington elite."

"Senators . . . and the rest of the Beltway crowd?"

Costanelli nodded. "You can't blame him. Those are the people who need his kind of services. And they have the means to pay for it."

"That can get pretty slimy. What kind of a guy is he?"

"Morally, I'd say he is to be respected. His Navy Seal training compliments his own character. He seems to be a good man. Your sister-in-law is fortunate to have this guy in her corner."

"Still, I need to catch up with her. Our adversaries continue to target her. If we can intersect one of their moves, I can find out who they really are."

"Corsica has strong suspicions about who we are dealing with. They desperately need your confirmation. That appears to be your best strategy," said the station chieftain, as he pointed to a console control. "Now, jump forward to their arrival in Boston . . . here."

Domenic moused and clicked through various catalogs of images, following Costanelli's urging. Another screen blinked and a series of map coordinates, street diagrams, and other supporting visual data appeared. "The Longwharf Marriott," said Domenic, punching up new keys. Instantly more data flashed across the monitors, giving him access to every possible kind of information about the harborside hotel in downtown Boston. Floor plans, security codes, accounting databanks, guest registrations, and even a detailed list of who was watching what pay-per-view films. Every detail about the Longwharf Marriott gave itself up to the watchers from the Knights of Malta.

"That's her room, right there," said Costanelli, using a laser pointer to touch the screen at a specific place.

"What about Etchison?"

"He apparently helped her get settled in and left last night."

"Not a good idea. . . ."

"Agreed. But we have tracked his activities—he's been busy. You can grab a printout if you want it. And by the way, he did some low-level snooping of his own."

Domenic smiled. "Really?"

"And if he's as good as he might be, he's probably getting some focus on your handling the funerals."

"I trust that all went well?"

"Yes," said Costanelli.

"Good, thank you for the help." Domenic paused, exhaled. "As far as our PI, he won't be able to go deep enough."

"No doubt, but if he's good, it's going to show up on his radar. It's going to make him think."

"Well, if he was really thinking, he wouldn't have left Kate by herself."

Costanelli shrugged. "He doesn't realize how good his enemies really are. He obviously believes he has made them untraceable, unreachable."

"As would most people . . . so," said Domenic. "We may have to save him from himself."

Costanelli pushed back his chair, stood up. I will leave you to sift through the data. Time is of the essence."

And it was. He didn't like the situation which had demanded Kate be left alone in the hotel—a bad miscalculation on Etchison's part. She was totally vulnerable, and presented a soft target. He knew he desperately needed to get up to speed on all new developments, but getting Kate out of immediate danger was primary. Everything would have to wait.

After getting the necessary gear from the station's QM, Domenic went out beyond the edge of the runways and launched his stealthy assault boat into the indifferent waters of Boston Harbor. Overhead, the approach lights of incoming jetliners peppered the sky and the decellerating cries their engines made sent vibrations through the water as well as the land.

He was perhaps ten minutes distant from the waterside hotel, and that distance seemed suddenly remote, unreachable. Notching the speed control into its highest position, Domenic hoped he wasn't too late. . . .

. . . as he still hoped now, when he released the lever which activated the superspring-loaded winch.

With a neck-jerking authority, the cable began to be

reeled in, yanking Domenic upward as though he were shot from a circus cannon. The winch's tiny but awesomely powerful spring would provide enough energy to retrieve him for one assault and one only. By grabbing the tensile line with his free hand covered by specially designed steel mesh gloves, Domenic had a rudimentary control over his ascent and his general target. . . .

. . . which was the plate glass window that was now filling his field of vision as it grew wider and higher, and he homed in on it with great speed. Arcing his head back, he jammed his boots forward. Like an armor-piercing shell, Domenic penetrated the glass in an instant of radiating, razorlike fragments. His aim had been a little off; his left boot grazed the back of Kate's head. His crash to the floor was enough to freeze-frame the three people in the room for an instant. He released the cable from its piton and raised his silenced Glock 9 mm to the woman's forehead.

Wheeling to his left, he squeezed off two quick shots into the face of the muscular woman. Her head was yanked away as if on puppet strings.

At the same time, the man had reacted automatically as well. Throwing himself into a rolling defensive curl across the bed, he disappeared into the space between it and its twin. In the midst of these moves he'd managed to launch his assault knife.

In the instant he dodged the weapon, Domenic knew the man would be using that precious second to reach for his own handgun. Kate slumped unconscious in the chair, a terribly vulnerable target. Domenic had no option; he heaved her sideways and down. As he did this, the man raised his weapon, sighting down the barrel.

And time stopped.

The world changed, becoming a dark tunnel, Domenic at one end, his adversary the other. His vision focused down to a single, all-important image. Everything had happened in the space of a few seconds, but Domenic's ability to isolate and react had the effect of distending time, giving him the powerful illusion of having *more* of it.

He raised his own weapon just as an explosion beyond the man literally blew the hotel door off its hinges. A roiling cloud of cordite and vaporized paint obscured the entrance to the room for an instant as both Domenic and his enemy turned to see the source of the attack. A man was standing in the threshold with weapons in both hands, one of them a now-smoking large-caliber assault rifle which had devastated the steel door with a concussive shell. His other hand held a small Israeli Uzi, which he'd already triggered.

Like a swarm of bees, the Uzi's slugs ripped into the space between the beds. The man crouched there began to rupture into fragments from the close-range burst. But Domenic did not have time to watch. He'd already launched himself back through the open window into the black water below. As he cleared the sill, he felt a stream of bullets slice off the heel of his boot like a surgeon's scalpel.

Hurtling downward, he cradled the briefest of wishes that the basin beyond the rock-strewn channel would not be too shallow. If it was, he'd never know it. . . .

PART
THREE

SIXTEEN

Paris

STREICHER

*S*omething odd was happening to him. Something as insanely pleasant as it was terrifying.

He was falling in love with a woman.

The thought had forced its way to the surface of his thoughts like a drowned corpse that refuses to sink. He didn't particularly like the simile's imagery, but it was damned appropriate. Streicher waited on an eighteenth century settee in the lobby of the Gounod Hotel several blocks off the Ile de France. He paged idly through the latest issue of *Paris Match*, but paid no attention to the words or photographs because he had only recently come to grips with the notion that he could be infected by something so mundane as romance.

Having reached his forties without surrendering his heart, he had long imagined he'd become immune to that strange and debilitating condition he'd seen overtake so many of his colleagues. But there was something different about Shahrnaz, or as she liked to be called, Nazy. She was very protective and sensitive about her name, and let him know right away she did not find his references to Hitler's National Socialist Party very funny. She had been hearing "Nazi jokes" all her life and was frankly sick of them. Her shortened name was a Persian affection much like the naming conventions in Russian, and she refused to be anything but proud of her name.

Normally, Streicher would have dismissed any such protests from a woman, because he simply didn't care enough. But this one, he knew, was not (as he often joked to his colleagues) "one of his females" . . . and for some reason, he'd found himself willing to respect her wishes regarding her name. Maybe this should be a signal to him? Was it a warning that he was somehow growing soft both in his abilities as well as his head? Is this the way an operative fades from the world stage? If not from a bullet, than a dizzying, self-deluding notion of *love*?

The thought actually unnerved him and he was deep in the act of analyzing it when he heard her call his name.

"Kurt?"

Normally, he *hated* that name, and never used it, never allowed anyone else to use it. To everyone, including himself, he was simply *Streicher*. But here she was getting away with it—because she'd told him how much she loved the sound of his first name, how it bespoke strength and wisdom and experience. Bullshit? Probably. But he was buying it, and on one hand he hated himself for it; on the other, he found it ironically amusing.

Standing up, he took her hand and kissed it. He enjoyed very much the employment of these archaic courtship customs. Partly because he'd never performed them till now, and also because Nazy seemed to delight so much in them. She would always smile broadly and give him a flirtatious flutter of her huge almondlike eyes. "Good evening, my dear Nazy," he said. "Hungry?"

"Why, yes, I could definitely enjoy something light."

He snorted in mock drama. "You always say that, and

you eat like you are going to the electric chair!"

She laughed and took his arm as he escorted her into the rococo dining room of the stately old hotel. She wore an elegant, but simply stated lavender dress which did very little to conceal her décolletage or well-exercised legs. She moved with an athletic grace and self-confidence he rarely saw in women, even though she expected (and received) an old-world chivalry from him and every man she encountered.

As they sat over the early courses with flutes of Veuve Clichot, he realized he was of two minds regarding the flow and direction of the evening. When he was with Nazy off-site, he avoided shoptalk if at all possible because he found he was enjoying the whole process of getting to know a woman who proved ever more fascinating at every encounter. But tonight, there were things he needed to discuss concerning the classified project.

"How are you doing with the encryptions?" he said after a slight lull in the conversation.

She rolled her eyes in mock frustration and paused to think of how she would phrase her answer. He hoped she wouldn't choose to comment on his breaching the subject of her work, and was pleased when she did not.

"Well, to say we have made no progress toward a final outcome doesn't really describe what we have been able to determine."

"Really? You mean 'no progress' can sometimes, somehow mean 'progress'?"

"You are playing word games, my dear Kurt. No, listen to me for a moment."

He nodded, gestured for her to continue.

"I think we are using the wrong terminology when we say *encryption* because I think we are dealing more with a new or unknown *language* rather than a code which needs to broken. While we have not come any closer to understanding the messages, we *have* been able to eliminate many avenues of pursuit that would eventually terminate in dead ends."

He considered her words as he continued to work on his *boeuf bourbignon*. "What kind of language? I thought you said it was Latin?"

"I said I had to *assume* it was Latin . . . in the beginning, at least."

"Do you have any clues?"

"Only educated guesses. Proto-Aramaic, maybe. Or perhaps a lost Essene dialect? We are still trying to pin it down. And of course there is the possibility that if it is a lost language, it may *still* be written in some kind of code."

"The old riddle within an enigma," said Streicher. "How wonderful!"

Nazy shrugged. "If you say so."

"I say nothing with any finality on this project. It is making me a bit crazy, if I can be candid. And my superiors are getting very impatient."

She looked at him as a school teacher might regard a recalcitrant charge. "Now, you very well know, Kurt, I am doing the best I can. Especially since the Guild compartmentalizes everything so much."

He could only nod in agreement at what she was saying. It was no secret. Guild policy had always kept each of its many components in almost total darkness regarding the doings and in many cases the very existence of any other operations. The fewer individuals who had total knowledge, the less chance of leaks and compromises.

"Nazy, I am beginning to understand how your mind works . . . is that your way of asking me to tell you more about the piece of glass?"

She took a sip of her champagne, smiled, and tilted her head in a way that could only be called coquettish. On some women, it would have appeared ludicrous, but on Shahrnaz, it was as intended: charming. "Oh, I suppose you could enlighten me a bit, but I think I already understand what we are dealing with here."

"Really?" Streicher returned her smile. "Care to share your speculations?"

"Few people know about the bombing of the Fatima chapel," she said very matter of factly.

Streicher did not try to hide his surprise. "But you obviously do. . . ."

Nazy shrugged as if this were nothing to be surprised about. "My sister married an historian, Siamak Barahmi, who teaches at Cambridge. He has written several books on the fascist movement in the twentieth century. At first I thought I should read them out of respect and courtesy, as well as a measure of curiosity."

"You wanted to see if your sister had married a brilliant fellow."

She winked. "Or a dull one."

"Of course, and you, being brilliant, could prove adequate judge of the question."

Nazy smiled. "Yes, I believed I was up to the task. And as it turned out, my brother-in-law is quite good. History in the tradition of Barbara Tuchman, if you know what I mean. . . ."

Streicher noticed her pause just long enough to let her semiesoteric reference dangle in front of him. She wanted to give him a chance to stand up and be counted among the erudite, and he rose to the bait with an air of studied indifference. "Oh yes, but to be truthful, I always believed *The Proud Tower* to be superior to *The Guns of August*."

His comment seemed to delight her and she gave him another approving, impish smile. "As have I! What a wonderful coincidence!"

"Yes," he said. "But you digress. . . ."

"Silly man," said Nazy. "You should know—digression is one of the most important ways we remain interesting!"

"Go on."

"Well, Siamak was very thorough. His research uncovered items not mentioned in many other texts on the subject. In the twenties, the fascist government in Spain and Portugal viewed the Catholic Church as its prime obstacle to gaining the favor of the common people."

Streicher smiled. "Yes, the more things change, the more they remain the same."

"Yes," said Nazy. "But you are speaking in a broader sense, yes? You mean to include all religions, don't you?"

Streicher shrugged. "Yes, I suppose I do."

She wagged her finger at him in mock disapproval. "You know, Kurt, if you had more of an appreciation of the spiritual, you would never feel that way again."

"I have survived these many years without it," he said. "I don't need it now."

She paused, gathered her thoughts, and continued. "One of the things that very much irritated the Portuguese officials at that time were the immensely popular pilgrimages to Fatima, to the spot where the Virgin Mary had appeared to the three children."

Streicher nodded. So far, she was right on track, and he would not be surprised to hear her continue with unerring accuracy. "I am familiar with the story," he said with a grin.

"Someone in the local government, perhaps a corrupted mayor or constable, incited some fervent party followers to sabotage the shrine at Fatima. It was a very small chapel built from donations of hundreds of thousands of faithful pilgrims. Right on the spot, in front of a tree, where the Virgin was to have originally appeared. They called it *La Capelinha*, the Little Chapel. It became famous in it own right because of the exquisite craftsmanship that went into its construction, most notably a spectacular stained-glass portrait of Mary. Legend says it was created by an anonymous artisan, who arrived in Fatima on the very evening the main window of the chapel had been laid, and plans were being made to hire a glazier. The artisan supposedly refused to be paid for his work, and completed the glass window containing the Virgin's likeness in one night. By morning, he was gone."

"That's correct. But few people know that much of the story."

"Yes," said Nazy. "There aren't many who have even heard of the chapel itself, much less know what happened to it, or what took place later."

"But you do."

"Only thanks to my brother-in-law. I told you he was good," said Nazy. "Anyway, the fascists were successful. One night . . . I can't remember when, but it was in the Twenties . . . they blew up the chapel with dynamite, totally obliterating it. Nothing left but splinters and dust. Except for one piece of stained glass . . . which contained part of Mary's face—her eyes."

"That's right," said Streicher, who nodded in agreement, and also to show how impressed he was with her knowledge. Although a part of him wondered if this seamless tale of a brother-in-law who just happened to be a brilliant historian was nothing but an artful construction. It was far more plausible to imagine Nazy doing her own research on the object she'd been given to examine. The family connection established her prior knowledge of the artifact, and kept Streicher from ever thinking she was a snoop, or worse, a spy.

"The local priest found the surviving fragment and gave it to his archbishop who proclaimed it's survival a miracle. The piece of glass made its way to Rome where it was examined and became known as 'The Eyes of the Virgin.' Nobody claimed to know where it has been for the last eighty years, and rumors of its supernatural power had been just that—rumors."

"Until . . . ?" Streicher said.

"Until . . . nothing," said Nazy. "That is all I know."

"But you do not believe you are dealing with rumor or superstition, do you?"

Nazy looked at him, smiled, and shook her head like

a disapproving mother, one of her signal gestures. "No more than you do, am I correct?"

"Turning the tables on me, are you?"

"I just believe in being honest with each other. It is obvious what is going on here. The Guild believes it has come upon something that *could* be a very important object, if—"

"Yes," said Streicher. "Several very big *ifs* could follow at this point."

Nazy appeared unfazed and did not hesitate to continue. "—if what the Vatican believes is actually true. . . . That Mary has used the artifact to continue to speak to humanity, as she once did through the children."

"All right," said Streicher. "Anything else?"

Nazy shrugged. "Well . . . as I understand it, there has been much conjecture about the actual content of the words which intermittently appear. They could be guidelines for living, clarifications of dogma, warnings, or even prophecies."

"I am impressed," said Streicher.

Nazy sipped her champagne. "None of the above have been verified, but several of the possibilities would be of obvious value to the Guild."

He looked at her without speaking for a moment. She was perfectly comfortable with the sudden lull in the conversation. Whenever he was with her, he found he was unconsciously wondering how much he should ultimately allow her to know about him. And on the other hand, he pondered how much she had been able to ferret out on her own regarding his background and his place and duties within the Guild. He had realized early on to never underestimate her abilities.

"Tell me something, my Nazy," he said softly. "Have you ever thought about how we . . . acquired the artifact?"

She looked as if she were about to respond with a casual answer, mantled in nonchalance and schoolgirl charm, but something stopped her as if she seemed to suddenly understand the subtler gradations of his question. "Well, that's an interesting query," she said. "I am not sure I have given it a *lot* of thought, certainly not as much as it may deserve. But, I am quite certain the Vatican did not *hire* us to conduct our schedule of examinations."

Streicher gave her the suggestion of a smile, and sipped from his glass.

She continued: "I . . . I know enough about my employers to understand several important things: one, the Guild is more than a large, multinational company, and two, it is probably better not to ask many questions about what goes on at levels above and below one's own."

"Now, that is a very good answer," he said. "One that makes me think you probably know much more than you divulged."

Nazy shrugged. "Given the perceived potential value of the artifact, I must assume it was acquired at any cost—even human life. I know what the state of the globe demands of those of us who wish to do more than merely *survive* in it, for those who would bend it to their will. It isn't something over which I have any control, and therefore I try to avoid thinking about it."

"In other words, you don't want to know."

"Something like that."

Streicher finished his flute and poured another from the iced bottle. "You know, my dear, it would be very easy for me to verify your story."

"My 'story'?"

"About how you know so much about the Eyes of the Virgin."

She chuckled as if truly amused. "I could save you lots of trouble. I have copies of all of my brother-in-law's books."

"You do?"

"Yes, of course."

"Here in Paris? At your . . . residence?"

She smiled and her large eyes almost sparkled. She

was *so* not afraid of him he found it as unsettling as he did exciting. "Yes, at my home here, outside of the city. Would you like to see them?"

Streicher liked her aggressiveness. They had been spending much time together, and it was time to advance to a more intimate level. "Yes," he said. "I would like to see them—tonight."

"Well, that can be arranged," said Nazy. "I am almost glad you have not completely believed me."

"Very well," said Streicher. "Let us skip dessert and be getting along."

"Yes," she said. "I think we can find a suitable replacement."

What they found was suitable indeed.

As Streicher was driven back to his hotel that evening, he allowed himself to enjoy the simple afterglow of their lovemaking. And that in itself was unusual for Streicher. He almost laughed out loud at his choice of words—*unusual.* No, it was more like *never.*

He could not remember the last time he had ever given a second thought to one of his sessions with a woman. Throughout his life, he'd enjoyed hundreds of women, and they'd been essentially interchangeable. They were like the thousands of quick meals he'd eaten while traveling all over the world for twenty years—something done of a basic need, but nothing exercised with any true aesthetic enjoyment.

Oh certainly, there had been some pleasure in it, but of such momentary nature, none of them had ever inspired him to think fondly of their union afterwards. For Streicher, it would have been no less absurd than him working up pleasant gustatory memories for his last Big Mac.

Sex had been one of those constant, but ultimately unfulfilling aspects of his nature. Like scratching an insistent case of allergic reaction to poison ivy, Streicher achieved no lasting or satisfying sense of relief. Driving through the streets of Paris reminded him of something pertinent. He'd heard that the French called the orgasm *le petite mort*—the little death, and had never really understood what the hell they meant by it. Knowing their penchant for satire and intellectual gimcrackery, Streicher had always imagined the reference had something to do with spending a bit of oneself with each ejaculation. . . . Some such pseudo-philosophical attempt at the truly profound.

For Streicher, he had always assumed a far simpler meaning—something that appealed to his Teutonic nature. Each orgasm was just another ending: of a mystery to be solved, a conquest to be achieved, another woman to be hammered and tossed aside. It was inevitable he should feel this way after the warning he'd received from his father so many years ago.

His father . . . one of those people he tried not to think about. Odd that the twisted old man should enter his thoughts at a time when he was feeling something akin to contentment?

Streicher had been ten or maybe eleven at the time, living in East Germany in a town called Friesen. His father had been employed as a truck driver for a freight hauler and was gone for long stretches of time. He was in his fifties by then and the work must have been getting difficult, and little Kurt's memories of father were largely those of a white-haired, bitter, and usually drunken and angry old man. He was rarely kind to his only child, a son born late in life to a second wife. But there was one afternoon when he really outdid himself, when he took it upon himself to teach his son one of those life lessons.

After coming home from school, little Kurt had been in the backyard playing with lead soldiers in a sandbox, when his father suddenly appeared. The old man was standing over him, but he was weaving slightly, a movement the young son had come to learn meant a recent stop at a beer hall. A rough hand had grabbed Kurt by his collar, yanking him to his feet.

"Come with me," said the father. "It's time I taught you something you're going to need to know."

And with that, little Kurt had been marionetted across the backyard to a rotting, slant-walled toolshed in the far corner of the property. The old man pulled open the doors and pushed his son into the cool shadows within. "It's time you knew about women," said his father in a loud, slurry voice.

And before Kurt could even ask him what he meant, his father lashed out his open-palmed hand and *slapped* him across the cheek with stunning force and speed. The blow sent tracers of shock and pain up his face and through his skull. A burning, throbbing explosion of agony enveloped the boy like a cloud and he staggered, his knees almost buckling.

"*That* is what women will do to you!" his father screamed, spittle flying from his mouth, his curled-back lips.

Young Kurt remained shell-shocked, and said nothing.

"They will tease you and even if some of them let you wallow like a stinking pig between their legs, they will still end up slapping your face! Their job is to humiliate us men," he said in a barely controlled rage. "To make us feel like the pigs we are!"

"Poppa . . ." he had tried to say something, but had no idea what words would be the right ones. All he knew is that he wanted his father to stop ranting, to leave him alone.

Then his father had turned and looked around the shed as if in a daze, until he saw a pair of hedge shears hanging on a bent nail. Grabbing them, his father held them in both hands, scissoring the rusty, but still menacing blades in front of his son's face.

"But that is not the worst of it, my little Kurtling," he'd said. "Oh, if the bitches were only satisfied with *that*! No-no-no! They never stop until they finish us off."

Kurt had been scared now. His father's eyes were white and far too round, his mouth twisted into an ugly shape. Suddenly he reached out and grabbed his son's elastic-waisted trousers and yanked them down.

"*That* is what they want," said his father in abruptly soft, low tones that were somehow more scary than all his yelling. He was pointing between the boy's legs as he snapped the shears together and continued: "They *hate* that little worm and that silly, ugly sack of ours . . . and never rest until they remove them completely. Come here, boy! Let me save them the trouble and do you a big favor!"

His father reached for him, but Kurt had seen enough, heard enough, and pulled up his pants and darted past the alcoholic lunge of the old man. He ran for what seemed like hours through the town, not stopping until he reached the forest. He stayed there until sundown, when his mother would be in the kitchen making their dinner, when it would be safe to go back.

And when he finally made his return to the house, his father had collapsed and was asleep on the davenport. The old man never mentioned the incident in the toolshed again. Young Kurt also believed it wise to never remind him, and the whole scene lay dormant and festering in his unconscious for the next thirty-five years.

Whenever Streicher allowed himself even a mental reference to the event, he did it with a sardonic nod of explanation regarding his own admittedly guarded personality. He knew he was classic casebook and textbook material, and the Freudians and the Jungians and all the other German doctors would dance around their fires as they sang the praises of his perfect pathology.

But he had learned over the years that there had been a hard kernel of truth at the core of his father's message. He had used it to armor himself against ever being hurt, and it had worked well for him. It was not until his father's death from emphysema that Streicher discovered some clues to what may have warped the old man's view of the world. The secrets coughed up by a dry-rotted steamer trunk in the basement were self-explanatory—armbands and caps and a clutch of military medals. His father had been an angry young man in his twenties during World War II, and had spent his time lugging a howitzer for an artillery company all across the Russian front. Ever since that moment of revelation, Streicher had felt something special for the strange man who had sired him. Something, if not actually warm, then at least cleansed by the tepid waters of understanding.

"We are here, sir," said his driver, bringing the sedan to a stop at the hotel.

"Thank you," said Streicher as he emerged from the auto and ascended the steps to the lobby. He had been wanting to think about his evening with Shahrnaz, had even figured that he would not be able to avoid it, and yet his mind had been taking him on a strange, nostalgic turn, had it not? And whenever he considered the woman who had touched him and threatened to change him as no woman ever had, he wondered if he could ever peel back enough layers of secrets and crimes. . . . If he could ever let her know the real person, the real Kurt Loren Streicher.

Nazy.

How different she was from anyone he'd ever known.

He smiled as he approached the elevators, wondering for the first time, perhaps, in his adult life, what another person truly thought of him.

SEVENTEEN

MATT ETCHISON

*A*fter the smoke cleared and he saw Kate slumped at a weird angle in the chair, Matt had a brief stab of loss and anger that he'd been too late. The room looked like it had taken a direct hit from a mortar shell, and his own firepower had been mostly responsible.

"Kate!" He repeated her name as he heard a rising cacophony of sound at his back—police sirens, fire alarms, the cries and shouts of other hotel guests. He'd notified his buddies at Boston Central that he would be putting his gun licenses to use, but he was fairly sure they weren't gonna be happy with his level of involvement in the crime-busting business.

Wading into the destruction he'd wrought, Matt reached Kate's chair. She sported a big abrasion across the side of her face, and she remained motionless as he touched her gently and eased her back to an upright position.

"Kate . . . can you hear me? You okay?"

Her eyelids fluttered and he realized he suddenly released a breath he'd been holding.

"Oh God . . ." she said. "I can't believe this. . . . I can't go through anything else. . . . I just want to die. . . . Please, God. . . ."

"Kate, come on . . . listen to me!" He thought about giving her a light tap on the cheek and thought better of it.

She looked up at him and the lights of recognition slowly came on behind her green-gold eyes. "Matt . . . oh God, what took you so long? It was . . . really bad . . ."

"Okay, relax, we can talk about it later. Plenty of time for that. Right now, we have to get you out of here."

He removed her from the prison of the chair, half-carrying her through the ruins of the room. As he guided her over the devastated door, Kate paused to look back at the broken-out window, framing the void of the night. She looked like she was going to cry or collapse, or both. But she drew in a deep breath and suddenly looked at him sharply. "Did you get all of the bastards?"

"Just one. The other guy—"

Kate paused as they passed into the hallway where people were still running from their rooms. Suddenly a couple of uniforms and several SWAT guys burst simultaneously from the fire doors. They had their weapons drawn and ready to fire. Matt knew the drill and threw down what he was holding, put his hands out where they could see them.

"Keep it right there!" yelled one of the cops, moving in carefully. There was a lot of screaming and noise in the background, and Matt knew he was probably in some trouble even though *he'd* been the one to call them.

"Take it easy," he said. "We're the good guys."

"We'll make the decision on that," said the closest uniform, still keeping his service revolver trained on a point in the center of Matt's chest. "Just don't move."

Matt complied. Kate looked at the cop with an angry expression. "Do I look like I'm going to shoot anybody?"

"Well, ma'am, I—"

"Can't you see we've been attacked!" she screamed. "Goddamn it, I've had it with all of you! Are you here to help us, or shoot us!? Because if you're going to shoot us, just get it over with! Because I've *had* it!"

Her sudden fusillade stopped everybody cold for an instant, and Matt was hoping they wouldn't follow her suggestion.

The closest uniform finally regained his composure after a second or two and told them he had no choice but to read them their rights—which he did.

And then they were taken down to the wagon for a ride to Central.

It was short ride and Kate was either too angry or too shaken to talk to him. Matt figured they would have plenty of time once they got things sorted out at headquarters. But before he and Kate had any chance to really talk, they had some serious explaining to do to Detective Tom Ryan and an FBI liaison by the name Marty Higgins.

They separated him from Kate as soon they reached the lower entrance to headquarters, and hustled Matt off to an interrogation room. He barely had time to seat himself behind the table when the door burst open to reveal a short, stocky guy in his early fifties. It was Tom Ryan, who looked like a miniature middle linebacker, and who'd known Matt for more than twenty years. Usually a nice, easygoing guy, Ryan didn't look too happy at that moment.

"What the fuck is wrong with you!" he cried as he slammed the door behind him. "You didn't tell me you planned to shoot the living-and-dead-Christ out of the place!"

Matt grinned like a kid. "Hey, if I'd known what was going to happen, I would have told you then. All I knew was that my client was in big trouble."

"From what I've been able to piece together, she's been in a world of shit for a while now," said Ryan. "Jesus Christ, Matt! We've got fuckin' cameras and TV assholes crawling all over that hotel!"

"Do you want me to talk to them?"

Ryan rolled his eyes, then began to pace the room like a big cat in a circus wagon. "Oh yeah, that's *exactly* what I need! Look, why don't you tell me what I can't find out in the files, huh?"

Matt took a few minutes to get him up to speed on all the events with Kate leading up to the hotel room scene. "When I reached the door, I knew I couldn't wait for you guys to help. She could've been dead or dying and I had to do what I did."

"Who are these people?" Ryan stopped. He leaned on the table, apparently finished with his ranting, and now ready to listen to details.

"I have no idea, but they're real pros. Killers. Operatives. Whatever you want to call them."

Ryan looked at him and shook his head. "And you have no idea who they represent?"

"None. It's like I told you—they obviously believe Kate Harrison has something they want."

"Yeah, I know, but the lady has no idea what it could be. That's what she's telling us; and I believe her."

"You got that right." Matt thought about the information Kate said she'd withheld from the police, and decided there was no percentage in mentioning a series of utterly cryptic numbers. Until she had some handle on what those numbers might mean, it probably was not a good idea to be throwing them around.

Ryan resumed his pacing, and the door to the sweat room opened to admit a tall, lean guy who had a very prominent chin and nose—so much so you couldn't notice anything else about him except the bland suit that was so ubiquitous it was almost a uniform worn by all functionary-level government employees. He walked to the table and sat down at the end opposite from Matt.

"Mr., Etchison, how do you do? I'm Special Agent Higgins, from the Bureau."

"I figured," said Matt. "They told me you'd be here. Do I have to repeat everything, or were you standing behind the mirror since we got started?"

Marty Higgins enacted a perfunctory grin. "Ah, no, I caught the whole show."

"How long before you get any results on those two bodies?" said Matt.

Higgins shrugged. "Hard to tell. We might get lucky and ID them, or then again, it could be like the damage you left behind in Eastman."

Matt nodded. "Yeah, I figured you guys would be in on that too. And I can assume the bad guys were anonymous?"

"Oh, totally," said Agent Higgins. "Like newborn babies. Like they'd never existed before you aced them."

"So what do you think this means?" said Matt. "Ever run into a scene like this before?"

"Not personally, but I'm aware of this kind of operation."

Ryan stopped pacing, looked from Higgins to Matt. "Hey, uh, pardon me—but I thought *we* were supposed to be the ones asking the questions."

"Aw, come on, Tom!" said Matt. "You know who I am! You know I'm not some nefarious type."

"That's true," said Marty Higgins. "But I'd say you're in over your head on this one, Mr. Etchison. The kinds of weapons these folks have used are not war surplus, third-world junk. Most of what we've found is top-drawer stuff, the best any government's arsenal can buy. I'm talking hi-tech and high cost."

Matt grinned. "If I'm so 'over my head,' then how come it's *their* bodies and *their* weapons that are lying around waiting for you to clean them up?"

Higgins threw up his hands. "Hey, it's always better to be lucky than good, but whoever is behind the moves against you and your client . . . well, they look very dangerous to us."

"Does this mean we're going to have your men protecting us?" Matt already knew the answer to that one, but he wanted to hear them say it.

"Well, let's just say we will be 'interested' in what you two're doing, that we'll be checking in every once in a while to see if you've learned anything."

"Yeah, so while you troll for international thugs, you throw us over the side like a bucket of chum, right?"

Higgins smiled. "Yeah, right."

"I think there's more we need to talk about," said Tom Ryan.

"I'm listening." Matt tried to look bored. He had an idea he knew what Ryan would be serving up as well.

"I can't have you and your client running around Boston causing the kind of mayhem you did at the Long-wharf."

Matt nodded. "Well, what do you have in mind? Would you like to keep us locked up? Or maybe get a restraining order on all the bad guys?"

Tom Ryan looked at the ceiling self-consciously. "Well, I was thinking more along the lines of you folks kind of, well, getting out of Dodge. . . ."

Matt leaned back in his chair, smiled. "Well, it's good that you brought that up, because that's exactly what we're planning to do."

"No, listen, I'm serious," said Ryan. "Boston is a big city, but it's also a small town. I can feel a lot of heat in a hurry, and I'm asking you to help me out here."

"Take our act on the road," said Matt. "If we're going to get killed, at least have the decency to get it done in somebody's else jurisdiction. Sure, Tom, I understand."

"Jesus, does it really sound like that?" Ryan pulled out a pack of Pall Malls, and Matt looked at them with genuine interest. Did anybody really smoke those things anymore?

"It sounds worse," said Higgins. "But it doesn't make

it any less true. And this is no knock on your people, Tom, but metropolitan police aren't trained to handle this kind of personnel. These people consider themselves *above* any law—in terms of their methods, their ultimate objectives. Whatever goes on among the 'little' people while they conduct their operation is of no concern to them. It's like knocking down an anthill while you're lining up your wedge shot out of a sand trap."

Matt had heard all this nonsense before. When he worked with the Navy, he dealt with the kind of "extreme force" units Higgins was doing his best not to describe in too much detail. Matt was fairly certain the Bureau had a few ideas who might be pulling the strings on this one, but there was no way he'd be getting them to give up their sources or even their suspicions. He decided to get the conversation grounded once again in things they could do something about.

"What about the guy who got away?" said Matt, directing the question at the special agent. "What do we have on him?"

Higgins shot a quick glance at Tom Ryan, and Matt grinned. That meant they *did* have something and were trying to decide whether or not to tell him. Matt shook his head. "Oh, you guys are so slick. Did you think I was was getting too old and too slow to keep up?"

"The guy who got away. . . ." said Tom Ryan. "We're pretty sure he wasn't with the other two."

Matt's eyebrows raised. Okay. That *was* interesting.

"You didn't take out the female perp," said Higgins. "She was killed by a different caliber slug, different weapon from yours and the . . . uh, bad guys, as you call them."

"Any idea who the mystery man might be?" said Matt.

"Not yet, but we will," said Higgins.

That meant they hadn't a freaking clue and probably never would. Good, thought Matt, because he had a very good idea the third element in the equation was Domenic Petralli. It made sense—especially when he tied in the business with the funeral arrangements for Petralli's wife and Kate's husband . . . and the phony priests and all the inconsistencies Matt had uncovered. He wasn't sure how Petralli was doing it, but everything pointed to someone with a vested interest in Kate Harrison or the information she *might* have access to. It was possible Petralli was in hiding somewhere, and had hired people to do the fake priest things, and even send in a heavy hitter to the hotel; or maybe the unknown guy had been assigned to keep an eye on Kate from the beginning.

He'd like to know if either of these guys had any clue on the whereabouts or the intentions of Domenic Petralli—a guy who was beginning to sound a hell of a lot more interesting with each new piece of the puzzle that unfolded. The simplest thing would be to just ask Ryan and his pals if they'd heard from Justine's husband, but then, he didn't want to go shining a light into too dark a place. If anybody should be talking to Petralli, Matt wanted it to be him and Kate. Nobody else.

"Well," said Matt. "That's too bad. Sort of complicates things, doesn't it?"

Tom Ryan shook his head. "I don't want to think there're too many more groups interested in killing you and Harrison."

"You?" said Matt, looking at his watch. "Yeah, well I'm not too crazy about that either. And by the way, are we done? As in—can I get my client out of here? Or do we need to call in the lawyers and the camera people?"

Ryan shook his head. "I think we can handle it here without you."

Marty Higgins gave Matt a card with some numbers on it. "Satphone stuff. You can pretty much reach me from anywhere to anywhere."

Matt smiled. "You mean like a 911 call?"

"Well, yeah, if you have to. But I was hoping you would use it to let us know if you come across anything we can use."

"You'll be the first guy I call," said Matt. "I promise."

Marty Higgins wasn't sure if he was sincere or not, but he figured a smile and handshake couldn't hurt.

"All right," said Tom Ryan. "Let's go see how Ms. Harrison's doing."

"Sounds like a plan," said Matt.

About an hour later, they were in Matt's SUV heading towards Matt's office in Arlington. The rear deck carried whatever the police had salvaged from the hotel room that wasn't being sequestered in the evidence room. He'd spent the time getting her up to speed—on the plans of the FBI, the possible motives of the guy who got away, and the business with the unknown priests arranging family funerals.

"It has to be Domenic," said Kate. "I don't think there's any question about that—only because there just couldn't be anybody else who would *care* enough to make it happen."

"I agree," said Matt.

"But it makes me wonder—just *how* is Domenic doing it?"

"Yeah, I was thinking the same thing. Either he knows lots of influential people, or he's not the guy we think he is."

"Probably a little of both," she said. "So, what's next?"

"I knew you were going to ask me that. I figure it's better to be a moving target than a stationary one, so it's probably best if we plan a trip."

"Where?"

"Not sure yet. But I want to be prepared, in case we have to move in a hurry. We're going to need stuff ready to go. You know—light luggage, toiletries, changes of clothes."

"Maybe we should do something about that now, while we're thinking about it," she said.

"Okay, there's a mall off one of these exits coming up. Good enough for what we want."

After a quick run through T.J. Maxx, Eastern Mountain Sports, and CVS Pharmacy, they were back on the road again. Matt couldn't stop working over what they knew and didn't know. "If we had any kind of lead on those sets of numbers you showed me, we might have a better plan. I'm assuming if anything had hit you by now, you would've told me about it."

"You assume correctly. But you need to give me more of a chance to contemplate their meaning. I've had a lot of distractions lately."

"True," said Matt. "But I have one more place we should look into. How far from here to your sister's place?"

"Well, Domenic had a condo downtown in the North End—he used it mostly as an office. And then they had the house in Somerset. Why?"

Matt shrugged. "Just an idea. You know the address to the condo?"

She did, and an hour later, they stood at the back door of a fashionable townhome on Baldwin Street. Years ago, it would have been called a "rowhouse." The back-yard was the size of a bedsheet, but there was a nice privacy fence of pressure-treated wood, stained with a muted natural color with a name like burnt sienna or copsewood brown or something like that. It was high enough to shield their presence and actions from anyone who might be looking, but the late afternoon neighborhood seemed quiet and totally uninterested in them.

"How are we going to get in?" said Kate.

"Break in, of course." Matt flipped open the valise he carried with him that looked like a carrying case for a notebook computer.

"Suppose he has an alarm system?" Kate looked past them to see if there might be anyone watching them.

He held up a small electronic device with an active matrix screen and a small calculator-sized keypad. "This will tell me what's going on in there," he said, and pressed it against the door. The screen flickered and several lines of numbers appeared on the display.

"Well?" said Kate.

"Well, he has an alarm and it's on and now we know how to disarm it."

"You mean turn it off?"

"Yes." Matt pulled out a small set of lock picks and worked them through the back door keyholes. After he'd sprung the tumblers and the door had swung inward, he entered, spotted the master panel, and keyed off the alarm.

"That is amazing," said Kate, who'd followed him in and was looking at the small device which Matt was returning to its niche in the bag.

"Yeah, well you can't exactly buy one at Home Depot. Your government spending your money for better espionage."

"So what're *you* doing with one?"

He smiled. "Trade secret, I'm afraid."

She shook her head, and surveyed the kitchen where they'd entered. "Oh God . . . looks like you aren't the only with one of those things."

The countertops were covered with the contents of the upper cabinets, the floors with that of the lower enclosures. Everything had been methodically tossed; Matt noted that it had the look of a careful and thorough search, not a quick, panicked destruction of anything that didn't look useful.

Not that the place didn't look ransacked; it did. As they walked through the rooms, the were dismayed to find every object not nailed down strewn across the floor. Whoever had done it had taken their time. Petralli's workspace, a large room with laminated counterlike desktops, standard computer gear, files and shelving, had been the target of the greatest scrutiny. There were papers everywhere. Charts, blueprints, spreadsheets, bound reports, uncountable file folders. It looked like a snow-drift after a nor'easter.

"Okay," he said. "I think we should get to work ourselves."

"What do you mean?"

"Well, it looks like our friends have already done a lot of the grunt work for us. All we need to do is check through this stuff and see if anything adds up."

"Oh, is that all?" said Kate, pushing a strand of hair from her face. He could detect a strain of defeatism in her tone. She was struggling now. She'd been battered and pushed and intimidated and threatened enough. Even though she'd proven herself to be tough and resilient, Matt knew if Kate didn't see something positive soon, she was going to pull down the shades and close up the shop—for good.

"This is all in a day's work," he said, trying to be cheery.

"Right, and how do we know that they haven't already found what we're looking for? How do we know they haven't taken it with them?"

Matt looked at her, grinned. It was time to stay upbeat. They'd reached a pivotal point and he had to maneuver them past it. "If they'd found it, they would have stopped at some point in their search," he said with fair confidence he was right. "It's obvious they went through every crack in the wall here. They didn't find what they wanted. That's obvious."

Kate contemplated his logic, nodded in acceptance. Good sign, that. "Okay, maybe you're right." She drew in a breath, exhaled. "It's just that . . . this could take so long, and I'm getting tired."

"We can take our time. It doesn't look like they'll be back." Matt took off his jacket, headed for the kitchen. "I'll see if I can make some coffee, whaddya say?"

Kate finally smiled, albeit a very small, perfunctory one. "Sounds good. I wish I could be more like you."

"Nah, you wouldn't like it. I get a lot of cavities and I'm starting to show the first signs of male pattern baldness."

She chuckled. Then: "All right, go make the coffee."

Matt watched her wade into piles of paper on the floor of the living room, where everything had been pulled off the bookshelves, and the pages of so many books had been leafed through and checked. She had gotten into the task at hand, and he suspected they were past the worst of it.

About four hours and many cups of Gevalia later, he *knew* they were.

"Oh my god!"

He was just getting started in the basement when he heard Kate's exclamation. He ascended the steps to the second floor office where Kate was emerging with a folder of papers in her hand. "What's the matter?"

"I think I found something!"

She sat on the first step of the stairs, opened the folder and showed him print-out with cells containing groups of four-digit numbers. There were hundreds of sets of numbers and they looked utterly meaningless. "Do you see it?" she asked with more enthusiasm than she'd generated in many days.

"Uh, no . . . I don't. I see a bunch of numbers. What else am I looking at?"

Kate smiled. "Whatever it is we're supposed to find . . . *this* can tell us where it is."

EIGHTEEN

Paris

STREICHER

"*E*xactly how much incompetence are we expected to put up with?" said Jagen Kerschow. He asked the question in a voice so soft, a tone so dripping with sincere concern, it was more than a bit scary. The nominal leader of the Guild was a lean, lupinely handsome man, despite his age and silvering hair. As usual, his clothes bore the marks of impeccable tailoring and his mannerisms bespoke centuries of European aristocracy, breeding, and elitism.

Streicher sat across the alfresco table from him as an endless stream of angry and animated Parisian motorists negotiated the small Rue de L'Esperance on which their sidewalk brasserie was located. Seated with him was the ever-present Renée Beauvais; many of her uncounted corporate amalgams were headquartered in this city. She made it clear to anyone who paid attention that she throroughly enjoyed flaunting her power and influence, and her ability to buy the attentions of even the most acomplished of men. That she now always accompanied Kerschow could mean only one of two things—she had been assigned to watch him by a competing faction of the Guild, or they had become lovers. She was an attractive woman, Streicher had noted. So the latter was as much a possibility as the former.

"Yes," said Beauvais. "I agree. Some of our colleagues are growing impatient. Even . . . angry."

Streicher sipped on his scotch, containing his anger. These arrogant fucks had no idea what he went through on an operation. "Listen," he said. "Do you think I am happy with the recent events?"

"You said you would take care of Petralli," said Kerschow. "But you have not even made an attempt."

"Petralli hasn't been our problem," said Streicher. "This private investigator has—"

Kerschow laughed. "A local Boston bumpkin has you by the privates!"

"He's a Navy Seal."

Beauvais pursed her lips mockingly. "Oooooh, is that supposed to be scary?"

Streicher's eyes narrowed as he smiled at her. "No offense, Ms. Beauvais, but he could bite out your throat while he was pouring you a glass of Cristal, and you wouldn't even realize it until—"

"That is quite enough," said Jagen Kerschow. "The point to be taken from all this is that we are facing formidable resistance and it is clearly time to send in the first string, would you not agree?"

"Yes, of course," said Streicher. "The decryption is virtually impossible without the correct key. Safavi-Martin says it is like the Voynich Manuscript."

"The *what*?" said Beauvais.

"One of the early manuscripts from the twelfth century. Full of weird illustrations and possible hints to its true meaning. Nobody knows who wrote it or what it says, but it was written in such a way that no known cryptanalyst has come close to cracking it. And it is believed it will never happen without a proper key, a comparison chart to other known languages or codes."

"Yes . . . yes . . . I've heard all that." Annoyance had begun to color her words.

Ever since he'd been called to this meeting, Streicher had been curious how it might play out. His superiors did not actually have any significant cards to play, and both of them knew this. Unless Shahrnaz accomplished a breakthrough or they obtained the key, they were at an impasse. The only real issue of the moment was whether or not the Guild believed they had anyone better equipped to make either of the above outcomes take place.

If they did, Streicher knew that would mean death for himself, Nazy and her staff. The Guild did not allow loose threads. Of course, if they ever intended to eliminate Streicher, they would have their hands full of trouble, and they must know that. He would never go quietly.

And so, his mission of the moment was to listen between the lines of what they were telling him. Almost two decades of experience in reading and reacting to the subtleties of human behavior had made him the unrelenting survivor he'd become. Despite the grim possibilities, Streicher continued to feel confident.

He sipped his scotch, looked Kerschow in the eye, and spoke firmly. "You are demanding that I take control of this, it is clear. So be it."

Renee Beauvais tilted her head coquettishly and levered her lashes slowly. "Do you think you are man enough for this job?"

Streicher refused the bait. "It would be unwise to deprecate the operatives we have lost in this effort. They were all excellent people."

"Time is of the essence here. Our statisticians have projections, charts, which are uncannily accurate," said Kerschow. "They tell us we are on the cusp of something momentous."

Streicher laughed. "If they are so good, what do you need with a piece of glass?"

Kerschow leaned forward, narrowing the focus of his cold, blue eyes, thereby enhancing his wolfish aspect. "Since Monte Cassino, our analysts have determined those Maltese bastards and the Vatican have either been preternaturally lucky . . . or they knew things the rest of the world did not know."

Streicher nodded. "I have seen the reports."

"Very well, then," said Kerschow. "Stop playing word games. You are aware of the serious and critical nature of this mission."

"No one wants it to fail," said Streicher. "We are presently dealing with those factors which inevitably appear in every plan—the x-factors, the ones which no one can foresee."

"Petralli is a ghost. He appears and disappears with impunity. Forget him. The other two are constantly available to you. Monitor them, see if they have any possibility of leading you to what we need."

"You don't need me to perform Level Three surveillance."

"And you don't need to be spending so much time in the labs," said Madame Beauvais. "Do not let affairs of the heart—or any other part of the body—affect the affairs of the mind."

And fuck you, too, thought Streicher as he stared boldly into her own gaze. Did she have any idea of what he was capable? He could make this woman writhe on the carpet in the most exquisite pain imaginable with nothing more threatening than a fountain pen, yet she dared think she could lecture him on his conduct. For a moment, he allowed his imagination to run wild and he unleashed an incongruous smile. It was a smile which Renee Beauvais somehow understood as she fought off a shudder that settled in between her shoulders.

"This is no simple surveillance," said Kerschow, interceding quickly. "This is a top priority. We believe the private eye and Harrison will eventually reveal data that may be useful."

"That is correct," said Beauvais, using the moment to cast off her anxiety and make an attempt to regain her perceived position of authority.

Streicher did not have much use for her, although he respected her immense wealth and range of control over so many aspects of industry and mercantilism throughout the world. Her presence in the Guild was necessary, by dint of her family's long-standing position as a world-class player in the global economic arena, but he knew it was always handled with great tolerance.

"Thank you for the clarification, madame," he said, looking from her to Kerschow. Streicher didn't care if the rumors about his superior and Beauvais might be true; he had to treat her with the same measure of deference tinged with a touch of arrogance he afforded other members of the board. He knew they considered him a necessary evil, and he knew if they ever decided he'd outlived his usefulness, he would be made quickly expendable.

But he had not been so blinded by their praise and their acquiescence as to assume he would be forever safe.

No, he had already put in place a safety net, invisible to all but himself; he had a contingency plan worked out to the hour and the minute. Should he ever receive any signal that his utility to the Guild had reached its eventual end, he would put his tactical machinery into motion. At that point, either he would escape . . . or he would take them all down with him.

"Streicher," said Kerschow, speaking softly. "We have an aircraft waiting for you at Orly. The usual arrangements."

"Very well," he said. He would be receiving his encrypted instructions after becoming airborne, but he already knew his initial destination would be Logan International.

A waiter had materialized to take their preferences for lunch, but Streicher stood up and nodded at Madame

Beauvais in a manner that oozed obsequious courtesy, then an extremely subtle suggestion of coming to attention for Kerschow. "I am afraid I must take my leave, sir. I have several loose ends to tie up before Orly."

"Very well," said Jagen Kerschow, whose expression seemed to indicate he was pleased with Streicher's actions and seeming acceptance of the assignment.

He didn't wait for any response from Renée Beauvais as he turned on his heel and began walking toward the closest intersection to hail a taxi. He would not be going anywhere until he had a chance to speak with Nazy, and the admission of this truth gave a moment of pause.

In all his years of unquestioning service, he had never once given any consideration to what anyone might think about his movements, his safety, or his accountability.

Now, it was suddenly different, and he did not mind a bit.

NINETEEN

Palermo

PETRALLI

Domenic emerged from the SkyFreight hangar and walked across the tarmac with his duffel bag. Despite sleeping through the transatlantic flight, he continued to replay the disaster at the hotel with Kate Harrison. Having to flee the scene before knowing if he had unintentionally killed her had burned in his gut like a piece of hot coal. That she had withstood the combined assaults of the enemy, himself, and her investigator proved to Domenic that his sister-in-law was a very capable survivor.

Later that evening, when he sent his report to Sforza by SkyFreight courier pack, he stressed his belief that she was safe with Matthew Etchison, who had been proving himself to be a formidable opponent for the enemy. Domenic did not wish to make excuses or be forced to defend his motives. He stated his belief as plainly as possible—protect the works of God first.

Just after he'd touched down in Palermo, he received a response by courier from his superiors. Sforza had confirmed his decision to come back to Europe without ensuring the insularity of Kate Harrison. The only drawback was not knowing if she indeed had any information that could compromise the secrecy and success of the entire operation.

The latest intelligence had revealed some substantial clues to the identity of the thieves of the *Capelinha* glass. Routine FAA security cameras at Baltimore-Washington International Airport, which were part of an experimental FBI face-recognition scanning operation, encountered a very famous identity in the world of covert global activity. In a totally random sampling of people passing through customs, the FBI's computers had pattern-matched the face of an individual flying to Paris with that of known international assassin and Level One operative, Kurt Loren Streicher.

Sforza's report went on to connect Streicher to the Guild, which everyone in Corsica already believed had to be the source of the theft. Only an entity as large and far reaching as the Guild could have learned the true secret of the Eyes of the Virgin in the first place.

But that had not been all of it. As Domenic continued to read the document, he found himself agreeing with the KOM's assessments. The Guild had not acted on any of the known information connected with the Eyes, therefore an important dual-track assumption might be made: The enemy had decrypted the code, but had chosen not to act; or, the enemy had no idea how to decrypt the messages, and better yet, no idea where to locate the data key.

Finally, the cleanup crew at the Wieznewski home had located the backed-up entries of the last laboratory work, and were enroute to Corsica. The latest messages could be decrypted with or without the glass. And so Domenic's priorities changed; reversed, actually. He did not need to rescue the Eyes first; he needed to retrieve the data key.

Easier said than done, but at least it presented him with a clearly delineated task. There was nothing worse than stumbling through an assignment when the objective refused to be clarified. They did not call his business *intelligence* for nothing. Knowledge was truly the greatest power, the most confident force he could wield.

After exchanging his SkyFreight coveralls for his own clothes, he left Palermo International through the main terminal. Better to become one with the thousands of tourists on late holiday. Sicily had become a favorite place to be in late summer and early autumn—and the more affluent workers of Germany, France, Switzerland, and of course, the States were showing up here in ever-increasing numbers. But it was growing late in the afternoon and the flow of passengers had slowed to reflect the more leisurely pace of the hours before evening. Although the tourists did not always understand or cooperate with the custom of an afternoon siesta, they did not have much choice when the shutters of almost every business closed them out.

Another Punta awaited him in the employee carpark, and he silently sent off a prayer of thanks for the efficiency of the KOM and all who worked in its service. Domenic drove the little car hard—the way it had been intended—all the way along the *autostrada* back to the city. As he approached the mountains which held the city by the sea like a pair of giant hands, he could see the sunlight spiking off the church spires of Monreale.

Si bella.

The only words for such a vision. A reminder of the power and majesty of his God, he felt himself smiling as he pushed the little Fiat to its limits. Twenty minutes later, he was down by Palermo's waterfront marinas on the harbor boulevard. He headed south on Corso Vittorio

Emanuele, angled left onto via Bottai, a side street so small and shadowed, a tourist might not even notice it. Several blocks of hotels and restaurants were tucked along the street, and all the cars of the locals were hiked up on the cobblestone curbs almost perpendicular to the street. There was a tiny cleft between two larger vehicles near the end of the row, and Domenic expertly maneuvered the Punta into the nonexistent space. No one would care. Driving and parking in Palermo was an endlessly creative endeavor.

Half a block from his car, he entered the Hotel Letizia, a small, narrow establishment covered with ivy and marked only by shuttered windows and flower boxes on the upper three floors. Entering through tall, double doors, he ascended a staircase to the second level where a thin young man with thick, long, dark hair and horn-rimmed glasses sat behind a small registration desk, reading a paperback book.

"Matteo, *ciao!*" said Domenic as he approached the service desk.

Matteo stood up and casually touched his index finger to his forehead and looked from side to side, but only for an instant. It could have been a thoughtless gesture, a social tic, but it was a subtle signal that they must be watchful of their words in the small foyer that served as the hotel's tiniest of lobbies. There could be others nearby who might be able to listen to their conversation. "Welcome, my friend," said Matteo. "Did you just arrive?"

"Yes. Is my room ready?"

"Quite ready, and the maid has prepared it for you." Matteo reached for a key from the pigeonholes behind him, then headed down the corridor beyond the desk.

Domenic nodded and followed him without another word. The Letizia had served as a safe house since World War II, and its walls, windows, and insulation had been specially retrofitted to shield it from probing ultra-tech surveillance. Periodically, the facility was re-

tested and "cleaned" of any potential security problems—
a task performed most recently by the "maid."

Once they had entered the hotel room and carefully
locked the door, Matteo shook his hand and looked at
him with typical Sicilian candor of emotion. "I have
been briefed on your mission, and I am so sorry to hear
what they did to your wife."

"Thank you," said Domenic, taking a deep breath. His
pain was not so sharp as it had been, but the dull ache
of loss was no less a part of him, as it always would be.
"She is with the angels now. I should be so fortunate
some day. . . ."

Matteo nodded, then after a pause: "You will be leaving tonight for Trapani? That is what they tell me."

Domenic had walked to a small washbasin in the corner of the room, and quickly splashed some water on his
face, scrubbed clean his hands. "Yes," he said, looking
back to Matteo. "And I'm supposed to take you with
me."

Matteo brightened. "Fantastic! I am so bored of this
place, this little place! I live in the most beautiful country in the world and I cannot get out to see any of it."

"Tonight you will. What is the latest on the Guild?"

"Nothing since the last courier messages," said Matteo, holding up his hands.

"So we have no idea whether or not we will have
company at Isole Egadi?"

"It is quite possible they still know very little. If they
are tracking your whereabouts, then your destination in
Sicily is still very much a mystery to them. If they have
a line on you, it remains moment-to-moment."

Matteo was right. If the Guild were watching him
now, they could make no plans—they could only react
to his movements by following, countering, intercepting.
And as long as he remained even a single step ahead of
them, he believed he had the controlling hand. He believed in the righteousness of his mission, which was
always easier if God was on your side.

He said as much to Matteo, who smiled gently. "Yes, I often have similar thoughts. And I ask myself, why does God bother with all the little messes? Surely He could intercede and do a better job of it Himself."

Domenic looked at him wearily. "I have discussed this exact concept with the Jesuits. Believe it or not, they claim St. Augustine foresaw the line of logic which would lead to the questions we ask. There is even a name for the 'argument' but I can't remember what it's called."

"Yes, I think I recall hearing it as well." Matteo grinned. "Jesuits! They all think they are so smart!"

"That's because many of them are." Domenic chuckled. "But I think God is constantly curious about us and the free will He gave us. Once He set us into motion and thought, He has been endlessly fascinated with watching what we will do next."

"But there remains the occasional divine intervention," said Matteo.

"Oh, I don't believe it's all that 'occasional',." said Domenic as he unpacked his few necessities from the duffel. "It seems to me that God and the Saints are involved in our lives every day, every hour, but usually in ways far less dramatic or obvious than the Eyes of the Virgin."

Matteo sat in a chair in the corner of the room considering this. "Which makes me wonder—why did that piece of glass become something so special?"

"I think it was a natural reactive product of the hate and the evil that created it in the first place," Domenic said. "It was God's way of saying that something good can spring from the rubble of *any* catastrophe. The Virgin Mother took what was essentially a negation of her love for us, and transformed it into a *gift*."

"Well said, my friend," said Matteo as he stood up, checked his watch. "Listen, I do not wish to interrupt you, but I did not take the midday meal. I figured you would be hungry from your travels, plus you would want an early start to Trapani."

"You're right about that. . . ."

"Good! Then we shall continue our theology lesson over an early dinner. I told Enrico we would be coming."

"Excellent," said Domenic.

He liked Matteo very much, and he owed him his life. He was that rare combination of intelligence and athleticism which made him an excellent recruit for the Knights. The only thing holding him back was his youth, his lack of experience. Domenic had met him on a training mission in Angola several years back. Matteo was part of a "team" of young men on a survivalist trek through the jungle north of Bembe, near the Zaire border, and Domenic was their instructor. Things had been fairly routine for the first three days of the mission until their group stumbled upon a secret staging area and arms stash of one of the more powerful Angolan warlords of the era. There was no time to explain their sudden appearance to the battle-hardened soldiers, who picked up their heavy assault weapons and started firing.

The survival team was practically unarmed, as well as outmanned by ten-to-one. It was worse than a turkey shoot, and all but two of them were literally cut into pieces by the pattern-fire of spanking new Kalashnikovs. Domenic escaped the initial onslaught with Matteo, then spent the next twenty-four hours on a headlong flight from the warlord's scout teams. The Angolans were on a desperate mission to catch them and kill them—the location of their munitions dump could *not* be compromised. The outlaw soldiers intended to track Domenic and Matteo down indefinitely until they found them and macheted their heads from their necks. That simple.

It was during the first night of their escape through the jungle heading vaguely north and west. He and Matteo had plummeted into an exhausted sleep in an outcropping of rocks by a small waterfall, when his companion *pinched* him awake. Domenic's training kicked in immediately and he did not make a sound as he tried to assess in an instant what was going on around him.

Darkness was almost total, but enough incident starlight provided him a dim view of someone standing on the ledge of rock directly over their heads. This was accompanied by the barely audible sound of mens' voices shouting back and forth a considerable distance from them. It was quite probable then that the man standing unwittingly over them was a point man, the advance scout. Domenic knew the man could turn around, or perhaps take several steps down onto the next ledge and he would discover them.

If Matteo had not somehow awakened, seen the intruder, and managed to *silently* alert Domenic, they would have been killed in a matter of seconds. The scout's feet shuffled across the rock, moved to step down, and Domenic knew this would be their only chance to survive.

Without working out a plan, Domenic lashed out with both feet, creating a lateral hammerblow across the scout's shins and lower legs. The shock and splintering pain of both shinbones cracking gave Domenic the seconds he needed to spring upward to grab the tottering man by the throat and crush his larynx with a single blow. In most cases, this would have been enough to subdue most men, but this intruder was huge—a lumbering, wide-shouldered hulk, who refused to collapse. As Domenic struggled to get his head and neck into position for a killing twist, the man reversed inside, facing him, to wrap him in a breath-crushing bear hug. Domenic felt his chest compress like a paper bellows so fast that dots of light began blinking in front of his eyes, and he knew he was only seconds from passing out.

Suddenly the impossible pressure on his rib cage was released and the intruder fell forward off the rock ledge, taking Domenic with him. Twisting as much as possible in midair, he deflected the full weight of the man's impact on him and the ground, and still managed to get body-slammed into the soft bank of the stream below the falls. As he struggled to his feet he saw the reason for the intruder's sudden collapse: Matteo's serrated commando knife was buried to the hilt at the base of the man's skull, where it had neatly severed his spinal cord, and passed all the way through to penetrate the front of his throat.

It was a brilliant killing move that Matteo had not yet been taught in his Knight's training. Afterward, he claimed he'd acted spontaneously and totally without conscious intent. It had just happened to work out, he claimed. And while Domenic believed him and his protests it had been nothing more than a lucky blow, he could never deny Matteo had saved both of their lives.

That had been five years ago, and now Matteo was in charge of the web of safe houses in Palermo and the surrounding towns. It was a cushy assignment in that it required little if any field work, but it was part of a "career path" reserved for the KOM hierarchy of tacticians and directors of intelligence. Matteo's brains had selected him out of the operative mainstream; he was obviously being groomed for the highest levels of the Order. There were only two reasons they were allowing him to accompany Domenic to Trapani: there was no one else available on short notice, and Domenic had requested him.

"I hope it's all right, but I asked Isabella to join us," said Matteo as they walked up the crowded Corso, crossing at via Roma, and ducking down a connecting street so narrow even the smallest Fiats could not enter. They joined a steady stream of pedestrians and the occasional motor scooter as the crowds eddied and swirled past storefronts and stalls of the *vucceria*.

"Of course! She is a lovely woman," said Domenic.

"Her presence will make our meal more civilized than we could ever dream to do ourselves."

Matteo smiled. They walked in silence to the end of the block and entered a small set of double doors. There was no sign to indicate the *ristorante* inside, and its owner preferred it that way. Only those patrons who already knew of its offerings need come by; there were plenty of alternate venues for the tourists.

As soon as they closed the doors behind them, Enrico, a portly, mustachioed man in his forties, glided up to them, clapping his hands together softly. He had a wide, toothy smile and crinkly eyes under bushy brows. He welcomed them with much animation and guided them to a table in the back room which had been quietly reserved and set just for them.

A raven-haired woman awaited them at the table. She had the bottomless brown eyes and full lips of many Sicilian women, but she was clearly no peasant or shopgirl. Isabella wore the tailored clothes of the successful business class; her jewelry was understated but elegantly expensive.

Everyone greeted each other with kisses and hugs. Domenic was happy to see Matteo with someone so special, who cared so much for him; but it reminded him he would never see Justine again. And there was nothing to do but wait for the feeling to subside. He did not want his own state of mind to diminish his genuine happiness for Matteo and Isabella, and he felt guilty for feeling sorry for himself.

The conversation during the serving of the courses was light, although underscored by a basic intelligence. Matteo's erudite references; the astute economic analyses of Isabella; and Domenic's political observations. But later in the evening, as they sipped Sambuca, Isabella challenged both of them.

"Domenic, I do not wish to sound harsh or accusative, but I am worried about Matteo."

Both men looked at her, but said nothing.

This did not seem to please her, so she pushed on. "What I mean is this: Every time you come to Palermo, Matteo disappears for days at a time . . . with *you*. I don't see him! I don't hear from him!"

Domenic had to keep from smiling. He could see where Isabella was going with this, and there would be no way to dissuade her of her suspicions.

"Isabella, please . . . I have told you. Domenic works for a company that does much work for governments— they have secrets! They have competitors who would love, like you, to know what we are doing!"

She looked from Matteo to Domenic, then back and forth. "I have heard this before and—"

"And you don't believe us," said Matteo.

"That is true; I do not."

Domenic could see a growing panic in the features of his younger colleague. He remembered having frighteningly similar conversations with Justine, and how stunned but also relieved she had been at Logan International when he'd finally told her his true identity and real employer. He wouldn't have told her then if he hadn't believed he would be the one killed that night, and he was desperate to have the data preserved. Justine had been his last, best, and only hope. He had pulled her into the loop and it had resulted in *her* death.

"Isabella," he said quickly, sensing Matteo had no idea how to proceed, "just exactly what is it you think Matteo and I do when we are off on a job for my company?"

The directness of the question caught her off her guard, obviously expecting more dissembling from both men. Isabella paused gathered her thoughts.

"Well, I am not certain. . . . I mean, I cannot say what you are really doing because I do not know. . . ."

Domenic pressed forward while she hesitated. "Exactly what is it you think we do? Seek out women for our pleasures? Do you really believe we are men like that?"

"No!" she exclaimed with a sudden passion, and Domenic could tell she was sincere.

"Thank you," he said. "Then what? Are we homosexual lovers? Could that be what takes us away for days at a time?"

"Dear God, no! That is even *more* impossible."

"Thank you, my love," said Matteo, regaining his confidence to contribute.

"Are we . . . master thieves, out doing bank jobs, securities, smuggling?"

"Please, that is so silly!"

Isabella had to grin, in spite of herself.

"Or, maybe we are international spies . . . professional assassins?"

Domenic knew that by giving breath and word to her suspicions, he could make them all sound so silly, so unreal. The only way to defuse her feelings was to take them head-on.

"I am so sorry. . . . How did you know what I was thinking? The crazy places my thoughts would take me. How could you know?"

"Isabella, I was married for a long time."

She nodded, clearly embarrassed. "I am sorry, Domenic, but then you must understand how frustrated, how . . . difficult to not have such thoughts."

"I do. Believe me."

"And there is something else," she said, raising her gaze to lock with his for an instant, then darting to Matteo as well.

"What?" he said.

"It is a feeling I cannot lose, I cannot stop going back to it," she said. "I feel the *danger*. I feel it surrounding you like a thick, clinging fog."

Domenic sipped the clear liquid that stung of anise and coffee bean. He had to be mindful enough here, not be too dismissive. "Well, that may be more wellgrounded. The construction business is not risk free, especially things like bridges and transmission towers."

He watched her receive and digest his response, and he could tell it was not what she wanted to hear. He and Matteo both promised her they would be careful, especially if she had been experiencing odd, premonitionlike sensations.

She looked at them with her huge, dark eyes, then shook her head. "I am so sorry I sound so silly, but sometimes women get feelings, and they learn to trust them."

"No one is calling you silly," said Matteo.

"I know," said Isabella, pushing her dark hair from her cheek. "That is why I am so very much concerned."

TWENTY

Palermo

KATE HARRISON

As the United flight touched down in Palermo, a wave of intuition passed through her like a chill, and Kate felt an eerie, incongruous sense of calm. It was as though she was being told by some outside force or agency she was doing the right thing.

She'd sincerely hoped the trip would not only solve their mystery, but put an end to the complete disruption of her life. She knew she hadn't even been allowed enough time to properly grieve over the deaths of Lawrence and Justine, but that didn't stop her from feeling guilty and troubled by it. She'd never admitted to Matt or herself how much she regretted not being at their funerals. God, she was so tired of it all. . . .

She had to stop at some point and start thinking about what was going to come next. Some very momentous and volatile events had changed her forever after; Kate had some very big decisions waiting for her, if she could just get past the whirlwind of weird events that continued to threaten her life and her future.

"Not a very big place," said Matt, who was looking

out the window at the Punta Raisi terminal. "I had no idea what to expect. Guess we get spoiled by the O'Hares and the Heathrows and the JFKs of the world."

"I would have been disappointed if it was a big, ugly cookie-cutter airport like all the other ones," said Kate, who had to admit to feeling as much like a tourist as an investigator. She'd never been to Sicily, but had heard that most people rarely visited the island only once; it was a place that lured you back with its subtle beauties and attractions from so many classic ages of history.

She followed Matt from the plane into the main building, which was probably smaller than the terminal in Manchester, New Hampshire, although it appeared much busier. She found the car rental desk and filled out the paperwork while Matt changed up some cash, then called ahead to make a hotel reservation in Trapani. He had insisted they pay for everything with cash, even though sophisticated surveillance could break into airline booking computers to scan for their presence on any flight anywhere in the world. His philosophy was to make it as labor-intensive as possible, rather than easier. Even if his pursuers could manage to track them to a particular city, they would then have a more difficult time finding the next thread of their passage. She was glad she didn't have to think about stuff like that and was actually tired of even having *him* thinking about things like that, but maybe only for a little while longer.

Maybe soon it would all be over. . . .

Because she could not use any credit cards, the rental agency required a large cash deposit, but Kate didn't care. At least money was one thing she didn't need to worry about. At this point, she simply wanted all this chaos to be over—she didn't care what that might cost.

"Okay, let's get to the car," said Matt. She watched his dark eyes endlessly scanning their surroundings, trying to maintain a full-alert status that might buy them a few more seconds should they need it. Kate could not help admiring not only what he did, but how he accomplished it. Matt Etchison was the product of keen conditioning and the best training in the world. Kate had learned she could depend on him, and not worry about him doing anything else stupid or irresponsible that men often did in her presence. He was a good man, and she was thankful for that.

They left the terminal just as the sun was going down and walked a short distance to a Hertz lot containing a row of Fiats and some other smaller cars which she didn't recognize until they were close enough to read the nameplates.

"Okay, here's ours," said Matt, pointing at a smallish, white Alfa Romeo sedan. Climbing into the passenger side of the car, she waited for Matt to fold his large frame into the driver's seat. Matt had mapped out their itinerary along the *autostrada* which connected the various towns and cities of Sicily, and was double-checking a small spiral-bound book of map pages.

"Okay, the A29 west till we get to A19, then into Trapani. Looks like a piece of cake."

They pulled out of the airport at Falcone-Borsellino, and slipped onto the Interstatelike highway. Although Matt quickly shifted through the gears and ran the Alfa's speed up close to 170 kph, at least half of the cars on the road ripped past them at even higher speeds.

"Things haven't changed much since the last time I was in Italy," he said with a soft chuckle as a low-slung sports coupe blurred ahead of them on the left. "These guys are the craziest drivers in the world."

"I know. Lawrence and I did a driving tour of Tuscany about five years ago. I'll never forget it. . . ."

Mentioning her husband saddened her with the terrible truth she tried to avoid, and it made her realize she hadn't dealt with the reality of his death yet. All the proper grieving continued to be held at bay, and it was only in vulnerable moments such as this one that she allowed herself to feel any of the pain waiting to curl over her like an icy wave.

"Hey," said Matt. "I'm sorry if I was the one who made that happen."

"It's all right," she said, inwardly surprised at how he'd picked up on her change of mood so quickly. "I did it to myself, and I think I need a dose of reality once in a while. When or if this mess ever gets over with . . . if I make it through to the other side, then I'm going to miss him terribly . . . and I . . . I *want* to miss him. Does that make any sense? Do you understand what I mean?"

"Oh yeah. It's like you feel like you haven't had time to do a very good job of it."

She glanced over at him, but he kept his gaze fixed on the road and the traffic. "I don't know if I could have phrased it like that, but that is exactly how I feel. Thanks."

Matt nodded, but didn't reply. He knew he didn't have to.

Kate continued looking out her window, trying to take in the panorama of the small coastal towns and the Mediterranean Sea beyond them. The road didn't follow the exact contours of the shoreline, and her view alternated between good and terrible. Plus, the day was slipping into twilight when everything shifted into indistinct grays. Matt didn't add anything else to the conversation, and it was obvious he wanted to stay focused on his driving, the road, and the fighter-pilot tactics of most of the other drivers he encountered. Kate decided he was probably right; she sat back and watched the scenery, trying to keep her mind clear of too many disturbing thoughts until it got too dark to see anything but the road and the path of the headlights.

When they reached Trapani after another hour, Matt stopped at the small, prearranged hotel near the waterfront. The proprietor had two rooms ready and Kate was so tired she hardly noticed the furnishings or even the size of the accommodation. It seemed like they'd been traveling for days, and she fell into an exhausted sleep where she dreamed Lawrence wasn't really dead, and she'd been dreaming the entire, chaotic saga.

But when the bright light of the Sicilian morning surged through the half-open shutters of her room, she was forced to accept what was dream and what was not. Showering and dressing quickly, she descended to the already busy streets of downtown Trapani, where the fishermen and vendors were gathering to transfer product and lire and even a few Euros. The smell of the salted sea surrounded her, blending with the animated language of the natives, and she thought she could easily live in a place like this. But for now, she had a job to do.

After meeting Matt at the corner coffee bar for latte and *pasta dolce*, they walked down to the dock to meet the morning ferry, a fairly high-speed vessel called the *aliscafo*. As its engines throttled down and it drifted towards its slip and gangway, Kate saw a man dressed in khakis, a blue chambray shirt, and one of those fisherman/journalist/photographer vests that makes you look so dashing and *au courant* no matter the time or place. He was tall and thin, and practically bald, and would have looked like a mathematician if he didn't have such a bronzed tan and an adventurously weathered look around his eyes. His name was Dennis Costello, and he was living proof that men who were losing their hair could still be attractive. The man was waving and smiling at them.

"I guess we stand out enough from the locals," she said softly.

"You bet we do," said Matt, who had spent considerable time checking on the credentials of Mr. Costello, the project director of the Marettimo Data Haven Facility. He'd been working at Kendall Structures for more than twenty years, ever since getting his masters from MIT. Lived outside of Boston with standard-issue wife, two kids, dog, fence, and aluminum siding. Couldn't look any cleaner. When Matt had told him he was representing Domenic Petralli's sister-in-law, he was more than eager to meet them and help them in any way possible.

The aliscafo came to rest against the wharf and Costello descended the gangway with his hand extended. "Ms. Harrison . . . Mr. Etchison," he said. "Good to meet you both."

After they'd reciprocated, Costello escorted them back onto the ferry for the return trip, and began a running commentary about the somewhat exotic location of the data haven they were building. "Actually, the choice of Marettimo Island is not so remote when you look at a map. Our client, a consortium of international communications companies, needed a centralized site. Marettimo is the hub of a great wheel with spokes coming to it in the form of undersea fiber-optic cables—from Spain, France, Italy, Greece, Turkey, the Middle East, Egypt, and all of North Africa."

"I can see it's a great spot," said Kate. "No wonder Domenic raved about it." She smiled as she gestured outward from the railing where they stood as the high-speed ferry skipped across moderate chop. They were headed west, toward a group of volcanic islands called the Isole Egadi.

"Oh, yeah," said Costello. "Before the new century got started, this place's main industry was fishing. Hadn't changed in a thousand years, I'd bet. But we came in and pumped some serious Euros into the Egadis and Trapani."

"How do the locals like it?" asked Matt.

Costello shrugged. "That's a good one! At first they *hated* us. Wouldn't talk to us, wouldn't supply us with a workforce. It was rough. Then we started bringing in Tunisian laborers and they started spending their payroll checks in Favignana and Trapani and even Villa Marettimo, and the natives started paying attention. Still took about two years, though, before they started talking, then finally signing up for the jobs which for them were very high-pay."

Kate and Matt used the opportunity afforded by the length of the voyage and Costello's garrulous nature to get a full-scale understanding of the data haven facility. Although it would not be fully operational for another year, its basic structure was practically complete: a giant cube, four hundred feet on a side, sunk into the center of a long-dead caldera, then covered over with millions of tons of reinforced concrete. The essential idea is to create a vault that can store information in a series of redundant arrays within a protective environment that could endure nuclear bomb strikes, electromagnetic pulse penetration, comet or asteroid impact, and just about anything else short of our G-type star going nova on us.

If that happened, Costello said with a wry grin, then all bets were off.

Data havens were springing up in various parts of the world, and Kate realized it was happening with an intentional lack of fanfare. She had known of their theoretical value years ago since they had been discussed in various tech-head journals and were always items found near the top of every ultra-tech company's wish list. She had also heard Domenic talk about them on occasion because they were one of Kendall Structures' specialties—she'd even mentioned it to Matt Etchison at some point.

When she began sifting through all the papers scattered through her brother-in-law's offices, her analytical side had unconsciously kicked in. Without realizing it, she was looking for anything that would make Justine's sequence of numbers mean something. A stack of CAD documents and printouts relating to the Marettimo Data Haven project had caught her attention, and she leafed through the complex diagrams, blueprints, reports, graphs, and dimensional models, not really knowing what she might be looking for.

When she saw the four-digit identifiers initially, she must have made a subconscious mental note of their existence (not even paying attention to *where* she saw them), but it wasn't until she saw them showing up in tiny print along the three dimensions of the building that she realized where she'd seen them before.

The Marettimo facility was elegantly simple in its basic design—a giant cube, composed of thousands of smaller cubes comprising its interior space. Clients would be assigned storage spaces, or cells, and their locations were identified by a series of four-digit numbers which described a cell in three dimensions within the larger structure.

When she showed Matt what she'd found, he believed she was probably correct, but there was one problem— her sister had given her *four* numbers, not three, which would be the normal way to describe a location in space. Convinced she was onto something, she played with the numbers, got absolutely immersed in the tsunami of paper, and prepared a list of possibilities to explain the extra set of digits.

But nothing had come clear, and that's when they decided to be as direct as possible, and contact the people who were actually going to be running the facility. Matt considered posing as the rep of a potential client for the DHF, but they didn't have time for him to get up to speed on the kind of technospeak and business savoir faire he would need to pull it off. After conferring about their limited options, they decided the time would be better spent ferreting out the contacts at Marettimo who would listen to their story and help in whatever way might prove feasible. The title of the Mister Number One at Marettimo was project director, and with Kate's help, they eventually tracked down a name to the title, Dennis Costello.

Although Matt regarded the information with suspicion, Mr. Costello claimed to be a very good friend of Domenic Petralli, and basically told Kate he would do whatever he could to help her. Nothing was too good for my pal, Domenic. . . .

Matt did a thorough background check on Costello, but Kate found it fascinating that Matt found evidence through his sources that Costello did a very exacting check on *their* bona fides as well. Everybody was being none too careful and everybody seemed like they were square, which was just the way Matt liked it.

And so Kate felt very comfortable setting up the meeting and actually going on-site. Her instincts insisted that whatever Justine and Domenic had wanted to tell her or give her would be found at the Marettimo DHF.

As the ferry skated past the largest island in the Egadi, Favignana, she continued to listen to Costello talk about the facility as if it were his beautiful new baby. She knew that although it would not be officially opening for another eleven months, the basic machinery and equipment was in place and was already functioning in "beta mode," which was a testing phase. Its basic design did not require clients to ever physically visit the facility, and most access would be accomplished by 1024-plus algorithmic encryptions, which would prove impenetrable to anyone without both the public and private decryption keys. Admittedly, Kate only knew enough about this aspect of the data-packet industry to be sketchy and probably dangerous, but she understood enough to know that Domenic had gone to great lengths to protect *something*, and she had almost been killed more than once trying to find out its true nature.

As she looked westward over the *aliscafo*'s prow, she watched the vague form of Marettimo gradually assume real shape and definition. Its original volcanic beginnings were still obvious, although many thousands of years had worn it down like an old shoe. The mountainous slopes were fairly barren; signs of human influence were seen along its coastlines—small villages where fishing was the solitary industry, the largest being Villa Marettimo. As the ferry zoned in on the town, Kate saw a large quay jutting out from the rocky shoreline. It looked so new and massive with hi-tech illumination towers, modern slips, and other electronic gear that it looked wildly out of place in a setting otherwise unchanged in centuries.

"That quay's the only thing you're going to see to give anybody a clue we've even been here," said Costello.

"Looks like it's enough," said Matt. "It's huge."

"Well, we had some pretty big vessels coming through here for a while. Lot of construction. We promised the governor we'd dismantle it when we're done!" Costello chuckled. "The people said they hope they never need anything this big."

The ferry eased up to one of the slips and several people in teal coveralls with yellow K-S logos on their backs secured it to the dock and extended a gangway. Dennis Costello excused himself and moved off to give the employees further instructions.

Taking advantage of the sudden private moment, Matt leaned close and whispered: "I don't see any security at all. Either it's concealed, or it's non-existent."

"Well, this place is fairly remote. It doesn't look like anything could sneak up on it without being noticed."

Matt grinned. "Don't kid yourself. This place looks *too* easy."

"This way," shouted Costello from the dock. Behind him, a small motorized vehicle, about the size of a golf cart but enclosed in a plexiglass dome and windshield, awaited them. It was painted in the teal and yellow colors of Kendall Structures.

After climbing into the cart, they were driven through narrow twisting streets flanked by stucco and stone buildings several floors high. Storefronts and houses all packed tightly along the tiny streets. There were few automobiles, more scooters, and an equal amount of pedestrian traffic. Most of the natives were dressed in drab colors, loose-fitting jackets and pants, and they paid no attention to the odd-looking vehicle negotiating their ancient avenues. Kate saw no children or teenagers.

Within minutes, they had cleared the outskirts of the harbor town and had begun climbing a wide, modern highway carved into the side of the island's principal slope. Obviously built by Domenic's company, the road carried them to an entrance cut into the side of the mountain. Here Kate saw the first evidence of any security—the usual chain-link fence, electronic camera surveillance, light towers, guardhouse. Beyond this were two ten-foot steel doors leading underground.

After a perfunctory clearance by two Kendall guards, the doors swung inward, and Costello drove them into the facility. The interior was as sterile and featureless as any standard movie-set underground installation. Cold, unfiltered lights revealed beige tiles lining a corridor with a concrete floor and various color-coded lines streaking it. Costello gave them a running commentary about the miles of tunnels honeycombing the place, statistics about how many tons of this, and how many thousands of that—stuff of absolutely no interest to her. Kate let it fly through her like radiation, and hoped Matt would keep in mind any info he thought might be important.

Ten more minutes and they reached a series of elevator bays, where Costello guided them to one on the end. They entered and ascended for a short time. When the doors opened, they looked out on what could be a floor in any of a thousand different office buildings in a thousand different cities. Kate noted that Kendall Structures' designers had a knack for the Totally Generic look.

Costello guided them through several turns until they reached a conference room filled with the requisite fake wood table and padded swivel chairs. Added touches were small pop-up monitors and keyboards at every seat. "Please, have a seat, I'll get Will." Costello smiled and left them alone.

"So far, what do you think?" she said.

Matt shrugged. "Impressive. But it looks like plenty

of other places I've seen. The only really interesting thing is the difference between the people on the outside of the island and the people on the *inside*—a couple hundred years at least. The symbolism is almost as severe as in a Kafka novel."

Kate grinned. Every once in a while, Matt surprised her with little asides like that which revealed there were layers, and then there were layers to him.

"They seem very eager to help us. Does that make you . . . I don't know . . . wonder at all why?"

Matt shook his head. "Not really. They checked us out. We're who we said we are. Plus—they already knew of you through Domenic. They knew you'd been in on the planning and consulting."

Just then the door opened and Dennis Costello entered with a sandy-haired man in his late forties. He had a long, pleasant face with eyes that suggested a slightly plaintive expression. "This is Will Paulson," said Costello. "He's one of the people who designed the layout and can tell you what you want to know."

Everybody shook hands and Kate jumped right to the heart of the problem by describing the data—the four sets of digits. "I received this information from my sister," she said. "She was told it was very important to the family, but before she could explain it any further . . . she was killed."

Paulson nodded. "Yes, I heard what's happened. And Domenic's disappeared too. He might have also been killed is what I've heard."

"No way to tell right now," said Matt.

"I . . . I was able to figure out from Domenic's notes that three of these number sets might be 3-D coordinates describing the location of a 'cell' in the facility," said Kate.

"That's right," said Paulson, glancing at the numbers as he plugged them into the keyboard in front of his chair. "Very good work."

"But I can't figure out the *fourth* set of variables. Is it a code or something?"

Paulson smiled. "Not really. It's a descriptor for the fourth dimension."

Matt and Kate looked at him, not understanding for an instant, then it hit her—*Of course!* "Time?" she said half-chuckling. "That's what it is? The *time*?"

Paulson lifted his hands in a open gesture. "It was a simple identifier, so that only the person who stored data in the cell would be able to reaccess. Our system will not retrace a location without the timekey."

Kate looked at her notes. "So Domenic stored something here at eight-fifty-four in the morning?"

"Or at night. We use the zero and the one as time IDs. All the other numbers are reserved for cell coordinate descriptors."

Matt had been looking from one to the other, not speaking. Kate knew he was playing the dumbfounded muscle man role, but she was pretty sure he knew exactly what they were talking about.

"When can we get access to the storage cell?" asked Kate.

Paulson smiled. "Right now. I have keyed in your descriptors and the system has locked in. Would you like to use a screen or print outs?"

"Eventually, I will probably want hardcopy but right now, I would like to have a few minutes to examine it with Mr. Etchison."

Paulson smiled, punched in a few keys, then stood up. "No problem. I have to get back to work anyway. It was nice meeting both of you. Give me a call if you need anything."

"That goes double!" said Dennis Costello as he also moved to exit the room. "I'll be waiting for you in the hall. Take your time!"

Kate watched both of them until the door closed behind them, then to Matt: "This is all kind of silly, isn't it? I mean—they designed this place. If they don't have a back door or a monitoring system to know exactly what kinds of data flow in and out of here, then they are a *lot* dumber than they look."

Matt pulled up a chair next to her screen, but he still looked at her as he replied. "I've been having the same thoughts, but how many companies would sign on to a facility like this if they believed their most valuable data could be stolen or breached?"

Kate leaned back, rubbed her eyes. "I don't know. . . . I don't know anything for sure. These days, when I look at *anything* too closely, it stops making sense to me."

Moving closer to her, so that he might look over her shoulder, he peered at the screen. "Okay, let's stop over-thinking everything. We seem to do best when we just *react*. So, what do we have here?"

She began to study the documents that appeared on her screen. There was a wealth of information, prefaced by an abstract and an outline, with references to something called *the Eyes of the Virgin*.

"This looks pretty weird," she said.

"Okay," said Matt. "Let's see what's what."

As Kate scrolled down the PDF pages, they began to read.

TWENTY-ONE

Trapani

STREICHER

*T*racking Harrison and her hired gun was so easy, he almost laughed out loud.

The thought amused him as he checked the cockpit instruments of the modified Nightbird attack-copter, also called a "black chopper" by the popular press. He was soloing out of the private hangar of the Khazar turbine plant in Bizerte, Tunisia, which was owned by a Guild consortium. The Nightbird was an amazing craft with terrain-avoidance radar, ultra-quiet whisperjet rotors, and enough armament to sink a battleship. He'd learned to fly helicopters when he'd been with the East Germans, and it was a skill which had served him well over the years, especially since he preferred working alone.

Once Harrison's passport had been logged at the Italian customs computer at Palermo, it set off a chain of what-if scenarios within the Guild's version of CARNIVORE surveillance (a worm that lives in bureaucratic intranet systems looking for specific keywords). After that, it was a simple matter to tap into the airport security cameras and do face pattern-match searches of everyone leaving the terminal until Kate Harrison was located. That linked them to a rental vehicle, and led to reestablishing the satellite recon. From that point, they were tracked right into the front gate of the Marettimo facility. The entire operation had taken less than twenty-four hours, and even though he'd expressed his displeasure at the assignment to Kerschow, he secretly enjoyed the excitement of a good hunt.

Everything was making sense now. The data haven off the coast of Sicily was a brilliant hiding place—blatantly obvious, but only once you realized the simple truth. There is an old espionage dictum that holds that the best place to hide anything is always out in the open, and Petralli had demonstrated the worth of the axiom.

Checking his watch, he noted several key points. Harrison and her goon had entered the DHF around noon. It was doubtful they would be staying in the facility overnight, but even if they did, it posed no large problem. Darkness now cloaked the island, and as his chopper approached in almost total silence, he could hover directly above the entrance gate with impunity. Even if the facility possessed rudimentary detection equipment (which he already knew it did *not*), the Nightbird's stealth characteristics rendered it invisible.

If Harrison and her companion left the facility tonight, they must do it soon to catch the last ferry to Trapani—where he could intercept them on the *autostrada*. If they stayed at a hostel on the island, his job would be even easier—any lodgings in the fishing village town would have absolutely *zero* security countermeasures.

Looking down, he saw the western coastline of the island slip beneath him. The moon was just rising over the Mediterranean Sea, sending out pale feelers across its fractured surface to be absorbed by the black bulk of the island. His craft made less noise than the crash of breakers on the rocky shore as he drifted over the data haven entrance like a dragonfly looking for prey.

His instruments revealed infrared heat signatures of a

guardhouse attendant and several smaller shapes in the nearby hills—probably scavenging cats or other small mammals. Streicher smiled, and eased down on the stick as he saw a small outcropping of basaltic rock higher up the hillside. It would be suitable for his purposes—a place to land the chopper, and which afforded him an unobstructed view of whoever entered or left the facility.

Sooner or later, Harrison would be leaving this place. Streicher would be waiting for her.

Twenty-Two

Trapani

PETRALLI

"*I* was told you would be here," said the fisherman. He was looking at Domenic and Matteo as if he really didn't want to notice anything about them he might remember later. Not many people chartered fishing boats after dark, and the *pescatore* clearly didn't want to know why.

"Good," said Domenic, paying him an outrageously high fee to ensure his disinterest but full cooperation. "Let's go."

"One more thing," said the fisherman, removing a folded SkyFreight LetterPak from his oilcloth coat pocket. "I was *also* told to give you this."

Domenic grinned as he took the unopened cardboard envelope. "*Grazie*. Now, away!"

Matteo stood with him on the deck as the old vessel's diesel clunked and chugged up enough revs to get them moving. Both men were dressed in black clothing, utility vests which concealed sidearms, and waterproof backpacks with more sophisticated weapons and gear. The moon was up and its quarter-light cut a path across the moderately choppy sea. That, plus light spilling from the wheelhouse windows was enough to read Sforza's update.

"What does it say?" Matteo watched as he checked the update.

"We were right. They made their way here on schedule, and reached Marettimo before we did. I wish we could have caught up with them beforehand."

"Sure," said Matteo. "If you wanted to risk regular comm channels. You've been doing it right using the couriers and letterpaks. Nobody can intercept anything."

"I know, I'm getting impatient. I just want to be sure Kate's out of danger."

"Well, we're almost there! We should be able wrap this up quickly, yes?"

Domenic shook his head, tapped the paper for emphasis. "Hang on—there's more. We've picked up taps from other cybersurveillance. That suggests Unfriendlies may also be tracking Kate's progress."

"Which means we may have company?" Matteo's expression changed from an easy grin to a concerned frown.

"It could mean anything. The Guild, or whoever else is tracking her, may have already been waiting on the island . . . or they may have already followed them in."

"Or they might be like us—en route."

"Sounds like the ingredients for quite a party," said Domenic. "You seen any action since Angola?"

"You know I have not."

"It was rhetorical, my friend."

Matteo did not reply for a moment. "I wish I had been a bit more truthful with Isabella."

"What?"

"In case something . . . you know . . . *happens* . . . then at least she would not be so surprised, so shocked."

Tapping him on the shoulder, Domenic smiled. "I understand how you feel, but think about what you're saying—what could you have said? *Oh, and by the way, my love, I might get killed while we're on this supposed business trip. No big deal. Nothing to worry over."*

Matteo looked at him, realized he was not making the best of sense.

Domenic shredded the memo and confettied it over the side. "All I wanted was to get Kate into a safe place. Then I could track down the glass without that distraction. I owe it to her, especially after the mess I made in Boston. And now there might be more trouble. She must be wondering what kind of thug her sister married."

"Stop punishing yourself," said his friend, pushing his thick black hair back from his forehead. "We're here to see that she will be safe."

The old fishing boat was belching and chugging its way up to speed and had cleared the harbor. The captain could probably pilot these waters blindfolded; the weather was calm and clear, and he would take the most expedient course to Marettimo. Neither Domenic nor his friend spoke for awhile, allowing themselves to be enchanted by the moonlit passage. There was something magical about the sea, and man's fragile relationship with it. One of Domenic's grandfathers had been a *pescatore*, and he wondered if the comfort he now felt might be some gentle stirrings of genetic memory.

As he stood with his hands on the railing, he felt a weird sensation pass through him. It reminded him of when he was a small boy and his shoulders would be feathered by a sudden chill or a shudder—and at those moments, his mother would say, *Someone has just walked across your grave.*

It was like that, and yet, it was not.

No, it was more . . . *physical* than that.

As if something real and solid had glided over him. Like a giant, coasting gull, or a huge bat. He thought of the Old Testament description of the Angel of Death floating down the streets of the Pharaoh's city, while those to be spared felt his cold shadow pass over them.

"Did you feel *that*?" He said to Matteo as he unshouldered his backpack and rummaged for a pair of night-vision goggles.

"No . . . what?" Matteo looked at him and then awkwardly from side to side. "What are you talking about?"

"I don't know," said Domenic, fixing the goggles to his head. "I had the feeling that something flew right over us, something *big*."

"Big like what?"

Domenic didn't answer. He was scanning the swath of the night sky ahead of the boat's prow. He'd almost turned his head too far to the left when he caught a slight glint of a heat signature—which his experience told him could be the residue from the baffled exhaust of a stealth aircraft. Keeping his head pointed in the right direction, he adjusted the magnification of the goggles. There . . . far ahead now and dwindling to the vanishing point, he saw it closing in on their destination.

"Damn," he said under his breath, which was about at close as he ever came to real cursing.

"Domenic! What is going on? What did you see?"

Removing the goggles, he looked at Matteo. "Black helicopter. Headed for the island. Just like us."

Matteo's eyes widened just for a moment. "Our adversaries?"

"It would seem likely. Not just anybody has access to that kind of technology."

"Do you think he saw us?" Matteo was looking into the inky sky even though he could see absolutely nothing.

"No. If he did, and he ID'd us, we wouldn't be here right now." Domenic didn't bother detailing how easy it would be to send a heat-seeker down the chum boat's exhaust funnel. "No," he repeated softly, "he didn't see us."

"But we saw him," said Matteo. "So, at least for the moment, we have a little bit of an advantage."

"Yes, but the question is—what do we do with it?"

Checking his watch, Matteo tilted his head toward the

captain in the wheelhouse. "Do we tell him anything? Could he be any help to us?"

"We tell him nothing. He would be *less* than useless." Domenic replaced the goggles to his pack.

"How much longer till we get there?" said Matteo.

"Too long. They've got a big jump on us."

"Can we notify Marettimo? They know you there; they'd listen, right?"

Domenic thought about this and what it meant. "We agreed to radio silence, but this is one of those out-of-bounds incidents. Something we couldn't have figured on. No contingent plans."

"What about ship-to-shore?"

"I thought about it, but we might be shooting ourselves in the foot."

Matteo looked at him. "Right—if they intercept our radio, then we give ourselves away. We lose whatever advantage—you know, our element of surprise—we might have had."

Domenic gestured with one hand dismissively. "Too risky. They could be waiting for us when we hit the shore. They could take us out before we even *reached*."

"Yes, a sitting duck."

"More like a *dead* duck." said Domenic.

"So . . . what do we do?"

Domenic thought about their dilemma for a few moments, knowing every second wasted could be critical. He had been avoiding using any of the latest technology for fear it might reveal his position or intentions, but the recent discovery left him little choice. If he did not make an attempt to track the occupants of the black helicopter, he could lose the entire advantage he'd been given.

"Okay," he said, as he returned to his rucksack full of gear. "Let's do it."

Matteo said nothing as he watched his superior. Retrieving a palm unit, he activated its screen and deployed its omnitracking mini antenna. Then he keyed in his algorithm. Within seconds he'd established a link with

Corsica via encrypted satellite. The problem with taking this risk was not so much getting his messages or incoming data intercepted—rather it was the possibility of giving away their position if someone was watching and listening.

He couldn't calclate those odds right now, and didn't care.

Too late, he thought, *I've already committed.*

He bypassed the voice-link to Corsica and requested body-heat tracking from the nearest geo-synch satellite. He plotted the last known position of the black helicopter and let the spy network CPUs do the rest. Within seconds, he had what he needed. Looking up at Matteo, who was looking very anxious, he expended a small smile.

"We're okay, I think."

"Tell me. . . ." said his young companion.

"We have a fix on the aircraft. Looks like it's sitting on the hillside near the main gate. One boogeyman on board—stationary. If he moves, we'll know where he's going."

"So what is he doing there?" said Matteo.

"Waiting for Harrison is the obvious answer."

Matteo shook his head. "This is like playing football with an anchor tied to your leg. If Harrison shows up and he moves on her before we can get off this boat—"

"Game over," said Domenic. "You didn't need to remind me."

"Now we place our trust in the Lord."

"Yes. And we ride this scow out to the island and we hope we're not too late."

"Do you have a best-case scenario?" asked Matteo sardonically. "Anything I can hold onto till we hit shore?"

Domenic thought about it. "Well, it is more and more doubtful our man is going in to attack the facility. That would be crazy—it would not advance the Guild's agenda, which is to get a key to reading *the Eyes*. Besides, the pilot does not have anything on board that would even scratch that place."

"Okay," said Matteo. "Go on."

"I also have a hard time imagining him storming the gates. You know—breaking in and not having any idea where he should be going. No, if it were me running the op, I'd have to figure it's a snatch and grab operation."

Matteo nodded in agreement. "Sounds logical."

We'll see, thought Domenic.

TWENTY-THREE

Marettimo

KATE HARRISON

Kate and Matt continued to scan the files from Domenic Petralli's data cell, transfixed by the unraveling of so many secrets.

One of the digital files contained a history of a church artifact called The Eyes of the Virgin, which had originally been part of a stained-glass window in a small chapel near Fatima, in Portugal. The window had been created by a mysterious craftsman, a glazier who appeared at the rectory of St. Anthony's Catholic Church very late on the evening before construction of the chapel was to begin. The craftsman said he'd heard the parish had not yet found anyone to design and install a stained-glass window, and he was offering his services. His work turned out to be exquisite, although he disappeared without asking to be paid.

The chapel, built to honor the Virgin Mary's recent appearance to three children from Fatima, was beautifully elegant in its simplicity. No one suspected it was a target of enemies of the Church.

But one night in 1922, the little chapel at Cova da Iria

had been literally blasted into powder by a squad of fascist hirelings. The bombers had planted so much dynamite that the tiny building had been almost vaporized. It was enough of a miracle that even a single piece of stained glass had escaped destruction. But when Father Julio Enrique picked up the fragment and saw it contained the lapis lazuli eyes of Mary, he knew he'd discovered something truly special.

Surely, he proclaimed, this was no accident. Father Julio wrote to Archbishop Ferdinando and told of his belief it was a divine sign from God and the Virgin. The archbishop requested that the village priest bring the artifact to Lisbon, where its preservation and captivating beauty stirred all who looked upon it. Near the end of 1922, the bishop wrote to the new Pope, Pius XI, asking that the artifact be examined by the Vatican's Commission on Miracles, and in November 1922, Pius XI responded by sending an emissary to Lisbon to examine the piece of glass.

When the Pope's representative picked up the glass, admiring the work, he witnessed a true miracle—the Virgin's eyes seemed to melt into the depths of the glass as though sinking into water, and words appeared in their place. The archbishop also witnessed the transformation, but neither man was able to read the message in the glass—a message from Mary, the mother of Jesus.

The emissary hand-carried the fragment of glass directly to Vatican City, where Pius XI examined it with a team of scholars, who determined the words were written in a dead tongue, possibly a dialect of the Essenes or of Aramaic, but no one could read it. Pius discussed the possible importance of this event in his first official document, *Ubi Arcano Dei Consilio*.

While under the care and watch of the Vatican, the message eventually disappeared, replaced once again by the hypnotically beautiful rendering of Mary's blue eyes. Years passed and no one could decipher the words copied from the glass.

Until 1931, when Pius XI had a dream in which he spoke to the Virgin. Afterwards, he awoke, although in a trancelike state, to write down a crude translation "key" that Mary had dictated to him. The key and the Eyes of the Virgin were sent to the Abbey of Monte Cassino where they were studied and guarded by the Benedictines, who were considered the best living linguistic authorities of all the Biblical dialects extant at the time of Christ. Their initial work on the material received by Pius XI resulted, in 1931, in the creation of a complex, but workable method to read whatever text may appear on the piece of miraculous glass.

It was at this time that the true nature and purpose of the Eyes of the Virgin was made clear to the Church. The original message, a short and cryptic passage, was finally "decoded" by the monks—it said: *A Beast is born in Germany and his loss is a victory.*

Initially, the real meaning of the message was argued in the highest circles of the Vatican, but the one with the highest credibility—that Adolph Hitler's loss to Hindenberg in the Chancellor elections of 1932 meant that he would eventually be a fearsome entity—proved to be terribly correct the following year when Hitler was "appointed" Chancellor and given dictatorial powers by passage of the Reichstag's Enabling Act.

A faction known as "the Marists" within the Vatican believed the message was a divine warning from Mary, whose always-prayed-for intercession was finally becoming a reality. When two other messages were received by the Benedictines over the next few years which accurately predicted the invasions of eastern Europe by Hitler's armies, and the rise of the Japanese military state, there were many Rome insiders who believed the End Times were upon the world.

This commonly accepted notion caused a curious fracturing within the ranks of the Vatican's most powerful leaders and advisors to the pope. One side argued that the best course of action was to do nothing—to accept the coming of the apocalypse and embrace the Creator; but an equally vocal and zealous group countered with the idea that Mary had given her people the information for a *reason*—so that mankind could take *action* against a destiny that was not immutable. Pius XI decided the only way to decide which faction might be correct would be to wait for the next message from the Queen of Heaven . . . and then make an attempt to act upon the information.

But no messages appeared until several months *after* Japan bombed Pearl Harbor, which many advocates of the do-nothing faction avowed as proof that Mary wanted no human intervention—otherwise she would have warned us of the coming Japanese attack.

This logic proved faulty because, the Eyes of the Virgin "blinked" again in the summer of 1942 when a message was widely interpreted to mean that Winston Churchill would be assassinated during a secret meeting with leaders of the French resistance in Madrid. The new Pope, Pius XII, instructed the Vatican Secret Service to work with the American OSS unit to convey what was learned to British Intelligence. Although the Vatican's "proof" was flimsy, Churchill himself was convinced there might be something valid in the prophetic message for one very good reason—only six people in the world even *knew* about the Madrid meeting. It was practically impossible for a handful of Benedictine monks to discover the details of such a plan. The British decided to stage the meeting with a "double" for the prime minister (an actor named Edward Rutherford), and succeeded in capturing the would-be assassin, Jean-Paul Levesque, who was the number-two man in the hierarchy of the Resistance. It was a top secret coup of the greatest magnitude, and the details of the operation have never been made public.

The overall effect of the incident, in terms of veracity and reliability of Vatican intelligence, had long-term repercussions within the deepest levels of government both in Britain and America.

During World War II, when the dreaded Nazi invasion force known as the *Fallschirmjager* commandeered the Abbey, the safety of the Eyes of the Virgin was a great concern of Pius XII, who made a point of receiving promises from both the Germans and the Allies that the Abbey would not be harmed. The Benedictine monks were also confident that Monte Cassino would be safe and made no effort to move their vast archives of church artifacts.

But Mary herself intervened.

A message appeared briefly in the glass warning of the destruction of the Abbey at Monte Cassino. The monks did not hesitate; the small band of Benedictines sworn to preserve the Eyes of the Virgin left the Abbey during the second week of March 1944, and under the order of Pius XII, entrusted the care and safety of the artifact to the Knights of Malta by delivering it to their fortress on the island of Corsica. Less than a week later, 229 B-17 Army Air Corps bombers dropped 600 tons of bombs on the Abbey and reduced it to a pile of rubble.

Once again, the Eyes of the Virgin had seen into the future.

Although the incident at Monte Cassino was viewed as a success, there was one negative attached to the operation. Nazi espionage agents took notice of the movements of the Benedictine monks who spirited off the glass artifact, and reported back to a special division in Berlin unofficially called the Office of Cultural Requisitions. It was claimed to be one of Hitler's favorite ongoing projects—to acquire by whatever means the greatest works of art and cultural treasures from all over the world. With the ultimate aim of making the "Thousand Year Reich" the repository of human culture's greatest artistic achievements, any and all rumors of possible "acquisitions" were marked with the highest priorities.

Coupled with this agenda was Hitler's abject fascination with the occult and the mystical. When the rumor reached him that the Vatican might possibly have access to an object—a relic, an artifact, a talisman, or whatever—which possessed the power of prophecy, the *Führer* became obsessed with finding out more about this curious and mysterious object.

Although the Office of Cultural Requisitions authorized a special search team to find any trace of the rumored artifact, the trail to Corsica ran cold, and the Eyes of the Virgin remained safe by the war's end. But the rumor endured throughout the next fifty years of geopolitical turbulence—especially when certain world-shaping events were oddly altered or interrupted or changed by last-minute forces. Suspicions persisted in some of the highest offices of some of the world's most secret centers of power that the Vatican may have access to information that was truly without precedent.

After World War II, despite a constant vigil, the miraculous glass revealed no new messages for many years. It became the common wisdom of its guardians that the Virgin Mother had not intended for humankind to become dependent on the artifact. It would be prideful and dangerous to presume humans were deserving of *any* miraculous intervention, and it was widely believed that whenever Heaven decided to contact the world, it should be regarded as a singular and wonderfully special event.

There were a handful of messages during the latter half of the century, but they became increasingly more complex—more difficult to decrypt *and* interpret. The situation had become critical when no consensus could be achieved regarding the meaning of the last two messages from Mary. At the conclusion of the last millennium, it was decided by the Vatican and the KOM to enlist the best minds of the Church to study the last series of messages to ensure they were understood.

Leo Wieznewski had been a member of the Knights

of Malta since being recruited out of Georgetown University, where he attended their graduate school in cybernetic theory. He had become instrumental in bringing the Eyes of the Virgin to the United States, to be studied at Potomac Systems Laboratories near Washington, D.C. He was also the designated guardian of the artifact when it was stolen more than a year ago in what appeared to be a gangland-style execution scenario at the Wieznewski residence.

But ultimate responsibility for the Eyes of the Virgin lay with the North American sector chief of the KOM, Domenic Petralli.

Turning away from the monitor, Kate looked at Matt Etchison with what must have been an expression of total amazement.

"This is the craziest stuff," she said. "My brother-in-law is what?—a medieval knight? A secret agent?"

"Sounds like a little of both," said Matt.

"I can't believe my sister knew about this? What did she get me into?" said Kate, trying to find something basic, something normal in all the information she'd been given . . . something she could hold onto that made regular, logical sense. "What have I gotten *you* into?"

"There's a lot more material here," said Matt. "I don't think we have much choice but to keep pushing through it."

Kate was feeling overwhelmed. Too much information was being thrown at her. She knew how her mind worked—always trying to solve problems on an unconscious level. It was a characteristic that had always served her well, but this time, she was getting swamped. It was too much to not only take in all at once; it was also too much to have to believe.

And yet, she had little choice.

"Okay," she said. "Let's go."

The last information Wieznewski's lab had been able to deliver to Domenic Petralli was a refined decryption key and a new message that had appeared in the glass. The message had not yet been decrypted when Domenic received it, and he decided it would be unwise to do so in light of the actual theft of the artifact. He sent message and key directly by satellite and buried fiber optics to his data cell in Marettimo, entrusting the code to its location only to himself.

"This can't be right," said Kate, looking up from the screen. "Somehow, my sister had the right codes."

"It was probably correct when it was stored here," said Matt. "Petralli probably didn't give the codes to his wife until the last minute."

"I'm not sure I follow you."

"We know the last time Petralli saw your sister was at the Rome airport. He obviously believed his life was in grave danger, and since he'd already stashed all this info, he was the only person on the planet who knew how to ever retrieve it. You with me so far?"

"Yes," said Kate. "So he sent Justine back to Boston with the location codes, figuring she would be safe. . . ."

"Right, but the bad guys were smarter than that, but not smart enough. They hadn't planned on your sister contacting you."

"And they must have thought they'd gotten what they needed from her," said Kate, shaking her head at some unpleasant memories. "Or they wouldn't have killed her."

"I know. That one bothers me. Either it was a mistake, or they believed they'd gotten what they wanted. Hard to tell now."

Kate nodded, collected her thoughts. "At least we understand something about what's going on now. No wonder somebody wanted that piece of glass so badly. The gift of prophecy, it's hard to imagine."

"That kind of information could be volatile in the wrong hands."

"And Domenic was trying to get this data back to the Vatican," she said.

"Sounds logical."

"So where does that leave us?" she said. "Since Domenic might be dead by this time, do we try to take it back to Rome?"

"That's probably a good idea. Although we still don't know who we're up against, and we have no idea how to reach these Knights of Malta."

"Somebody would listen to us. Couldn't we walk into the U.S. Embassy? The CIA? The FBI? Somebody would listen to us."

"Maybe. Don't forget how crazy all this sounds. You've been living it, so it's starting to make sense," said Matt. "But for everybody else, we've got a lot of explaining to do."

Kate looked at him and paused. She couldn't fault his logic, but as far as she could see, it didn't change things much. "I don't see what choice we have."

"Well, we have a few more," said Matt. "Like what about that message and the key?"

"What about it?"

"Well, I don't know about you, but I sure as hell want to know what it says."

She looked at him and grinned sardonically. "We might not have the facilities to do that."

"What do you mean—hardware, software?"

"Maybe both. Until I see the data, I have no idea."

"Okay, so let's take a look," said Matt.

Kate selected the rest of the files from the data cell and began scanning them while Matt sat impatiently beside her, not sure what he was looking at. From her initial impressions, there appeared to be files dedicated to specific decryption software not included with these files, but there were also PDF files of what appeared to be translation or decryption charts that looked like the kind of classic decoding documents used for centuries.

"I don't know. . . . It looks possible we have everything we need."

"Okay," said Matt. "How do we transfer this stuff? Or get it out of here? Transport it? I'm not sure I'm even asking the right questions."

"It looks like we can redirect it to another network server or basic CPU, or we can request a download and burn it to a CD."

"Normally, I would say we should send ourselves a copy to my website server, but it's possible their surveillance and intercept capabilities are too good."

"Meaning?"

"Meaning we should only trust ourselves with the data. Burn a CD."

Kate nodded, and she began keying in some commmands. "Okay, let's do it. I think we'll burn *two* copies. Just in case one of us doesn't make it or if you can think of a good place along the way where we could hide it."

"Good idea. I have a feeling we should get this stuff to the right people as soon as possible," said Matt. "I think as long as *we* have it, we're putting ourselves at great risk."

"I agree," she said. "But you know, I'm wondering if anybody is really the 'right people' for this kind of information."

"This is no time to get philosophical," said Matt.

"I know, I know. Let's go find Mr. Costello."

Less than a half-hour later, Kate carried a download of all the data on a CD in the side pocket of her all-weather jacket as she and Matt were being escorted to the egress of the facility by Dennis Costello. Matt carried a second copy in a document harness he always wore under his clothes when working. There was little traffic in the sterilized corridors, since they had lingered far past regular workers' hours.

"You won't be able to get a ferry back to the mainland till morning," said the project director. "But we maintain a suite of rooms at the hotel in town because of situations like this. So, please, be our guest tonight, okay?"

After climbing into the company vehicle and riding down the hillside, they entered the mostly dark, narrow streets of Villa Marettimo. They saw practically no pedestrians and fewer lights. When Costello stopped the small, electric-powered car in front of the Hotel Mattanza, Kate was surprised to see how small the building was. It looked like an old rowhouse that had been converted to a hostelry many years ago.

Once inside, the project director cleared them with Enzo, the thin and wiry proprietor; then Costello wished them good travels, and departed. Kate and Matt stood in the small foyer as Enzo, who spoke no English, gestured they should follow up the back stairs. The way was illuminated by kerosene lamps, which made the old stucco walls glow with deceptive warmth. There was the smell and dampness of the sea everywhere.

On the second floor, Matt was given the closest door to the staircase, while Kate's was at the end of a short hallway. "See you in the morning," she said softly.

Matt smiled and nodded as he pulled his door shut behind him. Kate entered her room and did the same. It was a narrow enclosure, barely big enough for a wardrobe, four-poster bed, and a small table with a pitcher of water and a washbasin. Brocaded wallpaper completed the quaint, nineteenth-century ambiance, and Kate imagined the room had not been redecorated since the house had been built.

She removed her jacket, took off her shoes, and was in the process of turning down the blankets when there was a knock at the door. More like a very soft tapping.

Kate. . . .

She heard Matt whisper her name. What could he

want now? Reaching for the knob, she wondered if it even locked on its own. So disarming was the room—she'd forgotten to even check. Then just as her fingers touched the doorknob, she felt it turn in her hand, and the door swung inward to reveal a tall, handsome man staring at her.

But it was not Matt Etchison.

TWENTY-FOUR

Marettimo

PETRALLI

*W*hen the boat softly thudded against the wharf, Domenic climbed over the gunwale to step carefully to the thick planking. Matteo followed and they awaited the captain, who had been told the rest of his job would be to drive them in an old pickup truck to the facility. He was nothing more than a hired man, who knew nothing of their intentions or identities. Corsica had in fact paid him an extra fee to be as indifferent as the stars which blazed above them in the blue vault of the night.

And so the man appeared to not notice the all-black clothing his passengers wore, nor the heavy canvas equipment bags, nor the bulges under their windbreakers which could only be holsters for weapons of formidable size.

"The truck is this way, signore," said the *pescatore*.

"No," said Domenic, who had received new target coordinates from his palm unit. "Change of plans. We are not going to the facility."

The man looked wary. "I was paid to—"

"To do what I need," said Domenic, pointing to an

intersection on a map of the town. "Take us here. *Now*."

Shrugging in assent, the man gestured for them to climb aboard. Matteo threw their gear into the cargo area and joined Domenic in the cab. The truck belched and smoked as it lurched into motion. The driver eased away from the docks and tucked into a side street that angled steeply up to the next concourse of streets, where the Hotel Mattanza awaited them.

Domenic had no choice but to believe he was truly an instrument of God's will. More than once in his career as an operative, he had succeeded when he should have failed—because everything in his plan worked almost *too* perfectly. It had not happened often, but on the few times when it had, Domenic had felt like a piece on a game board and nothing more. The sensation had been eerie, and in a way, terrifying. The conviction of being totally controlled, manipulated. Powerless under the steel grip of the Creator.

But he could feel it happening at that very moment, and his natural instincts were to fight against the notion. And of course it could all be in his mind, all a construction to explain how and why things were happening the way they were. Domenic felt as though everything—all the events and people and possibilities—were funneling down to an inevitable center-point, accelerated by the gravity of fate. If he concentrated on the concept, he felt dizzy, disoriented.

"We're not going to make it," said Matteo in a gritty whisper. "He's ahead of us. I can feel it."

"We know he is," said Domenic. "It won't matter."

As the truck angled hard into an alley to emerge at the opposite corner from the hotel, Domenic thought he saw the front door of the narrow building swinging in upon itself.

Could we be so close?

"Stop!" he said just loud enough to startle both other men. The driver punched at the brake pedal and everyone pitched forward. Matteo was already yanking at the handle as Domenic shoved outward. "No time! Take the lobby! The front stairs! I'll take the back. . . ."

"Okay."

"But don't do *anything* until I have you covered," said Domenic.

Both men dragged their rucksacks from the pickup's open deck, dropping them to the side of the narrow street. The driver stood mutely, watching them advance on the Mattanza and draw their weapons. Without a word, he slipped the shifter into gear and rolled away slowly and silently—but with great determination.

Signaling to Domenic with a smile as he held his weapon straight up, Matteo turned and slipped into the hotel.

Domenic sprinted around the side of the building where the entrance to the kitchen and service stairs were located.

It was dark, but light leaked from unknown places to give him the slightest suggestions of where and how to move. He could make out a small flight of steps to a stone porch, or dock, where supplies were delivered, and beyond it, a door.

There was a sudden absence of sound, of touch, but Domenic's vision seemed to harden to a new level of clarity. Looking up beyond the dock, he could see the narrow threshold, and Domenic felt as if he were now *floating* above the steps, rising like a puppet being lifted by its own strings.

The ascent was both rapid and endless. There seemed to be an infinite amount of time to decide what might come next . . . and also *no* time at all. Crossing the space of the dock, he reached the door, turned the knob.

Locked.

He pushed slightly against it, and could feel the barrier of a security crossbar on the inside.

No backup from here. The thought jacked through him with a jolt, but no panic. There was also no escape for the boogeyman, either.

But he had to get moving. Matteo was closing in without cover. Kate and Etchison could already be dead. Too many possibilities to weigh out now.

Just *move* it.

Soundlessly, he retraced his steps around the corner of the dark building, and the amount of light available was insulting. As he reached the corner, turning toward the hotel's entrance, he could see something suspended in the air in front of him. It was his arm, his hand, and his weapon.

TWENTY-FIVE

Marettimo

STREICHER

As the door opened, Streicher paused for an instant. The woman standing in front of him was not what he'd expected. Lean, angular, her hair tied back away from her face, she appeared wary and capable—not the soft society wife he'd absorbed from her dossier. She looked surprised, but not panicked. More concern than fear.

"What? I thought—?"

"Ms. Harrison—Kate Harrison?"

"Who are you?"

"I was sent by—"

"You called me *Kate* before, how could—?"

"Domenic Petralli sent me."

Streicher enacted his best smile, held up his open palms in a perfect gesture of helplessness. He wore a pair of hiking boots, Dockers, and a white, Irish cable knit sweater. He looked like an aging model for a mail order catalog.

The mention of the brother-in-law held her off balance for the moment he needed.

He had gone to her room first, without rousting her hired goon, because he wanted to avoid a raucous encounter if possible. When you were dealing with a guy who's an ex-Seal, you're dealing with trouble, no matter how tough you are. Streicher had known several Seals in his career and they could be, when pushed, the most dangerous, indomitable adversaries in the world. Although Streicher believed he could remove the Seal without great risk, there was no reason to take *any* risk if he could get what he needed from the woman, an infinitely softer target.

And then her hesitation was blinked away; she began inching the door closed and the subliminal twinge at the corner of her mouth told him she was ready to cry out for the Seal. Any second . . .

Moving quickly, he turned his shoulder so that he could knife his body between her and the door. His lead hand flashed out to cover her mouth and clamp down on her nose, simultaneously snapping her head back with just enough force to stun her and keep her from making a sound. As she staggered back, his trailing hand grabbed the knob and eased the door shut. The room was small, dim, and claustrophobic. A single kerosene lamp cast hard shadows across her face, but he could still see that her eyes had rolled halfway back into her skull. Despite this, she remained dazedly conscious.

Still moving as though choreographed, Streicher grabbed her by the hair and arched her back over his knee, still clamping down on her mouth.

"Hear this—" he whispered sharply into her ear. "I will put a bullet through your eye socket if you make a sound. I am removing my hand from your mouth now. Your choice: silence or death."

He didn't wait for her response, but continued to move with feline quickness, releasing her and removing a silenced Sig Sauer 9 mm from his belt at the small of his back. In less than a second he had it pointed at her left eye, which was dilating in wild anticipation. Barely risking any movement at all, she shook her head at him in tiny little twitches.

"Very well," he said in a very soft voice. "You may answer my questions. If you speak louder than a whisper, I will kill you."

She nodded.

"Did you get what you were looking for?"

She hesitated, and he inched the muzzle closer. "Do not even think about deception," he said with a courteous smile.

Exhaling, slumping her shoulders, she nodded.

"Good," he said. "You will give it to me now."

"I don't have it," she said without any hesitation, which meant she could be telling the truth. "Etchison does."

"That is very bad news," he said. "Because that means I have no need of you. Good-bye, Madame Harrison—"

"Wait!"

Streicher chuckled, but her sudden burst had touched him in an unexpected way. For some reason, the tone or the sound of this woman's voice had reminded him of Nazy, and just the thought of her changed his demeanor in the subtlest of ways. At light speed, questions passed through him—how would Nazy feel if she knew he was going to kill this woman? Did Nazy already know he was a killer? If so, did that mean . . . ?

Stop.

That kind of thinking was getting him nowhere. He had a task at hand, and he could not believe he'd been even the least bit distracted. "What did you get from the facility?"

"A . . . history, and a way to–to understand the messages."

"A key," he said.

She nodded.

"You have it on EM?"

"What?"

"Electronic media," he said harshly.

Blinking recognition, she began to speak when she heard a noise in the hallway beyond the door. Streicher heard it too—sharp, solitary, but not recognizable. Was it the *click!* of a weapon being readied?

"Yes," she said after the slightest pause. "A disk. In that waist pack. Over there."

A tilt of her head indicated a waterproof Waller & Sons belted pouch on the credenza alongside the bed, and he glanced at it for an instant. She'd told him all he needed to know, and he could now dispense with her, but he hesitated. Although there had been nothing to indicate anything amiss since he'd heard that single sound beyond the door, it was enough of a random event to make him reconsider his options.

And terminating this woman might be removing one of them.

With the Sauer 9 mm still aimed at her eye, he spoke in the barest of whispers. "Get it. Give it to me."

She began to move as if under water with a deliberateness almost comical; she gave new meaning to the hackneyed reference to no false moves. Unzipping the pouch, she retrieved a wafer-thin jewelcase with a small disk no larger than the dial of a watch. Then, reversing her movements, she drew as close as necessary to offer it to his free hand. Placing it in his change pocket, Streicher nodded and motioned her to move closer. When she did, he grabbed her by the hair, turned her into him as though practicing a ballroom move, until her back was pressed against his chest, her head tilted back on his shoulder where his weapon nestled her ear.

"Now, together," he said in a voice barely audible. He could feel her trembling. "We will move to the door. You will open it. When I step, you step. Try to get away and you die."

Like a dance couple in rehearsal, they mirrored their steps to the door, which she opened slowly. As the wooden panel swung inward, Streicher smiled as he saw the shape of a man in a shooter's stance revealed as if someone were unveiling a piece of statuary. Streicher recorded details in an eyeblink: tall, lean and muscular, long hair, and weapon—a small chrome .38 caliber.

Then there followed that freeze-frame moment where everyone looked at one another and struggled to grasp what would come next. In the space of an unmeasurably small tick of time, Streicher knew everyone now attempted to reason out their odds of living or dying, of winning or losing, of making the first mistake. Less than a second in their collective lives had passed, but Streicher knew the distention well, and had long ago learned to think and react within its oddly warped dimensions. He could see indecision lingering in the face of his young adversary and that was all he needed.

The other man would blink, quite literally.

Streicher *knew* this, and a calmness settled over him as he waited, all within that fractional slice of time. He need only watch the young man's eyes.

Blink.

Moving the Sauer away from the woman's head with a lightning-snap of his wrist, he fired twice; both slugs whispered across the small, confined space of the hallway, entering the man's forehead. Two dark entry points, like fang marks, appeared and the body tipped backward to the staircase, where it began a rough, noisy slide downward.

Enough noise to create notice in the goon's room. Streicher heard the Seal call out her name. Any moment and he would be opening his door.

Without a word, Streicher dragged her across the landing and down the stairs, past the corpse with a pair of leaking head wounds, to the empty lobby. Above them, the sounds of a door opening cautiously.

No way to tell how many enemies he was facing. No way to properly assess or react. Not his fault. Bad timing was part of his job. Either you learned to deal with it, or you died.

Dragging a hostage was clumsy and dangerous, but the shield effect had saved him already and it could do so again. He hated the anchorlike punishment of maneuvering the woman along on every move, but simply killing her might leave him too vulnerable.

Footsteps on the landing above. The Seal or someone else.

Stepping out into the street, he cut left toward the shadows of an adjacent alley where he had left a stolen Fiat idling. Twenty feet and he could jettison the baggage of the woman.

Ten feet. She was not straining against him, but had gone totally limp, giving up, sensing the death *coup* to come within the next moment.

"Move! Goddamn you!" he whispered as he dragged her to within a few feet of the corner, then adjusted the position of the Sauer for a clean shot through the temple. His hand twisted and—

—exploded in sudden agony!

As if a thick spike had been hammered through his palm, a torch of pain rushed up his arm like napalm.

Too many things happened at once: The woman fell instantly at his feet like a bag of cement, his weapon vanished as it fell from his hand, and he threw himself backward and into the cover of the alley.

His instincts had saved him. Two more slugs stung the leading edge of the alleyway. His right hand sang with agony, as if he'd thrust it into an open furnace. The first shot had dead-centered on his weapon and wrenched it violently from his grasp—good chance of broken or shattered bones, but he couldn't let that stop him. With his left hand he yanked open the door to the little car, and punched the accelerator.

As it leaped down the alley with a spin of tires and loose gravel, the rear window shattered in a spray of safety glass, followed by the windshield. A bullet buzzed past his ear like a blowfly as he neared the open street.

PART
FOUR

TWENTY-SIX

ETCHISON

*H*e wasn't even certain he'd heard something, but that was the most amazing part of his training—even when his mind was confused, there was this autonomic circuitry that made his body react anyway.

One of his superiors called it a *somatic sense* . . . and it was one of those things you could never teach or sharpen. It was simply an ability individuals possessed or they didn't.

Matt had been drifting off to a much-needed sleep and his mind was awash with a maelstrom of images and lines of text from all the information they'd been sponging up. Weird, mixed-up images, facts that now became blended with memories and impression—all the usual pre-sleep hypnogogia everyone experiences in that falling-off-the-cliff instant before we really go under . . . and it was at that exact moment, he heard the *pffftttt! pffftttt!* of what could have been a couple of mouse farts or silenced slugs.

But he hadn't actually *heard* it.

Too drowsy for that, his body had *absorbed* the sound,

processed it for what it might be, and sounded the alarms in the "gray room." Like a night predator, his eyes had locked open, and he was totally awake, alert. No other sound reached him. The walls of the old building breathed a deathly silence into him, and then suddenly, the unmistakable sound of a body collapsing upon an unyielding surface, sliding downward. . . .

He'd lain down in a pair of khakis and T-shirt, but there might not be time to get shoes on. Reaching under his pillow, his hand wrapped around his close-in weapon of choice—a .357 magnum, hollow-point load. He believed he could fire it as quickly as any smaller caliber automatic weapon, with equal accuracy and far more destructive power.

Like a dancer, he glided to the door, spent precious seconds slowly reversing the lock and latch, ready to ease it open while staying *away* from any direct line of fire. The door's thin, wood slatting was a deadly non-shield, and he fully expected it to splinter inward any second.

But it did not.

And he pulled inward on the knob, just enough to allow the slightest sliver of dim light from the landing to seep in. Nothing more than a slip of paper's thickness, but all he needed to see movement or shape.

Nothing.

Okay. No guts, no glory. . . .

Pulling the door fully open, he dropped and rolled, his weapon always trained in front of him, but the area was vacant, quiet. Matt edged to the clearance of the top step, peered over to see the prostrate body of a man halfway down. He sprang to his feet, checked Kate's tiny room through the still-open door.

Not good.

She was probably dead, and he could easily be next. But he had no choice other than to get down there and see what was happening. There was enough blood on the stairs to tell him not to bother checking on the guy he passed. The tangy scent of death in the closed space did not bother him; he'd seen plenty in his time, but he never lost the ability to feel the sting of loss and the hint of what greater mysteries it could hold. It was that single, dark, and impenetrable part of his life that would be his not-life. Unthinkable and yet he was always thinking about it.

As he reached the bottom step, his instincts rightly told him the lobby was clear, but a glance at the tiny registration desk also revealed a telltale, red-black spatter of a headshot across the back wall of the enclosure. Odds were high on it being the desk clerk, not Kate. He quickly made the time-management assessment not to check, but to get outside and see if—

The muzzle-fire of the first shot sounded like a canon as it shredded the total silence preceding it. Matt tilted his ear, tracing its source to a point somewhere to the right of the front door. As he moved in that direction, two more shots, but this time sounding more normal, more expected. Pressing himself against the frame of the door, he kicked it open, dropped and panned his weapon.

To his left, the crumpled figure of a woman who looked much too much like Kate, and a man in black bending over her.

Both of them seemed to be startled by the sound of his appearance. Kate's eyes widened into incredible whiteness as he raised his magnum toward the man and pulled the trigger.

TWENTY-SEVEN

"*Matt, no!*"

She could barely hear her own scream as she tried to stop him. The outrageous concussion of his handgun had been amplified by the closeness of the streets, and the flash from its muzzle filled a single frame of her vision with a star-like brilliance.

As she looked up, Domenic appeared to twist in the air, throwing himself up and across the space where she lay, making an attempt to square his body up with Matt. Then he was violently snatched up and back, so that his full weight was thrown down on her. She saw the black bulk of his body rush downward, and then everything went away. . . .

. . . for a time she could not measure.

When she was blinking again, seeing again, she could only make out the blurry image of something large and round hanging over her. Gradually the circle resolved itself into a ring of faces all looking down in her direction. A variety of expressions ranging from curiosity to concern to disgust. At first, she recognized no one—just the seamed and weathered faces of the islanders, and then she saw Matt Etchison, looming above the circle, then shouldering in between two of them. The sight of him triggered the previous moment, and she remembered Domenic had been killed. . . .

Opening her mouth to cry out, to say *something* (although, still fighting the disorientation, she was not sure what she wanted to say), she felt him put out a hand and gently touch her shoulder.

"Kate," said Matt. "You're all right. Just relax. It's okay, it's okay."

There was the sound of tires braking and scritching along the cobblestoned street as a vehicle arrived out of her line of sight. "Matt—you shot him," she finally got the words out. "What—"

"No," said another voice. Soft. Familiar. "He didn't do a good enough job of it."

The crowd had parted enough to let a second man enter the inner circle. Domenic. "But—!"

"Vest," said Matt, touching his own chest. "I hit him right in the Kevlar."

Domenic reached down to help pull her up to a sitting position. He looked haggard, older than she'd remembered him. An expected thought passed through her— his swarthy Mediterranean features would keep him handsome no matter how old he might grow.

"He should have gone for the head," said Domenic. "Then I wouldn't be here right now."

"How—?" Kate shook her head, trying to clear her mind.

"Told me who he was," said Matt. "And some of the villagers verified it. Seems that your brother-in-law is very well known in these parts—even if only by his first name."

"What about the man . . . the man who—?" she said, slowly standing up. She could see a car from the facility waiting for them beyond the small crowd.

"I couldn't keep up with him," said Matt. "He had a

vehicle; I had to make sure you were okay."

"He is long gone by now," said Domenic. "Helicopter."

Kate looked up at the dark sky. "Can't you . . . I don't know . . . radio ahead to the navy or somebody? Can't they shoot him down?"

"The 'navy' doesn't know about any of this," said Domenic. "Besides, it was a stealth craft—hard to find, even harder to shoot down."

"Who are they?" said Kate.

"We can talk about it back at the facility," said Domenic, who, along with Matt, guided her to the car. "Let's go."

The ride was a short one through the town and back up the hillside to the entrance gate. Dennis Costello met them inside and escorted them to the on-site infirmary to get cleaned up and checked by the company physician. Kate had not been seriously hurt by the intruder, but her face had swollen under some bad bruises and her right elbow and shoulder were slightly sprained when Domenic fell on her. She welcomed the medical attention, especially because it gave her extra time to compose herself.

As she sat on an examination table while a female PA wrapped her elbow with an Ace bandage, she was suddenly hit by the terrible, leaden truth of her husband's death. All over again, as though she'd just heard about it. And her sister Justine. The finality of it crushed down on her, and she felt an ominous sense of loneliness threaten to suffocate her. The sensation had come out of nowhere, and for the first time since everything started her mad, pinwheel journey across the world, she felt sorry for herself. Why not? It was one of those indulgences everyone grabbed for once in a while in their lives, and Kate had not taken the time to do this simple, selfish thing even for a brief moment. And while it didn't feel particularly good or ennobling, she knew it was a necessary part of the grieving process not altogether afforded her. Tears had not been in great supply, because she couldn't allow them, but now they flowed, and she wore them with dignity. By the time Matt came by to accompany her to the next destination, she felt somehow better.

Because Domenic represented the contractors for the massive building, he was well taken care of by Costello's staff even under the most normal of circumstances. The current situation elicited far higher concern and care, and since the nature of Costello's business hinged upon discretion, the project director was not pressuring Domenic to explain what had happened to the trio in any great detail. Costello's attitude was simple—if there was trouble, it could be dealt with.

Eventually he had them taken to an elegant suite of rooms where they could refresh themselves and speak freely. Kate was impressed—the suite was one of the facility's more attractive features to wealthy clients who wished to inspect or utilize the site personally. Stretching out on a leather couch, she tried to get comfortable. Matt Etchison poured Glenlivet over three glasses of ice, and served her and Domenic before taking his own.

They had spent a good couple of hours getting each other fully up to speed on what they had been doing independently, and while Domenic was not happy to hear about the loss of the disc, he was not surprised their adversaries had been able to pull it off. It was during this time that Kate learned to accept the truth about Domenic and his vows to the Knights of Malta, and that secret agency's place on the geopolitical landscape. It was not easy redefining the brother-in-law she always believed was a kind of seminerdy engineer who'd sworn off plastic pocket protectors, but had little hope of ever being considered suave or even the least bit dangerous.

But he was apparently very dangerous and very capable.

Kate was also surprised how correct some of Matt's conclusions had turned out to be. Based on a few observations and assessments, Matt had compiled a surprisingly accurate identity for Domenic Petralli—without being able to pin down his membership in a particular "SOG," as he called them—special operations group.

"But you still haven't explained who these people are," she said after a second scotch had begun to warm her throat. "This 'Guild' . . ."

Domenic exhaled slowly, drew a new breath. "It is not easy to explain them. They began as a loosely structured subculture of craftsman who banded together during the Renaissance to ensure the continuity and power of men like themselves."

Kate could not hide her surprise. "*That* long ago? It seems hard to believe."

"Not really," said Matt. "There are plenty of secret societies in Europe and Asia that are at least as old."

"And then there is always the Knights of Malta," said Domenic with a wry, but deferential nod.

"Yes," said Kate. "I wasn't thinking of the Church. . . . I mean . . ."

"I understand," said Domenic. "It is, I think, especially hard for Americans to truly accept institutions older than their own country. And I don't mean that as an insult or anything like that."

"Yeah," said Matt. "I've seen plenty of evidence of that. Really notice it when you travel with people who've never been out of the country."

Kate cleared her throat. "We're getting off track," she said. "You were talking about the Guild."

"Right," said Domenic. "A very interesting case. Having been . . . well, let's call them *participant-observers* . . . in the mercantile process for centuries afforded them a certain leverage, *and* a very specialized vantage point for studying how cultures preserve themselves—a true insider's view. Not only were they present at the inception of the industrial revolution, but I would bet they were probably the first organized group to fully comprehend what it was."

"Okay, I follow you," said Kate. "So they continued to arm themselves with information and tried to keep organized through all the wars and changes of power throughout the centuries and continents, right?"

"Yes, and you have to figure it was probably a very hard thing to do," said Domenic.

Matt sipped on his whisky and nodded. "Sure it was, but I'd bet they had it easier than most other groups trying to preserve themselves."

"Why?" said Kate.

"Because the basis of their survival was one of the single most important and universal items in civilization—" Matt tapped his pocket. "Money."

"That's right," said Domenic. "Trade. Commerce. Other than religion, it was one of the only things that transcended national borders. Other than food, it was the only other item that everyone needed to survive. The early leaders and organizers of the Guild understood this simple truth very, very well. Money not only became the glue that bound them together, but it became their most potent weapon as well."

"I see where you're going with this," said Kate. "But it still must have been really hard for them to survive. I can't even imagine how many rulers and kings and emperors we're talking about, but it has to be a ridiculous number."

"That is true," said Domenic. "But one fact is irrefutable—the Guild survived. Not only did it survive, but it prospered, for a very closely related reason. All those kings and emperors, and everybody else looking to conquer everybody else . . . well, they all needed two things: weapons and financing for their campaigns."

"And the Guild filled these needs?" said Matt. "How?"

"Don't forget," said Domenic, "where the original

members of the Guild came from—not only tradesmen and bankers but also *craftsmen*. As time went on the Guild became manufacturers, or even better, the controlling interest *behind* the manufacturers. The great European and Asian families of arms merchants that rose up in the eighteenth century were all started with Guild investment capital."

Matt went back to the bar and poured another scotch for himself. "That makes sense. These guys had to be amazing opportunists."

"They were," said Domenic. "And eventually the families and their businesses and their inventories became absorbed into the greater body of the Guild itself."

"These guys sound very scary," said Matt. "Because they can show up anywhere and look like anybody else trying to make a buck."

"They *are* scary, Matthew, and you've hit on one of their greatest strengths—they can be totally invisible most of the time, and no one can even suspect the manipulations they are exacting upon the world. And during the twentieth century, with the explosion of technology, the Guild has become even more powerful and less visible."

"You make it sound like they run the show," said Matt.

"In many ways, they *do*." Domenic tossed back the remainder of his glass. "They have learned how to make wars happen and make them stop; how to control the flow of money and credit and resources throughout the civilized world."

"These guys have been around a long time," said Matt. "From what you're saying, longer than any current national entities, right?"

"Yes," said Domenic. "That's definitely a legitimate view."

"So . . ." said Matt. "Nations, governments, sovereign territories, whatever you want to call them, are what?— necessary inconveniences to them?"

"Yes, the Guild is 'supranational,' if you will." Domenic stood up and walked to the bar for another drink as well. "They operate outside the bounds of national borders, and represent no official charter, constitution, or political agenda."

"Other than *control*," said Kate. "Apparently, they like being in charge of things."

Domenic shrugged, grinned ironically. "Who wouldn't?"

"So is there any way to stop them? You make it sound *hopeless*," said Kate. "This is giving me a headache just thinking about it."

Domenic smiled. "Because you are thinking in terms of 'stopping' them almost guarantees you never will."

Matt chuckled. "That sounds so very *Zen*, Signore."

Domenic shrugged. "Sorry, but in this case, it applies. You don't 'stop' the Guild as much as you go against the flow of its influences and *redirect* it."

"And this is successful?" said Kate, who felt at times like a medieval philosopher as she followed the conversation. Angels dancing on the heads of pins seemed far more sensible. The concept of an organization so vast and so old went against conventional wisdom, and was hard to accept. "What good does it do? And who is doing the 'redirecting'?"

Domenic looked at her, sipped from his glass. "The Knights of Malta are not alone in their efforts."

"What do you mean—governments?" said Kate.

"Well, yes, but you have to understand that there are those in governments throughout the world who often 'turn their heads' at some Guild interventions or manipulations. They do this because they may be in partial synch with Guild objectives."

"That seems unavoidable," said Matt. "There are other organizations that go beyond national borders—the Unilateral Committee, the Cambridge Club, the Consortium for Global Unity—and I'm sure there's more of them."

"Yes, there are," said Domenic. "But there are also

more groups like the KOM—not all affiliated with the One True Church, but with other well-established and powerful faiths. Islam, needless to say, is a hotbed of cabals, secret sects, and rogue entities. The Jews, Hindus, and Buddhists all have equivalent agencies at work."

Kate shook her head. "This is getting too complicated, too insane."

"It is necessary that you understand who your enemies are."

She let Domenic's last sentence sink into her thoughts. There was much sense in what he said, but there was something implied, something unspoken still bothering her. "Wait a minute," she said. "You're forgetting one important thing—important to *me*, anyway."

"What's that?" said Matt.

Domenic simply looked at her, waiting.

"I'm not sure. . . ." said Kate. "They've gotten all they could want from me—unless they want me dead—but they sound way too pragmatic for that."

"That's true," said Matt. "Killing you now gets them nothing."

"And you are saying what, now, Kate?" said Domenic. "That the Guild is no longer your enemy?"

She paused as she looked at her brother-in-law, the man who was married to her sister and who had lived a double life for as long as she had known him. Up until this moment, Kate had tried to keep that awareness at arm's length, but she was getting strong enough to face it, to deal with it now. And what did it really mean? She thought back over the years of all the family events he'd attended, all the backyard barbecues, the Super Bowl parties, the Thanksgiving and Christmas dinners, the baptisms and funerals and weddings, and everything else, and it was all a sham, all a deception. Here he was talking and drinking with her and part of him was a total stranger to her, to her sister. What kind of a man was he? What kind of person could live such a separate existence and never even tell his wife? And on top of everything, his double life becomes the reason for his wife's murder, the reason Kate's life had been ripped inside out. She was angry, but not really sure who should be the target of her anger. She didn't know what to think anymore. Was it this "Guild"—were they truly responsible for the chaos in her life—or was it Domenic?

He walked closer to her, his gaze never wavering. His hair was long and damp; he needed a shave, which emphasized the angularity of his face. He appeared concerned, saddened. When he put his hand on her shoulder, she controlled an impulse to pull away, but another part of her was not at all surprised at the reaction.

"It's okay to blame me," he said. "Are you wondering who your *real* enemy might now be?"

"How do you know I'm blaming you?"

He shrugged. "I would probably do the same."

"Domenic, I don't know what I should think. I'm not sure how I feel. I don't know what to do next. . . ."

"I understand," he said. "But we all must move forward with our lives, our destinies. I must not relent. I have to tell you that I am in this for the rest of my life."

"Domenic, what are you asking me—whether I want to *stay* in this insane chase?"

"Is that what I'm doing? I thought I was trying to see how you feel. I would never ask you to continue. You are correct about being out of the loop now."

"I–I think I want *out*. I want to go home, but I don't know what's waiting for me there. My life back there—it seems so small, so silly, after all I've seen, all I've done. I don't know what I want to do."

Matt Etchison looked at her, but remained silent. He must have figured this was a good time to be listening carefully, taking mental notes.

"I do not have much time," said Domenic. "The trail of the Guild 'op' will not stay warm very long."

"You have to go after him," said Kate. It was not a question.

"Yes, of course." Domenic appeared apprehensive. "Not only because we need to retrieve the glass, but also because they do not often expose themselves as they did tonight. This is a rare opportunity to track them, to possibly penetrate the Guild."

"Kate, it's up to you, now." said Matt. "You're calling our shots."

She looked at Matt, trying to figure out what he really meant. "I know that," she said. He was an ex-Seal and he'd been trained for the kind of job Domenic would begin. She'd be shocked if he didn't want to be part of whatever was to come. "I know what you're trying to say," she said. "Both of you."

"My job is not done, Kate," said Domenic. "And I feel like I let you down, in many ways. But you owe me nothing."

"He's right," said Matt. "But I have to be honest with you—I'm not sure I can just walk away from this situation now. I mean—knowing what we know about the glass and the prophecies and this 'Guild,' I'm not so sure we want them to have it."

"You *know* we don't," said Kate. "They're amoral killers."

Domenic checked his watch. He had been acting more and more anxious with each passing moment until now. "If you could excuse me, I have to contact Corsica—it's time for me to get an updated briefing."

Kate watched him gently place his empty glass on the wet bar and walk quietly from the room. Looking at Matt, she couldn't read his expression. "Do I sound like a whiny baby?"

"Not at all. You sound like somebody who's had enough, that's all."

"But I feel guilty. I feel like I'm letting Domenic down because I feel like this. And I don't think I could ever forgive myself if he goes and gets himself killed, while I'm heading back to the Boston social set. Besides, am I so silly to think this . . . this Guild would *let* me walk away? I mean I know about them. I know they exist. Would they let me live knowing that kind of stuff?"

"Good question. I doubt it."

"Yes, but it's Domenic my thoughts keep going back to."

"You didn't take any vows in a secret society." Matt walked to the bar, left his glass on the counter, unrefilled. "You didn't ask him and your sister to involve you in this mess."

"I know that," she said. "But maybe God did."

Matt looked at her as though he might grin, then thought better of it. "I didn't know you were that religious."

"Maybe I didn't know it either. But there doesn't seem to be any doubt that this artifact has some kind of miraculous power about it," she said. "I mean, there are people who believe in it enough to *kill* to get it, so I'm thinking maybe I should be paying attention. Like maybe, this is one of those ways God tests us."

"Yeah," said Matt. "I've thought about that myself. Why else would God let things like this happen? You know that old argument about why any truly loving God would let something like the Holocaust happen?"

"Maybe it's like Teilhard said—God doesn't run us around like puppets; he breathed life into us and gave us free will, and now he is waiting and watching to see what we will make of it all."

"Okay, and what—now you feel a . . . a calling? Do you think you're being asked to take a stand?"

Kate paused as she considered her answer. Matt had verbally expressed the question and the concept that had been lingering behind all her thoughts lately. She kept wondering what her purpose was, what her role in the greater scheme of events might really be. Although tempted to cling to her day-to-day existentialist outlook, she knew in some deeper place in her heart and mind it would not support her, would not sustain her. She had been forced to endure terrors and outrages she would have never imagined possible, and had indeed survived with her psyche fairly intact. She believed she was the stronger for the experience and had to admit to herself she now knew she was a tougher, more resourceful, and more resilient person than she'd realized. There was a part of her—a part that clung to her time as a young girl when innocence was still in vogue and she believed in the goodness of God—that welcomed the challenge to her lapsed faith. Especially now, when she would be entering a phase of her life where she was essentially *alone*, she realized she needed something to give her strength, to help her carry on without Lawrence and without Justine.

"Take a stand?" she said. "No, I'm not sure it's that simple, Matt. But I'm getting the distinct impression that if I leave now, I will be doing some kind of grave harm to myself. Not physically, of course, but emotionally and spiritually."

"I think I understand. Believe it or not, I am a fierce patriot. In the past, I used those convictions to help me do some of the things I needed to do. It's always been a source of strength for me—like a reserve tank that's never empty. It's something everybody needs, and few of us get it." He paused, seemed to stand a little straighter as he faced her, as if she deserved his respect and attention. "And I think you know that, Kate . . . because I think this whole thing has reached places in you that . . . well, nothing else has ever reached."

She smiled gently. "Matt, you have an odd way with words, but I think you're right. I think you helped me see what's going on inside. I can't call for plane tickets home. I know you want to see this thing through now, and I do too."

"I had a feeling you did."

"But there is one small issue that's really been bothering me."

"What's that?"

"Well, I've been doing all this soul-searching about what to do now, and whether or not all this really Means Something in my life, but . . . when I think about it, I'm really not needed here anymore."

"Hey, come on, now—"

"No, I'm not saying this to get rah-rah votes."

"I know that," said Matt, as he noticed Domenic reenter the room.

"Face it, Matt—you and Domenic don't need me stumbling along while you chase down the bad guys. I'll just get in the way. I don't bring anything to the table."

Domenic looked at her as if meeting her for the first time. "You underestimate your value, sister-in-law."

"What do you mean?" she said.

"For one thing, we may need you to do something with that data disc—when we catch up with it. I don't know—verify it, upload it, encrypt it . . . who knows? I just don't want to go following the perp and the disc into some hi-tech scenario that's over my head. We might need you for the unexpected snafu."

"True," said Matt. "We have no idea what we're up against."

"I'm not kidding," said Domenic.

Matt Etchison looked at her, then shook his head softly. "Kate, this isn't really about that kind of stuff. And I think Domenic feels the same way. He believes you are a larger part of this thing—divine or mundane, I don't think that matters. I don't think I'd be misrepresenting Domenic if I said he wants you to be a part of what happens for one reason—you deserve it."

"You mean I've earned my 'stripes'?" Kate said around a small smile.

"Yeah, I guess you could say that."

She looked at him for a moment, and realized he was more than a hired gun. Matt Etchison had become a friend at a time when she hadn't even realized she needed one. "Thank you," she said. "Now, let's get back to work."

TWENTY-EIGHT

STREICHER

*H*is flight back to Bizerte was uneventful.

The Nightbird's terrain-tracking radar skimmed the aircraft across the Mediterranean far below the detection ceilings of all but the most sophisticated systems—and they would have to be deliberately scanning for him. There was the possibility his escape had somehow been routed to the Americans with their OTS (orbit to surface) satellite weapons, but his flight was too short for them to detect, track, target, and intercept. He would be on the ground and the engines cooling before all of that could happen. Besides, the Americans would require verification and an awfully good reason to take him out—without the risk of compromising a defense system they believed was as "black" and Top Secret as they can be.

Streicher grinned as he considered his odds. No sense worrying about them. If they targeted him, there was nothing he could do about it. Death would be instantaneous and he would never know it had happened. Hence, don't even think about it.

But he *was* thinking about how close he'd come to failing the mission.

Never before . . .

The phrase kept reappearing in his mind, prefacing his thoughts as he replayed the entire sequence of events. It was an unavoidable habit, in which he checked himself and made notes on how an operation could be improved. There was always room for improvement, but . . .

Never before had he come so close to blowing it, to getting caught, to being *killed*.

In fact, his left hand had remained totally numb and useless until after he reached the chopper and taken off. As feeling and sense grudgingly returned to the shocked nerves, he felt intense waves of needlelike pain, which further reminded him of how close he'd come to total mission failure.

Failure.

The word had never been a consideration, an option. But . . .

Never before had he flirted with the fear he might be getting beyond the edge of proficiency.

Never before did he consider it might be true.

When he thought about how clumsily he'd handled the situation, he felt embarrassed, and was thankful it had been a solo. If his colleagues ever discovered how badly he'd performed, his stature among the fraternity of operatives would be tarnished beyond recovery.

Using the Harrison woman as a *shield*!

Streicher laughed aloud in self-mortification, and the sound echoed within the cockpit, emphasized by the whispery quietude of the chopper's specially baffled engines.

Never before had it been necessary to hide behind a skirt to save his incompetent hide.

Although there might be a reason, totally unconscious, why he might be more vulnerable, why he may have become cautious to the point of what he would have earlier consiered cowardice ... in one word: Nazy. *Could that be it? Does my mind not realize what my heart already knows? That I have something more important to live for?*

An interesting possibility, he admitted, but he could not use it as an excuse for the way he'd handled the mission.

And he'd left the job half-undone. By not removing the personnel, he left himself open for identification and possible targeting somewhere in the future. Granted, it remained remote, but even leaving a chance of the possibility was a grievous error—the mark of a bumbling *amateur*.

The last word hung in his mind like a repellent odor.

But how could he have imagined Petralli would take that shot? As all trained agents know, Petralli was certainly aware of the danger of making the far simpler head shot. In many instances, even though the brain was being destroyed, the autonomic nervous system will still react with a signal for the muscles to contract—causing, among other things, a finger on a trigger to squeeze down, creating a final discharge. Despite what heroes were expected to do in silly films, there were only a handful of people in the world good enough to make a surgical gunshot like that. And Petralli had been one of them.

The single *plus* to the evening's adventure had been its essential success—he had gotten the translation key.

After touching down at the Khazar plant's hangar, then a quick shower and change of clothes, he met the driver assigned to take him to Tunis-Carthage where he boarded a commercial flight for Charles de Gaulle International. He hated the countries of northern Africa and could not wait to be free of a place so hot, and so unrelievedly filthy. The data disc, wafer-thin and practically weightless, lay in the breast pocket of his lightly starched Brioni shirt, and that is where it would remain until he gave it to Shahrnaz Safavi-Martin.

But, and he smiled at the thought, there was something else he must give her first. . . .

TWENTY-NINE

*H*e'd just finished a debriefing with Sforza on the latest fiasco. There was no sense in worrying about electronic surveillance any longer. The Guild had collected the final piece of the puzzle. Sforza had left him on standby while Corsica technicians attempted to track the black chopper path away from Marettimo.

Domenic waited in front of a blank screen that might have blazed into life at any moment . . . and let his thoughts off their leash during the interim.

Although he was pleased to have Etchison and Kate onboard, he was greatly troubled by Matteo's death and the compromise of the translation key. At some point he would have to go back to Palermo to see Isabella, and it pained him to think of how she would handle the news. Right now, there was no time to deal with anything but the most urgent of business, and he had no idea whether or not Isabella would even be told why Matteo had never returned from a night when he'd suddenly vanished with his trouble-making friend, Domenic.

As he grew ever older, Domenic became less and less capable of dealing with death's many dimensions. He'd been involved with the death game for so many years now, and he feared it was catching up with him. As he sat in the privacy of a communications suite designed for clients visiting the facility, staring at the still-blank monitor, he found himself recalling the faces of so many he'd either killed or seen die—adversaries and friends alike. Their gray features planed and whirled and coalesced into a terrible, gray *absence*—as if all that dying had created this weird void, this vacuum, into which he would be absorbed. The effect was both numbing and horrifying and he fought to regain some control of his thoughts. He would rather feel the stinging sense of loss of a friend in Matteo, and the anchoring weight of guilt and blame in causing his death. He would rather twist and writhe in the prison of such self-torture than confront the black-hole nothingness of all those collective deaths. There was something about pulling them all together, creating a gestalt of such proportion, that seemed waiting to consume him, and he simply could not face such a Grendel right now.

Maybe not ever again.

As he tried to get comfortable with that notion, the screen blinked and Sforza appeared again.

"We called in some favors to the Americans," said his superior. "The aircraft settled in Bizerte, which is no surprise. Lots of covert materiel gets stashed in those camel junctions. They've caught a pretty good image of your man off one of their satellites."

"Which means what to me?" asked Domenic. Glancing at his watch, he realized time was becoming critical, and he hoped this conversation was leading somewhere important.

"It means several things—one, we should have a real identity to hang on this guy. If he's a known entity in anybody's database, it's going to help finding out where he operates. Two, if the Americans are as good as they claim to be at hacking into other systems, then we will soon have every airport camera at every terminal in Europe, Asia, and Africa scanning for the right face. If he's moving with the herds, we have a chance of seeing him."

"I thought it was policy to not bring other governments into the mix."

Sforza nodded. "Usually, yes, but this is a special circumstance. We can't rely on chance or our regular channels of espionage. We can't just sit on our hands and hope our man is dumb enough to give himself away."

"Hard to tell how dumb he is," said Domenic. "I almost brought him down because he was either incredibly bold or just stupid."

"How much do the Americans know?"

Sforza shrugged. "They're on need-to-know, of course. We told them one of the Vatican's most revered relics has been stolen and we suspect some sort of geopolitical ransom plot is unfolding."

Domenic chuckled. "Did they buy it?"

"The Americans are funny like that. Sometimes I get the feeling they don't care what the details actually might be. As long as they get a chance to test out their latest toys under what they like to call 'game conditions,' they're happy."

Domenic agreed. The Americans were great allies when they believed they were 'doing the right thing,' but they were far more interested in proving how smart and competent they were. If a dramatic confirmation of their abilities allowed them to help somebody along the way, well, that was fine; but their first priority was always to make themselves feel good about themselves. Very American trait, and probably not all that bad of one, when you thought about it.

"Okay," he said. "So we will eventually find out *who* this guy is, but we have other issues."

Sforza grinned without humor. "If there are any new messages in the glass, they will now be able to read them. I know that, Domenic."

"That's not what I meant—even if we *do* track our spook, how do we know if he will lead us to the Eyes?"

"There are no guarantees, but we are all desperate men, now. We have to pursue whatever avenue opens for us."

"Agreed. Any idea when we'll get our first report from our friends in red-white-and-blue?"

"The scans have been ongoing since the Guild's man left the island. We will be updated at regular intervals. In the meantime, get some sleep, but presume you are standing by. You may have to move at any time."

"Are you getting me resupplied?" said Domenic. "And what about transport?"

"It's being taken care of. Within the hour, we'll have a chopper at the heliport. The pilot will be on your command."

"Good," he said. The infrastructure of his Order had always been so precise, so dependable. He felt immediately guilty for even checking on their preparations. But he was not feeling as confident, as strong as he usually did—too many defeats could do that to you. After an awkward silence, he added: "By the way, I want to thank you for your patience with me. I know I have not been very 'productive' lately."

Sforza paused, and even though much nuance was lost through the resolution of the monitors, Domenic could read the understanding in the man's features. "I have known you a long time. You have done nothing to tell me you do not remain the best man we have in the field."

"We cannot withstand more failures. Our stature in the Vatican has surely been diminished," said Domenic.

Sforza grinned. "Perhaps, but I would not worry about that. They have no place else to go. They are—how do you say it?—'stuck' with us, yes?"

"Yes, I guess they are. Thank you," said Domenic.

"Pray for strength. God in His wisdom is constantly *testing* His faithful. We know this is yet another of those times."

Domenic nodded and signed off. He should give Kate and Etchison an update, but his instincts told him to wait until he had something concrete to go on. After he'd heard what she'd been through, there was little percentage in telling her he had nothing to tell her.

Speaking with his superior had fortified him psychologically, but he felt guilty because he had not been totally open with him. It was an unspoken assumption that any pursuit of the Guild's man would be performed solo; the subject of possible accompaniment had never even been broached. And Domenic had not wanted to tell Sforza that Etchison and Kate were planning to be included in any new developments—he didn't want to be turned down.

And now he felt terribly guilty. He was dissembling, and it troubled him.

Depending on what kind of information they picked up, he would have to decide whether or not to ultimately tell Corsica his intentions. There was an added complication: Even though Sforza still believed in his abilities, Domenic was not so certain. He knew he not only wanted Kate and Etchison to go with him—he needed them.

THIRTY

Paris

STREICHER

*N*azy was waiting for him at the international terminal's lounge. As he passed through customs, Streicher could see her standing beyond the glass windows, waving at him. The line moved slowly, an indication there was an officious, and probably new, employee making it his business to delay as many travelers as possible. Streicher carried no luggage other than a notebook computer, window dressing for his cover as a continent-hopping pitchman for a corporate international sales team. He expected no problems passing through even the toughest scrutiny because the Guild's tentacles reached deeply into even the most recondite places.

His only real concern, however, was time.

The more *time* he spent in the open gave his enemies an equal amount of it to ID him. With technology what it was, one could never be sure he was not doing something to compromise himself. Standing in a customs line was one of those places where you were afforded the cover of the anonymous queue, but also the vulnerability of having no actual place to hide.

And it was certainly not a situation in which you could allow yourself to look uncomfortable, and therefore suspicious.

It was okay to look impatient, and he did, until he was finally moved past the French inspector with only a cursory interest in the notebook computer. As he passed through the final gate, Nazy moved up to take him into her arms. She moved with such grace, it was as if she were gliding an inch above the carpeting. This woman was unique. In all his years of knowing hundreds of females, he had never seen one move like her, speak like her, project such an aura of confidence and basic sensuality. Her tailored suit was just tight enough to display her finely toned and exquisitely proportioned body, but loose enough to never be vulgar. Her hair and her makeup were also created to suggest passion just barely under control. She looked exciting without crossing over the edge to be brassy or cheap.

"Did you have a successful trip, my sweet one?" she said.

"Very," he said, kissing her with the discretion necessary for a public place.

"And your client—did he give you want you needed?"

"Actually," said Streicher with a sardonic smile. "My client was a she, and yes, she gave me exactly what we have been looking for."

"Were the negotiations difficult?"

Streicher paused for an instant before replying. Her questions were pointed, yet veiled. It was as though she completely knew what he'd really done to get the translation key, and was only toying with him. But that was totally impossible, and he couldn't allow himself to think that way. Their conversations had often led them into places where she could have asked him for details of his work, and she'd always backed off. In fact, he had not actually told her the objective of his trip, and it was not likely she knew what he'd been after. It had always been presumed her need-to-know status at the Guild installation would provide her with enough information to do her job, but also give her plenty of areas in which to speculate. She'd said things in the past (and so had he) to indicate that he was a powerful man within the Guild's hierarchy, and therefore a dangerous one. Rumors were popular grist in any organization, and she'd once confided to him that others at the Paris installation thought he might be some kind of corporate spy. Streicher could live with that.

"The negotiations were . . . not easy," he said with a smile that could only be called charming. "But as you know, I can be very persuasive."

Nazy giggled in that manner which beguiled him with its hint of playful sensuality. "Well, sir," she said, "do you think you could persuade me to accompany you to your hotel room?"

"Most definitely," he said.

Hours later, after an agenda of outrageous sexual antics, showers, perfumings, and changes of clothes, he sat with her in the hotel restaurant. They sipped on Veuve Clichot and spoke very little, acting as lovers often do when all that's needed is to bask in the afterglow of consummate pleasure.

Streicher looked at her dark features, especially her huge, almond-shaped eyes, and wished he did not have to initiate shoptalk, but he did.

"We must go to your lab tonight."

"What?!" Nazy chuckled, convinced he was joking.

"No, I am serious."

"Kurt Loren," she said softly. She was the only person in the world who addressed him in that way, and somehow, he found himself liking it. "What do you have in mind?"

He cleared his throat, sat up a bit straighter. "Not what

you think, my vixen. I have delayed the inevitable long enough."

"What are you talking about?" She leaned closer, and tilted her head in mock conspiracy.

"I have the translation key."

Her expression suddenly changed from playfulness to professional concern. "You are not joking."

"No."

"How did you—?"

"I will give you the details some other time. Let's go to the lab."

She was already reaching for her purse and pushing back from the table. He had piqued her curiosity and spurred her professional side. "You have found your own personal Rosetta stone!" she said with great excitement and pride.

"Yes, I suppose I did." He offered his arm in escort and they exited the dining room to the grand lobby where he informed the concierge he would be requiring a car.

When they had entered the taxi and were finally en route, she spoke again, barely containing her energy. "What does it look like? Another artifact?"

"No," he said. "It is digital."

Nodding, she looked at him. "So it has been processed previously by others."

"Yes, I suppose it has, why?"

Nazy looked at him as if explaining something elementary to a child. "Because it may have its own proprietary formatting, or it could itself be encrypted. Did they tell you?"

Streicher felt a sudden pang of anxiety spike through his mind. *What?! No!* "They?" he said distractedly. "*Who?*"

"The people who gave it to you," she said with some impatience. "Didn't they tell you?"

"I—I didn't think to ask," he said. *Goddamn!* There had better be no foul-ups with this one! He had purposely not yet reported in to Kerschow and Beauvais, and therefore, the mission was not officially completed. They would most certainly know by now that he'd been checked through Bizerte and Paris, but they would have no way of knowing details until he decided it was the proper moment to provide them. A full accounting was yet to be made, and if there were contingencies to be dealt with—such as formatting or *more* encryption, he could simply include the tasks in his final debriefing.

"May I see it?" she said.

Nodding, he reached into his shirt pocket and produced the thin plastic case through which the data disc was visible. Handing it to her, he said: "You can't tell anything from just looking at it, can you?"

She looked reproachful. "Please! You make me sound like a lounge act, a stage magician. Of course not. I just wanted to see it. That makes it more real, don't you see?"

"I suppose," he said absently as he looked out the side window of the cab where the crowded streets of the city slipped past in blurry streams of light. They would soon be in the neighborhood of the cobbler's shop and the entrance to the installation.

Nazy held up the disc so that it reflected the lights of the city and cast them back in spectral colors. "The human mind created this—It is so beautiful, isn't it?"

"Yes," he said without much attention. He was hoping there would be no more roadblocks, no more obstacles.

The taxi was pulling over to the curb. Through the glass, he could see the darkened windows of the cobbler shop.

Soon, he thought.

After enduring the various stages of security to actually enter the installation, Streicher was finally standing at the door to Nazy's lab. The corridors were practically empty at this late hour, but the few staffers who chanced upon them knew better than to address their presence at the lab. Even though he and Nazy were dressed in evening attire, their business at the installation would not be questioned.

He felt like a helpless child as he followed her into the lab. Now they had entered a world beyond his ken, and he felt immediate resentment as he watched her grow more comfortable, more confident as she floated through her natural environment. Such feelings embarrassed him because he knew it was silly and childish and indicative of his incessant need to be in total control all the time. His rational side knew there was nothing wrong with an occasional relinquishment of responsibility and capability to someone more suited for it. Just because that someone was a woman with whom he might be falling in love . . . well, it should not make any difference.

But somehow it did.

He stood beside her as she sat before her workstation, placed the data disc in a reader, and began to analyze it. Almost immediately, she paused to look over at him. "No encryption," she said. "That's good."

It was like he'd begun breathing again for the first time in a long, long time. "I expected as much," he said. Lying never bothered him before. Now the words threatened to lodge themselves in his throat.

Nazy returned to the console, keying and mousing through various levels of her operating system and applications. She chuckled softly to herself, then looked up again. "This is so simple really," she said. "The best ones always are."

"Best whats?"

"Substitutions and formats," she said. "We weren't dealing as much with a real code as another language, another communication system. When you look at language like that, everything becomes a series of patterns and rules."

"What does it say?" he said impatiently.

"Kurt, please!" she said, her dark eyes flashed and her gaze bore into him for an instant before returning to her work. "We're not there yet. I am still setting up the key. The entire pattern must be reformatted and what is called an overlay is being created. Even though we are doing it digitally, it does not happen instantaneously!"

"Excuse me for being so impertinent," he said without humor. He hated the sensation of being so helpless. Just standing there, looking at her work.

"Not much longer, really." Nazy turned away as her equipment chirped on without her. "The whole thing is what a mathematician might call 'elegant,' but not in a fashion sense. More of an architectural one."

"I understand," he said. "How much longer?"

She looked at him and shook her head. "Just about now. Here look—this is original text we scanned off the glass. See?"

"Okay . . ."

"Now," she said, pointing and clicking at various points on the monitor, "this will begin the integration and substitution."

The screen morphed through several configurations for an instant and then new text appeared.

"There it is! It works!" said Nazy as she began to read.

Leaning over her shoulder, Streicher joined her. As the meaning of the words sank in, he felt suddenly hollow, weightless, as if he might faint.

"*Oh my God!*" he heard Nazy say in a whisper that was one part reverence and another shock.

THIRTY-ONE

Kate was not accustomed to drinking scotch straight, even if it was Glenlivet.

"I can't!" she said, holding up her hand when Matt moved to refill her glass. "I need to be lucid in case Domenic has to tell us something important."

"I thought you've been very 'lucid'," said Matt, who allowed himself several more fingers of the pale, gold liquid.

"Thank you," she said. "I've always prided myself in being able to think clearly. I always thought I was one of those know-it-alls, ever since I was a kid. But this whole adventure has shown what a fool I've been."

"Not a fool," he said. "If there's anything I've learned, it's that there's always a *bigger* picture. Just when you think you have things figured out, you realize you don't. No big deal. It's just the way life is—if you're paying attention."

"You're always thinking positively," she said. "How do you do it?"

He shrugged, sipped on the scotch. "I don't know. It's

personality to some extent. Plus I think I had a good grounding as a kid. My mother was an Irish Catholic from Boston—that's a surprise, eh?—and she sent me to St. Ignatius, a Jesuit high school where we had to wear jackets and ties, and took subjects like Latin and Greek and philosophy along with all the regular stuff like chemistry, physics, calculus, Russian . . . you know, all the 'cake' courses."

Kate chuckled, but wasn't surprised. Matt's overall demeanor hadn't sprung into being when he joined the Seals. There had to have been a good foundation, and she was beginning to see the evidence as he opened up a little. "My father used to call them 'Jebbies.' He said they were just about the smartest people in the world."

"The Jesuits? Don't know about that, but they were sharp, I'll give 'em that. They taught me this interesting concept that's kept me together most of my life: *always ask the next question*. Never be satisfied. Always keep looking for more answers. Be curious. Never lose your sense of wonder."

"Sounds like they made quite an impression on you." She placed her empty glass on the table, and leaned back in the leather chair.

"Enough to make me want to go to Notre Dame, which I did on scholarship. Partly from grades and partly because I wasn't such a bad quarterback . . . at least at St. Ignatius. At Notre Dame, they didn't think much of my skills, so I spent most of my time just being a regular student."

"What then? How'd you go from that to being a Seal? And a detective?"

Etchison sighed. "Ah, Christ, Kate . . . that's a long story. Too long."

"Too long . . . or too painful?" She could read his expression enough to know she was on the right track.

"A little of both. I can give you the shorthand version; that's about all I can handle, okay?"

"Only if you want to."

"Back then, we used to play the Naval Academy every year—alternating between here and Annapolis. The games in the East would either be in Baltimore or Philly, and it was always a great trip to follow the team for that game. Parties all weekend in a big city. A good time, trust me."

"I think I can do that," she said with a smile.

"Anyway, in my senior year, we're at the Navy game in Baltimore, and we end up at a party that night with a bunch of midshipmen—mutual friends from both teams and that sort of thing. I meet this girl—I guess you'd call her a woman these days—she was a senior at the Academy, and she was going to be one hell of an officer. Her name was Ashleigh Thompson and she was originally from Detroit. I fell for her in a big way and by the time we were ready to graduate, I decided to join the navy and go to OCS. It was probably a dumb idea, but I did it. Couple years later we got married, had a great couple of years, until an F-4 on a training mission crashed at Norfolk, where we were stationed. The jet took out the air traffic control bunker where Ashleigh was the OD—they never found enough of her body for a burial service. After that, I joined the Seals, and hoped they would send me someplace where I could get myself killed."

"Matt, I am so sorry," she said after a short silence. Her words sounded so hollow, but she couldn't think of anything else to say.

"It was a long time ago. I'm all right with it now." He tossed back the rest of the scotch, wiped his mouth with the back of his hand. It was a hard, careless gesture, meant to cover any emotions he might need to hide.

"And your plan didn't work," she said, trying to get past the awkward moment.

"You mean with the Seals?" He grinned laconically. "Yeah, I turned out to be too tough to kill."

"Well," she said. "I know we haven't had much downtime, but I've been wanting to tell you *thanks* for all you've done for me. I couldn't have gotten through this without you. I would be dead without you, and I just wanted to tell you—you're unbelievably good at what you do."

He nodded, sat on the arm of the sofa. "Can I tell you something?"

"Sure, what?"

"I've never been involved in anything close to what you've dragged me through!"

"You're kidding, right?"

"Not in the least. And I gotta tell you—if I'd known ahead of time what we were going to be facing, I'm not sure I would have signed on."

"Sorry, Mr. Etchison, but I don't believe you."

"Why not?"

"Because if that's true, then we wouldn't be hanging around here now. We'd be on our way back to the States."

Without hesitating, Matt nodded. "True. You've got me there. But if you press me, I'm not sure what the *real* reason is."

"I can relate to that," she said. "I'm not really sure for myself, either."

"I have a feeling, at least for me, that it's got something to do with the religious spin this whole thing has taken. I mean, I don't know about you, but it pretty much took me by complete surprise. A religious relic, or whatever you want to call it, is the *last* thing I would have figured this was all about."

Kate nodded. It was weird to hear him saying things like this. She'd been having similar thoughts herself. "Yes," she said. "Me too."

"So anyway, I haven't been the most religious guy you'd want to meet, and, I don't know, maybe getting to the bottom of this would be a way to . . . I don't know . . . I'm not sure what word I'm looking for here. . . ."

"Validation?" she said. "Proof? Conviction, maybe?"

"Something like that. I'm not sure what I believe

about things like that. Haven't been sure for a long time. But these 'miracle things' kind of make me second-guess myself. I think maybe I owe it to myself to find what's really going on, and what it really means."

"Matt, that makes plenty of sense to me. I don't know why you were having so much trouble getting it out."

"I was having trouble?" He looked genuinely surprised.

"That would be my guess."

He grinned, then looked at the decanter of Glenlivet, and seemed to think about one more.

At the same time, the door to the suite opened and Domenic entered alone. His dark hair was pushed back from his face and his eyes belied how fatigued he must be. "Good evening," he said with a lopsided and forced grin. "I have good news and bad news."

"Does it matter which we get first?" said Kate as she and Matt took seats at the conference table.

"Not really." Domenic moved to join them, sat down with a sheaf of papers he'd been carrying. He pulled a faxfoto out of the mix and passed it to them. "We've been able to get an ID on our man."

"That's him. How'd you do it?" said Kate as Matt studied the angular and very Teutonic face.

Domenic summarized the American assistance. "They intercepted the digital information from the surveillance cameras at Charles de Gaulle International Customs. This guy has been in deep cover for a long time. Kurt Loren Streicher. He was known years ago as a young wolf in the East German *Krieg*, and there is something on him as a teenaged supporter of the Bader-Meinhoff gang. Later on, he became one of Egon Krenz's favorite lackeys. But his work in the Guild has been totally invisible, which means he's been extremely good at it."

"I'd say," said Matt.

"We also have this," said Domenic, producing another faxfoto of a strikingly beautiful woman—dark, athletic, Mediterranean. "Her name is Shahrnaz Safavi-Martin.

She works for a large French consortium of chip designers, laboratory equipment fabricators, and communications software engineers. Her specialty is cryptanalysis and encryption technology. We have an address for her on the Rue des Carmes near the Sorbonne."

"I see lots of pieces falling into place," said Matt. "This woman is somehow associated with Streicher?"

"They appear to be lovers," said Domenic.

Matt nodded. "Okay, so we combine that with her position at a 'consortium,' which I'd bet is owned and operated by the Guild, *and* her expertise in deciphering unknown languages . . . and I'd say we have a home run."

"Yes, but . . ." said Kate. "I'm assuming this is the good news. There must be something going wrong."

"You assume correctly. The bad news is that he and this woman were eventually tracked to a shoe repair shop near Pere LaChaise—on the Rue de Martignac."

Kate looked at him in obvious confusion. "What's so bad about that? Then you know where they are."

Domenic shook his head. "Not really. He entered the shop several hours ago. It was closed. And he hasn't been seen since."

Matt nodded. "So he could have figured out he was being tracked?"

"A possibility. If we follow that reasoning, then he could have broken into any building and slipped out a back entrance. But our sources *assure* us there is no other entrance or exit to the shop."

"Which means he's still in there?" said Kate.

"We hope so. Corsica is presently trying to tap into Parisian databases that may have records of the architecture, building codes, any permits for renovations, reconstruction, or anything else that might give us a larger picture of why that shoe shop is so important to Streicher. It is quite possible the shop is a front, nothing more than a portal. A gate."

"A gate?" said Kate.

"A disguised entrance, right?" said Matt. "They walk into a shoe shop and then what—get in an elevator or a tunnel that takes them somewhere else?"

"It's a possibility." Domenic looked through the rest of the papers absently. "That's a fairly standard method. Corsica is going to put a microscope on that neighborhood and keep us updated."

"How long will that take?" said Matt.

"Hours. Days." Domenic shrugged. "No way to tell."

"Why do I think we're not going to be sitting around here drinking scotch while we wait?" said Kate.

Domenic exhaled slowly. "They are making arrangements," said Domenic. "I am to leave the island within the hour. If you're still serious about—"

"We're serious," said Kate.

Matt nodded. "No guts, no glory, right?"

THIRTY-TWO

Paris

*T*he syntax and vocabulary were clumsy, which Nazy assured him was a characteristic typical of translations of ancient languages, especially obscure dialects complicated by cryptographic interpositions. But the sense of the text reached them with reasonable clarity.

The first two translations were of text Nazy had copied from the glass shortly after its arrival in Paris. The deciphered messages described events from the recent past: a cataclysmic eruption of the Soufriere Hills volcano on Montserrat which destroyed half the population of the island including the towns of Mongo and Fleming; plus the assassination of Valmore Reccared, the first president of the Economic Federation of European States.

Streicher noted the grammar of both notations were written in future tense. This validated Guild intelligence data, which indicated the artifact displayed prophecies or predictions. But it was the third and final inscription which stunned both Streicher and Nazy. . . .

Essentially it stated that before year's end, a small boat would motor into the mouth of the Potomac River carrying a black-market nuclear bomb. It would be detonated by a suicide squad of Middle Eastern terrorists onboard, and the city of Washington would be consumed in an atomic fireball.

No other details. No specific date. No names.

Other than Nazy's initial exclamation, neither of them spoke for several minutes. Even Streicher—who had spent the majority of his life in the center of a global maelstrom of violence, retribution, retaliation, vengeance, subterfuge, sabotage, espionage, and the occasional terrorism—was stunned by the abject *reality* of the message. In the deepest core of his being, he knew this was not parlor trickery or conjecture—this was the real thing: a simple statement of what was to come.

"Can this be possible?" said Nazy, finally breaking the delicate silence which had erected itself around them like a cage. She tried to manufacture a thin smile, but it never really happened.

"Yes, most definitely. It described things that have happened since we delivered the glass to this lab. You had the proof; even though you could not read it."

"Does anyone else know about this?"

Streicher shook his head. "How could they? We just applied the key, didn't we?"

"No," she said. "I mean, what about the people who . . . who 'gave' it to you? Did they get this information as well?"

"I don't think so. Didn't you tell me this last entry appeared after we brought it to you, here at the installation?"

"Yes, but—"

"No 'buts,' Nazy. You know what I am saying—we

are the only ones who have seen this most recent message."

Stepping back from the screen, she glanced at random objects in the lab, but without appearing to notice them. "I feel very strange, Loren. . . . I feel *scared.*"

"What do you mean?"

"It is hard to explain, but I am getting this feeling that I shouldn't be knowing about this, that I'm not worthy? No, maybe that's not the right word . . . not equipped, or *intended* to know it."

"Nazy—"

"No," she said, turning to stare at him. Her eyes appeared wider and deeper than he'd ever seen them. She was extremely serious. "No, I mean it. This is too strange for me."

If possible, she looked even more attractive to him when distressed. Was it a vulnerability in her he'd never seen before? Whatever it might be, he liked it. He reached out, touched her cheek. "Nazy, it is fine. You are just letting it get to—how do you say it?—your 'mystical' side."

Unfazed, her gaze flashed over him, through if she could. "You should pay more attention to things like this."

"Like what?" He smiled.

"Like things which may be of other-than-normal origin," she said slowly, choosing each word with care. "Things of the spirit."

"Yes," he said automatically. "Maybe you are right."

"You do not take me seriously," she said. "But you cannot be thinking about this with enough care. What do we really have here?! There are people who believe these are direct messages from *God!* Doesn't that mean anything to you?"

Streicher looked at her with the warmest of feelings. He didn't wish to do or say anything that would upset her further, or diminish her opinion of him. But he wasn't sure what she wanted him to say.

"I'm not what you'd call a religious man," he said softly.

"But you believe that message is true, don't you? That the city of Washington is going to be destroyed!" She looked terrified by the possibility. "All those millions of people—!"

"Yes . . . yes, I do." He heard himself say the words, but he wasn't sure why they were true. He had *no idea* why he believed in the predictions. "But I should also stress this: I believe I am doing what my superiors want, and I think it is more important to ask if *they* believe the message is true."

"So is that what we're going to do with this? Just give it your bosses and forget about it?" She looked increasingly *more* distressed, if that was possible.

"Well, I . . . I would assume so. That is what they expect, and it is what they pay me to do."

"How do you feel about this information?"

"Nazy, what do you mean—'feel'?"

Putting her hands on her hips, she half-rolled her eyes in frustration. "I mean what do you *think*—is that a better word choice for a *man!*?"

"I think it would be a . . . world-changing event. Nothing would ever be the same," he said. "And I mean far beyond the massive loss of life. Washington is the repository of an incredible amount of *information* on every conceivable subject relating to the security, military strategy, and geopolitical state of the entire country. But more importantly, there are agencies and entities within the city that control and monitor data impinging upon the operations of practically *everything* in the world. The material destroyed by the fireball would be very bad, but the accompanying EMP would be far more devastating to all electronically-stored information within a very large radius. Its loss could bring the world to its knees."

"I hadn't thought it through like that, but you are right—this could be an event to change the world forever. In so many ways, some we probably cannot even imagine." Nazy seemed to be calmer, more focused.

"It would make the terrorist attack on the World Trade Center in New York look like a couple of firecrackers going off. The implications have to be staggering. Far-reaching. It would take a while to think it all through," he said.

She paused, obviously digesting his assessment. "The World Trade Center—I wonder why the glass never warned the world about that?"

Streicher shook his head, looking perplexed. "Hard to comment on that," he said after a moment. "I mean, how do we know they *didn't* know it was going to happen?"

Nazy didn't hesitate. "Who's 'they'?"

"The people who . . . who gave it to us, of course." She looked at him, nodded with enough of a facetious expression to say *yes, I am sure you're telling me everything*.

Neither spoke for a moment, then she said: "Your bosses, do they know you have retrieved the key, meaning you've most likely deciphered the messages?"

He shrugged. "Indirectly, I would imagine that, yes."

"Which means—?"

"They know I checked through Tunisia, that I cleared customs in Paris this evening. They are probably assuming I have been successful." He gestured around the room. "Besides, they've known we were here since the moment we entered the installation. They know whatever they want to know."

"Not everything," she said. "They can't get into my equipment unless I let them. I am an encryption expert. They cannot even understand our conversation—if anyone is listening. Everything in my lab is filtered through a digital security net I designed and keyed."

He shrugged. "You're probably right. But they know we're here, and they know we're up to *something*."

"But you have not contacted them yet?"

"Not yet, no."

"Why not?" She looked at him with a new level of interest.

Nazy was such a smart woman, he had trouble anticipating what she might be thinking.

"I wanted to be with you," he said. "They have waited a long time. They could wait a few more hours."

"Kurt Loren . . . are you sure you didn't want to see what the messages were first—*before* you contacted them?"

Good question, he thought. It was something he must have dealt with unconsciously. "You are probably right. Most likely I did it without thinking about it. Natural curiosity, I guess."

She grinned but without humor. "You may fool *other* people talking like that, but not me—I know you. If you didn't report to them immediately, you did it for your own reasons!"

Streicher laughed softly. He couldn't help it. He wasn't laughing at her—and she sensed that—he was laughing as a child often laughs when caught in a silly lie or in a situation where guilt cannot be hidden. Shahrnaz had exposed him with her trenchant observation and he had no place to hide under its harsh, probing light.

"I am correct," she said with her hands on her hips. "Do not bother admitting it."

He shrugged in assent. "As we all know, knowledge is the ultimate weapon, the only real power. I make it a point to never turn away an opportunity to make myself stronger."

"Do you feel stronger now that you have seen this?" she asked.

"I'm not sure about that, but I did notice something that is making me wonder what all this really means. . . ."

"What do you mean?"

"Think about this—tell me what you think," he said.

"Read the previous message, the prediction about President Reccared. Read it carefully."

"I have read it," she said, "but I am not certain I—"

"The tense," said Streicher. "It says 'will'. It speaks in unequivocal terms that Reccared *will be* assassinated . . . *but it did not happen!*"

"But they tried!" she said. "I remember the attempt was stopped by the Guardia Nationale in Madrid."

She went on to briefly recount the capture and destruction of the death squads from Turkmenistan who had been dispatched to kill Reccared when he spoke at the Federation Parliament.

Streicher listened patiently. "Yes, yes," he said finally. "So do you see what I am trying to say?"

"Of course," said Nazy. "It means the predictions can be *changed.*"

"That is right," he said. "It makes me think that the . . . uh, previous owners of the artifact may very well have used it to alter the outcome of future events."

Neither spoke for a moment. The implications of what Streicher suggested would need to be studied, interpolated, but he was very much aware of the basic meaning to be extracted from the facts.

"My God!" said Nazy. "How many times has the history of the world been changed. Is it possible? What exactly is it we are looking at? What does all this really mean?"

"It means we need more time to understand it. There are things here that do not make sense, and other things that are too obvious. I am just not sure yet what it all means."

"I keep thinking we are in over our heads," said Nazy. "I cannot feel comfortable being the only ones who have this knowledge."

Streicher understood how she could say something like that, but he didn't share her apprehension. Having spent his whole life dealing with sensitive information, he knew he was equipped to shoulder whatever this latest prediction might mean.

"Nazy, we have no choice. The information is ours, and . . ." he added in a very soft voice, "and it will remain so for as long as we choose."

Without thinking, she backed away from him.

"What is wrong?" he said, reading her body language.

Shaking her head slowly, she put her hands to her temples as though suffering a sudden pain. "I don't know. I don't know. This is all too much for me. It is too unreal. And you seem like . . . like it's all right. I think you are more accustomed to this kind of information. Not me. Not me."

"Nazy, I understand how you feel, but I must remain within myself and my training. I have to decide what this means and how to go forward."

"Yes, yes, I know that. I just don't know what to say."

"Can you encrypt this?" he said, gesturing at the screen.

"What—the key, the translation?"

"Everything. Lock it up so only we can get at it?"

"Yes, of course."

"Do it. And make a copy we can take with us."

Nazy spent several minutes taking the necessary measures. He watched, wondering how upset she might really be. Psychological shock was a strange condition—you never knew how it might ultimately affect people. Nazy was such a well-grounded, competent person, he would expect her to get a grasp on what she'd learned and to begin to stabilize herself soon. In fact, Streicher would be surprised if she did not. But, he thought, regardless of how she continued to react to the current situation, he would stand by her. Although until this moment, he had not taken the time to consciously think it through, he had made up his mind to keep this woman close to him *no matter what the circumstances*. She had become an integral part of his life by a means even he could not explain, and he could no longer deny it. Streicher probably realized it fully when he saw her becoming so *troubled* with the information they'd uncovered ... and he felt himself actually *caring* about it.

In the past, very little could ever happen to him to evoke even a suggestion of compassion.

Finally, she turned from the console and looked up as she handed him a small gleaming disc. "Here," she said. "Do what you must with it."

As he accepted the disc and placed it in his shirt pocket, he said: "That will be something we can decide later."

"We?"

He was happy to see she'd grasped for his choice of that particular pronoun. "That is what I said, yes." He looked at his Rolex, then back at her. "It is time to leave this place. Nothing else for us here."

Nazy appeared surprised at his admissions, but said nothing. Carefully, she went about shutting down her equipment before indicating her readiness to depart.

They closed down the lab, exited the installation by retracing their path through the security corridor, sally-port and centuries-old tunnel. When they exited through the cobbler's shop, it was the middle of the night. No one else was on Rue de Martignac, but Streicher could not shake the feeling of being terribly exposed, vulnerable, and perhaps even watched. He guided Nazy to the nearest corner and tried to flag down a taxi.

The lobby of Le Grand was almost as deserted as the streets outside, and the graveyard-shift staff paid them little more than sleepy-eyed notice. It was not until they reached his floor that Streicher allowed himself to feel the absolute fatigue that had been closing in on him like an invisible fist for what seemed like several eternities instead of several days.

Nazy had been silent throughout the taxi ride and the ascent to his room, and he imagined her always-dancing mind moving through all the possibilities and nuances of what he'd shared with her. He also had been turning over his options, and wondered what kind of G-2 his colleagues and superiors had collected and were analyzing on *him* at that very moment. Despite what he'd told Nazy, it was questionable just how much Kerschow and his people might really know. It was quite possible they knew very little—other than the apparent success of his mission, his entry into France, and his stop-off at the installation. He would know more soon enough, but he knew he needed some time to digest what he'd learned and how the information might be used. If the messages were not carved-into-stone prophecies, if they could be altered because of this foreknowledge, then they were doubly valuable. He would have to make an effort to get an investigation started on the possibility that previous events had been somehow intercepted, changed, reversed, or even prevented altogether.

After entering his suite, he and Nazy literally collapsed into the king-sized bed. But unlike previous nights which promised excitement, this one ended in the welcome sleep of exhaustion, in the body and mind's almost immediate release of stress. . . .

. . . which had been so rapid, he had little memory of lying in the bed, of drifting off to sleep. And for that reason, when he felt himself being yanked into wakefulness, Streicher felt complete disorientation. There was a sense of floating off the firm surface of the bed, of being disconnected from the normal channels of sound and vision. He could see that the room was dark, yet it seemed to be giving off its own illumination, like niter on the walls of the blackest cavern. For a moment, he thought he might be suspended somewhere in that region between wakefulness and a trance, but another part of him knew he was awake, this being real.

Beyond the window, a soft rain streaked the glass,

individual droplets refracting moonlight into tiny lamps.
The door to the bedroom suite remained closed, but he
felt that it was somehow open just the same—as though
a threshold to another dimension. And as such, admitted
a vacuum that swallowed up all sound and sense.

He glanced over at Nazy, who lay sprawled in silent
exhaustion, deeply asleep and unmoving, then quickly
back to the door to the suite, which had become . . .
transparent.

Impossible, yes. But he was looking at it under the
clear light of total rational thought. The weapon beneath
his pillow lay untouched because there was a part of him
which must have understood that whatever approached
would be unaffected by such things. Sitting upright,
Streicher stared toward a growing rectangle of light that
had been a door, now incandescent and full of furious,
churning energy.

Throwing back his bedcovers, his feet had almost
touched the carpet when he noticed something. . . .

Something penetrating the burning core that had been
a doorway. He retreated back into the bed like a child
seeking the safety of his blankets and watched a figure
approach. Tall, liquid, still shapeless, but massive. Its
features were obscured by shadow and a curious stretching of perception. It was human, or at least humanoid,
and it moved with the slow grace of a jungle cat, pos-
sessing great strength and confidence.

It glided towards him, then stopped in the center of
the room. Through some trick of perspective, it appeared
farther away than it could be, and it seemed to tower
above him, despite the limits of the ornately paneled
ceiling. An aura swirled round the figure, a borealis, an
emanation, as though the figure drew all the energy from
the room and hurled it back in silent, graceful fury. A
self-contained light, like the heart of a birthing star,
burned inside the figure. No heat, but a light that was
cold and blue and beautiful.

Time stretched, sagged in the middle, and fell away from him.

Motionless. Transfixed like a bug under a pin, Streicher saw the flesh on his arms ripple under the glare of the figure's radiation. From a back room in his subconscious a panel opened and a phrase from his lapsed-Lutheran past drifted free.

This is a *vision*.

And a voice resonated through his skull, compelling, almost hypnotic.

No, it said. The voice was angry, yet calm. Oddly feminine, in that it suggested power usually associated with the masculine nature. Soft, yet terribly loud.

The single word *boomed* throughout the room, and he imagined it must be echoing down the corridors of the hotel. The windowpanes rattled in their frames like rice paper in the wind. How could Nazy sleep through this assault?

An odd detachment held him, as though he were a spectator to events that could not affect him. It was almost like watching a movie, and seeing yourself in the picture, yet sharing in everything the movie-self experienced. The vision held him almost physically. He looked down the length of his body to his feet. He seemed to be floating above the bed, and tilted forward at a bizarre angle. The sensation was giddy and unsettling. He felt as though he would fall forward over his feet, and the temptation to tuck into a roll was almost uncontrollable.

His rational mind had slipped its usual moorings to spin outward. Scenes from his past flickered across a ragged screen hastily thrown up across the back wall of his mind. Bad scenes. Suddenly embarrassing ones. Little snippets that captured his worst qualities: Duplicity. Venality. Disloyalty. Cruelty. Sadism.

His vision distorted and everything stretched away from him, he was suddenly looking across a vast plain, a limitless sea, punctuated only by pieces of his life.

Their peaks bobbed across the surface like warning buoys against far greater evils still below unseen.

Then the perspective changed, like a zoom lens being pulled back. Streicher reeled from the mock vertigo.

He stared at the shape that filled the center of the room, a fragile pearlescent shell that threatened to break apart in an instant of pure light. And then it gradually coalesced, assuming an utterly familiar configuration. Initially, just the outline, the white silhouette of a shape which brought comfort to hundreds of millions, of an image repeated in medals and panels and windows of . . . glass.

Streicher felt as if he were now floating off the bed, totally detached from everything else not just in the room, but the universe itself. He leaned forward, as if anticipating more . . . words or actions. . . .

But there was *nothing* else.

And with no advance indication, the shape vanished— as if a switch had been thrown, canceling its arcane power source.

"*Wait!*"

The sound of his own voice so startled him, his heart double-clutched in his chest, a big diesel truck hitting a hill in the wrong gear. Streicher blinked in the almost total darkness of the room, and tried to reorient himself. He was sitting up in his bed, facing the space between him and the closed door. A filmy layer of old sweat covered him in a pungent glaze.

Although he had no proof, he *knew* he had not been dreaming.

Nazy stirred beside. ". . . what? What did you say?"

"Nothing."

"Who were you talking to?" she said, now awake and up on one elbow, The faintest of window light reflected off her face, and he knew if he could see her clearly enough, the same was true for her of him.

"I . . . didn't say anything. . . ."

"Loren," she whispered, "you look terrible. What happened? You must tell me."

"Nothing!" he said in a low voice that was embarrassingly hoarse. "I saw nothing!"

Nazy looked at him, pausing, processing, thinking as always. Then: "I didn't ask you if you 'saw' anything."

"No, I mean—"

"So, *tell me* what you saw," she said confidently. "It is quite obvious you did, and also obvious it has scared you."

"Just a bad dream . . . a nightmare." He heard his voice crack, and even he could not believe the lie.

He hadn't been dreaming. Something had come to him just now. Something with a purpose. A purpose he clearly did not wish to think about. He'd sensed an intimacy, a closeness that made him more than uncomfortable. Something so powerful, so possibly terrifying none of us would ever want it to know us. Yet that Something *knew* him and appeared *only* to him.

For a reason.

He felt singled out by some incomprehensible power, and it terrified him.

"Kurt Loren," she said, "tell me what happened. Tell me now."

Nazy's words fell into the darkest core of him and burned like incendiary bombs. He *was* trying to deny everything, and the impossibility of it was taking him apart at the seams. Never in his life had he ever felt so shaken, so threatened. And when he searched for the reason for his terror, he realized what it was: He had *no idea* what the vision had been trying to tell him.

And in that moment, he knew he must share what he'd seen and felt with Nazy. In a sense, she was his only hope of making sense of what had just happened.

"Very well," he said, turning to face her. "Listen. . . ."

Thirty-Three

Paris

*W*hile they had been enroute to Paris in a Sky-
Freight cargo jet out of Palermo, Domenic tried
to answer as many questions and fill in as many blanks
as he could in the current and past history of his secret
Order and the Eyes of the Virgin. He was encouraged
and heartened by the scope and the depth of their concern and their willingness to believe what he continued
to reveal about the artifact. Of the two, Kate seemed
especially driven to find elements of faith to embrace.
This wasn't surprising in light of the tremendous pressure and trauma she'd endured—that had only *begun*
with the loss of her sister and husband. In the years he'd
previously known her through Justine, Domenic had no
idea of her toughness of spirit, and he was happy to
include her as part of his mission.

After arriving at SkyFreight's Charles DeGaulle commercial terminal, Domenic and the others were escorted
to the order's bunker beneath the company's main hangar. There he received the latest updates on their target,
which he shared with Kate and Etchison.

"He left the shoe shop?" said Kate. "In the middle of the night?"

"With the Iranian woman," said Domenic. "They were followed to Le Grand Hotel on Rue Scribe, across the street from the Opera House. They are presumably there for the rest of the night."

"Okay," said Etchison. "What's the plan?"

"We don't have one yet, but it looks like we should be able to occupy his space without much trouble."

Etchison nodded. "Yeah, as long as we're not being set up. . . ."

"We already have a second-tier team at the hotel," said Domenic. "It looks very clean. If we have a baited hook here, these guys are a lot better than we could ever imagine."

"Wait a second," said Kate. "Are we going to be killing this guy?"

"Not if we can do something else," said Domenic. "Optimum results would be a clean capture. We need to interrogate him, and convince him to take us to the artifact."

"Even though we have a good idea where it is?" said Kate. "Wouldn't it be safer to just go into that shoe repair shop and see what we can find?"

"We could," said Domenic. "But without intelligence on where it may lead or how to penetrate any of its defenses, we would be stumbling around in the dark. Our chances of success would be minimal. That is a last resort kind of option. If all else fails."

"By the time we hit it, odds are they would have moved anything sensitive out off-site," said Etchison.

"I'm not sure I get it," said Kate. "What're we planning to do—? Just walk up to his hotel room and knock on the door?"

"Basically, yes," said Domenic. "Either Streicher has no idea he is so visible, or he doesn't care anymore."

When he considered the possibilities, Domenic would be very surprised if Streicher was suddenly unaware of his high profile and visibility. Which meant . . . what?

It could be very much a trap. There was little reason to assume Streicher was acting alone—even though his record as an operative was normally solo. He had always worked in concert with a larger, controlling entity, and had given them no indication he was no longer affiliated with the Guild. Very few organizations, including most governments, had access to the technology, aircraft, and weaponry displayed by Streicher. But the question which continued to dog Domenic was whether or not the Guild understood the real truth about the Eyes of the Virgin— that its messages were *not* immutable predictions, that events and outcomes could be altered. If the Guild already possessed this information, then the value and the need to control the artifact would become even more paramount.

"What is the next step?" said Etchison, sounding impatient.

"Sorry," said Domenic, who realized he'd been silent and deep in thought. "I was trying to decide the answer to the same question."

"No more 'briefings'?" said Kate.

"From Corsica?" Domenic smiled. "No. I think they are relying on me to work out the details on their last one. We have a surveillance-and-support team in place throughout the hotel—roof, lobby, exteriors, and all exit passages. We have Interpol and the local gendarmes ready to evacuate the building on our call as reps of the *Servicio Segreto Vaticano*. Streicher is not going anywhere."

"Maybe he doesn't want to . . ." Etchison had been rubbing his hands together like a boxer growing anxious before a bout. "Maybe he's waiting for us to come waltzing in . . . ?"

"Could be," said Domenic.

"So . . . what are we waiting for?" said Kate.

Checking his watch, Domenic forced himself to grin. "Why should we be any different than any other great attack—? Dawn. What else?"

Thirty-Four

Rome

Jagen Kerschow

*W*hen his phone awakened him, he'd been in that strange and disturbing kind of dreamless sleep of old men—a state of utter *nothingness* in which his mind had no sense of time, of self, of existence itself. Jagen did not like to think about such a state of *nonbeing* because it sounded far too much like the death-sleep of eternity. Whenever he blinked open his eyes after a night of seeming nonexistence, he felt briefly shaken . . .

. . . as he was now.

"Yes . . . ?" he said in a voice that was half-croak.

"Sorry to disturb you," said the man at the other end of the line. A man named Aegajanian, a member of the Ruling Circle, and an equal to Kerschow in the Guild hierarchy.

"And yet you did," said Kerschow in a cool, controlled tone. He would not be goaded into sounding anxious or angry.

"Who is it . . . ?" said the voice of a naked, young woman next to him.

"Shut up!" he commanded, and she retreated into silence. "Continue," he said into the phone.

"Streicher has returned." Aegajanian went on to detail the possible transgression of the Guild's most highly regarded operative by listing his activities since passing through customs. He was particularly outraged by the encryption web which restricted Guild access to Safavi-Martin's lab and all its equipment, especially since they believed he had acquired the translation key, and had access to information the Guild did *not* have.

"And you want me to do *what?*" said Kerschow, when the other man finally paused.

"*You* are our security chairman—you tell me what should be done."

Kerschow had known Streicher for more than twenty years. The idea of the man becoming a rogue agent was unthinkable, laughable really. Everyone had been finding his infatuation with the Iranian woman amusing because they were so very familiar with his reputation and track-record with females. Was is possible he was so much in love with Safavi-Martin he'd let his penis interfere with standard procedure? Kerschow had enjoyed thousands of females and had come to the conclusion that none of them were worth the values men continued to assign to them. But that was the conclusion of old men everywhere, and had no bearing on what was happening at this moment.

As far as Streicher was concerned, there *had* to be a simple explanation for him not signing in.

"I am in Rome. Streicher is in Paris. I have field agents there who can reach him within thirty minutes."

Aegajanian cleared his throat. "I have spoken to Madame Beauvais and the other members of the Circle," he said.

Kerschow chuckled. "Oooh . . . I am so scared. . . ."

"We have a preferred action," said Aegajanian, preferring to ignore Kerschow sarcasm. "We want *you* to address this problem personally."

Oddly enough, this subtle "command" from the Guild's decision-making body fell into line with his own thinking. Because Kerschow had enjoyed a special relationship with Streicher for so many years, he felt as though he understood the operative better than just about anyone else in the organization. He believed Streicher respected him as much as the man was capable of respecting *any*body. Kerschow also believed in Streicher's loyalty. The man had been a prototype lone wolf—the kind of man who had no close friends, no close family, no one with whom he could share any of the normal things people need to share. That's why lone wolf personalities were so historically loyal—their work becomes their total *raison d'être,* and their dedication to any perceived superior who provides their work becomes very important to them. Streicher fit that profile very well, and Kerschow believed he could reach the man, and at least find out what might be wrong. He knew Streicher would not act irrationally; it was not in his nature.

"That will take time," said Kerschow. "Time we may not have."

"We have a Lear waiting for you at Fiumencino. A driver is on the way."

It had been many years since Kerschow had operated in the field. His days in the *Stadtenkorp*—West Germany's Secret Ops Unit from the sixties and seventies—were forty years in his past, but he felt an excitement at the idea of getting involved in the visceral operations of the Guild. His father's family had been in the armament manufacturing business for almost two hundred years, and while he'd been groomed for management, it had also been thought wise to give the young Jagen a background in covert operations. For the Guild to grow stronger in the modern world, his father and his colleagues had decided to prepare the next generation for as many contingencies as possible. Wise men, they had been.

For so long now, Kerschow had been disconnected from all but the most rarefied machinations of the world. Something his father would not have approved.

He hadn't realized until this moment how he hungered for something base, something raw and unrefined. He wore Ermenegildo Zegna suits, timepieces by Cartier, and Brioni silks. He dined at Maxim's and Il Maestro's, and he copulated with nineteen-year-old escorts from Swiss finishing schools and he was getting thoroughly bored with it all. A curious layering effect had, over the years, insulated him from the earthy graspings of the common humans, and despite having access to anything he wanted, Jagen Kerschow discovered a terrible absence within himself. When the entire tapestry of civilization becomes as flat and bland as a cheap board game, you know you are in trouble.

And here, by odd fortune, a respite from the insular boredom of his position presented itself. Kerschow would not hesitate. "I will be ready," he said, hanging up the phone.

"One more thing," said Aegajanian.

"Yes?"

"The woman, Safavi-Martin . . . she is to be kept alive. At all costs."

Kerschow chuckled satirically. "Really? Well, I am so glad you reminded me. Now why could that be the case?—wouldn't have anything to do with her unexpected encryption algorhythms, would it?"

"Jagen, I—"

"Shut up, you insulting idiot! Have you forgotten who you are talking to? I was astride this organization when you were still in soggy pants!"

"I did not mean to imply—"

"No," said Kerschow. "You did not. Tell the rest of the Circle I will take care of this situation. In my own fashion. Good-bye."

Punching off the receiver, he stood up and pulled on his dressing gown. As he walked toward the bathroom, the woman called out to him from the bed in a dreamy voice. "Something wrong, Jaggy?"

He turned back to her and remembered her for the afterthought she was. "Get out of here," he said softly.

"What!?" she sat up in the bed, her young breasts pointing at him as if in accusation.

"Get out, you *milchkow!*" he bellowed the words this time. "Before I put a bullet in you."

That was enough for the escort, who gathered her clothes off the lush carpeting and ran from the room in mincing little steps. Kerschow laughed at the sight, and he knew it was the first time in a long while he felt true mirth.

After returning from the bathroom, he called Pantagruel, his bodyguard, who slept in a suite on the villa's first floor. After giving the man a summary of what was to come and an inventory of items to prepare, Kerschow addressed the question of his own wardrobe. This was not the time for suits and silks. As he selected rugged wear which hung largely untouched in his armoire, it occurred to him that he may be entering an arena of not only intrigue and adventure, but also peril. Perhaps even death.

Looking in the mirror at his khaki and denim attire, Kerschow raked his fingers through his silvering hair and smiled. It was a toothy reflection of the look he might receive from the Reaper himself, and on one level, he knew he could actually welcome a glance from death.

And why might that be true?

Kerschow smiled as he pondered the answer to that question. Men and women who reached the pinnacle of human existence as he had done were unconsciously in search of new territories to explore. And there was only one place left . . .

Not that he did not care whether or not he lived. No, but Kerschow suspected he needed something profound or exciting to make his desire to live kick forcefully back into gear.

When he was a young man, he met an older man in a bar who'd been with the U. S. Marines at Guadalcanal. The man had a beat-up Zippo lighter with a scratched, but legible inscription on it which said: IN ORDER TO HAVE FULLY LIVED, YOU MUST HAVE NEARLY DIED.

For a long time, Kerschow never understood what the words on that lighter meant. But he learned many things become clearer when focused through the lens of a lifetime.

A discreet tap at his door announced the arrival of Pantagruel.

"Come in." Kerschow turned to greet the bodyguard.

The door opened slowly and a large man entered the room. More than two meters tall, Pantagruel's shoulders seemed impossibly wide as they V'ed down to his narrow waist and hips, giving his body an exaggerated angularity like a wedge of cheese. His Normandic features were also full of planes and angles, further enhanced by his retro-look flat-topped military buzz cut. He wore fatigues, and under a journalist's vest, two handguns in shoulder holsters. To say he looked formidable would be gross understatement.

"The car is arriving now," he said.

"I am ready. Where is the rest of the gear?"

"By the door. It is taken care of."

Kerschow nodded, turned back to his desk, where he kept a U. S. Army-issue .45 caliber automatic. It was heavy, unwieldy, and hard to fire with much accuracy, but it was his weapon of choice. After checking the magazine, he slipped several extras into the cargo pocket of his khakis. As he continued to hold the weapon in his right hand, he looked back at Pantagruel.

"I know what your job is," he said to the large man by the door. "But I want to make something clear. When, and if, we encounter any . . . friction . . . I want you to give me a chance to deal with it first, do you understand?"

"You mean verbally, right?"

"No," said Kerschow. "I mean in *any* fashion. If violence is required, I will be the one to sanction it by being the one to initiate it, do you follow me?"

Pantagruel appeared truly perplexed. "Actually, no."

Kerschow drew a deep breath, exhaled. "Let me make this as simple as possible. If there is trouble, save yourself. I am not so certain I will *want* to be saved."

The bodyguard's expression remained confused. "Sir, I—"

Kerschow was losing patience. "Maybe I should simplify matters by making the trip alone."

"That is not possible, sir. My orders are to maintain a radius of safety around you at all times. If you were to travel alone, I would be failing my obligation."

Kerschow shook a finger at him. "Well spoken. You have memorized your employee manual well. But I could contermand your orders at any time, you realize that."

"Yes, sir. But I would ask you to reconsider."

"Then, I will require your solemn word—you will not interfere with anything that we encounter, anything that may be happening to me . . . unless I give you permission or some sort of sign or indication that I wish you involved."

The large man exhaled with obvious drama. "Sir, I have taken an oath to the Guild. I cannot do that. I have a sworn duty."

"Pantagruel, I have known you for almost fifteen years. That is longer than most men remain with a wife."

The man straightened, as if called to attention. "Yes, sir."

"I have trusted you with my life," said Kerschow. His voice was low, measured. "And there have even been a few occasions when you have actually earned your money. Remember the bombings in Dublin? The conference in Rotterdam?"

"Yes, of course," said Pantagruel. The man fought the

impulse to grin or nod as he recalled moments of valor and performance.

"And I am compelled to thank you once again for those occasions," said Kerschow, ". . . and also to tell you how sorry I am."

"Sorry? For what?"

"For *this* . . ." said Kerschow as he squeezed the hair-trigger of the old Army .45.

The walls of the suite seemed to buckle outward as they refracted the sonic *boom* of the handgun. Its big slug, at such close range, tore through Pantagruel's massive chest with the force of a sledgehammer, and he was hurtled backward like a gutshot deer. The man's last act was to claw frantically at the entry wound as though trying to remove the bullet.

Kerschow watched the man sink to the floor, then calmly exited the room.

Thirty-Five

Paris

STREICHER

"You know what you saw, don't you?" said Nazy. Seated in an ornate, gilded, antique-white chair, and wearing a sapphire-green silk robe, she looked at him with eyes wide with wonder.

Streicher was standing by the door to the bathroom, arms folded. He wore a pair of sweatpants and a T-shirt. "Let's just say: I know what you think I saw. . . ."

"You described everything to me. How can you deny it now?" Nazy spoke evenly, he noticed; she was not mocking or badgering him. Good for that. He may have smacked her if she had found humor in his experience.

No, that is not correct. His *former* self might have struck her. The new "Kurt Loren" would seek out a more subtle way to communicate his feelings. God, he was making himself sick! But how else could he feel after a dream like that?

A dream with the power to unnerve him so completely.

A dream he knew in his heart was *not* a dream. . . .

"I am not denying anything," he said after a pause. "I

am not saying much of anything—in case you had not noticed."

"I have never seen you like this," she said.

"What do you mean?"

"Indecisive. Shaken. Scared." Nazy moved to his side, touched his face with obvious care. "This is not the man I have come to know."

"If you already see these things, I see no need to also admit them."

"You are so proud! What are you worried about, Loren? . . . that I might mistake you for a real human being . . . with real human feelings?"

Her words penetrated him as no weapon ever could. Why did it take so long for him to meet someone capable of reaching him the way she could? Random thoughts quarked through him, wondering how much of his life had been wasted in a psychic prison of his own device. How different could his entire life have been?

"Nazy, I need help," he said in a voice that did not hide the weakness he now felt.

"That is why I am here," she said, and kissed his cheek.

"You know, you asked me earlier what I believe I saw. . . ."

"Yes?" she prompted him when he fell silent.

"Well, I . . . I am actually afraid to *say* it! To say what I *know* I saw."

"And you want me to say it for you?"

"You—you probably do not even believe in such things."

Nazy looked at him reprovingly. "After this much sharing with me, you still do not know me, and that is disappointing."

"That is not true," he said, but he understood what she meant and felt stupid as well as weak.

"I believe in *all* of it. To me, there is no doctrine that can exclude the endless variations and possibilities of what simply *is*."

"Please, I am in no shape to discuss philosophy. Just tell me what happened to me. If I hear you say it, maybe I will be able to live with it. Then I can start dealing with it."

Nazy looked at him and shook her head. "You saw the Virgin! Is that so difficult for you?"

"I saw something that could have been the—"

"Oh, stop! You sound like a fool!" Nazy looked into him and appeared to be ready to cry. But she held on, letting the words out instead. "That artifact in my lab— where do you think it came from?"

"I know its history!" he said like a child trying to defend an indefensible act.

"And you think it was some . . . *accident* . . . that the only surviving fragment of an act of pure evil was a piece of stained glass that . . . that just *happened* to have the eyes of Mary on them?" She laughed in a way that was almost musical, maniacal, fearful, and psychotic; and he knew it was none of those.

"No, of course I am not stupid," he said. "I always felt it was a sign of some sort."

"A sign from *whom*? Why couldn't you finish the line of reasoning? Because it always led to the *un*reasonable?"

"Yes, that is it precisely."

"Where do you think the words on that glass have been coming from?"

"I . . . chose not to think about it."

Nazy looked at him, composed herself, and nodded softly. "And you wish me to do your thinking for you, yes?"

Streicher considered this. Is that what he was doing? "No, no," he said. "I only need your advice. Your guidance."

"Do you believe you saw the Virgin Mother?" Nazy's words passed through him like radiation.

Closing his eyes, Streicher could see the silhouette of Mary in the familiar pose which defined the "miraculous medal" of all Catholic schoolgirls, and the same likeness in the stained glass of *la Capelinha*, the little chapel in Fatima. There was no doubt of what he'd seen.

"Yes," he said in a deadened whisper. Unsure of what he *really* believed, but having no place else to go. "Yes, I do."

Nazy took a seat next to him, pulling the folds of her robe closer to her neck. "Very well. Now, tell me what it means—why did she appear to you?"

He knew what she was doing, but a part of him, the part which clung to the adult training and the depredations of his childhood, did not want to go there. He opened his mouth but no words would come.

"Speak to me!" she said in a commanding voice. "*Why*?!"

"Because I . . . I hold the power now." Streicher had comprehended the significance of his experience from the beginning, but had forced himself to keep the thoughts from the forefront of his mind. He had even accepted the possibility that he'd seen only a construct of his mind—hallucination, nightmare, psychotic episode, or some other kind of delusional or self-induced hypnotic state. But even if the vision had not been authentically divine, it still had *happened*, and therefore had meaning. But the meaning would not make itself clear. Even if he'd created the vision in his own mind, the primary question held him down like an anchor—*why*?

The old maxim "if God did not exist, we would have to invent Him" came to him, and he wondered if that was what he'd done in this case. He posed it to Nazy.

"You are unbelievable," she said. "You make me wonder why I am staying here with you now. Why I would bother."

"Nazy, please . . ."

"Please what?—tell you what to do?"

"Yes! Christ, *yes*!"

She exhaled slowly, looked into his eyes again, although this time she appeared to be searching for something. "You said something before about having the power . . . you were right. And you must decide how to use the power."

"That's it, isn't it. Simple, but so difficult as well."

"Do you want to see Washington destroyed?"

"Ideologically . . . ? It is not such a bad idea. The Guild has philosophical problems with all governments. The very nature of government is almost antithetical to—"

"Please," said Nazy. "Just answer the question—yes or no?"

"No, I suppose I don't."

"What about your superiors? Do you think they share your sentiment?"

"No, of course not. The resultant blow to world economies could be parlayed into unprecedented gains for the Guild. If there were outbreaks of aggression, even nuclear incursions, and some smaller third-world countries were essentially destroyed, the opportunity to manipulate market commodities such as oil and wheat could be the most comprehensive and lucrative in all of history."

"I take that as a yes, then? The Guild would allow Washington to be nuked?"

"Knowing them as I do, yes, I believe they would."

"You have the knowledge, which is definitely the power. Part of the power is knowing, or at least suspecting strongly that the predictions from the artifact can be altered, am I right?"

"Most definitely."

"Then it appears quite simple to me," she said. "Do you give the Guild this information, or do you give it to an entity who might be able to do something to change what is to come?"

"It is too much to ask of one person," he said.

"Explain yourself."

"Nazy, I have done many things in my life which may

lead to my damnation—a condition that, up until very recently, I would have never believed as real, or even possible. I have caused the death of hundreds, maybe even thousands of people. But this is a situation involving many *millions*. . . ."

She stood, pulled him close to her, holding his head against her breasts like a small boy. The warmth and the sweetness of her natural scent swept over him and he wished he could hold the peace of that moment forever. "That sounded very much like a confession," she said.

"It probably was."

Neither spoke for a moment. Then she leaned back to look him in the eyes yet again. "So, what is our next move?"

"I don't know, but leaving the hotel would be a good start. If we want to avoid crossing paths with the Guild, at least for now, we should—"

The phone rang.

Both of them stood looking at it with fear and confusion. It was the middle of the night. Who would be calling now? Who even knew how to reach them?

Getting up, he approached the writing desk opposite the bed, picked up the receiver. "Yes?"

"Monsieur Streicher, please forgive me for calling at this hour," said a familiar voice.

Familiar, yes. But he could not place it. Too much to think about right now.

"Who is this?"

"I am so sorry, Monsieur! This is Roland LeClaire."

The name suddenly registered—LeClaire was the proprietor of the Grand Hotel. "Monsieur LeClaire, what—?"

"There is no time," said the caller. "My night manager just called me in a panic. They have just received orders from the Surete to evacuate everyone on the third, fourth, and fifth floors!"

Streicher grinned. "Everyone *except* me, yes?"

"That is correct, sir." LeClaire cleared his throat,

spoke in a hushed tone. "Monsieur Streicher, I have no idea what is going on. And, I swear to you . . . I have no desire to be told. All I know is that you have been a frequent and highly regarded guest of our hotel for almost fifteen years. One of our finest patrons. I believed I, at the least, owed you this call. But discretion is—"

"I never heard from you, Roland. Thank you very much indeed."

"You are welcome, sir. Godspeed."

Streicher hung up the phone, looked at Nazy. "It appears as if we have been located."

"What? By who?"

Streicher shrugged. "No way to tell. The authorities are in on it, but they could be pawns for the Guild or . . ." He paused, realizing he'd never mentioned Petralli or the Vatican, and that there was much he had yet to share with this special woman. And now, it occurred to him, he may have run out of time.

". . . or the people you stole it from," she said, finishing the sentence.

"Not to put too fine a point on it," he said coolly.

"And why do I have this nagging feeling it was the Catholic Church?"

"Perhaps because it *was . . .* ?"

Nazy stood by the door. "And you are honestly surprised you had a religious experience? Kurt Loren Streicher, there may be no hope for you."

Streicher nodded as he got up, started pulling on some clothes. "You'd better get dressed. I have no idea what we're in for."

Nazy moved quickly, slipping into baggy jeans and a sweater. She was putting on a pair of running shoes when the door to the suite's foyer thumped several times.

"Stay here," said Streicher, reaching for a silenced Sig Sauer he'd kept by his pillow.

"Wait!" she said, grabbing his arm, but he ignored her, moving from the bedroom to the dining room, and finally to the foyer.

The door thumped politely again.

"Yes, wait a minute . . . what is it?" said Streicher affecting a tone of someone roused from sleep.

"This is hotel security, Monsieur," said a voice from behind the door. "The hotel has received a bomb threat, and we must evacuate the building."

"Very well, I must get some clothes on," Streicher said with mock irritation. "But I'll have you know—this is ridiculous!"

"I am sorry, sir," said the voice. "But there can be no delay. We must get everyone out immediately. . . ."

"Yes," said Streicher, as he angled away from the steel door, his right arm extended as his head turreted to look down the plane of his shoulder through the Sauer's sight. "Please, come in. . . ."

THIRTY-SIX

Paris

HARRISON

Kate had been pressed against the hotel's corridor when the door opened inward. She knew she didn't belong there, and her only job was to stay out of the way. But after what she'd been through, she *wanted* to be in for whatever happened, especially since her sister and her husband had already gone far beyond anything she'd so far endured.

Standing off on each side of the threshold were Domenic and Matt, both armored (as was she) in Kevlar vests and helmets. At each end of the hallway, by the fire stairs and the elevators, small detachments of Parisian SWAT teams waited in backup mode. She wondered what kind of connections Domenic enjoyed to have them fall into line so easily. Apparently, the power and resources of the KOM were far greater than anyone would ever expect. A worthy opponent to an invisible juggernaut such as the Guild.

As the door cantered inward, slowly like the entrance to a vault, she heard a woman shout. "Don't do it! No!! Don't kill him!"

And then—silence.

It had been so unexpected that Domenic and Matt hesitated, and she figured it had to be a trap, a ruse. And no one moved, no one fired their weapon. If anything, Kate pressed herself closer to the wall as she continued to watch Domenic for a cue on what might be next.

"It's over, Streicher," he said, still staying out of a direct line of fire. "Stand down."

The sound of a woman sobbing, whispering something in a language Kate did not recognize, followed by the loud click! of an automatic handgun's clip being released. She heard it thump upon the thick pile of the carpet. Domenic and Matt moved instantly after that, both pushing into the room.

Following with more caution, Kate peeked in the doorway to see Streicher standing in the center of the room with his left arm holding a dark-haired woman close to his chest, a fragile embrace. His right arm hung loosely at his side, his hand empty. By his feet lay a handgun and a loaded clip of ammo.

Turning to look at Kate and the others, the woman stood as tall as possible, shoulders back. "Thank you," she said. "Everything has changed now."

"Can you please step away from him," said Domenic as he hinged back the visor of his helmet.

She did so, and Matt searched Streicher for any other weapons. Then, he did the same to the woman, who proudly allowed the personal intrusion. Kate knew she had to be the crypto-specialist, but she hadn't expected her to be so striking, her presence so . . . commanding of respect. Kate could tell from this woman's bearing, she was someone special.

As he was doing this, Domenic signaled to the support teams still out in the corridor and one of their officers rushed up to the open door. After a quick and whispered discussion, the French police departed.

"They'll be standing by in case we need help," he told Kate as he had her close the door to the suite.

His frisking completed, Matt nodded and escorted both captives to the nearest chairs where he stood behind them, his weapon still in hand.

"Okay," said Domenic, standing in front of both of them. "We need to talk."

"Signor Petralli," said Streicher, his gaze unable to hold eye contact. "I told my superiors I would someday kill you. It sounds very . . . silly now."

Kate remained standing as she regarded Streicher, wondering if he had been the one to kill Justine or Lawrence. And if not by his own hand, had he been the one who'd authorized those monstrous acts? He looked so weak, so helpless now. Nothing like the cunning machine-like figure described to her. What had happened here? How did he become so deflated? But that didn't matter, really. He was part of the organization that had ripped her life inside out. She felt a churning in her chest, and she knew she would have to concentrate on keeping her emotions in check. There was a part of her that wanted to throw herself across the room and claw out his eyes.

"You have something that belongs to us," said Domenic.

"The disk is in the other room. On the desk." Streicher sank his face into his hands.

To Kate, the man looked beaten, utterly defeated. He bore little resemblance to the surly, arrogant intruder who'd been ready to kill her on Marettimo. Again, she had to wonder what had happened here.

Domenic shook his head. "That key is of no use to us. We have the original—and it is pretty obvious you have already used it."

"That is correct," said the woman. "I am Shahrnaz Safavi-Martin, and—"

"We know who you are, Madame," said Domenic in a dismissive tone. "We want our artifact back. Can you give it to us?"

"Yes, I can," she said calmly.

Neither Matt nor Domenic could hide expressions of surprise. Her response had been totally unexpected, and Kate immediately suspected some kind of trick. But the woman sat looking at them with nothing which belied any subterfuge.

"Do you have it here?" said Matt.

Safavi-Martin shook her head. "No, it is still locked down. At my lab."

"At Francosoft," said Domenic. It was not a question.

"Yes," she said with a lift of her eyebrows. "You know of it?"

Domenic nodded. "We also know how you get through the back door."

Streicher looked up at everyone and chuckled. "I don't know about any of the rest of you, but this conversation is starting to bore me. Everybody already knows what everybody else is saying."

"Too bad," said Matt, who looked like he wanted to take the guy's head off and was just barely keeping himself under control.

Ignoring him, Streicher looked at his companion. "Nazy, I just want to get this over with. Why don't you just tell them everything . . . ?"

The woman looked at Streicher with the eyes of an intimate. Kate recognized the expression, and she was struck by the odd truth of it. But how could a woman of such intelligence be attracted or involved with a cold and brutal killer like Streicher? It didn't make sense.

"Yes," said Safavi-Martin. "I will do that. . . ."

And she did.

Kate, Domenic, and Matt sat in total silence listening to this calm and articulate woman. Each word revealed her own passion and belief in what she was saying; each sentence underscored the incredible story they'd all been pulled into. It was now obvious to Kate this woman was deeply spiritual and her attachment to Streicher an attempt to save him from himself. When the woman told them the latest prediction she'd extracted from the glass, Kate could feel a cold mantle of shock and silence embrace them.

"Jesus . . . !" said Matt. "Did it say anything about when?"

Safavi-Martin was about to speak when Domenic cut her off. "It never does. It never has. . . ."

"You are very familiar with the artifact?" said the woman.

"Yes, I am."

"Streicher believes the events it describes are not so much prophecies as . . . *possible* futures," said Safavi-Martin.

Matt seized on this as he directed a hasty question at Domenic. "Is that *true?* Can we stop it? Can we change it?"

Kate watched Domenic as he wrestled with the choice of revealing more of what he knew or understood . . . or believed. He was normally self-contained and quietly in control, but now he was obviously in conflict, having difficulty concealing his agitation. "I don't know," he said.

"That's bullshit!" said Streicher, exploding out of silence. "You stopped Reccared from being killed by the Basques! You knew about it because the glass told you it was going to happen."

Matt looked at Domenic. "Is that true?"

He paused for a few seconds, then nodded. "Yes. We placed twenty-four-hour protection and surveillance on Reccared—with the intention of picking up any advance activities. Of any would-be assassins. We knew it would happen. It was just a matter of when."

"How did you know for sure?" said Kate. "How did you know the glass was always right?"

"Because . . ." Domenic paused as he chose his words carefully. "Because we have received enough information from the artifact to know it is . . . accurate."

"You believe God is giving you these messages, right?" said Kate.

"Yes, of course."

"Why?" said Streicher.

"I don't know." Domenic cleared his throat. "It had been the subject of theologians for more than seventy-five years."

"How often do you receive them?"

Domenic shook his head as if clearing an errant thought. "More often than you would imagine."

"And you want me to believe you change human history on a regular basis?" Streicher looked at him with an expression that seemed to be a combination of hope and disbelief. And Kate could certainly understand that kind of thinking. As she sat listening to Domenic and the interchange with the others, she felt herself hoping that everything being spoken of was *true*. How much she *wanted* it to be true. She felt like a little girl wishing that a fairy tale could be real.

"No," said Domenic. "We are not even close to being so fortunate. But there have been enough times—over the last eighty years—to give us hope, and to convince us to carry on."

"What happened at the World Trade Center?" said Matt.

Domenic looked embarrassed as he paused again, then: "Not as bad as it *could* have been. . . ."

"What?" said Kate, remembering the horrific live video of the jetliners and the collapsing towers. She and Lawrence had stood in front of their television, arms around each other, unable to speak. "What happened?"

"You see," said Streicher to Safavi-Martin. "I *told* you—"

Domenic drew in a breath, closed his eyes for a moment as if recalling a bad dream. "In the past, we have attempted to warn whatever particular governments may have been involved. But you must understand it is a very delicate procedure. You cannot just walk into the power centers of the biggest governments and tell them you have . . . predictions you *know* will come true.

"People are skeptical," Domenic said, after a pause. "And bureaucracies complicate things even worse! It is always a nightmare to route urgent information up-channel through the maze of agencies and departments. You all know that."

"So what happened on September eleventh?" said Matt.

"We know now that the U.S. was getting lots of weird warnings about a terror attack," said Domenic. "Some fairly specific stuff from the Sudan, more from a Saudi underground group, a batch of intercepted communications that didn't make sense until after the fact, and of course, our *own* efforts to tell the right government people what was going to happen."

"They ignored you?" said Kate.

"Not so much ignored as our warning getting fouled up with all the other information that was working its way up to the proper desks. Some of the other data was just as specific as that from the glass, but the dates were wrong! Nobody's warnings agreed with anyone else's, don't you see?"

"Go on," said Safavi-Martin.

"When we realized we wouldn't be getting much help, we did what we could on our own. We managed to get one of them grounded in Chicago. It never took off. It was supposed to take out the Sears Tower."

"Oh my god . . ." said Kate.

"And the one that went down in Pennsylvania—we'd been able to get two of our operatives onboard. It's target was the Capitol Building. We stopped another one from Dallas—it put down in St. Louis. The FBI kept a lid on the details of that one, but it was supposed to take out the Golden Gate."

"You mean the FBI knows about that glass?" Matt sounded openly skeptical. "They *believe* you?"

"It is not open for 'belief,'—we are dealing with an

observable entity," said Domenic, who gestured at Streicher and Safavi-Martin. "These two have seen it. They *know*. And the FBI knows *enough*, and so do some other high-level organizations from countries we can trust—they know our information is good. After the last set of events, they have little choice but to trust us. *Without* questioning our sources."

Kate looked at Streicher and spoke to him for the first time. "Why did you think that such a gift would... would still be a gift in the hands of people who would *steal* it? Didn't it ever occur to you that—"

"Listen," he said, cutting her off. "In my job, I tried not to *think* too deeply about anything. I was a good little soldier, lady, that's all. I did what they told me to do. Do you think I cared whether or not God would be angry with me or my bosses?"

"So what changed your mind?" asked Kate.

Streicher's anger slipped away like air out of a balloon. "A lot of things. Let's leave it at that."

Domenic looked at Streicher. "That is fine with me," he said. "We're going into the Francosoft building—you can help or you can stay in custody, I don't care."

"I can help you," said Safavi-Martin. "So will Kurt."

"*Kurt?*" Matt smirked as he repeated Streicher's name. Kate could see that Matt was just looking for an excuse to do something ugly to him.

"We have no time to waste on this," said Domenic. "The amount of resistance is a direct relation to the amount of time we give the Guild to prepare for us. At this point, they have no idea what we know or what has happened to their man on the scene."

"We really don't, either," said Matt, which meant he was not ready to trust Streicher or his lady-friend even a little bit.

Kate didn't feel as much danger from either of them. If this was all part of an elaborate scheme on the Guild's part, she would be stunned at their ability to construct something so artful. Something had obviously happened to crush Streicher's will, and Kate felt fairly certain it had been something greater than Safavi-Martin's spirit.

"Depending on how much resistance they have in place, I can probably get you inside the building," said Streicher. "Shahrnaz can clear you to her lab. Getting out will probably be a problem."

"We have faced many problems, for many years," said Domenic.

"Do you have a plan?" said Streicher.

Domenic looked at him impassively. "We will."

THIRTY-SEVEN

Paris

*H*e had to give this guy credit—Petralli was as
highly trained and as efficient a warrior as Matt
had ever met. His years in the Seals had taught him to
not expect limits from anybody who made it through the
training, and going along with that was the idea that
nobody else was as tough as you. You never expected
to meet anybody as good.

But Petralli was that good.

Matt could see it in the way he took control. He turned
the suite into a mini-war room, used laptop and satphone
equipment to establish encrypted communications with
Corsica and the Order's chief tacticians. The ability to
size up a situation and work out a rapid solution could
not be taught, only developed.

Whatever access the KOM had to surveillance data
must have been state-of-the-art because Domenic was
provided with three-dimensional drawings and interior
photography of the Francosoft installation, plus plans,
blueprints, and scans of every structure within a mile of
the building in every direction. There were also sum-

maries of e-mail, phone, and fax intercepts; satellite prints of traffic movements; sonic-vibration transcription from geosynch laser "analysis" on windows of the target structure; and air traffic control flight data in and out of the Paris airports.

Petralli absorbed the flood of information as quickly as any field general could do it, then consulted with his Corsica support team. The key to success, as far as Matt was concerned, was the level of interference they would meet with French authorities and actual resistance from any forces the Guild could marshal in a short time. Petralli considered the reports on the size of the Francosoft internal security team, the possibility of the Garde National de Paris being in the pocket of the Guild, and any other hostiles that might keep them from entering the lab.

He and Matt decided they would be the only ones armed as they entered the installation. Kate had declined the option to carry because she didn't feel confident enough to do anything effective with it. She had enough insight to realize how lucky she'd been so far. After a little refining on some details, Domenic was ready to go.

"We can still get inside before it opens to regular staff," said Petralli, checking his watch out of habit as he addressed everyone in the suite. "But we have to get moving. Streicher, we agree with your belief the easiest entrance will be through the old shop-tunnel. If you do not provide the access codes, we will employ shaped charges to disable the sallyports."

"I have already transcribed them and given them to you. You don't even need me," said the German.

"Yeah, but you're still coming with me," said Matt. "I wouldn't have it any other way."

"In addition," said Petralli, "we have Corsica working through legal channels to get us authorized backup by the Surete or the Army, but that might not come through in time. Magistrates *hate* being awakened in the middle of the night. And storming the headquarters of the largest business in the country is a lot different than assisting in an immigration arrest at a hotel. We also have a chopper of our own commandos enroute, and it will be a close call, but they should get here before the building opens for the morning shift."

"Looks like we have a lot of possibilities, but I wouldn't be counting on much help from *any* of those guys," said Matt.

"I'm not," said Petralli. "We'll take anything we get as a bonus, but at this point, we have to figure it's just us."

He then looked at Safavi-Martin, who'd insisted on being called Persian, rather than Iranian. Matt had known lots of people from that country who shared her preference. Who could blame them? Better to be identified with a spectacular culture of the ancient world than a band of fundamentalist thugs from the modern one. She'd made a point of explaining her nationality when Matt had innocently remarked on what an interesting name she had.

"You will be expected to decrypt your lab security, get us access to the artifact, and finally destroy any sensitive data in the Francosoft system."

"Yes, I am clear on what you want," she said.

"Good," said Petralli. "Anything short of what I need simply can't be tolerated. We are prepared to do everything the *hard* way, but . . . that will remain up to you."

"I have no intention of disappointing you," she said.

Petralli didn't bother to reply, other than to pull a large pack onto his back. Matt did likewise and helped Kate suit-up a smaller bag of gear. As per Petralli's briefing, they exited the hotel room single-file with Petralli in front, followed by the Iranian woman, Streicher, Kate, and Matt.

He liked it that way just fine.

SAFAVI-MARTIN

As they crosshatched the deserted backstreets of Paris in a rental van, she asked herself a single question: *If she had known ahead of time what would be happening in her life, would she do anything differently?*

And the answer was a simple no.

Nazy had always believed herself too curious to turn away from anything unknown to her. The world revealed to her because of her association with Streicher had been so all-consumingly *alien* to all she'd ever imagined she accepted her life being forever changed with both eyes fully open. She invited the change because she knew that change is how life constantly renewed itself. And she believed that whenever we learn more about the world, we learn more about ourselves.

And she had indeed learned much. For so many years, she had allowed her profession to control and define her. When she met Streicher, she at first had figured his bad-boy persona was simply that—an act he employed to interest and attract a certain kind of woman. And by the time she realized he was not just a corporate errand-runner with dreams of being James Bond, it was too late.

For both of them.

Now she stood on the brink of an abyss. If she slipped off the edge, there would be nothing more. At least in this turn of the wheel. And that would be so tragic because she had only recently understood how rich and deep and exciting her life could be.

"The shop is on the left. The next block," said a hand-cuffed Streicher who was seated in the right passenger seat, next to the tall American, Etchison. Nazy was seated next to Kate Harrison, whose ash-blonde hair was pulled back in a functional ponytail. Her Celtic face had a fresh, clean look that did not need makeup, but the stress of the impending confrontation could be seen in the incipient line around her eyes, making her appear older than her years. Seated behind everyone was the stocky, shorter undercover agent from the Vatican—the one man whom Nazy truly feared. He was a true believer, in the classic and psychological uses of the phrase, and therefore the most dangerous because he was always willing to die for his faith and his God.

"Here," said Streicher. "We can stop here."

Nazy peered out the window at the narrow backstreet. Other than intermittent pools of lamplight, the avenue was very dark. Dawn remained almost an hour away, and she could detect no movement or human presence on the street. The doors opened and Etchison guided them toward the entrance to the cobbler's shop, which was several steps below the narrow sidewalk.

Petralli moved quickly to the front door, locked with a standard key and tumbler mechanism, and pulled a small electronic device about the size of an instant camera from his utility bag. She watched him hold the instrument against the lock, over the key slot for several seconds until a soft *beep!* punctuated the darkness, followed by a solid *clunk* as the lock surrendered to technology.

"Wait," Petralli whispered to the group, then vanished into the black void of the shop's interior. Although he could not have been gone for more than thirty seconds, it could have been thirty minutes to Nazy, who felt so exposed, so vulnerable standing in a circle with the others. As her eyes adjusted to the light from the stars and a distant street lamp, she could see everyone's faces clearly. If anyone was looking for them, they were an obvious target.

"Okay, move it!" whispered Petralli, holding a small, but powerful flashlight. He personally ushered Streicher into the lobby of the small shop, guiding him his upper arm.

"Through here . . . all the way into the back," said Streicher, as he led the group past the counter and register area, into a room full of pigeonholes and a large workbench. At the back wall of the shop, Streicher indicated the concealed electronic switch that moved the wall to the side, allowing access to a tunnel of great age. Nazy remembered Streicher telling her that it had been dug by Guild members centuries ago.

She allowed herself to be guided along the passageway in single-file behind Petralli and Streicher, followed by the Harrison woman and Etchison. Everyone moved in silence, slowly, and with obvious caution. There was no way to know if their movements were being monitored and if anyone was expecting them or not. There could be many different factions on both sides of the conflict marshaling their resources and rushing to the place they were headed . . . or there could be nothing in wait for them, depending upon the timing.

Regardless, Nazy felt like they were diving headlong in to the center of a maelstrom.

STREICHER

Any other time in his career, he would have felt humiliated by the handcuffs and the prisoner-like treatment at the hands of Petralli, but Streicher was surprised to discover that he really didn't care anymore. Although he'd had a tough time articulating himself and his true feelings—his emotions, if you will—he knew that he'd been changed in some weird and terrifying way. He knew something had, for want of a better word, transformed him or as the religious would say, *converted* him.

As Petralli urged him onward toward the sallyport in the distance, Streicher continued to examine his thoughts. He wasn't sure if he wanted to actually *believe* he'd seen the Virgin Mary, but his rational nature insisted it did not matter what or who he'd seen. There were plenty of philosophers, such as William James or de Chardin who would argue that any "religious experience" originates and culminates within the subject— which meant to Streicher the cause didn't really matter, only the effect. Which was this: He'd undergone a change significant enough to change his entire way of dealing with the world. Between his involvement with Nazy and the exposure to what may be a divine power, he now valued human life, when only weeks earlier, he did not.

Looking up, he saw they were more than halfway through the tunnel. Their column moved slowly because Petralli stopped to listen for any other presence every once in a while. Interestingly, Streicher had no idea who or what might be waiting for them. If his superiors trusted him as implicitly as they'd done in earlier operations, then the installation could be practically deserted. If Kerschow believed otherwise, there was no telling what might be awaiting them.

But in a most important sense, it did not matter.

What happened to Petralli, the artifact, the Guild, and everyone else except Nazy simply didn't matter any longer. Streicher was out of it. Whether he survived this or not, he was retired. Known only to him were stashes of cash in various denominations in various locations. He'd been shrewd during his years of solo work, and had realized his was not an occupation he could do well in his twilight years. Devising the terms of his own retirement pension had been a necessity, not just a good idea. And now, all he found himself thinking about was a chance to send his life off in a different direction. With Nazy. With a new understanding of what it meant to be alive. With a real reason to want to *be* alive. Of course, they would be needing new identities as well, and he had cultivated many foolproof sources for any papers he or Nazy might ever need. All he wanted now was the chance to make it happen. . . .

"Okay," said Petralli. "We're coming up to the gate. Get over here."

"If there is anyone watching, they have already picked us up on camera," said Streicher. "This is your weakest position."

Petralli nodded. "I know. Just get the outer door open, I'll do the rest."

"As long as they haven't had time to cancel my access information."

"We're going to find out, aren't we?" said Petralli. "Move!"

Streicher was pushed up to a small alcove where the video-recognition lens awaited his image. As he did this, Petralli had unshouldered his bag and pulled out a small weapon which Streicher recognized as a RM-30 concussion grenade launcher. Etchison had also advanced to the face of the steel door, holding a steel piton and a hammer. As Streicher stared into the optical scanner, Petralli dropped to one knee in firing position.

They would know at that moment whether or not the program still recognized Streicher's distinct pattern-matrix, and therefore whether or not access was still assured.

PETRALLI

A sound of unseen bearings smoothly set into motion. Domenic watched down the sight-line of his weapon as the heavy, burnished metal door began to slide. If Streicher's description proved accurate, there would be a well-lighted pass-through chamber and a second door which would open once they had entered it and allowed the first door to seal them in.

To allow this to happen would be as disastrous as it was unwise, and Domenic had a solution for it.

The heavy steel panel moved away, locking into its stopped position, and Etchison wedged the piton into the space between the trailing edge of the door and the metal track upon which it traversed. One whack with the hammer, and the door was jammed open. Simultaneously, without hesitation, Domenic depressed the launcher's trigger, dispatching the mini-missile in a flash of white heat. Then, throwing himself to the left of the opening,

Domenic dodged the blast of the second door being obliterated.

Through the roiling cloud of debris-dust, he could see the red glare of emergency lighting syncopated to a pulsing alarm klaxon. There could be no hesitation now, the element of shock and surprise would only allow them a very short window. If there had been a welcoming committee on the other side of that door, they had been taken out—or at the least disabled for an instant.

And that was all Domenic needed.

Rushing through the debris cloud, armed with a Kalashnikov assault rifle, he laid down a pattern of automatic fire to reduce the opportunity for any rapid retaliation then threw himself into a forward roll which exited him past the sallyport's devastated inner door and into a carpeted foyer that opened into a wide corridor. He fired in the direction of the corridor as he dropped as low as possible to the floor. Since he lay low, above most of the rising smoke and dust, his vision cleared quickly enough to assess the effects of his first wave.

Against the concrete block wall opposite the inner door lay many bodies of security personnel caught in the initial blast or from his first pattern of automatic fire. More stilled figures littered the corridor to his right. The left appeared vacant.

"Let's go!" he yelled back to Etchison, who had been awaiting a signal to advance.

The sound of footsteps through the sallyport was followed by the sight of shadowy figures moving quickly through the dust. Domenic counted them off as Streicher and Etchison were followed by the two women.

"Stay low!" he said, then he watched Etchison push Streicher forward with enough force to send him flat on his stomach.

"That should be low enough." said Etchison. "Stay there till we want you to move."

"Practically no resistance," said Domenic. "What do you make of it?"

The ex-Seal shrugged. "Only two things it can be. Either they weren't ready for us . . . or it's a—"

"*Trap*," said Domenic. "Right, but when and where?"

"One thing for sure," said Etchison, looking over the layout. "We can't maintain this position while we talk about it."

Domenic nodded, and signaled the others to fall in behind them. He knew what Etchison meant, and they were far too exposed. They needed to reach the first agreed-upon objective—the entrance to the wing which housed the crypto-labs, and which would provide them with a defensible position.

Looking back over his shoulder, Domenic saw the Persian woman staring at him with expectation. "Now," he said, and watched her take the cue to slip past them, into the lead. The open space into which she half-jogged remained clear, other than a residual, thinning layer of dust and smoke; but he doubted it would remain so. He motioned the others to follow closely as he and Etchison maintained a vigilant, aggressive stance with weapons waist-high.

As they moved down the wide corridor toward the entrance to the lab wing, Domenic had an instinctively bad feeling about the way things were going. He'd been involved in operations like this too many times in the past to not have acquired a sense of how they should *feel*, how they play out. There are certain resonances that stay with you, that become part of those synaptic learning experiences you can't ignore. He'd discussed this kind of awareness with others in his profession and the people with longevity knew exactly what he was talking about. He hated the popular media reference to a "sixth sense" kind of silliness, but it was something damned closed to that kind of cognizance. Some people had this subtle ability to sense when an adversary was close by— a proximity sense; others had an acute sense of timing and coordination; and others had a broader, less-definable sense of the *rightness* of how something should feel. Domenic believed in those extra levels of perception because he'd seen and felt them work too many times in the field.

And this operation just didn't *feel* right.

He wouldn't be surprised if he scuttled behind one of these walls and discovered they were nothing more than painted stage flats, propped up by plywood and two-by-fours. Of course, he knew that was not the case, but it was that kind of sense—of things not being what they seemed.

He was following close behind Safavi-Martin as he approached the point where they needed to turn right through a set of double swinging doors. There were windowed panels halfway up, like those separating wards in a hospital wing, but no light emanated from the lab. Crouching below the glass, Safavi-Martin pushed gently, ready to enter.

"Nazy!" cried Streicher. "Wait! Don't go in alone!"

She paused, waited for Domenic and the others to scramble forward. Streicher moved next to her with a look of concern Domenic found incongruous as well as intriguing. He and Etchison had slung their assault weapons, replacing them with handguns, which would be more suited to any action in the enclosed space of the lab.

She looked at Domenic, waiting for his signal.

He nodded as he pushed inward on the doors into the darkened space. Despite his lingering sensation of something terribly *wrong*, Domenic realized he had no choice but to press on. As the others slipped into the foyer of the lab's entrance, Etchison flicked on a small penlight, its beam lancing the shadows in search of the digital keypad that would unlock the next door and get them closer to the artifact.

When the thin beam of light crossed the face of a man standing in the far corner, Domenic was not surprised, and in an odd way felt almost relieved his instincts had not failed him. At the same instant, the lights burst on, momentarily stunning and blinding everyone. It had been enough, however, for Domenic to see the Uzi in the man's hands—a weapon with a firepower that was absolutely withering in its ability to inflict horrific damage to a maximum number of targets in fractional seconds.

"Stop!" said the man.

And nobody moved.

Domenic looked at the man, who appeared to be in his early sixties, but lean and fit. He projected an aspect of elegance, of manicured appreciation for the best in life. Chiseled jaw line, steel-blue eyes, and silvered hair combed straight back. That he did not look like the stereotypical operative did not, however, make him appear any less lethal. And familiar, thought Domenic, who flipped through mental dossiers of suspected Guild members, trying to make the man's identity. His training demanded this of him—knowing your enemy always helped you understand how to defeat him.

"Your weapons, gentlemen . . . you will please place them carefully on the floor."

Without hesitation, Domenic and Etchison ungripped their handguns, unshouldered the rifles.

"Good . . . good," said the man. "I anticipated building security being no match for you, and so I exercised patience."

Streicher looked at the man with an unreadable expression. "You are alone?" he said, holding up his hands in the chromed cuffs. "Get these off of me. I can help."

The man looked at him and smiled. "It appears as if you have been a great help already."

Standing straighter, a subtle nod toward a military posture of attention, Streicher spoke evenly. "They already knew everything. Do not underestimate the abilities of these two. Safavi-Martin, she is the only one with direct access to the materials, to the encryptions. I had to ensure her safety."

The man stood silently for a long, awkward moment,

his hands still leveling the Israeli automatic weapon at the group. He appeared to be evaluating Streicher's words, sizing up the situation. "Streicher, I appreciate your concern, but I have backup on the way. I will not be alone for long."

Domenic paid close attention to the exchange between Streicher and the Guild man. The mention of backup had been purposeful, and Domenic wondered if the Guild had anticipated commandos from Corsica on the way to secure the building if necessary . . .

"Kerschow, do not be an ass," said Streicher in a low, angry tone. "Get me out of these."

The man looked at him. "You have the 'key'?"

"You know we do," said Streicher.

Domenic understood this exchange as well. The Guild man, whose name, Kerschow, had been unknown to him, was here to retrieve the key and whatever information he *knew* Streicher had uncovered on the previous, and presumably unauthorized access to the lab.

"Ms. Safavi-Martin," said Kerschow. "I assume you are still employed by Francosoft?"

"Why yes, of course," said the Persian, trying to sound surprised.

"Then I would ask you to please come here to open the lab."

Without looking at anyone, or doing anything that might compromise her position, she approached the key-pad and entered her encryption code. She was good, Domenic thought.

There was a soft, electronic chime as the lock disengaged and the door to the lab opened. Safavi-Martin waited for a nod of permission from the man with the Uzi, who gave it with a disingenuous smile, then she entered the room and turned on the lights.

"If you would all join me. . . ." said Kerschow.

Domenic waited until Kate and Etchison moved past the threshold before doing so himself. Streicher was next, followed by their captor. Domenic was trying to assess the chances of he and Etchison somehow over-powering him. The Uzi was known for its hair-trigger and lethal spray of small slugs. It was the perfect weapon for its present deployment and a great equalizer when odds were not close to even. Despite Kerschow's age and possibly slowed reflexes or instincts, Domenic did not like their chances against the automatic weapon. But he had to do something, and—

His seditious thoughts were abruptly suspended as he passed completely into the lab and saw the white plastic-and-glass cabinet on one of the tables in the center of the room. Suspended and held by rods and clamps so that it appeared to float in the middle of the cabinet was a shard of glass. And in the center of the piece of stained glass, the fragment of a woman's face—a pair of sky-blue eyes that stared in all directions.

The Eyes of the Virgin.

The sight and the thought iced through Domenic like a blade, and held him for a moment. Seeing it like this, a stolen captive, made everything so much more real. These people had actually done it, and now he had come so close to retrieving it and now there was a great chance he might fail. His heart ached for the what might await them. To stand before the artifact and feel so helpless was more than he could bear.

And he knew he must do something.

KATE HARRISON

As she stood with the others, she noticed that no one, not even the man called Kerschow, had spoken. *Every-one* had fixed upon the piece of stained glass, penetrated as it was by probing lamps and surrounded by lenses and sensors. There was something special about this piece of glass, of that there could be no doubt.

Kate could feel it. It was like staring into the suddenly flung-open door to a furnace and feeling the shock and the power of what raged within. They all could feel it.

And the sight of the eyes . . . eyes which were so . . . *arresting*.

Yes, she thought. The perfect word to describe them.

The experience of seeing the artifact had for the moment removed her attention from the current crisis, but it couldn't hold her indefinitely. Her heart had been hammering and although she'd looked repeatedly to Matt for a sign or an indication of what they should do, he'd been unable to give it to her.

And Streicher . . . he was worrying her.

He'd never convinced her of his sincerity, and had been happy when Matt insisted on not only keeping him in the cuffs, but also being personally in charge of him. He obviously had a familiar relationship with the gunman, Kerschow, and Kate had no clue where his loyalties or interests now lay.

She knew she wanted to *do* something, but had no idea what that might be.

"Very impressive," said the gunman after what seemed like a interminable silence. He looked at Domenic and grinned. "No wonder your people wanted to keep it all to themselves."

"Do you really think it would be of any use to you?" Domenic spoke softly, as though engaging a philosopher.

Kerschow reacted with mock-surprise. "Did you actually believe you had no obligation to share this gift with the rest of humanity? Why, Signor Petralli! Such arrogance. Such pride! Did not your Pontiff remind you that 'Pride goeth before the Fall'?"

"We used it in the service of Good," said Domenic evenly, and in that moment Kate felt so proud of him and his stout-hearted belief. He was a true soldier of faith and of God. She was sorry she hadn't known him better through the years, and felt a sadness that he had always been little more than an insanely busy, always-traveling brother-in-law. He was such a special person and she had a terrible feeling that none of them would survive this incident . . . and there was so much she realized she wanted to say to him. About Justine, about herself, about him and what she'd learned from him in such a short time.

Kerschow ignored Domenic's comment as he regarded Streicher and Safavi-Martin. "We know you were both here earlier. I need the decoded material. I need the key. I need everything."

"You want the glass, too?" said the woman.

The gunman nodded. "Oh, yes. I don't believe it would be safe here any longer, do you?"

"No, I suppose not." She moved to another workstation and pressed a few keys on a console board. "I will need to deactivate the cabinet before I can open it."

"Good. Get to it." Kerschow looked from Safavi-Martin to Streicher. "The data disc."

"I have it. Get me out of these things, for Christ's sake!"

The gunman exhaled slowly. "You know, Streicher. You should be the first one I shoot. We cannot reward people who do not follow procedure."

"When have I *ever* been accused of following procedures?" Streicher had resumed his oily, confident manner, and Kate wanted to claw at his eyes.

Kerschow looked at Matt, gave a brief dramatic shake of his head as though he grew tired of dealing with childish nonsense. "You . . ." he said as he raised the barrel of his snub-nosed gun just enough for everyone to notice. "Take them off. And, please, I don't want to use this just yet."

Matt did not hesitate, reaching into a vest pocket to retrieve the cuff key.

When he'd clicked the lock on both cuffs, and the second one fell from Streicher's wrist, he didn't flinch when Streicher lunged out with his fist and caught him flush in the jaw.

"Thank you," said Streicher, who turned quickly to

Kerschow. "I can kill him right now. You don't need him. You don't need any of them."

Kate watched Streicher as Kerschow considered this. "Actually, you are only partially right. I think Signor Petralli will be of use, as well as an amusement, to our interrogators."

Streicher thought for a moment about this. "You are probably right. Although I have learned enough to penetrate their web—with or without anything he might give us."

Now *that* was weird, thought Kate.

Just as she was beginning to accept Streicher's turn back to the Guild, and wonder what death would actually be like . . . he says something that could be just *wrong* enough to be a signal to Domenic and the others. Streicher had no way of learning anything about Corsica . . . so what was he saying? And why?

"Give me the data disc," said Kerschow to Streicher. "I will not ask you again."

Streicher nodded, reached into his pocket, and gave him the small, plastic-encased wafer.

"What about you?" Kerschow turned and spoke to Safavi-Martin. "Open it. Now."

"It is ready," she said, retrieving a small ratchet from the workstation and approaching the cabinet. Several turns on each corner connector were enough to break the gasketed seal on one of the glass panels which hinged upward on silent hydraulics. As she did this, everyone's attention again became fixed, held, arrested as the artifact appeared suddenly fragile, vulnerable.

"Excellent . . ." said the gunman. "So beautiful. . . . You will remove it from its moorings, please. And give it to me."

Kate watched the Persian woman carefully go about the task, as did the others. It was a moment which everyone could not resist giving their full attention. Safavi-Martin carefully removed the padded clamps of polished steel, one by one from the artifact. When it was free, she held in her hands as if were the most delicate membrane, a thing of gossamer that might fragment away in a soft breeze.

"Give me that," said Kerschow, reaching out with a casual hand to snatch it from Safavi-Martin's cradling touch.

Kate could hear herself gasp as he did this—for two reasons. His irreverent action . . . and also the result of it. For an instant, as the glass settled in his palm, it gave off sudden, white-heat starburst of light.

A sudden, brief but effective, distraction.

Followed instantly by a muffled explosion. Although far away, it resonated through the walls and the foundation of the building. Gunfire and random cries filtered down the corridors. KOM commandos, the Guild . . . or both.

Someone yelled out something, but Kate couldn't make it out. And then everyone was moving in all directions. She felt Matt's arms encircle her from behind, holding her, turning her, and as gently as possible, he carried her down to the floor, covering her like a shield. Twisting, she looked up to see Streicher lunging backward toward the entrance to the lab—where Matt and Domenic had shed their weapons.

Kerschow had taken his attention from them in that instant to look at the glass which had flashed so brilliantly, like a miniature sun. It was a single frame of confusion and disorientation; and Kate knew what would now come from Domenic, whose training had kicked in at the same moment. Only Safavi-Martin stood stunned, unable to move or react.

Like the strobe-light flash of a photograph, Kate's mind captured the scene and locked it away in her memory.

But there was more to come.

She could do nothing but watch as Domenic moved in on Kerschow, trying to get inside the radius of his weapon. Distracted, the gunman didn't have the time to aim and fire the Uzi with his left hand.

But he did reach the trigger—

—and fired off a random burst before Domenic hit him like a middle linebacker and forced him down.

As the volley of slugs ripped through a wall of equipment and both men crashed to the floor, Safavi-Martin backed as far away from the fray as possible. Matt's body lifted from her as he clambered up to help, giving Kate a clearer view of the silver-haired Kerschow struggling to throw the dead weight of Domenic from his chest. As he rolled off and onto his back, Kate could see a huge, black stain soaking through the side of his shirt. Kerschow was sitting up now, struggling to pull the automatic weapon from under Domenic's body as Matt reached his feet.

"Kerschow!"

The gunman looked up past Kate and Matt to Streicher who kneeled in the doorway behind them, holding an Army .45 in a classic shooter's stance. As Kate dropped to the floor, Kerschow squeezed down on the Uzi.

Streicher fired a single shot.

—which hit his prey in the right shoulder with incredible force. In an explosion of bone and flesh, the man was whipped around and slammed to the floor as if he'd been hit by a sledgehammer.

Sounds of conflict in a distant part of the building seeped in to fill the terrible silence that followed. She heard the Persian woman cry out in an unrecognized language as she looked past Kate to where Streicher had been.

Looking back, she saw his body, supine and twisted into an awkward death pose. A row of bullet wounds had stitched out a deadly pattern across his chest and neck. All the blood brought a sudden memory-flash of Kate's sister, and she felt tears exploding from her eyes.

Not now, damn it! Not now!

Matt pulled her up and rushed toward Kerschow and Domenic, but they were not as fast as Safavi-Martin who had dropped to her knees, half-crawling, half-dragging her way to the stunned and wounded Kerschow. She was screaming and cursing in another language, her features warped into an insane rage.

"Wait a—!" yelled Matt as she twisted the Uzi from the man's hand, redirected the muzzle into the center of his face, and squeezed the trigger.

His head collapsed like a piece of rotten fruit and Kate reeled back, away from the carnage. She was vaguely aware of Matt rushing forward to Safavi-Martin and Domenic's stilled form. She kept thinking he was still alive, but she had no idea how . . .

. . . or why.

EpiLoGue

Kate Harrison

*S*he was never clear on the sequence of what happened next, but despite her shattered psyche, she has always remembered all the events.

Memories of:

—Safavi-Martin quietly sobbing as she crawled away from the ruined corpse of the man called Kerschow to that of Streicher. Kate feeling so utterly helpless as the woman lay her head across the man's ravaged chest.

—a handful of Maltese knights slipping through the double doors, and instantly assessing the situation.

—Matt Etchison bending over Domenic and telling her he was still alive.

—her hearing the words and not allowing them to mean anything. At least not at that moment.

The idea of saving Domenic seemed too absurd, too difficult. As if one more cruel trick awaited to be played. It wasn't until much later—long after the commandos had carried him off in a stretcher, after all of them had been evacuated from the rooftop by helicopter—she believed Domenic Petralli would survive.

All those things remained a vortex of jumbled images and sequences. Only one thing remained which Kate *knew* happened last. Matt Etchison pointed to the artifact as it lay on the carpet, just beyond the stilled grasp of Kerschow.

The Eyes of the Virgin had clouded over in a total absence of color and image. Replaced by a terrible darkness so complete Kate knew it would be forever. And she wondered at that moment if it represented a final message to the earth and its inhabitants—that we were finally on our own, that our spiritual mother could no longer hold our hand, that she'd been forced by our own violent nature to let us go. . . .

She had been pondering the answers when Matt touched her shoulder. "It's time to go," he said. "We have one more job to do—in Washington."

THE WASHINGTON TIMES (AP) Coast Guard officials verified yesterday that an "open-sea interdiction" took place four and half miles south of Tangier Island to affect the seizure of a tugboat entering the Chesapeake Bay, on a heading for the mouth of the Potomac River. A quick check of the vessel's registry revealed it had previously been owned and operated by the Kosnac Floating Derrick Corporation, but had been decommissioned several years ago. It was then purchased through the Hall Brokerage by Acmed Ibn Al-Hazzad, a Saudi Arabian entrepreneur. Unofficial reports indicate that lethal force, implemented by members of a U.S. Navy SEAL team, was required during the board-and-seizure operation. Additional reports speak of a single piece of cargo being removed from the unauthorized vessel, but it has yet to be identified.

THE LONDON TIMES (REUTERS) In the most recent series of anti-Christian, Turkmenistan terrorist attacks, the Sivisli Chapel in the Guzelyurt valley region of Cappadocia, Turkey was bombed shortly after midnight on December 8th. "The explosion was so terrible," said the building's sexton, "the only thing we found intact was a single piece of stained glass."